SILENT
WITNESS

Gallatin Warfield

HEADLINE

First published in Great Britain in 1994
by HEADLINE BOOK PUBLISHING

10 9 8 7 6 5 4 3 2 1

British Library Cataloguing in Publication Data

Warfield, Gallatin
Silent Witness
I. Title
813.54 [F]

ISBN 0–7472–0735–6

Phototypeset by Intype, London
Printed and bound in Great Britain by
Mackays of Chatham PLC, Chatham, Kent

HEADLINE BOOK PUBLISHING
A division of Hodder Headline PLC
Headline House
79 Great Titchfield Street
London W1P 7FN

For My Mother, Caroline Kirwan Warfield,
An Artist In Her Own Right

ACKNOWLEDGEMENTS

I would like to express my sincere gratitude to Larry Kirshbaum, President and CEO of Warner Books, for his tireless efforts in the editing of this book. He was a thoughtful and patient mentor who encouraged me to do my best. Thank you for having faith in me.

I would also like to thank my agent, Artie Pine, and my editor, Joan Sanger, for their steadfast support and assistance throughout. Their labors have been truly appreciated.

In addition, I would like to thank friends and colleagues everywhere for their warm reception of *State v. Justice*. Your letters and comments were duly noted, and adjustments made, where appropriate. Thank you all.

And finally, I wish to thank my wife, Diana, for being there when I needed her, allowing me the luxury of writing through the long hours of countless days. To her I say, I love you.

They drew all manner of things –
everything that begins with an
M ... such as mousetraps, and
the moon, and memory ...

Lewis Carroll,
*Alice's Adventures
in Wonderland*, ch. 7

PROLOGUE

The young man entered the store and, on appearance alone, his intentions were innocent. Or so it seemed to Addie Bowers standing behind the counter. When the small brass bell above the door tinkled, she looked up from her newspaper and smiled. A customer at last. It had been a slow day so far.

Her husband Henry was busy restocking canned goods on the shelves above the soft-drink cooler. When the bell rang, he didn't even turn round. Addie would handle it, just as she had done for the last forty-two years in the small grocery and dry goods shop that stood on a lonely stretch of Mountain Road.

'Hello.' Addie's blue-eyed smile was like pale sunshine on a spring day. 'What can I get for you this afternoon?'

The man approached the counter, but said nothing. His gaze shifted to a row of pump-action twelve gauges in the gun rack.

Addie's smile continued. 'Interested in a gun?'

Henry had stopped his restocking chores. He was a gentleman of the old school, kind, trusting and soft-spoken, but he held his strength in reserve. He had been a front-line infantryman in the war, and had taken his share of incoming shells. That had left him with a certain cynicism that Addie didn't possess. He could always smell an enemy approaching.

Henry lowered himself from the step-stool and walked towards the counter. Something didn't feel right. 'You're gonna need some ID,' he said from behind the customer's back.

The man whipped round suddenly, and plunged his hand

1

into a military-style fatigue coat. Then he pulled out a large black handgun and pointed it at Henry.

The old man's eyes widened in surprise. 'What the hell . . .'

Addie began to shake. 'Don't hurt him,' she whispered.

'Where'd you get that?' Henry said, canting his head towards the giant pistol.

The man shrugged, then moved to the side. He motioned Henry to join his wife with a few abrupt flips of the gun barrel. Then he yelled towards the front door. 'You comin'?'

There was a pause, and then a second man cautiously entered the room and joined the group.

'You must be crazy,' Henry said to the first man. 'Stone crazy! And *you* . . .' he looked accusingly at the companion. '*You* . . .'

The gunman remained silent, while his companion stepped back, awaiting orders. He motioned Addie and Henry towards the back wall with another quick jerk of his gun-hand.

Addie's sudden intake of breath sounded like a sob.

'You got no need for that,' Henry pleaded.

The gunman looked him coldly in the eye, and raised his weapon. 'Please . . .' Addie begged. 'Please just take the money.' Her voice trembled as she spoke, and Henry reached over and gently took her hand.

'The money,' Addie whispered again.

But the gunman kept them moving towards the deep recess of the store, ignoring the cash register on the way.

The school bus was in a state of controlled bedlam. Ellen Fahrnam had taken her second grade class to the Crystal Grotto limestone cave for a field trip, and now they were winding down Mountain Road towards town. In late May, when the school year was about to close, trips like this eased the transition to summer vacation. Teachers and kids could leave the classroom in company time and explore the countryside. As the bus rocked around the curves, the back rows began pumping up and down with excitement. Miss Fahrnam had said they could stop at the Bowers Corner grocery store for a soft drink, and maybe Mr Henry and Miss Addie would let them visit the small pets zoo behind the store.

The ringleader of the impromptu wave in the seats was eight-year-old Granville Lawson, son of the county prosecuting attorney Gardner Lawson. A blond-haired boy with a crop of freckles across his nose, Granville was a pint-sized perpetual motion machine. 'Goin' down to Bowers'! Goin' down to Bowers'!' he chanted, as his seat-mates picked up the refrain. The store was one of his favourite places, and he couldn't keep still. It had been months since he and his dad had stopped by there. He always got a lemon lollipop from Miss Addie, and Mr Henry let him open the rabbit cage and hold his choice of long-eared creatures.

'OK, kids, we're almost there!' Miss Fahrnam shouted over the din. 'Let's put on our polite faces and stop the noise!'

The bouncing slowed, but one boy kept moving as if the order had not been given. Granville had recognised the fruit grove at Sandy Junction. It wouldn't be long now! Just two more big curves, a patch of woods, and they'd be there. He interrupted a bounce to get his bearings. The bunnies were waiting.

Henry had been ordered to kneel on the floor, and when he hesitated, the gun was pointed at Addie. 'Don't hurt her,' he said. The threat worked. Henry did as he was told.

Addie was prodded down beside him. 'What are you going to do?' she asked, her voice quaking.

Henry was silent. He now knew exactly what lay ahead. He turned to look at his wife, his expression strangely calm. 'Ad, I love you,' he said softly. He was still holding her hand, and he squeezed her fingers as he spoke.

The gun barrel was pressed to the back of his head. He could see the reflection of horror in Addie's eyes as the weapon clicked.

The bus pulled into the parking lot beside the store. It was empty and quiet. The road was clear of traffic also; nothing moving in either direction. It was a normal Thursday afternoon at the western end of the county. The farmers were off feeding their stock, and the office workers were still at their jobs in town, fifteen miles to the east. Bowers Corner was deserted.

Miss Fahrnam had restricted the flow at the door of the

bus as the kids crowded to get out. But, somehow, Granville had twisted his way to the head of the line. He was the self-appointed leader of the expedition. He and his dad were regular customers of the store. He promised the other kids deals on sodas and candy, and bragged about his expertise with the rabbits. This qualified him to lead the charge into the front door.

Henry's body was sprawled face down on the floor, and Addie was convulsed with hysterics, trying to revive him.

The gunman grabbed her shoulder, and tried to pull her back, but she kept grappling with her husband's lifeless form.

She was finally yanked back to a kneeling position. 'Why?' she screamed. 'Why are you doing this?'

The weapon clicked again.

Granville had broken from the pack, and was up on the porch before Miss Fahrnam could assemble the group into an orderly column.

'Granville Lawson!' the teacher called. 'Come back here!'

The boy had his hand on the door handle. He was a good child. Respectful. Polite. He usually followed the rules. But he had a streak of impulsiveness that sometimes pushed him across the line. Today he couldn't wait. He had to be first.

The door popped open, and the bell clanged a single 'ping'. Light footsteps flew across the floor, and suddenly stopped.

'Miss Ad—?' Granville was face to face with the kneeling Addie. He looked up, to a shadowy figure behind his elderly friend, then back to her eyes.

A gentle greeting somehow squeezed through her tears. And then, as Granville watched in horror, the gun went off.

PART 1

Whispers in the wind

CHAPTER 1

It was 5 p.m., and State Attorney Gardner Lawson was still in court. A three-week arson trial was finally winding down, and the defence were about to rest their case after their last alibi witness had finished telling his bogus story to the twelve men and women sitting in judgment. Gardner had meticulously manoeuvred the defendant, a three-times convicted arsonist, towards conviction, and the only thing left now was the coup-de-grâce.

Gardner stood up. He was forty-two years old, but his body was lean and toned. His eyes were dark brown, and his black hair was laced with silver threads. Well-tailored, confident, self-assured, he looked like a trial lawyer. He always commanded attention when he spoke, and this, as well as a brilliant courtroom record, had won him multiple terms as the elected State Attorney.

'Mr Karr, you say that you saw the defendant at the Mill House sometime around 9 p.m. Is that correct?' Gardner walked towards the witness stand as he spoke.

'Yup,' the witness said nervously.

'And what were you doing at the time?' Gardner rested his arms on the rail and eyeballed the man behind it defiantly.

'Just hangin' out. That's all.'

Gardner shot a glance at the jury. They had heard this same patter before, from six other witnesses. Six other hard drinkers who spent all their time and money guzzling booze at the Mill House bar.

'Did you happen to consume any alcoholic beverages while you were there?'

'Objection,' Public Defender Rollie Amos said half-heartedly. He'd made the same objection before, but it had been overruled every time. Alcohol impairment is a fair avenue of inquiry, but if he kept quiet, his client could accuse him of lying down on the job.

'Witness may answer,' Judge Simmons said wearily. He knew that the defence attorney had to play the objection game. A lawyer had to protect his client, but he had to protect himself also. If he failed to raise a point, his own client could attack him later for incompetence.

'Uh, might'a had a beer or two,' the witness mumbled.

Gardner gave the jury a sceptical look. 'One or two beers?'

The witness shrugged. 'Sumpthin' like that . . .'

Gardner walked to the trial table and picked up a piece of paper. Then he flashed it by the defence attorney and handed it to the witness. 'How about ten beers, Mr Karr? Isn't that what you really drank that night?'

The witness squirmed in his seat. Gardner had just confronted him with his bar bill. 'Uh, this ain't right,' he finally said.

Gardner took the paper from his hand and held it aloft. 'Are you denying you drank ten beers?'

Karr was caught. If he denied it, he'd be a liar, and if he agreed, he'd be a drunk. He decided to hedge. 'I jus' said that bill ain't right.'

Gardner plonked it on the rail and pointed to the top. 'It's got your name right here: Bill Karr. What's wrong with it?'

The witness was outmatched, but he was not going to quit. 'They got the number wrong. Wrote it down wrong . . .'

Gardner pushed in close. 'We have the bartender on call, Mr Karr. Think before you answer again. How many beers did you have that night?' The witness squirmed again, but didn't answer. His options were gone. 'How many, Mr Karr?' Gardner repeated.

The witness remained silent, his face down. Gardner tossed the bar bill on his trial table, glanced at the jury, and sat down. 'No further questions, your honour.'

The courtroom was sparsely sprinkled with spectators. The victims of the arson were there, and a few retired townies. But, other than that, the seats were empty.

Gardner had been too wrapped up in his work to notice County Police Sergeant Joseph Brown enter the courtroom.

8

'Brownie' was a detective in the department and close personal friend of the prosecutor. The black officer had put his life on the line many times for Gardner, and there was no question that Gardner would reciprocate in an instant.

Brownie moved to the front row and sat down. As Gardner worked the witness, he tried to catch his attention.

Gardner finally noticed the officer when he returned to his seat. As their eyes met, an icy hand seized Gardner's heart. Brownie's face looked like a wrought-iron mask. He'd seen that expression before, on Brownie and on others. The 'bad news' look. He swallowed, and motioned Brownie forward. Something devastating had just happened. 'Brownie?'

The officer grimaced. 'There was a shooting out at Bowers Corner,' he whispered, 'Bowers both dead . . .'

Gardner paled. The Bowers, Addie and Henry, dead? He looked to Brownie for a softening of his eyes, but there was an even darker expression of pain. Gardner's heart began to race. There was more . . . 'And?' He tensed against the words.

'There was another victim . . .' Brownie was stalling. 'Still alive, but med-evaced to shock-trauma . . .' There were tears in the officer's eyes.

'Who? Goddamn it!' Gardner shouted.

The courtroom fell silent, as if everyone suddenly knew what Gardner didn't.

Brownie put his arm around Gardner's shoulders. 'Take it easy, man. He's gonna be OK . . .'

Gardner stood up. He was trembling, and his face had drained to a dull shade of grey. 'Granville?'

Brownie tried to restrain him. 'Gard! He's gonna make it!'

But it was too late. Without asking leave of court, Gardner bolted from the room, blasting through the swinging panels at the base of the gallery and slamming past the outer door with a double blow of his fists.

Assistant State Attorney Jennifer Munday had just heard the news about Bowers Corner, and she didn't know what to do. Gardner was more than her boss. They had been lovers for the past year, ever since they had joined forces on a sensational murder case that had rocked the county. Before that, they had been friends and colleagues, developing an

9

attraction that neither had acted upon until it spon-
taneously erupted into a heated affair. And now they were
so deeply imbedded in each other's lives that the pain of one
instantaneously affected the other.

Jennifer was on the telephone in her office, trying to get
information. 'Yes, Officer Lowell, I do understand . . .' The
cops were not giving out many details. 'But the boy . . . What
about the boy?' Jennifer brushed her dark hair behind her
left ear, and adjusted her glasses. 'How is . . . he?'

Granville came with the Gardner package, but he had
never interfered with the relationship. Jennifer had become
his surrogate stepmother. She loved the boy. He was so full
of spunk. A miniature Gardner, that's what she saw whenever the blond head popped into view.

'OK, OK. University Hospital, Baltimore. Shock-trauma
unit.' She was jotting notes as she spoke. 'No. I don't know
where he is right now. He left the courtroom. Never came
back here.' Her words were slow and deliberate. 'Please let
me know if you hear something. I'll be at the office number.'

Jennifer hung up the phone and lay back in her chair.
The sun had just dropped behind the western ridge of the
Appalachian mountain range that bordered the outskirts of
town, and the orange glow from its aura suddenly lit up the
room. She shaded her eyes, and looked out of the window.
The pointed church tower in the square, illuminated from
behind, looked like a black spear against the sky. An ominous symbol.

Just then, Jennifer flashed back to a chill November day
at Bowers Corner. The five of them had spent the afternoon
around the wood stove in the store, rocking in the old-
fashioned chairs that Addie kept for visitors. Gardner was
badgering Henry for war stories. Granville was alternating
laps between Addie, Jennifer and his dad. And they were all
drinking hot chocolate.

'What was your scariest moment?' Gardner asked.

Henry rocked back and took a sip from his china cup, his
eyes closed briefly in thought. 'Came face-to-face with a
German tank,' he said sombrely.

Gardner perked up. The others kept rocking. 'What
happened?'

'It was two days after the invasion. Near St-Lo. We had been moving for fifty hours non-stop. Most of the men were so dog-tired they were asleep on their feet . . .'

Gardner was listening intently, stroking Granville's head as the boy curled in his lap, listening also.

'They told us to set up a gun position on a road outside town. Anti-tank unit.' Henry could see it clearly in his mind as he talked. 'It was a foggy morning. We set up the gun and then some of the guys lay down for a rest.' His voice became agitated. 'All of a sudden, we could hear it. Clank! Clank! Clank! Out of the fog. Clank! Clank! Clank!'

Granville stirred, and Gardner calmed him with another stroke of the hair.

'Then we could see him. Big Tiger tank, 'bout a hundred yards away, rumbling out of the fog. Clank! Clank! Clank!'

Addie and Jennifer were now absorbed in the tale, their eyes bright with expectancy.

'Tried to wake two of the gunners, but they were too far gone. Couldn't even kick 'em awake.' Henry was rolling, caught up in his own story. 'Then he opened up with his 50-calibre. Rat-ta-ta-ta! Tracer bullets flyin' past us like lightnin' bugs. One hit Charley Jones in the head, and he went down . . .'

Henry stopped suddenly, leaving his audience in suspense.

'Well?' Gardner said anxiously. 'What happened?'

The old man took another sip of cocoa. 'Got a shell in the breech, and pulled the cord. Boom! Like ta' knocked out our eardrums. Then another boom! Even bigger. Got 'im in the turret and blew it clear off. Smoke. Fire. And a poppp-poppp-poppp! as his ammo went off. That woke the boys up good. There wasn't any sleeping after that.'

Gardner praised Henry for his bravery, and Granville shook his hand. They drank another round of chocolate and thanked the fates for saving Henry's life.

Jennifer's mind wandered back as she realized that the bullets that had missed that day in France had finally found their mark. Henry was gone. And Addie too . . . She picked up the phone and dialled long distance. 'Shock-trauma, please.'

'Trauma Center.'

11

'Calling to inquire about a med-evac patient, Granville Lawson.'

'The county boy?'

'Uh-huh.' Jennifer suddenly pictured Granville on a trolley, plugged with tubes and wires.

'He just arrived. Can't tell yet. All I know is that he's alive but unconscious.'

Jennifer's lip trembled, and she began to cry. 'Can you . . . Can I . . .' She couldn't go on with the call, so she hung up. Granville and Gardner were linked by a secret lifeline. If the boy went under, the father would follow.

At 9.30 p.m. the commercial section of the town was deserted. The shop owners and workers lived in the residential zone that stretched from the base of the mountains to the foot of Court Avenue. Beyond that, the square containing the post office, the courthouse, St Michael's church and four low gothic-style office buildings made up the heart of the town. After sunset, when the work-day chores had ended, the heart stopped beating.

The Bowers killing had hit Brownie hard. He, like many others, had been captivated by the old couple, and had done his share of time in a rocker by the stove. Who on God's earth would ever want to kill them? And Granville . . . Comatose in the hospital, injured in the same insane outburst. What the hell had happened out there?

Brownie shuttled his crime lab van through the silent streets at the centre of town, en route to the 'strip' on the southern outskirts. It was a string of country-western bars, liquor stores and pool parlours where muscled farm boys and townie toughs came to strut, drink and tangle violently as they acted out their daily frustrations.

He tried to analyse the case as he drove. He'd been to the scene earlier and received a briefing from the other investigators. There were no witnesses. By the time Miss Fahrnam entered the store, the Bowers were dead, and Granville was unconscious on the floor. She and the children went into hysterics. The 911 call was almost unintelligible. Screams and wails, and on and on about the blood. It took the cops a long time to get anything out of anyone, and what

12

they got was worthless. No one saw anything. And all they heard was a loud bang. No car. No running footsteps. No hard evidence. No obvious suspects.

Brownie had taken it upon himself to tell Gardner. He wanted to ease the shock, to let him down slowly, but it hadn't worked out that way. The prosecutor had lost it, and now, in retrospect, Brownie scolded himself for not anticipating his reaction. After the courtroom scene, he had followed Gardner to the State Police barracks, and to an empty helicopter pad where the Western Maryland chopper had been parked only moments before. It hadn't taken long to get it airborne, heading eastward towards the hospital. The State cops respected Gardner as much as the county boys, and when he asked a favour, they could never bring themselves to turn him down.

So now it was going to be up to Brownie to track the killer. The county detectives were still working the scene, and the State Police crime lab had sent reinforcements, but from what Brownie had observed in his brief visit to Bowers, it was not promising. There was only one clue out there that gave him some hope. Behind the store, Brownie had found some smeared footprints in the dirt. Too messed up for any kind of ID, but clear enough to peg as recent. And one of the prints was unusual: the heel had been dragged across the ground before the foot came to rest. It had grabbed Brownie's attention immediately. There was at least one person in town who walked with a boot-dragging gait: a nasty punk with a record for violence named Roscoe Miller.

Brownie had begun the investigation in the usual way. He made a list of the local thugs who might be involved: bad guys who did this sort of thing as a career, and whose whereabouts that afternoon had to be checked. He had seven names on his list, and the alibis of three had already been verified. One was in jail in a neighbouring county; one had left town weeks ago; one was in the hospital recovering from an overdose. The next name on Brownie's list was Roscoe Miller.

Brownie pulled his lab van into the parking lot of Carlos' Cantina, a honky-tonk joint at the top end of the strip. The cinderblock building was bordered in red and green neon, and the sign was dotted with yellow lightbulbs. He adjusted a uniform button that had popped loose at his midriff. He was stocky, but not fat, and the cut of his dark blue outfit showed the outline of well-defined muscle. He liked to eat, but it hadn't softened him. 'Time for some cowboys and indians,' Brownie said to himself as he entered the door.

The gang at Carlos' were milling around in the smoke that filled the void between the bar, jukebox and pool table, and they glared at the intruder as he marched in. Brownie returned the cold stares and walked to the bar. He was not easily intimidated.

'Evenin', Carlos,' he said to the tan face behind the counter.

'Sergeant.' The owner nodded politely.

'Lookin' for Roscoe Miller,' Brownie said, turning to peer into the cigarette haze. 'Seen him tonight?'

'Roscoe?' The owner's ears seemed to prick up. He was a man who always needed to know why.

'That's the one,' Brownie said casually. 'Need to talk to him.'

'Hasn't been in,' Carlos replied. 'Hey, Willy, seen Roscoe today?'

A smoky face turned toward Brownie with a 'What's he done now?' expression. 'Nope,' the man grunted.

Miller was well known to the local police. His rap sheet included strong-arm robbery, car theft and disorderly conduct. When there was trouble, he was usually near by. But he always got a hot-shot lawyer, and skipped around the fringes of conviction, usually ending up with probation.

'Roscoe in hot water again?' Carlos said with resignation.

'No,' Brownie replied. 'Just want to talk to him. That's all.'

Carlos shot the officer a sceptical look. 'What's goin' on, Brownie?' He could see emotion seething behind the solid facade.

'Had a shooting at Bowers Corner,' Brownie said gravely. 'Two dead, and a little boy hurt bad. Lawson's son.'

Carlos' face paled in the dim light. 'Heard about that,' he said. 'You think Roscoe's involved?'

Brownie leaned across the bar. 'Not that I *know*.' Roscoe was not an official suspect; at least, not yet. 'I just want to talk to him. Just talk.'

Carlos nodded silently, and Brownie left the bar. In about twenty minutes, everyone in town would know that Brownie was looking for Roscoe. Including the man himself.

The man walked into the bathroom and flipped on the light. Its harsh glare hurt his eyes. He turned the tap, and a thick stream of water poured out. Then he washed his hands.

Over and over in the frothy flow he soaped his knuckles and fingers, scouring, kneading, rubbing until the skin was almost raw. He was obliterating the marks, destroying the proof. He glanced at his face in the mirror, and smiled. He was back to normal, under control . . . now.

Earlier, he'd almost lost it. He pictured Henry, and Addie struggling, and the sudden, startled eyes of the little boy. But he'd brought it off according to plan. The get-away was clean, out of the back door, down the old trail into the ravine. It was a piece of cake, and no one had a clue. Just as he'd planned.

The man cut off the water and pulled a towel off the rack. The bathroom was quiet, the only sound now the drip of the tap. But . . . His thoughts became troubled. Someone could talk. Give information to incriminate him . . . He flashed back to a stark grey jail cell. He'd been there before. More than once. And he didn't like it at all.

He left the bathroom and pulled out his wallet. In the lining was a business card with the name of a man who had saved his ass on more than one occasion. A lean, mean, legal machine: the toughest lawyer on earth.

Gardner's face was pressed against the glass of the intensive care unit. On the other side, Granville lay still and quiet in a large metal bed, his head swathed in bandages. The monitor was flashing numbers as his heart rate fluctuated, but there was no respirator. He was breathing on his own.

Gardner was in agony. He'd visited countless scenes like this before, on occasions where he and the victim's family kept vigil while a broken body lingered in the breech. He'd comforted, and reassured and counselled, but he was insulated against the big hurt. His profession saw to that. There was a separation between emotion and intellect. And

15

Gardner always held himself on the side where logic, not feelings, ruled.

The doctors were coldly sympathetic: medical versions of Gardner's prosecutorial self. The head physician was named Jenks, and he was the first to speak to Gardner, outside the unit's white enamel door.

'Mr Lawson?'

Gardner nodded. He was struggling with his new role on the victim's side of the aisle. Words were scarce.

'Your son is stable. He has concussion, a hairline fracture to the temporal region of the skull, but he's still unconscious.'

Gardner didn't react. He knew the verbal gobbledegook by heart. 'Let me see him,' he said shakily.

'In a few moments. We're still running some tests . . .' Dr Jenks was blocking the door.

'Goddamn it, let me see my boy!' Gardner said, his voice threatening. To hell with protocol! He needed to be in there.

'Take it easy, Mr Lawson,' the doctor said firmly. 'When the tests are done, you can go in.'

Gardner took a step forward. 'Get out of my way!'

Jenks could see that there would be violence if he didn't give in. 'All right! But quietly.'

'Yeah,' Gardner said gruffly, pushing past him into the room.

The mark on Granville's forehead caught Gardner by surprise. He had been briefed by the State cops on the flight down. The Bowers had both been shot execution-style. There was a contact pattern on the back of each skull, with extensive exit-wound damage. But Granville had not been shot, they assured him over and over. He had just been banged on the head.

Gardner thrust past the attending medics to the top end of the bed. Granville looked peaceful, his pale skin smooth, but in the centre of his forehead there was a purple mark. Gardner fixed on it at once, as its ugly circular pattern was very familiar. He'd seen it in a lot of homicide cases. The bruising had blurred the edges, but there was no question as to what it was: the imprint of the barrel of a gun. He stroked Granville's cheek and whispered 'Dad's here' and replayed happier moments in his mind when they were together. But

16

the boy remained still. Gardner stayed by his side, held his hand, and talked softly, and promised that he'd find the man who committed this vicious act against his son.

And then they asked him to wait outside the room. 'He can come to at any time . . .' the doctors said. 'Just stand by out there. You can see fine . . .' So he waited by the glass, looking at his boy, praying for his eyes to move – a tiny flick of his lashes that would let his father know that the vigil was over.

'Gardner!' A female voice suddenly snapped his attention away from the glass. He looked down the corridor to a figure approaching at a run. It was Carole, his ex-wife, Granville's mother.

Her dark curly hair was tousled, her eyes were red, and her makeup had smeared. 'How is he?' she asked breathlessly. With no access to a police chopper, she'd raced by car down from the county.'

'He'll be all right,' Gardner said, pointing into the intensive care unit.

Carole brushed by, and pressed her face against the window. 'He— He looks . . . dead.' She sobbed.

Gardner put his arm round her shoulders. 'He's asleep. That's all. Doctors say he can wake up any time now . . .' He kept the arm in place, reassuring her with a firm squeeze.

'What happened to his forehead?' Carole quavered.

Gardner swallowed. 'He was hit with a gun.'

'God,' Carole moaned. 'Who . . . ?' She wanted to ask who did it, but the sentence wouldn't come out.

'Don't know yet,' Gardner said. 'Police are investigating.'

'But they'll get him,' Carole said.

'Yeah,' Gardner whispered. 'They'll get him. And then they'll hand him over to *me*!'

CHAPTER 2

It was 10.45 p.m., and Brownie was still on the move. Further up the strip he'd found two more rowdies on his checklist, and satisfied himself that they weren't involved in the Bowers shooting. Each had a credible alibi. But Roscoe Miller had not yet been located. He was an N.F.A. man on the police blotter: No Fixed Address. A rolling stone who never stayed long in one place. Finding him was usually a matter of luck.

Brownie backed the lab van out of the Triple Seven Bar's parking area, and headed back towards town. As he passed Carlos' place, he did a double-take. There, on the apron, was a familiar red truck. He pulled in next to it, jumped out and shone his flashlight into the cab. It was empty.

He entered Carlos' front door and scanned the smoky room, focusing immediately on a muscular form deep in the murk, a man bending over the pool table. The cue came back for the shot, but Brownie seized the end and locked it still with his grip.

'What the fuck!' The man whirled round to see who had the guts to disrupt his game.

Brownie pulled the cue out of his hand with a jerk, and dropped the thick end to the floor. 'Evenin', Roscoe,' he said calmly.

Miller stood up straight and put his hands on his hips. He had dark unkempt hair, light blue eyes and a trail of tattoos running down each arm. He smiled at Brownie. 'Well, if it ain't nigger Joe Friday . . .'

Brownie stayed cool. 'Need to talk to you, Roscoe.'

The other patrons at the bar froze, and the jukebox was between tunes. The room was silent, expectant.

Miller leaned back against the rail of the pool table. 'I'm busy right now. Come back tomorrow.' He smiled sarcastically and looked into the crowd. Several wanna-be punks laughed in the background.

Brownie stepped closer. 'Afraid I'm gonna be unavailable tomorrow, Roscoe.' His voice was icy. 'Got to go down to the morgue.' Brownie moved up and pinned Miller against the table. 'We have to talk *now.*'

Miller was in a spot. He was being challenged in front of his peers. He had to respond, but he had tangled with officer Brown before. The man was like a slug of pigiron. Miller subtly reached behind him for another cue, and a crony deftly slid it into his hand. Then, without warning, he swung it towards Brownie's head. Like lightning, Brownie blocked the blow with the cue in his hand and snatched the second cue from Miller's fist. Then he jammed it across the man's neck and slammed him down to the pool table.

'Ughhh . . .' Roscoe's air was cut off.

'I'm not here to play games,' Brownie said calmly, applying pressure to the cue. 'You're gonna talk to me, or get locked up for assault. You decide.'

Miller's eyes started to bulge. Brownie pushed himself away, and Miller sat up. The crowd hesitated, then drifted back into the smoke.

Brownie patted the flap of his sidearm. 'No more trouble, OK?' Miller rubbed his neck and nodded. 'Now, let's go outside where we won't be disturbed,' Brownie said.

Miller stood and glanced around, but there were no seconds in sight. Then, grudgingly, he started to shuffle slowly across the rough wood floor.

Outside, the air was cool for late May. A half moon had just risen above the flat roof of the bar. Brownie directed Miller to his truck as a prelude to a consent search. If Miller agreed to a look at his personal effects, he couldn't complain later about an illegal search. That was the trick.

They reached the truck, and Brownie turned Miller round. 'Where were you about 4 p.m. today?' Miller didn't answer. 'I said, where were you this afternoon?'

Miller stood fast. 'I don't hav'ta answer that . . .'

'Take it easy, Roscoe.' Brownie decided to slow down. 'Just

tell me where you were, and we'll call it quits.'

Miller looked up. 'Why you want to know?' He was sweating.

'Two old folks got killed today.'

'And you think *I* did it?' Miller asked, his expression one of shock.

'Didn't say that,' Brownie said quietly. 'Just want to know where you were at the time.' As he spoke, he glanced over Miller's shoulder into the truck.

Miller moved left to block his view. 'You still sound like you're accusin' me . . .'

Brownie's patience was almost gone. He could see Addie and Henry in his mind's eye, flat out on the blood-soaked floor of their grocery. 'One more time, Roscoe! Where the fuck were you today?'

Miller's eyes turned ice cold. 'Go to hell! I'm not telling you shit . . .'

Brownie suddenly lost it. With a move like a rattlesnake, he leaped on Miller and wrestled him to the ground. 'You're gonna tell me, or I'm gonna break your fuckin' neck!' Miller was pinned under him. 'Tell me, motherfucker!' Brownie screamed.

Miller had stopped struggling, but was eyeing Brownie with defiance. 'You're crazy, man!'

The words had no effect. Brownie pulled Miller to his feet and shoved him away. 'What are you hiding in the truck?' he said, pulling his nine-millimetre from its holster.

'I don't believe this!' Miller groaned. 'Get the fuck away from there!'

Brownie moved to the door and tried it. The lock was down, the window up. 'Open it!' he ordered.

'Where's your warrant?' Miller knew Brownie was in dangerous legal territory.

'You gave me consent!' Brownie bluffed.

'Like hell!' Roscoe yelled back.

'OK, have it your way,' Brownie said calmly. With a flick of his wrist, he smashed the driver's side window with the butt of his gun. Then he pointed the weapon at Miller's face. 'Lie down on the ground. Put your hands on the top of your head, and don't move until I tell you.'

'You're really gonna be sorry...' Miller said. 'You better not fuck with me...'

'Down!' Brownie ordered.

Miller kneeled, then went to the prone position as instructed. Meanwhile, Brownie had entered the truck and was busy rummaging through its interior, holding the gun on Miller as he worked.

The bar crowd had heard the commotion, and were now poised in a semicircle around the truck.

'Call my lawyer,' Miller hollered. 'Somebody call Kent King...'

Just then, Brownie emerged from the cab. 'Yeah. Call Kent King.' He straightened up and unfolded his fingers. 'Roscoe's gonna need him big time!' Brownie moved his palm into the light, exposing the items he'd found in the glove compartment. Three brand new twelve-gauge shotgun shells.

Gardner stood alone outside the intensive care unit at 2 a.m. Carole had become tired, and moved to a nearby seating area to wait. The corridor was quiet, disturbed only by the passing of an occasional nurse. Nothing had changed since the afternoon. Granville was still stable, but asleep.

'He moved!' Gardner yelled suddenly. The small bandaged head had slowly rolled to one side. 'Nurse!' he called.

There were footsteps in the corridor as robed figures flowed from all directions. Carole had also stood up in the commotion, and come to the glass. They were quickly allowed entrance by a doctor; Gardner on one side, Carole the other.

In a flash, Granville's eyes came open. Blurry at first, then steady, they searched for a familiar face. A small hand came out, and touched a larger one reaching to meet it. A weak smile materialized between the bandages as the small hand gripped the larger. And then, the first two words, 'Hi, Dad.'

Gardner's hand trembled as he felt the movement of his son's fingers against his own. 'Gran...' he mumbled. His

22

voice croaked as he bent down to kiss the boy's barely exposed cheek. 'Gran . . .' And they all began to cry.

Dawn was approaching from the southeast quadrant of the county – the Apple Valley side. Pink waves of clouds had been building on the grey horizon for the past half hour, and soon they would crest and pour molten sunlight into the green trough between the ridges. It was a peaceful time, when cows gathered by the barn and alarm clocks buzzed in the farmhouses. But the peace wasn't evenly spread. In a foggy meadow below Mountain Road, a stranger had returned.

He hadn't planned to come back. He was going to stay clear of the area at all costs. But it had been a bad night. The cops were restless and, the way they were going, it was not going to take them long to put it together.

He had to act now, still under the cover of semi-darkness, against the rules he'd laid down. The cops had gone crazy. The goddamn prosecutor's kid! That's what had set them off! It was all over the local news. 'Lawson! Lawson! Lawson!' What luck! Of all the brats in the world who could have interfered, it had to be the prosecutor's kid. So much for planning . . .

He cut in and out of the saplings at the edge of the woods, and found the entrance to the trail. The light was stronger now. In no time the narrow strip of trees would be lit up, and there would be nowhere to hide. He had to get in and out in a hurry. The rocks and fallen logs began to look familiar. It had been a quick decision at the time to ditch the merchandise. If he'd been caught with it, then it would have been over. 'The fruits of the crime,' his lawyer had said. 'Never get caught with them.'

The big boulder with a Y-shaped indentation marked the exit point. He left the trail, trying not to stir the underbrush or get snagged on the brambles. Then he saw it. An old oak with a rotted core. The bark was firm and the wood strong for six inches all around, but there was a gaping wound on one side, and the innards had crumbled to sawdust long ago. He looked at the sky. Dawn was just moments away. He approached the tree and thrust an arm

23

deep into the wound, up, high inside.

Grasping an object, he twisted it from its niche within the hollow tree. If they got their hands on *this*, it could be real trouble. He grunted and pulled a twelve-gauge shotgun from the dust. Attached to the trigger guard was a crudely marked tag: 'BOWERS SPECIAL $189.95.'

He checked the hole, and smoothed the surrounding fall-out with his foot. The sun had broken the plane of the far ridge. Time to move. In twenty minutes, this link to the crime would be severed for good, hidden where no one would ever look. He was back in business.

Gardner and Carole sat in the doctor's room awaiting the verdict. They had stayed with Granville all night, comforting and soothing, holding his hands, giving support as much for their own needs as for his. But now it was morning. Granville had dozed off peacefully, and they felt comfortable taking a break.

They were told to go to the head neurologist's office. He had made a complete examination of the child, and could give some answers to the parents. There were some other patients to check, but he would be with them soon. The walls were bare, the furniture spartan. This was obviously a part-time job for the doctor. With his background, he probably had a plush private practice somewhere in the suburbs. The hospital work was loose change.

Gardner and Carole sat in silence, on the verge of exhaustion. Suddenly the door swung open and the doctor entered. He was in his fifties, tanned and healthy looking. 'Mornin', folks, I'm Wilson Robertson.'

Gardner stood and shook his hand, 'Gardner Lawson, and this is my . . .'

Carole extended her hand. 'Carole. Granville's *mother.*'

'OK . . . OK . . .' The doctor was smiling. The news could not be too bad. He sat behind the narrow metal desk, and laid a clipboard on the table. 'Your boy is very lucky. There is not going to be any permanent physical damage. He'll have some short-term side-effects, but in the long run he should be fine.'

The listeners broke into smiles. That was terrific news.

24

'How long does he have to stay in hospital?' Carole asked.

'Another day or two,' the doctor answered. 'We'd like to keep him under observation, just to be sure there's no brain swelling. And we'd like to get him started with the therapist.'

'Therapist?' Gardner interrupted. 'You said he had no long-term injury. Why does he need a therapist?'

Carole's face mirrored the same concern.

'I said no permanent *physical* injuries. There may be some mental problems.'

'What kinds of mental problems?' Gardner's voice sounded like cross-examination.

'Too soon to say for sure,' Robertson said. 'Violence-induced traumas in children can take their toll. All we know at this point is that he's begun dissociation . . .'

Gardner suddenly saw the full picture. This often happened in child abuse cases. A hurt is so overwhelming that the child represses it deep in his subconscious mind. Unable to deal with the reality, the child makes it all go away. But it doesn't leave; it stays inside and festers. Gardner had been so caught up in the physical part that he'd forgotten about this ominous aspect.

'He took a hard blow to the head,' Robertson continued, 'and there was a weapon involved, but that's not the problem. It's what he *saw* that we have to deal with . . .' His voice faded, and the room went silent. They were waiting for him to continue, but he had stopped.

Gardner caught his eye. 'And what was that, Dr Robertson? What did he see?'

'I'm afraid that's the problem. At this point he's unable, or unwilling, to say.'

'So what can we do?' Carole asked.

'Start therapy as soon as he's feeling better. I've got several people on staff who can see him here, then he can continue with someone local when you go back home.'

'But what can *they* do?' Carole continued.

Robertson smiled wanly. 'Try to make him feel better. Deal with the shock. Ease him back to normalcy.'

Carole looked at Gardner, then at the doctor again. 'But what about his memory? You said he can't remember. Are the therapists going to try to *make* him remember?'

The doctor glanced down at his chart. 'He'll be given a chance to get it all out,' he said.

'Why?' Carole asked suddenly. 'So he can go to court?' She looked at Gardner. 'Are you going to make him testify? Is that what you're trying to do?'

Gardner tightened his jaw. 'No!' He hadn't even thought about it. So far, they had no suspects and no case. Court was the last thing on his mind.

'Promise me you won't make him testify,' Carole said.

'God, Carole . . .' Gardner answered.

'Promise me!'

Robertson stood up. The conversation had gone past him. 'Unless you have other questions about the boy's treatment . . .'

'Thank you for all you've done,' Gardner said.

'Yes, thanks,' Carole echoed.

The doctor left Gardner and Carole alone in the room. 'Please tell me you won't make him go to court,' Carole repeated.

'I'm not planning to,' Gardner said hesitantly.

'But you might?'

Gardner did not answer.

Brownie entered the main lobby of University Hospital. It was 10.15 a.m., and he'd pulled an all-nighter. The Miller lead had not panned out. The man had stonewalled in interrogation, and Brownie had to admit to himself that the link between the shotgun shells and Bowers Corner was just speculation. They were not even sure that any shells had been taken from the store. Even the preliminary forensic work came up negative. After several tedious hours at the station, Brownie had had to let Roscoe Miller go. Then he made the three-hour drive to Baltimore.

He had an 11 a.m. appointment at the medical examiner's office to observe the autopsies of Addie and Henry. But, first, he wanted to stop by the intensive care unit to check on Gardner and Granville. According to the doctor he'd spoken to earlier on the phone, things were looking up. The elevator carried him to the ninth floor.

Brownie spotted Carole at the end of the long corridor, and

26

ran down. He spoke politely to her, and moved on to find Gardner by Granville's bed.

'How're ya feelin', young man?' Brownie asked.

'Head kinda hurts . . .' Granville replied.

'Think this might make it better?' Brownie pulled out a giant chocolate bar from his uniform coat pocket, and Granville's eyes widened.

'Don't know if he's allowed it quite yet,' Gardner said.

Brownie pretended not to hear. He began to peel the foil from one end.

Carole entered the room, and looked over his shoulder. 'Maybe we should ask the doctor,' she said softly.

Brownie kept peeling, then broke off a small piece and extended it towards Granville's mouth. Gardner and Carole looked at the child. His face was beaming, his eyes the brightest they'd seen since he woke up. Brownie put the candy in Granville's mouth. Then he looked at Gardner, and winked. 'This boy's gonna be just fine.'

Brownie had now gone over twenty-four hours without sleep, and he was starting to flag. After the autopsy, he could get some rest at the University Inn, where the county had reserved him a room. But, until then, he had to try to stay alert, to see if the bodies contained any clues that might help him get the investigation back on track.

The medical examiner's facility was located in the sub-basement of University Hospital. As Brownie entered, the odours of chemicals and death entered his nostrils, and revived him like a shot of ammonia. It was an eerie place, deep underground, lit by greenish fluorescent tubes. On more than one occasion he'd picked up clues that the pathologists had missed. To complete the investigation, he had to observe the autopsy. But it always gave him the creeps.

Addie and Henry lay on parallel stainless steel slabs, naked, their bodies grey with age and post-mortem pallor. Their blood had been drained, and their skins looked like candle drippings.

'OK, OK, I'm comin' . . .' A voice emerged from the office, followed by a white-uniformed figure. 'Grandma and grandpa, you're next . . .'

27

Dr Gladys Johanssen was known for her non-stop witticisms. The pathologist was too abrasive for live patients, so she had buried herself in the ME's office for twenty years. Whenever she autopsied, it was one wisecrack after another until the job was done. Penis size. Cause of death. Even stomach contents were grist for the joke mill. She always laughed in the reaper's face.

'Mornin', Doc,' Brownie said.

Gladys frowned when she saw his expression. 'Know these two, huh?'

Brownie nodded. 'Real, real good.'

'OK. I get the picture.' She dropped her smile, and picked up a scalpel.

Brownie moved into his observation position behind her. All in all, Gladys Johanssen was a pretty good technician. Quick, efficient and keen-eyed. And, on the right day, amusing as hell.

The procedure moved swiftly through the internal organ phase. The Bowers each had a list of congenital ailments associated with age, but none was life-threatening. In fact, their bodies had held up remarkably well. A lot of years left on the meter, Brownie sadly noted.

Gladys moved to Henry's wound, and Brownie edged closer. She turned his head to the side, and exposed a hole in the back of the skull. 'Contact shot.'

Brownie could see where the exhaust gases of the gun barrel had blown a star-shaped pattern of gunpowder into the skin round the hole. 'Large calibre,' he said.

'At least nine-millimetre, maybe larger.' Then Gladys went to Addie and checked the same area. Another star. Same sized hole.

'Identical,' Brownie said.

'Same gun. Same point of entry.'

'Same shooter,' Brownie cut in.

'That's my conclusion. A precisely calculated act.'

Brownie sensed a theme. 'You sayin' it was premeditated?'

Gladys gently put down Addie's head, and turned to face the officer. 'Was it a robbery?'

Brownie bunched his brow. 'Don't know yet. No money gone from the till. Maybe a shotgun taken. Possibly some shells. Not really sure.' He looked at Addie's hand. She still had on her diamond ring.

'This wasn't a robbery, Sergeant Brown.' This was two decades of autopsies talking. 'It was an execution.'

Brownie had been thinking the same thing. It was a clean shot to the head each time. No last-minute act of desperation. Whoever did it went to Bowers Corner to kill. The robbery, if any, was secondary. 'Check for fragments,' he said, pointing to the wound. The crime scene boys had not found any intact bullets at the store, only minute fragments, as if the bullets had disintegrated on impact.

Gladys inserted her forceps and drew out a slender piece of lead, then held it under a mounted magnifier. 'Incredible,' she whispered. The greenish glow of the overhead lights was picked up by the blood-stained metal.'

'Shredded,' Brownie said.

Gladys put that fragment on a dish, and extracted another one. It was bent and twisted in the same way. 'No way you're gonna get a ballistics ID on this,' she said solemnly.

'That must'a been the whole idea,' Brownie responded.

'Huh?'

'He customized the ammo, so it'd come apart when it was fired,' Brownie said. 'I think you're right. The son-of-a-bitch went there to kill.'

It was late in the afternoon, and Gardner was still at Granville's bedside. He hadn't slept for two days, and had barely moved out of a twenty-foot radius of the boy's room since he'd arrived at the hospital. Carole had gone to see her mother in the Baltimore suburbs. Father and son were alone.

'Dad?' The boy was propped up against a massive puff of pillows. 'When can I go home?'

Gardner shifted in his chair and patted Granville's knee. 'In a day or two. Doctors have got to be sure your noggin is OK. Then mom'll take you home.' Granville squinted, as if he were in pain. 'Son?' Gardner sensed a problem.

'Am I going to die?' the boy asked suddenly.

Gardner winced. Death was a subject they'd never really discussed. It was always 'Grampa or grandma went to heaven.' No one ever *died*. 'No,' he said with a nervous laugh.

'You're not going to die. You're going to live to be a hundred.'

But Granville didn't respond. He was lost in thought.

'You're not going to die, son,' Gardner repeated. No force in the universe was going to harm the boy. Not now, or ever.

CHAPTER 3

Joel Jacobs looked out of the thirty-third-storey window of his Manhattan law office. The sun was low in the west, and deep shadows now lay in the parallel canyons below. There was a layer of smoke across the Hudson; soon it would cut the light in half and bring dusk to the island before its appointed time.

Jacobs was in his early sixties. He worked out regularly in the gym on the fifth floor, and could go the distance with men a fraction of his age. Thick white hair and alert brown eyes were his most striking characteristics. He wore an expensive tailored suit, and topped it off with a red bow tie. After thirty-five years of practising law in the uptown jungle of the city's courts, he'd finally made it to the top.

Jacobs, Zinmann and Kale was one of the most prestigious and powerful law firms in the country. They were known as the three wise men, and Joel Jacobs was the wisest of them all.

'Mr Wellington Starke on line three,' a liquid female voice said over the intercom on his mahogany desk.

'Thanks, Rachel,' Jacobs replied, picking up the phone. This was it. His bread and butter.

'Wellington!' Jacobs' voice had a hearty timbre, full of authority and control.

'Joel. Thank you for taking my call.' The voice was affected, the man obviously well-bred and cultured.

There was a slight hesitation in the caller's voice that made Jacobs sense that something was on the way. He waited, but Starke said nothing. 'What can I do for you today?'

'Did you receive the retainer?'

31

Jacobs picked up the generous six-figure cheque. 'Have it right here.'

'Good. Just wanted to make sure you got it.'

'Sure did. Thanks. Anything else on your mind?'

Again, there was a pause, as if the caller was dealing with a problem he didn't quite know how to raise, even with his long-term counsellor. 'Uh, no, not really . . .'

Jacobs knew that he couldn't push. Sooner or later it would be delivered to him. He decided to drop it. 'How's Joanna?'

'She's fine. Playing tennis every day at the club. Getting quite good, actually.'

'And Jessica?'

'Still at school, but getting ready to graduate. Can you believe it, Joel? Jessie a college graduate . . .'

Jacobs smiled, remembering a tiny freckle-faced blonde running around the table while he conferred over a stack of files with her father. 'Unbelievable, Wel. She's really grówn up.' The lawyer hesitated. There was one more Starke to inquire about. One more name on the family list. 'And the boy? How's he making out?' Wellington Starke the fourth. The only son. Namesake and heir to the family fortune.

'Doing fine. Just fine.'

'Still at the boarding-school in Maryland?'

'Yes, sir. Prentice Academy. He's a senior, but he's not going to graduate until next fall. The transfer messed up his credits, and they have to hold him over.'

'Too bad about that,' Jacobs said, 'but he's OK?' There was a touch of concern in his voice.

'Yes. So far. Grades are, uh, not the best, but they're acceptable, and he's made some friends . . .'

'Good.'

'He's on the skeet team. Best shooter on the squad, they tell me.'

Jacobs smiled sceptically. 'Coming right along . . .'

'Yes, I'm happy to say. A credit to the family name.'

'That sounds great,' the attorney replied. 'So we're making progress across the board?'

'So it seems. Just wanted to say hello. I have to pick up Joanna now. You know how she gets when I'm late . . .'

'OK, Wel. Thanks for calling. It's always good to hear from you.'

Jacobs hung up the phone and leaned back in his leather chair. As anticipated, the sun had vanished in western haze and the shadows had blended into a blanket of gloom. He reached out and flicked the chain on his Tiffany lamp, laying out the retainer cheque in the oval light spot on the desk. Something was in the wind, some monumental crisis in the Starke family. And the fee for his services had been paid in advance.

The lights were burning late at the State Attorney's office. By 8 p.m. things were usually battened down and quiet in the second-storey suite of rooms the prosecutors occupied in the courthouse. Most official functions ceased at 4.30, but tonight was different. There was a killer on the loose, and the Prosecutors were playing catch-up.

Gardner and Jennifer were seated at the small conference table in Gardner's private office. The setting was like the den of a county home, decorated with duck prints, regimental curtains and a walnut desk. All were reflections of Gardner's heritage as an eighth-generation Lawson in Maryland.

Gardner's eyes were creased with fatigue. Except for a brief nap in the helicopter on the return trip to the county, he'd not slept for fifty hours. He'd reluctantly left Carole to tend to Granville, assuring himself and the boy that he could return at a moment's notice if needed. After the autopsy, Brownie had briefed him on the progress of the investigation, and the news was not good. He had no choice but to come home and assume command. Jennifer had been handling the office chores since he'd bolted out of the arson trial. She'd completed the case for him, and brought in a guilty verdict. Then she'd set up a command post for the coordination of the Bowers investigation, opened a case file and lined up witnesses. And now Ellen Fahrnam, the teacher who made the 911 call, sat nervously in the conference room, waiting to be interviewed.

'She's convinced it's her fault,' Jennifer said softly. The assistant prosecutor was keeping pace with Gardner's sleep deprivation, but it didn't show. Years of early rising, healthy eating habits and exercise had conditioned her not to need much sleep. She looked as though she could go another two days without rest.

33

'I told her not to torture herself,' Gardner replied.

'But she *is*,' Jennifer said.

'Let's get it over with,' Gardner said wearily.

Jennifer rose, and returned with Granville's teacher. An attractive woman with short curly blonde hair and a shapely figure, she was a model of classroom decorum. When she saw Gardner, her lip began to tremble. 'M-m-m-m-ister Lawson, I'm so, soooo sorry . . .'

Gardner rose and extended his hand. 'It's OK, Miss Fahrnam, I really appreciate your coming down this late . . . Please, *please* understand that in no way do I hold you accountable. I mean that.'

She shook his hand and sat down opposite the State Attorney. 'But . . .'

'No more,' Gardner said firmly. 'You had nothing to do with it.' He picked up the written statement she'd given to the police and handed it across the table. 'I just want to go over your observations. Some time has passed, and maybe you can be clearer on a few of the details.'

'I'll try.' Her voice was weak.

'Good. Now let's take it from the point you heard the shot,' Gardner said gently. 'Are you familiar with firearms?'

'No. Not really.' She looked confused.

'Well, how did you know it was a shot? Have you ever heard a gun being fired before?'

'No. Not in person. Only at the movies, and on TV.'

'But you specifically said you heard a gunshot,' Jennifer cut in.

'Yes,' Miss Fahrnam answered.

'So you knew what it was as soon as you heard it,' Jennifer continued. 'You were not drawing a conclusion later, after you saw the bodies.'

At the mention of the word 'bodies', the teacher's lip began to tremble again. 'Uh, no . . . Yes. I— I don't know!'

'OK, OK, that's all right,' Gardner interrupted. 'Let's go on. Please, Miss Fahrnam, I know this is difficult, but we have to know exactly what you saw. When you entered the door, what was the first thing, the very first thing, you noticed?' He tensed. This was the only person beside Granville who might have seen something. The only other eyewitness. A fleeting shadow. A colour. A shape. Anything would help.

The teacher's eyes went blank again. But she was still calm and composed. Suddenly her expression switched to horror. 'The blood!' she shrieked. 'The blood! Oh God, oh God, oh God!'

Gardner and Jennifer were caught by surprise, as she lapsed into hysterics. Gardner, in particular. He'd already tried to avoid the scene. The nightmare reality of Granville's face against the barrel of a gun. Now, as the teacher screamed her guts out, Gardner's soul chimed in with an anguished wail of its own. He was too close. Too goddamned close. He thought he could handle it like the others, detached and professional, but now he knew he couldn't.

'God! God! Godddddddd!' The teacher was over-hysterical now. Jennifer hugged her.

Gardner wanted to help Jennifer comfort the witness, but he couldn't. As the door to Bowers Corner had cracked open in her mind, he had peered in too, and what he'd glimpsed left him as horrified and speechless as the teacher. Jennifer had got Miss Fahrnam to a state of quiet sobbing, but Gardner was still reeling with the effects of her outburst. He shuddered, and looked at the limp body in Jennifer's arms. If the scene had that effect on the teacher, what in God's name had it done to Granville?

The county lay in the westernmost region of Maryland, an area dominated by hills, mountain ridges, cliffs, valleys and flatlands. Shaped by prehistoric subterranean upheavals and contractions, it was bordered by two major ridge-lines. The town had sprung up in the central valley, and had become the centre of the county's universe. The population was as diverse as the land itself. Farmers predominated, but there was a growing class of entrepreneurs and professionals in and near the town, and that class included the lawyers.

Kent King, a Baltimore attorney who had moved to the county five years back, was the undisputed tiger of the defence bar. A skilled courtroom technician and trial counsel, he knew the law and how to apply it to benefit his clients. His philosophy was to fight and win, and never to compromise. And he gave Gardner Lawson hell anytime he could.

Ironically, Lawson and King were more alike than they were different: slightly distorted mirror images of each other. Both were tall, dark and trim. Both were highly intelligent. Both were intensely combative. But Gardner fought for the State, and that left King to defend the other side.

King pulled his Jaguar into the lot at Carlos' Cantina. Miller's truck was there, a plastic sheet taped over the driver's side window. He entered and found Miller at the pool table. Miller followed the lawyer to the parking area. They stopped by his truck.

'There it is, Mr King,' Miller said angrily. 'That's what Brown did after he beat me.'

King surveyed the truck, then studied Miller, 'Where are your injuries?'

Miller frowned, 'Huh?'

'You said you got beat. Where are your bruises?'

Miller raised his tattooed arms. 'Here somewhere.'

King seized both Miller's wrists. 'I don't see any. Are you sure he *hit* you?'

Miller shuffled his feet. 'Yeah.'

King let go of his wrists. 'Don't bullshit me, Roscoe! If Brown wanted to hurt you, there'd be some damage.'

'He did, no shit. I want you to file charges.'

'OK,' King said, 'we can do that. It'll be uphill, but we can do it. Too bad you don't have any marks.'

'He took pictures,' Miller said suddenly.

'What?'

'Photographed me. All over.'

King let out a sigh. 'They can *prove* you weren't hurt when you came in. Your word isn't going to cut it.'

Miller blinked, and leaned back against his truck. 'He did hit me . . .'

King crossed his arms. 'Sorry, Roscoe . . .'

'What about my window?' The young tough did not want to quit.

'We may be able to do something with that,' King replied. 'Get me an estimate, and I'll draft a claim. Now, tell me about

36

the interrogation. Did you give a statement?'

'I didn't tell them nothin',' Miller said. 'I didn't *do* nothin', so there was nothin' to tell.'

King nodded. 'That's good.'

'Nothin' to tell,' Miller repeated. 'But they're after me . . .'

King's expression turned thoughtful. 'Not to worry. They screwed up by hassling you. There was no legitimate reason to bring you in, and no probable cause to take the shotgun shells. If you're ever charged, nothing they've got so far can come into evidence.'

Miller stepped away from the truck and put his head close to King's, 'So I got nothin' to worry about?'

The defence attorney gave him a piercing look. 'I wouldn't say that. Two people were killed and the prosecutor's son was injured. You really think they're going to go easy on the investigation?'

Miller paled. 'Uh, how is the boy? How's he doin'?'

King hesitated. It wasn't clear where Miller's concern was coming from. 'He'll pull through, but his head may be messed up awhile.'

'Huh?' Miller's interest was still intense.

'He can't remember what happened.'

Miller sighed. 'But he's gonna live?'

'Yeah,' King replied. 'He's gonna live.'

Miller stopped talking. There was something very serious on his mind. 'You're gonna represent me, right?' he finally said.

King frowned. 'On what?'

'The case. If they try to pin it on me?'

King's frown intensified. 'Murders are expensive, Roscoe. I don't think you can afford the fee.'

Miller smiled. 'That ain't gonna be a problem.'

'No?' King was surprised. He knew Miller usually struggled to scrape together the fee for a minor assault.

'No,' Miller said resolutely. 'In a couple of days I'm gonna have plenty of money, and then all you have to do is name your price.'

Gardner and Jennifer lay in the four-poster bed in Gardner's townhouse bedroom. Snug beneath a quilted blanket, they had assumed a 'spoon position' with Jennifer's slim body nestled behind his. His breath was forced, the rhythm of exhaustion. She held him across the shoulder, and pressed her face into his neck.

Ellen Fahrnam had really shaken him up. 'I can't run this investigation,' he told her after the teacher left. 'My objectivity is shot. I can't think straight.'

'What are you going to do?' she had asked.

'What the hell *can* I do? Somebody's got to get this thing going. Before that maniac kills again . . .'

'What about me?' It just popped out. She had given it no thought, but it was a logical answer. She could captain the case. Gardner had trained her to be a pro. She had the basic moves down pat. The only thing she lacked was experience.

'You?' Gardner's voice had carried surprise, not condescension.

'Me. I can run the investigation, and you can advise me . . .' She was making it up as she went along. 'I think I can keep my perspective.' A fleeting vision of Granville's face flashed through her mind, and she swallowed. 'I think I can . . .'

Gardner had tried to smile, but the pain did not allow more than a brief upward turn to the corners of his lips. 'I don't know if I can stay out of it,' he said solemnly.

'You won't have to,' Jennifer replied. 'You'll still be there, just not up front.'

Gardner's silence signalled his agreement. There was no other choice, really. He was too emotionally involved to lead. And now he was asleep by her side, snoring deeply while she lay awake, wondering if she could make good her promise.

Gardner's sleep was deep, but not without dreams. As Jennifer clung to his back in the waking world, he was locked in a bizarre prison somewhere on the other side. There was no structure, no bars or gates. It was far away in a flat-surfaced desert whose white sand stretched endlessly to an undefined horizon. Beyond the horizon was the nothingness of space.

He and his companions were trapped. They were watched and controlled by faceless beings who set them tasks that had no reason. Gardner was the leader of the prisoners. In the centre of the scene was a wall. A single panel of stone, standing alone. In front of it was a line of chairs.

Suddenly there was a commotion. The ritual was about to begin. The keepers yelled at him to move. To mount the chairs, and scale the wall. Gardner helped the weak ones to climb, pushing their feet, pulling their hands. He was the strongest. The only one who could get them out of the danger zone. But there were not enough chairs.

Hurry! Gardner screamed. Hurry! They're coming! He tried, but he couldn't help them all. Several people were stuck on the sand, terrified. Hurry! he screamed. But it was too late. The keepers had arrived with the dogs – giant snarling beasts that fed on human flesh. In an instant they were ripping and slashing with their teeth, tearing the help-less ones to shreds. Their screams were lost in the growling chaos. And Gardner clung to the top of the wall and watched, unable to save them.

Purvis Bowers sat at his computer and tried to work, but he couldn't concentrate. His aunt and uncle lay in Frame's Funeral Parlor, and they had nothing to wear. Delivered this morning from the morgue in Baltimore, they were still naked. They needed clothes to be buried in, and Purvis had been asked to supply them.

The thirty-five-year-old accountant was the only son of Henry's deceased brother Burton. A small man with a sharp mind, he had grown up in the town's backwaters. He was a genius with the numbers of commerce. He loved numbers, and he could always find a way to make them sing.

Purvis had set up a solo accounting practice after his father died, crunching digits for everyone up and down Main Street. He'd saved a lot of money for a lot of clients, but his ambitions stretched beyond the county line. He saw himself someday at the head of a giant corporation, giving orders, poring over reams of billings that his numbers had created. And in his dream he was away, far away from the town, in a city that he owned. Picking up his telephone, he dialled.

'Frame's Funeral Home,' a female voice answered.

'Ms Frame, It's Purvis Bowers.'

'Hello, Mr Bowers.'

'Hello.' He took a breath. 'I got your message.'

39

'About the clothes.'

'Yes, ma'am. About the clothes.' His voice was hesitant.

'Is there a problem, Mr Bowers? We didn't know who else to call.'

Purvis was the closest relative to Addie and Henry. They had had no children, and their siblings were all dead. In a crisis, he was the logical choice.

'Ms Frame, I was wondering if you could send over someone from your place to see about the clothes ...' Purvis asked. 'I just ... It wouldn't ...'

'I think I understand, Mr Bowers,' the lady replied. 'You'd rather not go over to the store. With the shooting and all, I *do* understand.' The line went silent. 'Mr Bowers?'

'Yes, Ms Frame?'

'That right? You'd rather we pick something out for them?'

'I'd appreciate it,' Purvis said. He sounded relieved.

'We can do that. What about the key? How are we going to get in?'

'The police will help. If you call the station, they can let you in.'

'All right. Don't you worry about this now, Mr Bowers. Don't you worry at all. We'll take care of everything. Addie and Henry are going to look just beautiful.'

'Thank you, Ms Frame,' Purvis interrupted. 'Bye.' He hung up, and rubbed his cheek. Then he picked up the receiver again, and dialled.

'Kent King's office,' a voice answered.

'This is Purvis Bowers. May I speak to him?'

'Moment, please.'

'Yeah?' King sounded rushed. 'What's up, Purvis?'

'I need to shelter some money,' Bowers said. 'Can you help me out? It has to be legal.'

King sighed. 'How much?'

'A lot of zeros.'

'How sheltered do you want it?'

'Out of sight.'

King laughed. 'Make an appointment. We'll talk about it.'

Brownie stood on the porch at Bowers Corner and looked down Mountain Road. There was a short curve, then a straight stretch, then another curve that snaked into the woods. That was north. In the other direction it was more or less the same: excellent sight distance for at least two hundred yards before the road disappeared. That provided plenty of advance warning for a criminal. He put his hands on his hips. The fucker must have gone in blind, with no look-out on the porch and no wheel man in the lot. He had had no warning that Granville was on his way.

Pushing open the front door, Brownie looked in. The rockers beside the stove were still, the room dark. The shelves were still stocked with food. Nothing had been disturbed. It was in, do the job, and then out. But why no eyes out front? The planning had been meticulous, up to a point. There were no fingerprints, no shell casings, no intact bullet fragments, no hairs or fibres. And there was no apparent motive.

Twelve paces marked the distance from the door to the spot where the bodies were found. It would take about ten seconds at an adult's leisurely walk, seven or eight at a child's run. Ellen Fahrnam had reported hearing a shot almost immediately after Granville had entered. She'd panicked, and hesitated before going in. Add another five or six seconds. Then, with her entry, perhaps cautious, perhaps hurried, add seven seconds more. Twenty seconds. It all took place in less than twenty seconds: Addie's execution, Granville's injury, the escape. The last part was well planned. The look-out part may have been sloppy, but the retreat was worked to perfection.

Brownie skirted the chalk lines on the floor, and walked to the rear exit. It was three paces to the door. That would take one and a half seconds at a run. He opened the door and looked out. There was a narrow passage between the pets' zoo cages and the base of a steep hill behind the store, then twenty yards to the end of the yard, a rocky ten-foot drop and, finally, the wilderness: thirty acres of trees stretching down a long inclined slope to a meadow on the other side. It had been scouted and then searched by two squads of patrol officers, and later followed up by the dog team. But, not surprisingly, they hadn't found a thing. A forty-minute head start was all the bastard had needed. And now he could be anywhere.

41

He walked round the building to his lab van. There was something very strange here. The perpetrator seemed to be a bungler and a genius at the same time. Some aspects were brilliant, others not so smart. The characteristics of a schizoid personality. Brownie stopped suddenly and slapped at his side. 'That's it!' A man intelligent enough to plan so well would not have left himself unprotected. He would have covered all angles, and that meant he could not have done it alone. There had to be at least two people involved, or it would never have been attempted. One smart, and one stupid. A schizoid *team*!

Two men stood on the skeet range of Prentice Academy, below the main campus. It was late afternoon, and the gothic tower of the administration building blocked the path of the falling sun. Modelled on a British university, the school was an academic enclave for the wealthy and high born, an architectural masterpiece of cloistered courtyards, stone dormitories and leaded glass windows.

'Pull!'

A clay pigeon suddenly twirled through the air like a miniature flying saucer. IV Starke took aim with his shotgun, smoothly guiding the barrel along the trajectory and then slightly ahead.

'Blam!' The pigeon was instant dust.

'A good one!' the coach, Thomas Randolph, yelled.

Starke lowered the gun, and adjusted his dark glasses. 'Show me a double,' he called to the concrete pit ten feet below.

There was an adjustment in the bunker. 'OK. Ready!'

Starke steadied the gun at his chest. 'Pull!'

This time two saucers spun out, one high, the other low. The shooter tracked the low one first. 'Blam!' Another puff of dust where the pigeon had been. Then he aimed at the high one, just now dropping from its apogee. 'Blam!' Dust again. Starke lowered the gun, and smiled. 'Any questions?'

'Not from me,' Randolph said, 'but Sutton Hill may have some next week. They're already grumbling about your eligibility.'

Starke's smile faded. He was twenty years old, and not yet

out of high school. A re-tread, some joked. Rolled in and out of a slew of northeastern prep schools, now the stalwart of the Prentice Academy skeet team. He was a handsome young man, with bright blue eyes and a conservative close-cropped haircut. The teachers found him polite and reserved. He was no Einstein, to be sure, but his bookwork was passable.

'You think they'll disqualify me?' Starke asked.

'They'll try. Division rules cut off participation at eighteen.'

The student frowned. 'Do they have to know? I mean we're not gonna volunteer it or anything . . .'

'Well, I'm sure as hell not gonna tell them!'

Starke grinned and shouldered his weapon. 'Good. I'd hate to miss the meet because of a Mickey Mouse rule.'

The two men started walking towards the main campus. As they neared the running track, Starke hesitated. The grounds crew were laying in cinders from a two-ton dump truck. Several workers leaned on shovels, while others raked the black sooty granules from the upturned bed. Their backs were turned, but Starke's eyes widened slightly when he saw the man in the middle.

'Coach, I have to get back to my room. Something I forgot to do.' He started to leave the path and cut across to the dormitory in a course that would take him far clear of the workmen.

He'd taken three steps when the coach yelled, 'Starke!'

Starke whipped round suddenly. The coach had a look of reprimand on his face. 'Sir?' His voice wavered slightly.

'The gun, Starke. You forgot the gun!'

Starke let out his breath and squeezed the shotgun in his hands. Weapons were off limits everywhere but the range. When not in use, they were locked in the rack in the coach's office.

'Uh, sorry, sir,' Starke said, handing over the gun. Then he bolted and ran straight to his room, never slowing or stopping, or even turning his head.

PART 2

Suspicions

CHAPTER 4

A week had passed since the murders, and the doctors had finally released Granville from the hospital. They had done all they could do; now it was up to time and therapy to complete the healing. Carole had brought him back from Baltimore and sequestered him in the safety of the large brick house on Watson Road that Gardner's ancestors had built. It was still owned by Gardner, bequeathed to him in the same tradition that all firstborn Lawson sons had received it. But title to the property currently carried no privilege. Carole had won the right to live in the house for five years following the divorce, and Gardner was barred entry, except by permission of his ex-wife. Not surprisingly, she had not let him inside since the day he was ordered to leave.

Gardner knocked on the heavy panelled door, and Carole opened it a crack and peered out. 'Hi,' he said into the narrow gap.

Carole attempted a polite smile. 'Hello.' The door came open, but not wide enough to permit Gardner in.

'How is he?' Gardner asked.

'Better,' Carole answered. The door stayed in place.

'May I see him?'

'Yes, of course,' Carole said civilly, but the door still blocked his path.

Christ, Gardner thought, can you ever give it a rest? The shredded fabric of their relationship was never going to be mended; they both knew that. All that mattered now was Granville.

'Go round the back, and I'll send him out,' Carole said finally, realizing that Gardner had expected to come inside.

'Things are a mess, and I haven't had time to straighten up.'

He glanced over her shoulder into the front hall. It was immaculate. 'OK.' Then she closed the door.

Gardner walked round the porch and turned the corner. Spring was in full bloom now, and the lawn furniture had been set up in the English garden behind the house, just as it used to be. He watched several birds hopping across the grass, and let his mind drift as he settled into the porch swing.

'Hi, Dad!' Granville opened the back door and ran out to greet his father.

'Gran!' Gardner gave his son a big hug. Then he pulled back so he could see the boy's face. The mark on his forehead was still visible, but it was beginning to fade. 'How're you feelin'?' Gardner was still holding the child by his shoulders.

'Head's a little sore . . .' Carole had said he was still on medication, but the dosage was being reduced.

Gardner gently ruffled the boy's soft blond hair. 'Good thing you've got the patented Lawson hard head. Takes more than a little bang to keep us down!' He looked into Granville's eyes for a reaction as he spoke, but he remained passive. The 'bang' reference had gone right over him.

'Did you get the books?' Gardner had sent him a large stack of games, puzzle and colouring books.

'Uh-huh.'

'Did you do any of them yet?'

Granville shook his head. 'Uh-huh.' His pale face went blank for a moment.

'How come?'

'Didn't feel like it.'

'Will you do some?' Two weeks earlier, Granville would have torn through the puzzles immediately. He loved them, especially the mazes.

'Uh-huh.' His eyes had lost their usual sparkle.

'Come up here,' Gardner said gently, pulling the boy up on his lap. 'Do you know how much I love you?'

Granville put his arms round his father's neck, and drew his knees up, almost into a foetal position. He didn't answer.

'I love you,' Gardner said again.

But Granville said nothing. He squeezed his dad's neck

48

tighter, put his head against his chest and lay there quietly for a long, long time.

They sat in silence, the hug substituting for words. Gardner could feel the tension in Granville's body, and he had a sudden anticipation that the boy would convulse hysterically like Miss Fahrnam and let everything spill out. But it didn't happen. The memory stayed inside. After half an hour, Gardner encouraged Granville to get the puzzle book. With father leading, and son listlessly following along, the two of them threaded mazes and connected dots for another half-hour. Finally, time was up.

'Granny!' Carole called from the back door. 'Come get your lunch!'

Granville stood up in response to the command, and gave Gardner the 'Sorry, gotta go' look. Mom was in charge, and their time together was always regulated by her.

Gardner grabbed him tightly. 'I'll be back to see you soon,' he said against Granville's hair.

'OK, Dad.' Then the boy dashed for the door that Carole was still holding open.

Gardner watched Granville disappear into the house. 'Bye, Gran,' he called. But the door closed on his words.

Brownie was on his fifth stop of the morning. Another witness interview in the Bowers case. One more name on his student list. The children who had gone on the field trip were now on an abbreviated school schedule. He had wanted to talk with the kids, one at a time, to see if they might remember something that could help the investigation. Miss Fahrnam's hysteria had left a jagged hole in his crime scene report; her observations were disjointed and incoherent. Maybe one of the little people could do better.

But the parents stood in the way. Every single one had barred the door. 'I'm sorry,' they said. 'We don't want little [fill in name] involved. This is too traumatic. He/she didn't see/hear anything. He/she can't help. Please find someone else.' In response, Brownie had argued, 'If you won't help, the killers could hurt other innocent people.' 'Too bad,' they said. 'Not our problem. Sorry. Very sorry, but please go away. We do not want our child in court.'

49

So the first four attempts were strike-outs. Children can't be forced to give statements like adults. In fact, they cannot even be approached without parental consent. And police rules decree that parents who do not allow their children to cooperate in a case will not be compelled.

Brownie knocked on the door of a suburban cedar-roofed house on Meadow Lane. A new development built in the past ten years, the properties were expensive. And most of the residents of the neighbourhood were upwardly mobile county professionals.

An attractive African-American woman answered the door. 'Yes?'

Brownie let loose one of his blazing smiles. 'Ms Dorey?' The woman nodded cautiously. 'Sergeant Joe Brown, county police. Like to speak with you about Jenneane.'

The woman stepped out on the low cement platform that bordered the door. 'Is this about the shooting?'

'Yes, ma'am. Wondered if I could ask her some questions in reference to what she heard or saw that day.'

Ms Dorey seemed to be sizing Brownie up, letting her dark eyes roam his wide body for a moment, then lock on to his face. 'That's all she's been talking about for four days. On and on about what happened . . .'

Brownie felt a surge of elation. Maybe this was a change in his luck. 'Is she home?'

The woman shook her head. 'No. She's at school.'

'Thought they were holding the kids out,' Brownie said with surprise. 'For counselling.'

Ms Dorey cracked a sceptical smile, 'Ahh, the counselling . . .'

Brownie cocked his head. 'You don't buy that stuff?'

'Jenneane doesn't need it,' the woman answered. 'She's very advanced for her age.'

'So maybe you and Mr Dorey wouldn't mind if I had a few words with her after she gets home?'

A frown creased the woman's pretty face. 'There's no Mr Dorey,' she said solemnly. 'Just Jenneane and me.'

Brownie's eyes glanced down at the wedding ring he had spotted earlier. 'Sorry, ma'am. I thought . . .'

'It's OK,' she replied. 'Everybody assumes . . .'

50

Brownie waited for more, but her voice trailed off, and she seemed to be staring at his badge. 'Uh, Ms Dorey, would it be all right if I came back later and spoke with Jenneane?'

She was still staring at his badge. 'That would be fine, Sergeant Brown. I'm sure she'd be glad to tell you everything she saw.'

Brownie thanked her and returned to his van. On the way back to the station, he placed a patched-in call to the school principal's office. 'Miss Kearns, this is Joe Brown.' He was speaking to the elderly secretary who had known him since childhood.

'Hi, Brownie.'

'Can you do me a favour?'

'Sure. I'll try.'

'Do you know Jenneane Dorey? Second grade student?'

'Sure do.'

'What do you know about her parents?'

She hesitated, then spoke. 'Moved here two years ago from Washington D.C.'

Brownie shifted the microphone in his hand. 'Whole family?'

'No. Just mother and daughter.'

'What about Mr Dorey?'

'He died a year before they moved out to the county.'

Brownie sensed tragedy. 'What happened to him?'

'He was a D.C. police officer . . .' Brownie visualized the woman's eyes on his badge. 'Killed in the line of duty.'

Brownie thanked her and clicked off the mike. The family of a dead cop. Daughter a possible witness. A touchy situation at best. He took a deep breath, and gripped the van's steering wheel. Maybe they finally had a break in the case.

Purvis Bowers hung up the telephone, and opened the drawer to his desk. A lawyer had rung, an estate attorney from Pennsylvania, asking about Addie and Henry's will. Some long-lost cousins had got word of the shootings, and were overcome with instantaneous grief. They wanted to convey their condolences, and make an incidental inquiry: what, exactly, could they expect to receive as bequests?

His aunt and uncle didn't have a will, Purvis said. At least,

51

he didn't know about one. They were simple people who lived simple lives. They didn't need that kind of paperwork. Everything they owned was owned jointly, and whoever survived would get it all. If they both died, it really didn't matter who got what. That's the way Addie and Henry looked at things, he said, so it was not surprising that they never drew up a will.

He reached into the drawer and pulled out a large yellow envelope. The distant cousins were a surprise. He hadn't anticipated their appearance. He was the sole heir. That's what he'd always thought. The only green leaf on the family tree. He opened the envelope and extracted a smaller one. This one was sealed, and he slit the seam with a letter-opener. He pulled out a creased document and smoothed the wrinkles, rapidly reading down the page. Then he turned to the next sheet, then the next. When he was through, he folded the pages and put them neatly back in the envelope, pausing long enough to read the inscription at the top left-hand corner:

LAST WILL AND TESTAMENT
LAW OFFICE OF KENT KING.

Purvis put the envelope back in the desk drawer, then picked up the telephone and dialled long distance.

'Cooney and Clearwater,' a dulcet voice answered.

'Mr Cooney, please.'

'Thank you, sir. May I say who's calling?'

'Peter Baker.'

'Thank you, sir. One moment, please.'

There was a brief pause, then a man came on. 'Tom Cooney.'

'Mr Cooney, this is Peter Baker. Did you receive my letter?'

There was another pause, and the sound of shuffling papers. 'Yes, Mr Baker. You're inquiring about an account.'

'Yes, sir. It's outlined in my letter. A client of mine needs to make a stock purchase.'

'And you want to know if we can keep the stocks in street name, and maintain your client's identity strictly confidential?'

'Correct, sir.'

'You are aware of the federal reporting requirements. Tax ID numbers, IRS notifications . . .'

'Yes, sir.'

'But the specifics of ownership you do *not* want mentioned in the account.'

'Precisely.'

There was another pause. 'How much did your client want to deposit with us, Mr Baker?'

Purvis smiled to himself. 'Five K plus.'

'Five thousand dollars?' The voice sounded irritated.

'No. Five hundred K. Five hundred.'

The words were met with silence. 'Five hundred thousand?' Cooney asked.

'Yes, sir. Cash.'

'Mr Baker, I think we can swing it. Might have to bend a rule or two, but I'm certain we can guarantee your client's anonymity.'

Purvis smiled. 'Good. Thank you. I'll be in touch.' Then he rang off, and got up from his desk.

The Veil Valley Professional Center contained two side streets that veered off the main road where Kent King's office was located. At the far end of the southern branch lay the County Outpatient Clinic. On its second floor was the Family Counselling Unit.

Gardner was familiar with the place. On many occasions he had watched from behind the one-way mirrored glass as young abuse victims were treated by the therapists. He'd always gone there to assess the possibilities of going to trial. Some kids were so messed up that they couldn't communicate at all. On those cases, he did everything he could to negotiate guilty pleas. But there were others, where the children were more articulate about their ordeals. They talked freely with the counsellors, and were able to explain what had happened and who did it. Those children were candidates for court. But now he was behind the glass, watching his own son. What he saw was making him very uncomfortable.

'Let's talk about what you like to do for fun,' Nancy Meyers said. She was a middle-aged woman with shoulder-length grey hair and glasses, a licensed mental health social worker and an expert in child trauma. Gardner had seen her in action many times over the years, and as a therapist, she was about the best.

Granville sat in the middle of the floor with his legs crossed under him. The walls were lined with shelves filled with toys. Dolls. Space planes. Building blocks. The ambiance was strictly juvenile. Anything to break the ice, and get the children on common ground with the therapists.

'How about it?' Nancy said gently. 'Tell me what you like to do.' She was sitting beside him, wearing slacks and a tee-shirt, trying to put him at ease.

Granville sat immobile. 'Watch TV,' he said suddenly, his head down.

'OK.' Nancy's voice was as soft as a lullaby. 'And what do you like to watch on TV?'

'Captain Freedom.'

'OK. Anything else?'

'Monkey Shines.'

Gardner could see that Granville was slow to respond. Why do I have to go to talk to someone? he had asked before they came. It had been easier, down at the hospital. They had all dressed alike, in white smocks, and the boy could not tell a shrink from a surgeon. He'd had three sessions, and not even realized it. But now he was home, and his head had stopped hurting, so why did he have to go see some dumb ol' lady?

'You like cartoons?'

'Uh-huh.' He was staying monosyllabic.

'Do you like to draw?'

'Granville's head finally came up. 'Sometimes.'

'Well, would you like to try some drawing now?' Nancy picked up a sketch pad and some coloured pencils, and put them beside him.

Behind the mirror, Gardner tensed. Art therapy was a device often used with severely traumatized kids. They were so beaten down, so repressed, that they could not even speak the words. What had happened? Who did it? The questions could not be answered. At least not with words. But sometimes they could draw what they could not say. And the drawings spoke for them and revealed the horrors that they could never, ever, utter aloud.

Granville picked up the pad and laid it across his knees.

'Draw anything you want,' Nancy said in a hypnotic voice.

Gardner pressed close to the glass to get a better view of the pad. Granville was situated just below and to the left. He sat there with the pad on his knees, but did nothing.

'Go ahead,' Nancy prompted again.

Granville fidgeted with the pencil, and hunched across the paper. Nancy and Gardner waited patiently. Soon, Granville put the pad down on the floor.

Gardner pushed his forehead against the glass. The page was empty.

Jenneane Dorey was a wide-eyed, alert eight-year-old. Her hair had been plaited by her mother, and she wore a bright blue jumpsuit. She fidgeted with one of her plaits as she talked to Brownie seated at the kitchen table. Mom was in the living-room, watching the evening news.

'Did you know my daddy?' she asked, looking at the detective.

Brownie smiled. 'No. Afraid not.'

'He was a narcotics officer.'

Brownie was beginning to understand what her mother had said earlier. This child was mature beyond her years. Her words were grown-up. 'I heard about him. He was a good man.'

Her eyes showed no grief, no clouding over like her mother's. She had accepted the loss as if it was natural. Daddy was home, and then he wasn't. If the hurt was there, it was long buried.

'Jenneane, I'd like to talk about the day you went to see the cave,' Brownie said, easing the subject matter back on track. 'Do you think we can talk about that?'

The little girl nodded. 'All right.'

'Good. Now I'm just gonna ask you a few questions, and, if you can, maybe you can answer them. OK?'

Jenneane nodded again. 'OK.' It was clear that she liked Brownie, and trusted him. She would try very hard to help.

'After you left the cave, you got on the bus, right?'

'Yes.'

'And do you remember where you were sitting? In the front or the back of the bus?'

The girl twisted her hair, and answered immediately. 'Right at the back. By Wendy.'

'Wendy Leonard?' That was one of his earlier witness rejects.

'Yes. She and me are friends. We always sit together.'

'OK.' Brownie made a note on his steno pad. 'And did you sit by the window or by the aisle?'

'Window.' Again, there was no hesitation.

'And did you look out of the window while you were driving from the cave, or were you talking to Wendy?'

'Lookin',' she said, 'and talkin'.'

Brownie smiled, 'Was it more lookin' or more talkin'?'

Jenneane switched plaits. 'Lookin' and talkin' . . .'

'OK.' Brownie got the picture. Two eight-year-olds chatting and sightseeing as the bus cut its path through the countryside. 'Did you see any cars pass as you were going down to the Bowers store? While you were looking and talking to Wendy.'

'Couple.'

'OK. Now, do you remember anything about the cars? What kind they were? What colour? Anything at all?'

'Two cars and a truck,' Jenneane said.

Brownie blinked. This was unbelievable. Such recall. And from a kid, no less. Adult witnesses seldom came out with that kind of detail.

'Jenneane, are you sure? Two cars and a truck?'

'Uh-huh. A blue one. A black one, and a red one.'

Brownie was writing furiously. It was incredible, but it might be true. Traffic was scarce on the western end of Mountain Road. Maybe the vehicles somehow imprinted themselves in her fertile young mind. He had to follow it up. 'Jenneane, do you remember which way the cars were going? I mean, did they pass you going the same direction, or were they coming the other way?'

This time she hesitated, as if she were trying to piece the scene back together. 'Two of 'em goin' the other way, and one zoomed past us . . .'

Brownie was still writing. 'Now, sweetheart, can you tell me which one passed you? Car or truck?'

'Truck.' No hesitation on that one.

Brownie tensed. 'And can you tell me what colour it was?'

'Red. Old red truck.'

Brownie let out his breath. 'Did you see any people, driving or inside?'

She looked up, as her mind scanned the scene again. 'Guy was in the back . . .'

'In the back?'

'The place where they carry stuff.'

Truck bed, Brownie noted. 'Now, Jenneane, can you tell me what he looked like? Do you remember that?'

She squinted her large brown eyes. 'White guy. Like the boy on TV. You know, Randy Sands.'

Brownie squeezed his pen. Randy Sands was a teenage idol with a primetime show, Hollywood High. He had distinctive features, dark hair and piercing blue eyes. The girls went nuts over him. But the poor guy had one nasty flaw that no one knew about. He bore an uncanny resemblance to a no-good shit named Roscoe Miller.

Brownie wrote MILLER in large letters on his pad. Another possible link! It looked like his initial instincts might have been right. 'Jenneane, did you ever see the truck again? After it passed you?'

'No.' Her response was quick.

'How about at the store? Did you see it anywhere near the store?'

'No.'

'You're sure?'

The girl gave Brownie a teasing look. 'I didn't see it ever again!'

That sounded positive. If it *was* Miller's truck, they must have pulled off on a side road, parked it and walked to the store.

'OK,' Brownie said. 'Now, when you got to Bowers Corner, what did you see?'

Jenneane lowered her head. 'I was still in the bus . . .'

'When the Lawson boy ran inside,' Brownie interjected.

'Yes, but I looked out the window . . .' Her voice faded.

'And what did you see?'

57

'Didn't see anything . . . Heard some bangs.'

Brownie glanced up from his pad. *'Bangs?'*

'Yes. From the store. Bangs.'

'How many bangs did you hear, Jenneane?'

'One when we got there . . . Then one more . . . Then another after Granny went in.'

Brownie looked into her eyes. They were steady. Honest. 'You heard *three* bangs? One, two, three.' He extended three fingers to illustrate.

'Yes. The window was down, and I put my head out, and I heard 'em.'

Brownie wrote THREE SHOTS on his pad. This was new information. Fahrnam had reported only one shot. The elderly, hard-of-hearing bus driver, none. And he'd not heard from the other kids. 'You're absolutely *sure* you heard three bangs?' Brownie repeated.

'Yes,' Jenneane said, 'I'm sure.'

Brownie underlined THREE. They knew one shot went into Henry, and another into Addie. That left one unaccounted for.

'Listen to me!' Roscoe Miller yelled on the phone. He was parked at Carlos' Cantina, using the pay-booth beside the building. The glass had been busted out on the lower panels of the enclosure, but the equipment still functioned. He kicked a jagged shard with the toe of his boot as he spoke. 'I want my money!'

The voice on the other end was subdued and calm. 'Take it easy. You'll get your money. Just be patient.'

The booth was shrouded in darkness. The dome light had burned out long ago.

Miller's face contorted in anger. 'Goddamn it, we made a deal!'

'And it will be honoured,' the voice replied.

'How long?' Miller was still seething.

'Soon. I can't say exactly when.'

'Shit!' Miller spotted a familiar blue van slowly glide by on the street. It slowed, but did not stop. He pulled away from the phone, then came back.

'What is it?' The voice was still calm.

'The cops. That bastard Brown again!'

'Where?'

Miller craned his neck out of the booth. The van had turned the corner, and headed west. 'Just drove by. Probably checkin' up on *me*.'

'Why?' The tone of voice was clinical, as if what he'd just heard was no big deal.

'He's after my ass!'

'Still? He doesn't have a thing on you.'

'He's not gonna give up tryin'.'

'Don't sweat it. Just be cool.'

'I'd be a lot cooler if I had my money!'

'I told you before not to worry. You'll get the money.' The voice was steady.

'You got three more days,' Miller replied.

'You'll get your money.'

'Three days.'

'Good-bye, Roscoe.' The calm voice ended in a click.

'Damn!' Miller smashed the phone against the metal hook, bouncing it off, so it jumped and twisted like a headless snake.

How could he have got himself into this? He was a tough guy. Always in charge. Always ahead of the game. But things had been switched around. He'd lost control, and there was not a hell of a lot he could do about it now.

Bowers Corner looked eerie at night. With no interior lights to soften the outline, it was as imposing as a witch's castle on a stony mountaintop. The roofline jutted with sharp angles where the gables joined the structure, and the antique glass in the attic windows reflected a rippled moon.

Brownie parked his van by the porch and got out. His meeting with Jenneane had exceeded any possible expectations. For some reason, the child had absorbed the day of the shooting like a sponge. All it took was a gentle squeeze, and the details had squirted out like rainwater.

The Miller angle was puzzling. If it *was* him, why was he riding in the back of his truck? He guarded that piece of junk like a Rolls Royce. It would be odd for him to turn it over to someone else, and then to take a seat in the bed. That didn't sound like the Miller he knew, but it was a beginning. Maybe now he could start to put together a case that was more than speculation.

Brownie mounted the porch and inserted a key in the lock. The tumblers clicked, and the glass door creaked open. He shone his flashlight into the room, and looked for the switch that would illuminate the brass fixtures on the wall. He found it, and threw the small toggle. Nothing. He crossed to the far side and tried the one by the back door. Again, nothing. There was no power. Someone had shut it off.

In the beam of his flashlight, somewhere in there, was the evidence of a third shot. The field detectives had assumed only two shots and never scoured the perimeter for another bullet. Brownie had thought the same thing, and had not wasted time poking around the shelves. But Jenneane's recollection was not to be ignored.

Walking over to the position where the bodies were found, Brownie began sighting possible trajectories. The shooter's back had been to the rear wall. That much was obvious. The bodies had both lain with their heads towards the front door. He sighted forward and down, to the place where the fragments were found, on the floor several feet past the victims. Brownie turned slightly and aligned himself with the chalk mark where Granville had fallen. It was at right-angles to the other bodies. He stepped back and imagined the gun barrel pointed at Granville's head. Then he sighted twenty degrees to either side. Then ninety degrees up. Then ninety degrees down. Following those sight lines he walked to the shelves that intersected the path. But nothing had been disturbed.

Brownie went back and adjusted the angle so that Granville would have been facing directly towards the spot where Addie was shot. Projecting trajectories from that location brought several additional shelves into view. He carefully examined each one, finally arriving at a high shelf by the front door. Using a chair as a stepladder, he slowly went from bottom to top, turning cans, moving boxes, looking for any sign of a bullet's path. When he reached the top shelf, his light picked up a metallic glint on the side of a soup can. He grabbed it and pulled it out. There was a slight crease on the

60

side, enough to cut the red paper and expose the silver of the can. He pushed the other cans aside and illuminated the wall behind the shelf. There was a hole! A jagged hole blasted into the plaster. Brownie had a sudden vision of Addie and Henry's shattered heads at the morgue. He swallowed hard, and shone his light into the hole. As far as he could see, it was empty. He pulled out his penknife and inserted it into the opening. He probed and probed, looking for the bullet, but it was gone. Someone had got there first!

Gardner and Jennifer sat at the dining-room table of the townhouse, staring across their plates. Gardner's baked chicken had been barely touched, and he repeatedly rubbed the back of his neck, a sure sign that the tension of recent events had lodged in his shoulder muscles. The interim police report lay to the side of his place mat, creased and rumpled by repeated handling.

'Do you want more tea?' Jennifer was trying hard to maintain the appearance of normalcy. She had never seen Gardner so depressed as he'd been after visiting Granville.

'Uh, no. No thanks, Jennifer.' Gardner was lost in thought.

'Are you going to finish that, or do you want me to wrap it for tomorrow?' Jennifer asked.

Gardner pushed at the plate. 'I'm done. Just can't eat right now.'

Jennifer stood, and cleared her place. Gardner began to stand, but she motioned him down. 'No. You sit there. I'll take care of it. I have a surprise for dessert.'

He flopped back into his chair. 'Surprise?' A brief smile flickered on his lips. Jennifer was a jewel: a brilliant attorney and a loving companion. She was tough as nails in the courtroom, and soft as satin at home.

She soon returned with a chocolate eclair, his absolute favourite.

'Thank you,' he said, pulling her down for a quick kiss on the cheek. He took several bites of his dessert as Jennifer watched. When he had finished, he picked up the police report. 'Did you read this thing?'

Jennifer moved to a side chair, where she could see the writing. 'You put me in charge, remember?'

61

Gardner turned to the last page. 'No suspects,' he quoted. 'They're not even referring to Miller as a suspect.'

Jennifer touched the page, and traced the words that Gardner had just read aloud. 'Brownie's hunch does not make him a suspect.'

He nodded. 'But his instinct's usually right on the money. I can't believe they don't have more evidence than this!'

Jennifer's hand moved to his arm. 'Relax, Gard.'

'God!' Gardner groaned. 'Two people gunned down, Granville injured, and they still haven't got any suspects!'

Jennifer rubbed his arm. 'Gard . . .'

'We have to do something. We, uh . . . You . . .' He corrected himself. 'It's killing me, just sitting here . . .'

'It was your decision to step aside, and you know it was *right*,' Jennifer said. 'I'm meeting Brownie tomorrow. He has some new leads.'

Gardner looked up. 'Leads?'

'A new witness. Possible identification of Miller and his truck near the crime scene.'

'Why didn't you tell me?'

'Because nothing's certain yet. I'll brief you after I get the facts.'

'But . . .'

'Obey your own directive. Please,' Jennifer said. 'It'll make it easier on both of us.'

Gardner started to protest, but stopped, and grabbed the arms of the mahogany chair. 'It's hard to do that,' he said more calmly.

'I know.'

'I'm sorry I got testy,' Gardner said.

'That's OK,' Jennifer replied, moving over and sitting on his lap. 'I *do* understand what you're going through.'

'But what if the witness doesn't pan out?' Gardner had slowed down, but he couldn't quit.

'We'll deal with that when it happens.'

'But we still need an ID. A *crime scene* ID.'

Jennifer squeezed his neck and felt the tension.

Gardner closed his eyes. The investigators could search and search, but only one person could really solve the case. One person. The only eyewitness to the crime. Granville.

CHAPTER 5

Granville was curled up in his bed, dreaming about Uncle Henry's bunnies. He had been home for three days, and all his dreams had been dark and spooky. But this one was sunny. He and Dad were at the Bowers Corner pets zoo. Granville looked into the first cage. A large white furball with the reddish eyes was looking out through the wire bars. His nose twinkled as he sniffed. Granville smiled, and turned to see Dad. He was gone. Suddenly, a shadow came across the sun. Granville turned to the cage. A man stood on the other side of the enclosure. He was dressed in black, and was so tall that Granville couldn't see his face. It was getting dark, and the rabbit in the cage began to hop around. The man opened the top of the wire and reached in. The bunny scurried to get away, but he was caught. It was getting darker and darker. Granville looked for Dad again, but it was too dark to see. The bunny was struggling. Kicking and squirming to get away. There was some writing on the side of the man's hand. Granville yelled at him, but he wouldn't stop. The bunny was shaking, its eyes wide with terror and pain. Dad! Dad! The darkness was turning to red. Red. Wet, sticky red all over. Dad! Dad!

Carole awoke, and ran to Granville's room when she heard him scream. She had been warned that this might happen. Nightmares were a common aftermath of trauma. She had left the nightlight on and kept the door open, just in case, but the strangled voice still startled her.

'Granny. Granny!' She shook his small body gently. His head was damp, and he'd twisted his covers into a tangled mess.

'Mom . . .' He put his arms round her.

'It's OK. You just had a dream,' she said, stroking his matted hair. 'Just a dream.'

Granville blinked away the sleep. 'I got scared.'

'You're fine now,' Carole said. 'No one's going to hurt you.'

The boy hugged his mother tightly. 'Can I sleep with you?'

Carole didn't answer immediately. Her son was eight years old, well past the stage where he had to cuddle with mommy in order to go to sleep. He'd graduated to his own room long ago, and not only accepted it, he liked it. Now he was slipping backwards. Since the day of the shooting, ever so slowly backwards.

'Can I, Mom?'

'Yes, Granny, you can.' Carole could not resist his pleading look. 'But just for tonight. Tomorrow you have to go back in your own bed.'

They gathered Granville's teddy bear, and walked down to Carole's room, holding hands. The clock on her dresser said 2.15 a.m. She pulled back her covers and let her son slip inside. Then she got in next to him, and reached for the light.

'No. Please, Mom.'

Carole considered switching it off anyway, but she retracted her hand. Granville was not playing games. The bedside lamp would burn all night because, among other things, Granville had developed an aversion to the dark.

The law office of Kent King was situated in the Veil Valley Professional Center, near the county's up-market doctors, dentists and attorneys. King had been the first tenant there when it opened two years before, and he had selected the prime location, a suite of first-floor offices at the head of the main thoroughfare. His large two-sided sign could not be missed as the people came and went to have their teeth drilled or their taxes prepared. Sooner, or later, they came back to Veil Valley. And, most of the time, it was to see King.

'Mr Edwin Charles to see you, sir,' his secretary called over the intercom.

King leaned back in his tufted leather chair. 'Thanks, Tanya. You can send him in.'

The door opened and a distinguished-looking man entered. He was in his late fifties with metallic grey hair, wearing wire rim glasses, and tweed from shoulder to foot.

'Mr Charles, please sit.' King motioned to a captain's leather chair.

'Thank you.' Charles eased down into the seat. 'You know who I am,' he began. 'Headmaster of Prentice Academy.' King nodded. 'Been there twenty years,' Charles continued smoothly.

King did not blink. The man's name was synonymous with the Academy. 'What can I do for you?' he asked.

'Can you tell me if you drew up some documents for Henry Bowers?'

King frowned. Client dealings were confidential.

'Uh . . . A bequest to the school. Henry planned to leave us some money when he died . . .'

King interrupted. 'Mr Charles, I'm not at liberty to discuss communications with my clients.'

'But he's dead,' the headmaster replied.

'All the more reason,' King answered. 'He can't defend himself against false claims.'

Now Charles was frowning. He pulled a piece of paper out of an envelope in his lap, and passed it across to King. 'We talked about it. Quite some time ago. Henry and I. He loved the school. What we were trying to accomplish there . . .'

King looked at the paper. The date at the top was seven years earlier. $500,000 was written in large print in the middle of the page.

'Henry guaranteed it. When he passed away, we could get the money. That's what he said.'

'Who wrote this?' King asked.

Charles hesitated. 'I did,' he finally said. 'But Henry signed it. At the bottom.' He pointed to an H with a squiggly line after it. 'There. Right there.'

King shook his head. 'You're not suggesting that this thing is enforceable, are you?'

'Uh, no. I don't really know. That's one reason I'm here. Henry told me he was going to get it written up in proper legal form. Did he see you about it?'

King shook his head again. 'Mr Charles, I'm not permitted to say. If I did draw up any papers, or if I didn't is a private matter. But it's really a moot question, isn't it?'

65

The headmaster's expression turned quizzical. 'I mean,' King continued, 'Henry didn't have that kind of money. Half a million? That's ridiculous!'

A shadow passed over Charles' face. 'You're sure about that?'

King smiled wryly. 'He was broke.'

'But Henry said . . .'

King smiled. 'Saying and having are two different things. I'm sure his intentions were good, but you cannot give what you haven't got.'

Charles looked confused. He had not expected this. 'Anything else?' King asked. 'Anything else I can help you with?'

Charles' face was still blank. 'Uh, no . . . I guess not.'

King stood up and handed his business card across the desk. 'Well, if you ever need any legal advice for yourself, you know where to call.'

Charles stood, and took the card. 'Thanks, Mr King. I may just do that.'

The meeting ended on that note, and Charles left the room. As soon as he was out of the door, King dialled the number for Purvis Bowers.

'Hello?'

'This is King. Mr Edwin Charles just paid me a visit.'

There was a pause. 'What did he want?'

'Money.'

'What did you tell him?' King did not reply. 'What now?' Bowers asked.

'We just sit tight,' King said. 'If he makes a formal claim, we'll have to defend it. But don't worry, Prentice Academy won't get a cent.'

'You're sure about that?' King went silent again. He hated anyone to question his advice. 'So we're OK?' Bowers persisted.

'So far. Just pray that no one digs too deep.'

'I will,' Purvis replied.

'Good.' Then King hung up the phone. Their moves had been well planned; the money was safe, and it was all legal. With a little luck, the police would rush past it in their search for the killer.

'Call your next witness,' Judge Danforth ordered from his

lofty bench in courtroom one. It was mid-afternoon, and the minor shoplifting case had dragged on all day. The assistant public defender, an inexperienced recent appointee, was making her debut against Gardner Lawson. So far, the blonde twenty-six-year-old had effectively stood her ground.

But Gardner had fought back. Despite his lack of enthusiasm, he could not let this rookie best him on her first try. He was sleepwalking through the case, barely able to concentrate, but he knew how to draw on his storehouse of experience. And now he was about to call his main witness, the store detective who had caught the defendant stealing a pair of designer jeans.

'Stuart Ingram,' Gardner said wearily.

A uniformed man in his early thirties took the witness stand, and was sworn in.

'State your name for the record,' the clerk droned.

Gardner's mind was far away. He was barely listening, hardly aware of the trial or the people around him. The voices were hushed, like distant whispers. He was lying in the hammock back at the Watson Road house, six and a half years ago. The sun lit his face as he rocked slowly from the shade into the light, and the tall pine trees whistled in the soft wind. He was peaceful. Content. Suddenly something touched his arm. 'Da-da.' Granville had escaped his crib, crawled down the stairs and gone to find his dad. Gardner smiled, and pulled Granville up into the hammock, laying him across his chest, belly to belly. The boy hugged his neck, and together they continued to rock from the shadows into the light.

'Mr Lawson!' Judge Danforth shouted. 'Ask a question! We can't stay here for ever!'

Gardner shook off his daydream and stood up. 'Uh, Mr . . .' He had to look at the report to find the man's name. 'Mr Ingram, please tell the court by whom you are employed.'

'Cran Mart.'

'Is that Crandall Market Incorporated? A licensed enterprise doing business as Cran Mart?'

'Yes, sir.' Exact corporate identity was a crucial element of proof. Without it, the case could be lost.

'Uh, and were you working on the . . .' Gardner had to scan

the report again for the date '. . . fourth of September?'

'Yes, sir. I was.'

'And in what capacity?'

'Undercover shoplift patrol.'

Gardner opened a plastic bag and pulled out a dark blue pair of jeans. 'Let me show you this item, and ask if you can identify it?'

The witness took the jeans, and looked at a dangling tag. 'It's one of ours. Sportswear.'

Gardner slowly walked back to his table. 'Can you be more specific?'

'Cran Mart's.'

Gardner rubbed his neck. 'More specific than that?'

'Crandall Market Incorporated, trading as Cran Mart.'

'Thank you.' Gardner's mind was wandering again. Now he was at Bowers Corner, the last time he had taken Granville to see the rabbits. 'Uh, can you tell the court when you last saw that item?'

'On September fourth, a customer placed this pair of jeans in a shopping bag, and left the store.'

Gardner was still watching Granville and the rabbit in his mind. 'Was there any attempt to pay for the item?'

'No, sir.'

The rabbit was kicking, and Granville was holding on for dear life. 'What was the value of the item?'

'Thirty-nine ninety-five.'

'And there was no attempt to pay?'

'None, sir.'

Gardner leaned back in his chair, and placed both hands over his eyes. The images were still coming on strong. 'And you apprehended the customer?'

'Yes, sir.'

Gardner leaned forward, and scanned the report. 'Uh, and he, uh, he confessed to taking the jeans?'

'Yes, sir, he did. After he got caught, he said he'd like to pay for them, but I told him it was too late.'

Gardner ran his finger down the report. 'Uh, and the item, again . . . the item was the property of whom?'

'Cran Mart.' The prosecutor glared scornfully at the

witness. 'Sorry. Crandall Market Incorporated, trading as Cran Mart.'

'Thank you.' There was a long silence.

'Anything more, Mr Lawson,' Judge Danforth asked impatiently.

'Uh, no, sir. Your witness.' He glanced at the PD.

The ingénue stood up. 'No questions, your honour.' She was smiling broadly.

'Any other witnesses, State?'

Gardner checked his notes. 'Uh, no. No other witnesses. We rest.'

The assistant PD was on her feet in a flash. 'Motion for judgment of acquittal, your honour!' Her expression was one of triumph.

'Grounds, counsel?'

The PD's smile broadened. 'There has been no identification of the defendant as the person who took the goods, Judge. That's an essential element, and it's missing.'

Gardner suddenly woke up. She was right. That detail *had* been omitted. It was something a good prosecutor never left out, but today he had.

'Response, Mr Lawson?' Danforth knew it was all over, but he wanted to give Gardner a chance to pull it out.

'Uh, there was, uh, an implied ID . . .' Gardner stuttered.

'There must be an actual, unequivocal identification, or the case fails,' the PD interjected smugly.

Danforth nodded, and the prosecutor knew it was no use. An identification is the cornerstone of conviction. Without it, the prosecution is dead.

'Motion granted,' Danforth said solemnly. 'Case dismissed.'

Gardner rose, and extended his hand to the Public Defender. 'Nice job,' he said without enthusiasm.

She smiled. 'Thank you.' After all she had heard about Gardner, it was too easy. This was definitely not the man she had expected.

The prosecutor gathered his books and slowly walked towards the door. He pushed through it, and left the courtroom. He'd quit the Bowers case because he couldn't be objective. And now the malaise had spread to everything else.

IV Starke sat on the bed and punched a set of numbers into his cordless phone. His dorm room was of standard boarding-school dimensions: short in length by shorter in width, a warren for sleeping and studying, and not much more. But Starke's was opulent in its decor, decorated with fancy curtains, bedspread and pillows, with a state-of-the-art sound system, computer, television, VCR and leather easy chair. And, of course, there was a telephone.

The other students had to use the pay phones in the lower corridors of their dormitories. The rules were strict in that regard. But Starke's father, a wealthy contributor to the annual fund, had suggested that they be set aside for his son. And thus he became the only kid in town with his own private communications network.

The line buzzed, and a female voice answered. 'Maria, this is IV. Let me speak to Dad.'

A moment later, Wellington Starke came on the line. 'Son?' There was a hint of concern in his tone.

'It's me.'

'Haven't heard from you for a while.'

'I've been busy.'

'On school work?'

'Uh-huh.' Starke wanted to get right to the point. He knew his dad was going to bust an artery when he got the news, so he figured he'd get it over with. 'Uh, Dad, I might get put on suspension . . .'

Wellington took a deep breath. 'Suspension?'

'Yeah.'

'Why, son?' He was trying to control his anger.

'Uh, had a problem at the skeet meet. They say I threatened one of the judges.'

Another deep breath on the phone. 'Did you?'

'No!' He raised his voice. 'Those creeps tried to disqualify me!'

'So what did you do?'

'Nothing!'

70

'They don't suspend for nothing,' Wellington replied. 'You must have done *something*.'

'All I did was suggest it might not be a good idea to keep me out of the meet.'

'That's all?' Wellington knew there was more.

'Well, I was sort of holding a shotgun at the time.'

'Oh, God!'

'They said I pointed it at the chief judge, but I didn't! I swear! They just wanted me out because they knew I was gonna win!'

The deep breaths were coming faster over the line. 'When are they going to make their decision?'

'Tomorrow morning. Headmaster Charles is having a meeting with the athletic association. If those guys push it, Mr Charles says they're gonna have to bust me.' There was a plea in his voice.

'OK, OK, OK.' His father let out a long plaintive sigh. 'I'll see what I can do.'

'Thanks, Dad.'

'OK, OK.' Wellington sounded weary from the conversation.

'Oh, yeah, Dad. There is one more thing.' Silence on the other end. 'I'm gonna need some money.'

'You got your trust cheque this week.'

'I know, but . . .'

'My God, son, it's ten thousand dollars!'

'I know, Dad, but . . .'

'Don't tell me you've spent it all!'

'I need some more.'

'How much?' The exasperation became resignation.

'Twenty.'

'Twenty?'

'Yeah, Dad. I'm on the hook. I need another twenty grand.'

There was no reply, but it didn't matter. The old man was going to come through. He huffed and puffed, but he always came through. What else was he going to do? Say No to his only heir?

Young Starke said good-bye to his dad and hung up. He smiled, and thought about tomorrow. If things took their normal course, his problems would soon be solved.

Granville was on the floor of the therapist's office, and Gardner was again watching through the two-way glass. Nancy Meyers had tried to run the routine again: small-talk, playtime and drawing. Granville was still taciturn and uncooperative, not interested in talking, not interested in toys, not interested in drawing. They were nearing the end of the session, and nothing had been accomplished. 'Here,' Nancy said. 'Take this and draw me a nice picture.' She handed Granville the pad that he'd previously rejected. 'I hear you're a great artist. That's what your dad and mom told me.'

She was right, Gardner thought. The boy had some talent. He stayed within the lines in his colouring books, and his freehand sketches were remarkably able.

Granville took the pad across his knees, and scraped his pencil across the page.

'Good!' Nancy exclaimed.

Granville then crossed back with another line.

'OK,' Nancy said. At least he was drawing *something*. Suddenly Granville's hand began moving rapidly, and he scribbled up and down the page.

'Good. Good!' she encouraged him.

Granville was drawing furiously now, and Gardner strained to make out the image. Finally, he put the pad down and crossed his arms.

'Bravo!' Nancy said.

Gardner looked at the marks on the page: nothing but a bunch of meaningless scrawls. Elliptical lines that went round and round a central point, then crossed over each other.

'What is it?' Nancy asked.

Granville shrugged his shoulders.

Gardner studied the page. The drawing looked like a jumbled attempt at an atom symbol. Nothing coherent about it at all. What was Granville trying to say?

The crime laboratory at police headquarters was equipped with most of the modern devices that forensic scientists had developed in recent years. There was a fingerprint classification computer, a chemical substance analysis kit, a digital breathalyser, a high-powered microscope and a wide assortment of eavesdropping, wiretapping, and long-range surveillance gear.

Brownie had put in a requisition every time a new gismo came on the market and, in deference to him, the department usually came through with the funds. His latest toy was a laser latent fingerprint reader. With it, prints that were invisible to traditional collection methods miraculously materialized under the intense light beam. He'd had it only a short time but, so far, it had been used to solve a drive-by shooting and a string of commercial burglaries.

He had already dusted the dented soup can from Bowers Corner with the black powder that would cling to the skin oils left behind. That's what a latent print really was. A residue of body oil in the shape of the ruts and ridges on the end of the finger. The powder adhered to the oil, and the print emerged. But sometimes the touch was so brief, or the amount of oil so slight, that the powder didn't cling. When that happened, the old method was useless. The only other hope for developing the print was the laser.

Brownie placed the can in the chamber and sealed the lid. Then he dimmed the overhead light, and adjusted the eyepiece on the machine. Finally he triggered the switch, and a whirring sound was emitted from the cylindrical unit as the laser powered up. Zap. Zap. Zap. The beam pulsed against the can. Searching. Probing. At each pulse, a simultaneous macro-photograph was snapped. Zap. Zap. Zap. The can rotated on an internal turntable, so that the beam could reach every square inch of the can. Finally the circular motion stopped, the zap, zap, zap quieted and the whirring sound cut off. The procedure was complete.

He withdrew the film canister and placed it on the table. The person who removed the bullet at Bowers had to have touched the can. There was no way to get to the wall without pushing it aside. If the laser did its job, it would not be long before he had a print. And then, all he had to do was put a face to the wobbly lines.

'Brownie!'

He turned and greeted Jennifer as she entered the lab.

73

Dressed in jeans and a light jacket, she was in her field outfit. 'Ready?' she asked. They were supposed to review the Bowers evidence, then drive to the crime scene.

'Give me a minute, OK?' Brownie asked, as he carried the laser-print film over to the closet-sized darkroom. 'Let me set these in here, and then we can get started.'

Jennifer said OK, and walked over to an examination table against the wall. Brownie had laid out the bullet fragments on a white cardboard sheet. Uneven and splintered, there was no semblance to a cone shape, but he had tried to piece them together to get an idea of the overall dimensions.

'Really strange,' Brownie said suddenly, over her shoulder. 'Never seen a bullet like that. Not in today's market.' Jennifer leaned in to get a clearer look. 'Too much lead there,' he continued. 'More than a .357, I'd say. And look at that.' He poked a long twisted splinter with the point of a pencil. 'That's an old chunk of metal.' He emphasized *old* as if it had some special significance. 'Museum piece.'

Jennifer turned and faced Brownie. 'What does it mean?'

'It means that it didn't come from an ordinary gun. No way. Came from something special, a unique piece of weaponry.'

Jennifer blinked behind her glasses. 'What kind, Brownie?'

'Don't know. Not yet . . . But I'm workin' on it.'

They sat down at the centre table. Brownie had laid out the police reports, the autopsy photos and the pictures he had taken of Roscoe Miller the night he was picked up. Together they went over each item, and Brownie summarized his conclusions as they went along.

It had been a pre-planned hit. Although it had the appearance of a robbery, there was no money taken. Addie and Henry's inventory records were so poor that they couldn't be sure if any merchandise was missing. The shotguns and shells appeared to have been disturbed, but they couldn't say for certain if any of those items were removed. The shells in Miller's truck were run-of-the-mill twelve-gauges. They could have come from anywhere and, without a serial number inventory list, they could not be traced to the store. Brownie had checked the numbers on the boxes at Bowers, and compared them to the tracking numbers on Miller's shells. They were from a totally different series. The method of execution was professional. Clean. Deliberate. But there were some amateurish elements, such as allowing the perimeter to be penetrated by a child. This has led to the two-man theory.

Brownie was about to continue, when Jennifer stopped him. 'Motive,' she said. 'What was the motive?'

Brownie shifted in his seat. 'Been working on that. I tried to get bank records, but the Bowers apparently never used one.'

Jennifer showed surprise. 'No bank?'

'No. Not as far as I could tell. Couldn't find any record of an account.'

'So they only used cash . . .' Jennifer's mind was racing.

'Uh-huh.'

'Maybe they saved some. Kept it at the store.'

'Could have.'

'And someone knew it, and killed them for it.'

Brownie puckered his wide forehead. 'That's where I have a problem. If they were saving money, they wouldn't have kept it in the store. At least not downstairs. This thing went off too fast. The killers were in and out. Nothing upstairs was touched, and there wasn't enough time to do everything and still grab the money.'

'So maybe they left it, and came back later.' Jennifer was making notes as she talked.

Brownie's thoughts suddenly jumped to the hole in the wall above the shelf. 'Well, *somebody* went back.' He then filled Jennifer in on the midnight visit to the store, the hole, the can and the laser machine.

'So we have a shot at a fingerprint!'

'If Speedo over there is working properly,' Brownie answered, jerking his thumb towards the laser, 'we'll know as soon as the photos come out.'

'How much money do you think they had?' Jennifer asked suddenly.

'Don't jump too fast, Jennifer,' Brownie warned. 'We don't know for sure if they had any. That store was not exactly a money machine.'

'But it's the only possible motive,' she argued.

'So far,' Brownie replied. 'There could be something else.'

Jennifer picked up one of Roscoe Miller's pictures. 'So how does he fit in?'

Brownie scowled. 'He's the shooter. I know it. Worthless piece of . . .' He caught Jennifer staring. 'Uh, excuse me, Jennifer, I just . . .' He stopped talking. He was a tough, almost nerveless, cop. He cussed and spit, and fought, and got down and dirty with the best of them. But, with women, he was a gentleman.

'If Gard were here, you'd say it,' Jennifer continued. 'But I'm running this case. He put me in charge. Now do me the favour of treating me the same way you'd treat him.'

Brownie's magic smile exploded on his face. 'Piece of shit!' he said.

'Thank you,' she said softly, breaking into a grin. 'Now let's get back to work.'

They spent another hour outlining the evidence, discussing Miller's tentative ID by Jenneane Dorey on the day of the murder, why he might be riding in the back of his truck instead of up front, and his clammed-up attitude from the moment Brownie had first accosted him.

'I *know* Miller did it,' Brownie said. 'I just can't prove it yet. Even a positive ID by Jenneane Dorey doesn't put him at the scene, only near it. We've gotta get something more specific. Like Roscoe flashing a handful of money . . .'

'So we're back to the money again,' Jennifer said wistfully. 'What's your plan on that?'

Brownie flipped a page on his note pad. 'Put out a teletype . . . Check if any of the local jurisdictions have seen Roscoe with cash. Ask around the neighbourhood . . . Tomorrow I'm meeting the nephew, Purvis Bowers. He was Henry and Addie's accountant. He must know about their finances.'

'Sounds good,' Jennifer said in a distracted voice. She had just focused on one of Miller's photos. 'Why did you take this one, Brownie?' It was a close-up of his hand, showing an evil-looking skull-and-bones tattoo across the wrist.

Brownie picked up the glossy print and studied it. 'Bastard claimed I beat him up, but look . . . Not a scratch.' Jennifer was still staring at the skull. 'Ugly damned thing, isn't it?'

'Charming,' she said.

Brownie picked up the photo. 'Jennifer, if you saw something like that for the first time, you think you might remember it?' She nodded. 'Me too. Sucker sticks out like a neon sign.' Jennifer looked into Brownie's eyes. 'And if Roscoe was waving a gun around, tattoo like that might just get stuck in your face . . .'

'Or in your mind,' Jennifer said suddenly.

'Right,' Brownie answered, and walked out of the lab.

CHAPTER 6

'Push me, Mom!' Granville yelled. 'Please!'

The swing set behind the Watson Road house was one of the first things that Gardner had bought to celebrate his son's birth. It was 'a child lives here' symbol. And, as Granville grew, he was out there all the time.

'Push me,' Granville called again.

Carole watched from the porch as the boy allowed the swing to lose its momentum and die. In the past week, he'd continued his backward slide. He had insisted on sleeping in her bed every night now, and today, he couldn't even keep the swing going by himself. This was normal, the therapist said. The increased clinginess was a natural by-product of the shootings. Carole stepped into the yard and took Granville by the waist.

'Push, push!' Granville chanted.

'OK,' Carole said. She drew him back and released him, allowing a gentle forward swing.

'Do what Dad used to do!' Granville begged. 'Ride under!'

Carole's mind flashed back to Gardner pulling the swing way, way back, then running forward, pushing it up over his head, and releasing it. She's always hated it; the steep angles were too dangerous. She'd even made Gardner stop doing it.

'Ride under, Mom!' Granville was still lobbying for the high ride.

'No, Granny. I don't like it.'

'Please?'

'I'll give you a big push instead,' Carole said, shoving harder.

Meanwhile, in a wooded strip two hundred yards below the house, a pair of eyes was watching. The man adjusted his binoculars, and tried to keep the face of the little boy in view. Because of the angle, and the motion of the swing, it was hard to do. But, at the top of the ride, as he stopped for a fraction of a second, the face was perfectly framed in the circular lens. That was him. The little shit who had walked in at Bowers. Sticking his nose into a situation that was none of his business.

The swing dropped back, and the face disappeared. Then it returned. No memory, huh? No ID? I don't believe it. He *knows*! The bastard *knows*. The little shit should have gone the same route as the Bowers. A two-hundred-eighty grain shot to the head.

The man shifted his position on the ground. A nice set-up the prosecutor had. Ex-wife and son in a big house in the middle of nowhere. So remote. So accessible. The address was no secret, and with all of the trails and woods and back roads in the area, it was a piece of cake to sneak up on it. The face popped into view again. No way the kid's sick, the man thought. He's a normal jerky little kid. A witness. Nothin' but trouble . . .

Just then, he detected movement past the house, and shifted his glasses to the parking area. A county police car was pulling up. The man ducked, and retreated into the woods. Can't remember? Bullshit! The cops are working on him. They've got nothing else to make the case. If he shoots off his mouth, it's all over.

The man was sprinting now, dodging trees and bushes to retrace the route he'd taken in. The image of Granville haunted him as he ran. Something had to be done. One more hit. Wipe that goo-goo expression off the little bastard's face with another look down the barrel of his gun. One more face-to-face. Only, this time, he'd get more than a bruise between the eyes.

Purvis Bowers was already at the store when Brownie arrived. They had agreed to meet at 10.30 a.m., but Brownie decided to get there early and walk the perimeter again. At 10 o'clock, Bowers was parked out front and waiting. He got out of his grey compact car when he saw Brownie's door open. Wearing a blue polyester suit and a knit tie, he looked like a character in a thirties movie.

'Mornin' Mr Bowers,' Brownie said with a smile. 'See you're a bit early.' Bowers nodded. 'Been inside yet?'

Bowers shook a 'No', adding, 'You people took the key.'

'You didn't keep a spare?'

'No. Police told me they didn't want anyone in the store but them.'

That was correct. The initial investigation team had confiscated all the keys to the store, and Bowers had signed a statement that there were no others in circulation.

'Do you have any problem going inside with me now?' Brownie opened the door with the key he had brought, and turned to face Purvis.

The man was standing at the bottom step. 'Is that really necessary? You never said anything about going inside.'

'I'd appreciate it if you would,' Brownie said gently.

Just then, the noise of a vehicle erupted around the western curve in Mountain Road. A beat-up red truck approached at high speed and Brownie and Bowers both turned to look at it. It slowed suddenly, as if to stop, then picked up speed again when it came opposite the lab van. The driver was shaded by the cab, not clearly visible. In an instant, it had flown by and vanished into the wooded grove to the east.

'You know that guy?' Brownie asked.

Bowers had not moved a muscle since the truck first rounded the curve. 'Huh?' he said absently.

'Miller. Roscoe Miller. You know him?'

Bowers removed his glasses, and probed an eyesocket with his knuckle. 'Miller?'

'Yeah, Roscoe Miller. You ever seen him before?' It was a question without accusatory intent.

'I might have run into him a couple of times . . .'

Brownie's ears pricked. 'Yeah? Where?'

Bowers unbuttoned his coat. 'Around town. Here or there . . .'

Brownie made a mental note. Bowers and Roscoe. Maybe it meant something. He decided to let it ride for now. 'Let's go inside.' He changed gears, and led Bowers into the store. This time, when he hit the switch, the lights came on. They walked past the cash register, and stopped. The blood had

81

been scrubbed and the stains removed, but the white lines on the floor remained. 'Heard you did some accounting work for your aunt and uncle,' Brownie said suddenly. 'That right?'

Bowers took several steps away from the chalk lines. 'Yes.'

'Did they deposit their income in a bank?'

'Bank?'

'Yeah,' Brownie said sarcastically. 'Bank. A place where people keep money.'

Bowers crossed his arms. 'They did use Western National occasionally, for cashing cheques they received.'

'But did they *deposit* their receipts?'

'No. Not that I'm aware of.'

'Never had a bank account.' Brownie's statement was really a question.

'No,' Bowers reiterated. 'Uncle Henry had a problem with banks. He never trusted them.'

'So how much cash did your aunt and uncle have?' Brownie had done so well up to now, why not hit the central issue head on.

Bowers took another step away from the lines. 'How much money?'

'Yeah,' Brownie repeated. 'How much cash?'

Bowers did not respond. He was thinking. 'Why are you asking me these questions?' he finally said.

'I'm doing a murder investigation,' Brownie answered firmly. 'I have to ask questions.'

'But I already gave a statement to the other officers. Told them everything I knew.'

Brownie motioned him outside, and they walked to the porch. 'That was a preliminary report. They didn't ask you about your aunt and uncle's finances. If they had some money stashed away, big money, it might have been the motive for the shooting.'

Bowers turned round suddenly. 'They told me it was a robbery *attempt*. No one said anything about money being taken.'

Brownie leaned against a porch post. 'I'm working another angle. Maybe it was *more* than an attempt. Maybe something was actually taken. Some hidden cash . . . That's why we need to know what they had.'

Bowers closed his eyes for a moment. 'Can you answer the question, Mr Bowers? Did your uncle have some money hidden away?' The man remained silent. Brownie sensed a problem. 'How much money did they have?' he repeated.

'Am I under arrest or anything?' Bowers asked suddenly.

Brownie recoiled in surprise. 'No, of course not! But if you know anything about any secret money your aunt and uncle had, you'd better tell me now. If we turn it up later, *you* might be implicated!'

Bowers turned and started walking rapidly towards his car.

Brownie jumped off the porch and headed him off. 'Please, Mr Bowers, give me a break. Tell me what you know about the money.'

Bowers said nothing. 'Well?' Brownie was still waiting.

Bowers looked past him towards the car. 'No.'

Brownie's face reddened. 'Why not?'

'I want to talk to my lawyer first. Before I answer any more questions.'

'Who's your lawyer?' Brownie asked.

'Mr Kent King. Now, if you would please get out of my way, I'm going to leave.'

Brownie's question still hung in the air. He'd touched a nerve with Bowers. Maybe there really *was* a money trail that led back to the killings. He stepped back and let Bowers pass. He had no authority to hold him. 'Give King my regards,' he said sarcastically.

Bowers started his engine and drove off without answering.

'King?' Gardner had just been briefed by Jennifer on the Purvis Bowers impasse. It was noon, and he had returned from another court appearance on a misdemeanour case.

Jennifer was now working full-time on the Bowers investigation, and Brownie had rung her immediately after Purvis had cut and run at the store. 'He said he had to talk to his attorney before answering questions about the money,' she continued.

'Damn King!' Gardner pounded his fist on his walnut desk.

83

'Always in the middle of everything . . .'

Jennifer winced. 'Take it easy.'

'Let me see the file,' Gardner said gruffly, ignoring her admonition, and she pushed it across the desk. He opened it, and thumbed the pages rapidly. 'No bank. Never used a bank . . . Big deal!'

'Brownie seems to think it's something . . .' Jennifer was trying to get a handle on Gardner's mood swings. Ever since the shootings he'd been up and down daily. It was really beginning to get tedious.

'So the new theory is that Addie and Henry were hoarding cash,' Gardner said sarcastically, 'and they were killed for it!' He'd been around the Bowers long enough to see how they lived. They were simple, very simple. They had an old car, old clothes, old everything. They never even owned a colour TV, Henry used to brag. And now, suddenly, they were Rockefellers, wiped out for their dough! 'This was a flubbed robbery attempt, Jennifer. You're getting off track.' She resisted the temptation to argue. 'And King is going to push you all around all he can, just for kicks. You know the way he operates.'

Jennifer was still struggling to control herself. 'Gard, you put me in charge because *you* can't handle this case. Both Brownie and I think there may be an angle with the missing money. We want to pursue it.'

Gardner's face went dark. 'You're both wrong. This is a dead end, I'm telling you.'

Jennifer looked at the door to make sure it was closed. 'Listen to me. As long as I am in charge, *I* decide how to run this investigation. Please keep your negative comments to yourself!' Gardner looked as if he'd just been slapped in the face. He picked up the telephone. 'What are you doing?' she asked nervously. His expression was diabolic.

'Calling King.'

'Don't do that!'

He pulled the phone closer, as if to protect it from her reach. 'Uh, yes. Good morning. This is Gardner Lawson. Let me speak to King.'

Jennifer stood up and leaned over the desk. 'Don't do this!'

Gardner ignored her. 'Kent, Gardner. You have a client named Purvis Bowers?'

Jennifer gripped the edge of the desk to keep herself from throwing a punch. Gardner could never relinquish control. That was obvious now.

'OK.' His voice was smooth and reserved. 'We may have to bring him in before the Grand Jury . . .' He flashed a coy look to Jennifer. 'Right. The financial situation.'

Jennifer fired back a cold stare.

'No?' He gave Jennifer a smug smile. 'How about immunity, then? Transactional immunity for full disclosure?'

That was it. Jennifer reached across the desk and slammed down the hook with her finger.

'Whaaa?' Gardner suddenly realized he was cut off. 'What do you think you're doing?'

'What the hell do you think *you're* doing?' Jennifer snapped back.

'Trying to save this case!' Gardner snarled. 'You want the financial data, and I'm going to get it for you.'

'I didn't ask you to do that,' Jennifer said sternly. 'What if Bowers was in on it? You gonna walk him? Huh? Did you think of that?' Gardner frowned. It was obvious that he hadn't.

'King calling back on line one,' Gardner's secretary, Miss Cass, announced over the intercom.

Gardner glanced at Jennifer, and reached for the phone. She blocked his hand and picked it up.

'Mr King, this is Jennifer Munday.'

Gardner sank deep in his chair, and covered the side of his face with his hand.

'We are not in a position to offer immunity to anyone.' She looked at Gardner. His fingers tugged at his cheek, drawing down one eye. 'You misunderstood Mr Lawson, and if you believe that he made such an offer, you can consider it withdrawn.'

Gardner could hear King's explosive response.

'Sorry, he's stepped out.' Jennifer uttered a few closing words, and hung up. Then she looked at Gardner like a mother about to discipline her child. 'Don't *ever* do that to me again, Gard! I mean it.'

He didn't answer.

The phone rang in IV Starke's dorm room, and he picked it

up. 'Hello?' It was late afternoon, and classes were done for the day.

'Starke? It's Joel Jacobs.'

An unexpected call. 'Mr Jacobs . . .' He put down his magazine, and sat up on his bed.

'Your dad asked me to call. Heard you had some trouble on the gun range.'

News travelled fast in New York, especially between Wellington Starke and the master. 'Yeah, but it's OK now. They decided to drop the whole thing.' Thanks to Dad and you, he was tempted to add.

'No suspension?'

'No, sir. They didn't even make me apologize. Said it was just a misunderstanding.'

Jacobs cleared his throat. 'Was it?'

'Huh?' Starke didn't catch the meaning.

'A *misunderstanding*.' His emphasis on the word suddenly crystallized the question.

'Oh. Uh, no. I mean yes.'

'So you didn't point the weapon?'

'No sir!' This time he was emphatic. 'It was, sort of, in their direction, but I never pointed it.'

'You've gotta be careful!' Jacobs said suddenly. 'Do you have any idea of the consequences of that sort of thing?'

Starke went silent. 'I said I didn't do anything dangerous. Don't you believe me?'

This time Jacobs paused. It was as if he was counting to ten. 'I believe you, son,' he said with considerable effort. 'But if that gun had gone off, all your dad's money couldn't save you.'

'It didn't go off!' Starke said defiantly. 'I knew what I was doing!'

'That's what I'm afraid of,' Jacobs replied. 'Your smart-ass attitude is gonna do you in one of these days. Get yourself under control!' That was definitely an order.

'Uh, I'll try, Mr Jacobs,' Starke said meekly.

Jacobs was about to hang up, when Starke stopped him. 'Uh, Mr J., can I ask you a question?'

'Yes. Go ahead.'

'If something major happened, would you be there for me?' His tone was ominous.

'What do you mean?'

'I mean what if someone said I did something *really* serious? Would you defend me?'

Jacobs cleared his throat again. 'You're gonna have to be more specific, son.'

'I mean if someone *really* did get hurt, and they said I did it. Would you be my lawyer?'

'Did you do something else?' Jacobs did not sound pleased.

'No!' Starke's voice suddenly tailed off. 'But there's people . . . people around here who don't like me. I'm afraid they may try to set me up or something . . .'

'What the hell are you into?'

'Nothing! I swear it! But I'm afraid . . .'

'What of, son? You've got to tell me!'

'Just say you'll represent me, no matter what. Please?'

'You know I will . . .' Jacobs was comforting now.

'Good. I feel a lot better.'

Jacobs waited for more, but his young client stayed silent. 'You'd better come up to New York. I think we need to have a long talk.'

'Can't do it. Got two more weeks of school. Then I'm goin' to Nantucket.'

'I suggest you try to fit it in. It's *very important.*'

Starke made an excuse that the dinner bell had rung, and told the lawyer he had to run. 'I'll try to come up.'

'Do more than *try*, son,' Jacobs commanded. Then he said good-bye. Starke put the phone down and looked in the mirror. Why would they want to mess with someone as cool as him? He was rich. Smart. And powerful. Anyone would be stupid to try to take him down. But, if they did, he could always call on his New York reinforcements.

It was 10.30 p.m., and Roscoe Miller was well on his way to being drunk. He had money in his pocket and sex on his mind, so he had hurtled up past the State line to a notorious roadhouse known as the Drive Inn. Situated on the main interstate highway, the gaudy red-roofed saloon attracted truckers, coal miners and straying housewives. Supported by a two-hundred-room motel that backed up to the parking lot, the place was ideal for a night out, and Miller had no intention of leaving until he had got what he wanted.

He stood by the end of the bar, mouthing the end of a long-necked beer bottle. The honeys were out in force, and his eyeballs probed the dusk for a likely target. Miller never had a problem with women. They liked his dark skin and his bright eyes. Some even said he looked like a TV star. And that made it easy for him to score.

'How' do!' He spotted his mark sitting at a table by the dance floor. She had long, curly blonde hair, bare flesh spilling out of a ruffled shirt, and a curvy butt polishing the seat in time to the music. He shuffled over, and leaned down in her face. 'Evenin'.'

She looked at him, her eyes as blue and hypnotic as his own, her face youthful and smooth. 'Hello.' She was a nineteen-year-old farm queen, beautiful and bubbly. And she was ready.

'Excuse me!' A male voice suddenly interrupted his move from behind. Miller turned round, and found himself confronted by a hulking miner.

'Whut the hell do you want?' Miller was not at all intimidated. Back home, he ate punks like this for lunch.

'Cain't talk to her,' the miner said. 'She's with Charlie.'

Miller glanced back at the table. The girl was alone. Then he turned and put his hands on his hips. 'I don't see no Charlie.'

The miner also put his hands on his hips. 'He's on night shift.'

Miller smiled. These West Virginia bozos! Letting their women out under guard. 'Too bad for Charlie,' he said sarcastically, then turned back to the girl.

'Guess you didn't hear me,' the miner said as he grabbed Miller's shoulder.

Miller whipped round and delivered a kick to the miner's groin with the metal tip of his boot.

'Agggg!' There was a scream of pain as the man went down.

Instantly, six other grimy look-alikes converged from the bar. Miller took a defensive position and reached into his jacket pocket. The miners began to approach, their faces set with the look of revenge.

'You-all gonna die!' Miller barked as he pulled out a handgun.

The men froze. After what had just happened to their friend, there was no question this guy was serious. He was one crazy motherfucker.

Miller stood calmly as the miners gathered up their fallen comrade and retreated to the bar. Then he stuffed the gun back in his pocket, took the blonde by the elbow, and pointed her towards the back door. He had some heavy-duty plans for the rest of the night.

The sunlight was streaming into Appalachian Park from a cloudless sky. For a weekday morning, the place was under-standably deserted. Dads and mums were at work, and kids were at school. The only movement, except for the darting birds en route to their nests, was from two lone figures in the middle of the ball field.

'Catch it!' Gardner shouted, as a baseball arched high into the air and dropped towards Granville's outstretched glove. A day off from the office had been mandatory, after yesterday. He and Jennifer had barely spoken the night before, and he knew if he went to work, he'd be tempted to get into the Bowers file again. So, he and his son were playing hooky at the park.

'Awww . . .' Granville juggled the ball, and it dropped to the ground.

'That's OK,' Gardner yelled. 'It was a good try. Throw it back, and I'll hit you another.'

Granville gave the ball a mighty heave, but there was little power behind it. Gardner had to run up to fetch it, then backtrack to the batting area. It was strange, really. The two of them in that situation. Granville was unfit for school, and Gardner was unfit for work. Both were psychologically wounded. Gardner pondered that point as he held the ball in one hand and swung the bat with the other. A child could not even walk into a grocery store and be free of a visitation from hell. Predators were everywhere, and every time they struck, the consequences were unfathomable.

'Get it!' Gardner yelled as the ball squibbed off his bat and bounced across the ground.

Granville moved to the side and positioned himself in

front of it, the way his dad had taught him. Suddenly the ball hit a rut, and jutted off at an angle, striking Granville on the knee. He dropped the glove and fell backwards, ending up sitting on the ground.

'Shake it off,' Gardner yelled. 'Get up, and shake it off.' Granville stayed down, rubbing his knee. 'Gran! Get up.' The ball had not hit him that hard. But the boy didn't get up.

Gardner walked over, and plopped down on the grass next to his son. 'You OK?'

The boy had tears in his eyes. 'Uh-huh,' he said weakly.

Gardner pulled up the child's trouser leg, and exposed his knee. 'Where'd it hit?'

'Here.' Granville pointed to a spot, but there was no mark. The skin was clear.

Gardner rubbed the area gently with the tips of his fingers. 'Sometimes the ball doesn't go where we expect,' he said softly. 'Sometimes it takes a crazy hop.'

Granville looked up through his tears. 'I'm sorry, Dad.'

Gardner was not expecting that reaction. 'Sorry?'

'Uh-huh. I know I'm not s'posed to cry.'

'Who told you that?'

Granville pulled his trouser leg down, and stood up. 'You did. You said to pretend it didn't hurt . . .'

Gardner stood up also. He'd told Granville to pretend the ball was a marshmallow that just mushed when it hit.

'But it *did* hurt!' Granville continued.

Gardner picked up the boy's glove and handed it to him. 'I never said it wouldn't hurt.' He put his hand on Granville's narrow shoulder. 'You just can't let it stop you from playin'.' Just then, he was struck with the irony of his own words. The comment could just as well have referred to himself. He was on sick leave, too, out of the game. He had been preaching perseverance and tenacity all his life. But, lately, he'd quit.

He took his son's hand and led him to a nearby bench. They sat down, and Gardner looked into Granville's wide brown eyes. 'Gran, I need to talk to you about something.'

'What, Dad?' Granville could tell that his father was about to discuss something important, and he started to squirm.

90

'I want you to think real hard,' Gardner began. 'Real, *real*, hard . . .'

'What is it, Dad?' The boy's voice quavered.

'I want you to think about the day you got hurt,' Gardner said softly. 'Tell me what you can remember . . .' It was time for the prosecutor to find out for himself how much the only eyewitness really knew about the crime.

PART 3

Suspects

CHAPTER 7

Gardner leaned against the bench's backrest and looked at his son. Granville's legs dangled, and he nervously traced a semicircle in the air with his right foot.

'Gran, I want you to think back to the day you got hurt,' Gardner began. 'Do you remember going to the cave?'

Granville's foot speeded up its circular motion, and he gripped the edge of the bench with both hands. His eyes were cast down.

'Do you remember the cave?' Gardner repeated. This was definitely against the rules that Nancy Meyers had decreed: there should be but one inroad into Granville's troubled mind, the therapeutic course prescribed by her. No interrogation. No pressure. But the investigation was stalled, and the killers were still on the loose. They might decide to come back for Granville. Gardner couldn't wait. He had to act now.

'Gran?' Gardner took him gently by the chin and turned his face. 'I really need you to talk to Dad.'

The boy hesitated, but finally made eye contact. He appeared to be holding his breath. It was obvious that even a benign reference to the day of the murders could cause an electrical storm to erupt inside his brain. Granville's eyes broke contact almost immediately, as if they were searching for a safe haven away from his father's words.

Gardner felt a surge of frustration. The information was there, inside his head. But the boy was too scared even to turn in that direction, much less confront what lay inside the door.

'Gran.' Gardner tried to ease away from the urgency of his previous words. 'We don't have to talk about that now. Let's talk about something else.' Going in head first was not the way, he thought. Maybe he could sneak around the side.

Granville's face slowly turned back, and it seemed that he was breathing again.

'What say we go out to Simpson's pet store and look at some pups? Would you like that?'

Granville nodded. Since the 'talk' began, he hadn't said a word. 'Great,' Gardner continued. 'Maybe we can find one just like Minnie.'

The sun suddenly burst through the overcast in Granville's eyes. Minnie had been the family dog back when he, Carole and Granville were a family, a docile golden retriever with a mother complex, who allowed her tail to be pulled and stood in for a riding horse on many occasions. After the divorce, she'd found a home with a family across town, and blended in there as if she'd never known the Lawsons. But she was sorely missed. By Gardner, in his separate life. And by Granville, whose love for the dog went deeper than anyone knew.

'Remember the bally-wally?' Gardner smiled as he recalled teaching Granville how to make Minnie fetch. They'd nicknamed an old beat-up tennis ball 'bally-wally', and they would chant that phrase as they went out to throw the ball for her to race after, snap up in her mouth, race back and drop at their feet. 'Bally-wally! Bally-wally!' Granville would sing, and Minnie would go crazy. Jumping and leaping in anticipation of the chase, before the ball was even thrown. Just the mention of the words 'bally-wally' would send Minnie into hyper-space, running in circles, to the delight of Gardner and his toddling son.

Granville was smiling now. 'You gonna buy one, Dad?' he asked.

Gardner grinned. The tactic was working. 'We can look. Maybe if we find one like Minnie your mom might let me get it for you. But you know they've got some other animals there too.' He tensed. He did not want to shift subjects so fast that Granville would realize he was being manoeuvred back to Bowers Corner.

'Uh-huh.' Granville was still throwing Minnie the bally-wally in his mind.

'They've got snakes, and gerbils, and hamsters and rabbits.' Granville stopped smiling. Gardner let his breath out slowly. 'You love rabbits, don't you, son?'

Granville went silent and began to swing both feet. He gripped the bench with his hands, his face cast down again.

'What's your favourite? White or Black?' The feet speeded up. Gardner swallowed hard. 'You used to be real good at catching them. Remember?' He was back at Bowers. The feet were now a blur of motion.

Granville was struggling. It was as if he wanted to help his dad. He really wanted to, but something was standing in the way.

'Uncle Henry said you were the best catcher he ever saw,' Gardner said softly, looking at his son as the word 'Henry' was uttered.

The feet kept up their pace, and Granville gasped aloud. Tears began squeezing from his eyes and dribbling down his cheeks.

'So did Aunt Addie.' Gardner's heart felt like breaking as he said the dead woman's name, but he had to keep pushing. Granville was trying. Trying hard.

Suddenly Granville stopped swinging his feet and looked into his father's eyes. Tears were splashing everywhere. 'Dad!' he screamed. His voice sounded as if it had come from the bottom of a well.

Gardner scooped him into his arms, and hugged him, and kissed his head, and told him again and again that it was OK.

But, inside, he knew he'd made a start. Agonizing as it was, he'd have to keep going, pushing Granville until the menace revealed itself. So that dad could destroy it for ever.

'Got it!' Brownie yelled. The results were back from the laser fingerprint job on the soup can, and there, in photograph number six, was the fuzzy oval outline of a latent print on the edge of the label. He steadied the photo under his laboratory magnifier and examined the photo close up. 'Yeah. Yeah. Yeah,' he said to himself. Inside the faint outline was a network of interconnecting lines, the ridges, whorls and bifurcations of the print. There was enough there to make a comparison.

He removed the photo and placed it on the optical imaging receptor of his classification computer. After several adjustments of the light-dark control, he finally had it suitable for a feed into the system. 'OK, let's roll,' he said, pushing the enter button which allowed the computer to store the pattern of the print into memory.

Then Brownie moved over and sat at the console, activating the 'compare and classify' control. The screen responded by flashing a series of lightning-fast images of fingerprints into view as thousands of prints in the same general subcategory were juxtaposed on the one he had just fed in. The fingerprints of local felons and miscreants were on file there, but the system was also tapped into the Maryland and FBI data banks which provided access to almost a million more prints.

'Come on, baby,' Brownie sweet-talked the machine. 'Come on. Give it up.'

It seemed as if the computer was running the entire gamut of loaded prints. The pattern was changing faster and faster, as the optical imager came up short on the comparison each time. Finally the images began to slow down, and then they stopped. There was an audible 'beep', and the word UNKNOWN appeared on the screen.

'Shit!' Brownie whispered, giving the console a gentle whack with the palm of his hand, 'You done let me down, baby.' He moved the switch to the review mode, and ran the numbers on what the machine had just done. 'OFFENDER FILE COMPLETE', the summary said. The print wasn't in the file. That meant that the person who had left it had no criminal record.

Brownie rose and went to the case file on the lab desk. He ruffled the pages and pulled out Addie's and Henry's prints that were lifted at the morgue. In a minute the comparison was run, and the result was negative. Neither Addie nor Henry had left the print. 'Who else?' he said. Then a thought struck, and he hit the keys to access the law enforcement officers' prints stored in the personnel files of the department. The place had been swarming with cops after the shooting. Maybe one of them had touched the can.

Again there was a whirring sound as the unknown print went up against the hundreds of prints in the personnel file. Suddenly there was a double 'beep'. A match!

Brownie dropped the case file and raced to the screen. 'POSITIVE COMPARISON' was captioned at the top and, at the bottom, the name of the person who left the print. 'Son-of-a-bitch,' he moaned. The print belonged to SERGEANT JOSEPH BROWN. Himself.

It was late afternoon, and Jennifer was at the State Attorney's office, scouring the police report on the Bowers case for the thirtieth time that day. Sitting at Gardner's desk, in the privacy of his inner sanctum, she had been absorbed in the file for hours.

She leaned back in his leather chair so that the air-conditioning vent in the ceiling could blow some coolness across her face. The weather was heating up outside, and moist tendrils of summer were somehow finding their way inside the building. She closed her eyes.

She missed Gardner. He was like a petulant child sometimes, bent on having his way, but she couldn't freeze him out for long. Her heart was too soft to hold the anger that flared when he got bull-headed. She opened her eyes and focused on the photo perched on the corner of the desk. Granville was laughing, and his hair was flying as his father had caught him zooming down the hill at Watson Road on his bike. The boy was always in the middle. Caught between mom and dad in the break-up. And, now, between dad and a killer.

Jennifer snapped forward and flipped the file open to the bank records that Brownie had obtained. Gardner had belittled the monetary connection, but she and Brownie were convinced that, somehow, money was at the root of the shootings. The report was specific on one point: there was no bank account in the name of either Henry or Addie Bowers. Not in Western Maryland National. Not in Mountain Federal. Not even in Apple Valley Savings and Loan.

Jennifer picked up the phone and dialled Brownie's number at the lab. The line buzzed twice, and a familiar husky voice answered: 'Brown.'

'It's me, Jennifer.'

'Afternoon.' There was an uncharacteristic sadness in his tone.

'Catching you at a bad time?' she asked.

'Uh, no. Not really.'

'What's wrong?'

'I did something stupid.' The response took her by surprise. 'Spent the whole afternoon lifting my own fingerprint off that soup can.'

'What?' Jennifer wasn't following.

'Ran the latent print through the computer and it came back registered to Sergeant Joseph Brown. Don't even know my own damn print!'

'How did that happen?' Jennifer's voice was sympathetic.

'Don't know. I swear I never touched that can. I know better than that. All the damn evidence I've collected, never made a dumb move like that one.'

'So you touched the can, so what?'

'So that was my big lead. Chance to find out who dug the slug out of the wall.'

'No other prints on the can?'

'Nope. Just the thumbprint of a dumbass cop!'

Jennifer knew that Brownie was trying too hard. That's probably why he'd screwed up. His relationship with Gardner was so close that his objectivity was slipping too.

'OK, Brownie, that's done. We've got to get back on track.'

'I hear you.' The professionalism was returning.

'I want to talk about the bank records. I've been going over them, and I need to confirm a few things,' Jennifer said.

'Shoot.'

'You ran every bank in the area on the Bowers, right?'

'Every one.'

'And there were no listed accounts for Addie or Henry Bowers.'

'Correct.'

'What type of accounts were you looking for?'

'Cheque. Savings. Business accounts.'

'How about safe-deposit boxes?' Jennifer asked.

'Them, too.'

'What names were you searching under?'

'Henry R. Bowers and Addie S. Bowers.'

'Any others?'

'No. What are you driving at, Jennifer?'

'Did you run Purvis Bowers?'

'Not yet.' It was on Brownie's list, but he'd been side-tracked with the print search.

'Can you get a summons out on Purvis' bank records? As their accountant, maybe he did Addie and Henry's banking in his name.'

'Thought about that,' Brownie answered. '*He* could have the account. That might answer the question of why he got so squirrelly out at the store. Maybe he's the bagman for their secret stash.'

'Well, right now, he's our only live lead,' Jennifer said.

'Purvis?'

'Yes. I think he's the key at this point.'

'So what do you suggest we do?' Brownie asked.

'I'm going to subpoena Mr Bowers to appear before the Grand Jury,' Jennifer said resolutely. 'No immunity. No deals. He'll have to talk. You check out his bank records at the same time. Maybe we can catch him in a lie, and force out the truth.'

'King won't like that,' Brownie said solemnly.

'Screw King!' Jennifer snapped, sounding more like Gardner than herself. 'Bowers has to tell us about the money or face an obstruction of justice charge. And King can't protect him.'

'Now you're talkin'!' Brownie chuckled. 'I'll run the records summons, and you get your subpoena out on Purvis, and we'll be cookin'.'

'OK.'

'One more thing.' Brownie's voice dropped. 'How's Gardner doing?'

'So-so. Up and down. You know.'

'Take care of that boy,' Brownie said. 'Stick with him. He'll come round.'

'I'll try,' Jennifer whispered. Then she hung up the phone, pulled out her legal pad and began drafting a Grand Jury subpoena for Purvis Bowers.

Gardner and Carole had been called to Nancy Meyers' office

101

for a conference. Granville had been to four therapy sessions now, and she needed to talk with the parents about his progress.

'We seem to be off to a slow start,' she said. 'He hasn't yet adjusted to being here.'

Gardner had seen Granville's listless reaction on the floor of the therapy room, and his senseless scribbled drawings.

'How's he doing at home?' Meyers looked at Carole.

'Quiet. Almost morose,' Carole said.

'And with you?' She turned to Gardner.

'About the same,' Gardner replied. He said nothing about the tears at the playground.

'We'll just keep at it, then,' Meyers said, 'Slowly, slowly, slowly. I'm sure he'll start to relax before long.'

'How long do you think it will take?' Carole asked.

Meyers fiddled with her pen. 'No telling . . .'

Gardner lifted a paper bag he'd brought with him from the floor to his lap. 'I've noticed you have a lot of toys, but I didn't see one of these . . .' He pulled a large white stuffed rabbit from the bag and set it on the therapist's desk. 'How about putting this in there during Gran's next session?'

Carole gave Gardner a quizzical look. 'What's that for?'

'It's his favourite animal,' Gardner said.

'But it'll remind him of Bowers Corner!' Carole protested.

Nancy Meyers picked up the rabbit and studied it. 'That might be OK,' she said. 'I could put it on the side, make no reference to it. He could go to it only if he wanted to . . .'

'But,' Carole said, 'won't it just get him upset?'

'Not necessarily. He may take some comfort in it. Not all memories of the Bowers were bad.'

'But . . .' Carole was still trying to protest.

'Good idea, Mr Lawson,' Meyers continued. 'This might be just the gentle stimulus we need.'

Gardner was in the yard behind his townhouse, fiddling with the barbecue, when Jennifer arrived at dusk. They'd exchanged few words since the flare-up at the office, and Jennifer approached cautiously. He was dressed in shorts and a tee-shirt, and his face still radiated the glow of the mid-day sun. He looked more relaxed than he had earlier.

Jennifer let the screen door snap against the frame to alert him to her presence.

He looked up from the half-scraped grill top. 'Hi, Jen.'

She forced a thin smile. 'Getting ready to cook something?' In the course of their tiff, coordinating evening meals had been overlooked.

'Thought I might throw on a few burgers . . . You hungry?' Gardner's grilling techniques were as impromptu as some of his trial tactics. He liked to fire up the coals, toss on the meat, poke 'em, flip 'em, close the lid, sip a martini, open the lid and redeem the remains. Remarkably, like many of his off-beat courtroom manoeuvres, the results were usually favourable.

'Let's eat,' she said tentatively. There was still a barrier between them, despite his obvious overture of peace.

Jennifer went to the bedroom and changed into shorts and a halter top. She loosed her ponytail from its black cloth band and shook out her dark shiny hair. When she returned to the yard, the smell of the burgers was beginning to replace the cool grassy odour of the summer evening.

Gardner snapped up the lid, and retreated from the burst of heavy smoke. Then he flipped one of the burgers and closed the top again. Jennifer sat at the round patio table, and he joined her. They were on opposite sides, looking at each other in silence.

'We're going after Purvis Bowers,' Jennifer said suddenly. 'Brownie and I are convinced he's hiding something. I'm bringing him before the Grand Jury.'

Gardner's relaxed expression changed. He was obviously not pleased. 'That's not going to do it, Jennifer,' he sighed. 'This was a robbery that went sour, not some diabolical family plot.'

'How can you say that?' Jennifer asked.

'Twenty years, Jennifer. Twenty years of robberies. This was a robbery attempt . . .'

'Brownie doesn't think so!' Jennifer retorted.

'Why not?'

'It was too deliberate. Too well planned . . . And nothing seems to have been taken.'

103

Gardner frowned. 'It got interrupted . . .' He couldn't finish the sentence.

'I thought you trusted Brownie's judgment?'

Gardner put his elbows on the table. 'I do, Jennifer, but . . .'

Jennifer began to say something, but held back. She took several deep breaths and calmed herself. 'Well, Mr Lawson, how do you propose we proceed, then?'

Gardner looked into her eyes with resolve. 'Granville,' he said.

'Granville?' She was shocked.

'He saw the killer,' Gardner replied.

'But he's . . .' Jennifer was searching for a polite way to describe his condition.

'I think he's starting to remember,' Gardner cut in. 'He broke down today when we talked about it.'

'But you're not supposed to . . .' Jennifer stuttered.

Gardner scowled. 'Not supposed to what? Talk to my own son? Not supposed to give a damn that he was beaten and two of the nicest people on this earth were killed? Not supposed to interfere with the investigation? What? What am I *not* supposed to do?'

Jennifer's discomfort was mounting rapidly. She wanted to say that he was not supposed to get involved in the case, but she couldn't. 'You might hurt Granville,' she said at last.

'What?' Gardner replied. 'More than he's hurt right now? The boy's a mess!' Jennifer sat stoically, not responding. 'While you and Brownie fool with Purvis Bowers, the killer is still on the street, and it won't take him long to realize he's got a potential witness . . .' Jennifer nervously fluffed her hair behind her ear. 'We don't have any time. No more damn time!'

'So you're going to try to force it out of your son?' Jennifer said accusingly.

'You got any better ideas?' Gardner snapped.

Jennifer fell silent. There was no reasoning with him. Nothing she could say or do was having any effect. She got up from the table. 'This isn't getting anywhere,' she said sadly. Then she went through the house, got into her car, and drove away.

Gardner numbly walked to the barbecue and kicked open

104

the lid. Dense smoke erupted. Gardner picked up the fork and probed the grill. When the smoke had cleared, he could see that the burgers had both been burned to a crisp.

The next morning Gardner was still on leave from the office. He and Jennifer had slept separately for the first time in over a year, and he spent a restless, fitful night alone in his big bed while she lay in Granville's narrow bunk down the hall.

Gardner drove over to Court Avenue, and parked beside the doughnut shop on the corner. They served good breakfasts, and he had often eaten there in the lean post-divorce days. He sat at the counter and ordered his meal: two eggs over easy, hash browns and country sausage. The patrons were mostly elderly retirees, talking quietly over coffee. The working people had already eaten and gone to their jobs. And in the courthouse down the street, the 10 o'clock docket was now being called.

Suddenly the door clanged open and a man entered. Dressed in a tailored suit, he looked out of place. He walked over to Gardner and tapped him on the shoulder.

Gardner turned, and confronted Kent King. 'What a way to start the day,' he groaned inwardly.

'Gotta talk to you, Lawson,' King muttered. He did not look happy.

Gardner smiled coldly. 'I'm eating breakfast, Kent. Please don't bother me.'

King didn't budge. 'What's this about a Grand Jury summons on Purvis Bowers?' Gardner shrugged. 'You promised him immunity . . .'

Gardner shook his head. 'Haven't you heard? I'm not running things. Jennifer Munday's in charge.'

King smiled coldly. 'Bullshit!' Several elderly faces suddenly turned towards them.

'It's true,' Gardner said calmly. 'I'm out of the case. It's a matter of record.'

'Bullshit!' King repeated. 'You're tryin' to pull a Reagan. No accountability for your own decisions . . .'

Gardner crossed his arms. 'What's your point, Kent? My eggs are getting cold.'

'The point is, that we had a deal. My guy does not say a word without immunity. *You* said it first . . .'

'Maybe I wasn't authorized to say it,' Gardner answered. His arms were still crossed.

'Bullshit!' King barked. 'You are the elected State Attorney. You cannot abdicate your responsibility.'

'It seems that I did. If you've got a problem with that, you'll have to take it up with Jennifer.'

King stood there fuming. 'You're a wimp!' he said suddenly.

Gardner swallowed, and lowered his arms to his sides. 'What did you say?' His jaw was getting tight.

'I said you're a wimp,' King repeated. 'Letting your girlfriend cover for you . . .'

Gardner stood up. 'I don't like your tone of voice,' he said, balling one hand into a fist.

'And I don't like this charade,' King answered. 'I'm *sorry* your boy got hurt. *Really* sorry, but that's no excuse for abandoning your job. Purvis Bowers is innocent. You're way off base trying to jack him up.'

Gardner stood in silence, his first still balled. He agreed with what King said, but he could never admit it to his face.

'I know you feel that way, or you'd never have made the immunity offer,' King went on. 'Why don't you go to your office and get this thing under control? You're the boss, goddamnit! Why don't you act like one?'

'I'll think about it,' Gardner finally grunted.

'You'd better do more than think!' King replied sternly. Then he pushed out of the door and left Gardner alone with his breakfast.

Gardner pushed the plate away. He'd suddenly lost his appetite. Maybe King was right. Things *were* out of control. Maybe it was time to get back in the saddle.

It was 2 p.m., and the Franklin National Bank on South Avenue was about to close its doors for the day. The granite building had been around as long as the town – for centuries, it seemed. Brownie raced up the marble stairs, trying to sneak into the building before the security guard at the door turned the key.

Summonses had been issued for Purvis Bowers' financial

106

records at every bank in town. So far, nothing had turned up. This was Brownie's last chance to find something tying Purvis and Henry to the suspected cache.

Brownie slipped in just in time, and made his way to the manager's office. In uniform, it was obvious he was on official business. 'Mr Wilkins, please,' he told the brown-haired secretary who was parked in front of the office door.

'In reference to what?' The woman's tone was cold.

'Serving a summons,' Brownie said with a smile.

Her eyes remained blank, as she notified her boss. Brownie grinned at the woman, but she still didn't react. Soon the door opened, and the officer was ushered inside.

'Judd Wilkins,' the elderly manager said, extending a withered white hand.

'Joe Brown.' Brownie clamped it gently, releasing it before he broke any bones. The man looked like an antique brass fixture, an employee since day one.

'We need to locate some records,' Brownie said, handing over the papers. 'All the accounts of Purvis Bowers.'

Wilkins sat down to peruse the summons. Brownie took a chair opposite, and waited.

'Purvis Bowers,' Wilkins said.

Brownie's ears pricked up. 'He has accounts here?'

'Yes, sir. He's got several.'

Brownie smiled. 'Can you let me see the files?'

The old man nodded, and gave an order to his secretary through the intercom. She soon returned and dropped a stack of papers on his desk. Wilkins handed them to Brownie. 'That's the whole lot.'

Brownie scanned the pages. Cheques. Business cheques. Savings. A safe-deposit box. He was about to go on when he noticed a second name at the top of the deposit-box signature card. A co-signer! His heart began to race. There it was – the missing link! Purvis and Henry on the same account. He handed the document across the desk. 'What do you know about this one?'

Wilkins took the page. 'Henry Bowers,' he said sadly. 'Poor Henry . . .'

'What's the story on him and his nephew sharing a box?' Brownie asked.

Wilkins put the paper down. 'Years ago, Henry had a lot of them.'

Brownie was interested. 'A lot of what?'

'Boxes,' Wilkins said. 'Safe-deposit boxes. Must have had eight or ten in the beginning. Thirty, forty years ago . . .'

Brownie leaned forward. 'Boxes? With an S?'

'Yep. Let's see . . . Had at least eight deposit boxes when he first started. Then, as the years went by, dropped 'em one by one.'

Brownie eased to the edge of his seat. 'Ever say why he needed so many?'

Wilkins flashed a reprimand with his eyes. 'We never pry, officer Brown. What goes in is their business.'

Brownie put his hand on the desk. 'So, all those years, you never once peeked while he was opening a box?'

'Of course not!'

'Take it easy, Mr Wilkins. We have to get a handle on why Henry needed so many boxes. Didn't seem to be a wealthy man.'

The manager looked down at the summons, 'You'll have to ask Purvis Bowers about that. After Henry got down to four boxes, he added his nephew to the signature card as the primary account-holder.'

'Do you know the reason he did that?' Brownie interrupted. At least it explained why no accounts were found in Henry's name alone.

Wilkins scratched his balding pate. 'Sumpthing about taking care of Addie if Henry got sick. Seems he got a bad check-up one time, and the next thing we knew, Purvis was on the boxes and Henry was just a co-signer. He only went to it 'bout once a year.'

'May I see the entry card?' Brownie asked. Wilkins handed it over. Brownie sped down the sheet. It had been signed each time the box was opened. Sure enough, Henry *had* come in only once a year. And each time had been the middle of August. 'What's the status of the box now?' Brownie inquired.

Wilkins pulled another paper from the file. 'Closed,' he said. 'Purvis Bowers closed it. Within the past few weeks.'

Brownie let out his breath and leaned back in his chair. The questions were over.

'Should get the originals to you first thing tomorrow morning,' Wilkins said. 'Meantime we'll run copies. Is that OK?'

Brownie said Yes, and turned for the door. His head was awash with new information. Henry had eight safe-deposit boxes. Eight! Enough room to keep a ton of cash.

The security guard let him out, and he hurried down the steps into the afternoon sun. Henry was rich, after all. OK, he could handle that. But there was still a burning question: where in hell did Henry get that much money in the first place?

Deputy Sheriff Amy Falcon drove her white county car down the shadowy corridor of evergreens. She had drawn the duty at roll-call to serve summonses in this sector of town. It had taken her most of the afternoon to catch up with the names on her list, and now, as evening approached, there was one final name to cross out.

Purvis Bowers' house lay at the bottom of a dead end in the Cedars section of town. The structure, like the other relics on the shaded avenue, was gothic and austere. Most of the homeowners were shut-ins or recluses and, along the secluded street, the voices of children were never heard. It was sterile and deserted most of the time; that was just the way the neighbours liked it.

The deputy manoeuvred her car through the curve at the end of the cul-de-sac, and backed up so that the rear of her vehicle was perpendicular to Bowers' driveway. A small sedan was parked beside the house, so deputy Falcon ran a tag check on her mobile computer console and confirmed that it belonged to Purvis Bowers. He was at home.

She walked up the winding brick path, and stepped on to the wide wooden porch. The blinds and curtains were drawn at every window, and the door was shut. She rang the bell and waited, rocking back and forth nervously, wishing that Bowers would hurry so that she could drop the papers on him and leave. The place was giving her the shivers. There was no answer, so she tried the bell again. Again, nothing moved.

'Mr Bowers?' Her voice rattled the glass in the front door. Again, nothing.

The deputy walked to the end of the porch and looked

round the corner. There was a screen door to the rear of the house that seemed to be sagging off its hinges. Something was wrong. Not only was the door hanging, it had a large jagged hole cut in the middle of the screen.

Falcon ran over to it, and shuddered to a stop. '425 to dispatch!' she screamed into the radio strapped to her epaulette. 'Dispatch!' Her voice sounded like a siren.

'Dispatch here. What's your problem, 425?'

She had drawn her sidearm, and pushed the screen door aside. 'Got a man down!' she yelled breathlessly, scanning the area for any sign of movement.

'State your 20,' the voice on the radio said calmly.

Deputy Falcon looked into the kitchen. She could see a man on his back, just inside the door, a hole in his midsection. '426 Cedar Road,' she whispered into the mike. 'Bowers residence.'

'Do you need medical assistance?' the voice asked.

Falcon walked to the body and bent down. The tiled floor was visible beneath the area where his chest used to be, and there was very little flesh connecting the top half of his torso to the bottom. She gagged, and ran outside.

'I say again,' the voice repeated. 'Do you require medical assistance?'

The deputy choked back a burst of bile in her throat. 'Yeah,' she said weakly. 'You'd better send someone for *me*.'

CHAPTER 8

Nancy Meyers led Granville into the playroom and shut the
door. 'How are you feeling today?' she asked.

'Fine,' the boy replied.

'Want to pick out a toy or two?' She nonchalantly waved
her hand towards the shelf on the far wall. The stuffed rabbit
had been placed on the bottom level, right at the
end.

Granville glanced over, as he usually did before declining
the offer. Then he did a double-take.

Meyers watched as he focused on the new addition to the
toy collection. 'See anything you like?' she asked softly.

Granville's eyes were locked on the rabbit, but he didn't
move.

'Want me to get it for you?'

The boy shook his head.

For several moments, it stayed that way. Granville eyeing
the bunny, and Meyers silently observing. Finally she spoke.
'Do you want to tell me anything, Granville? Like how you're
feeling right now?'

The boy turned away from the shelf and shook his head
again.

'Well, what *can* we do?' She said merrily. No sense in
pushing it.

Granville tentatively raised his head. 'Drawing,' he said.

'OK.' Meyers produced the pad and pencils, and handed
them to him.

Granville shifted his body away from the toy shelf, and
propped his elbow on the floor. Then he began to
draw.

Meyers watched attentively from the side. His strokes

were slower, and more deliberate than before, but the shape was the same. A criss-cross of ellipses, with no apparent design.

Word spread rapidly that there'd been another murder, and soon the quiet street where Purvis Bowers had lived was choked with emergency vehicles all the way out to the main highway. Jennifer had been phoned at the State Attorney's Office, and she'd notified Gardner in a terse call to the townhouse. It did not take them long to converge on the scene, and, as the shadows deepened, Jennifer, Gardner and Brownie gathered on the porch of the old house to discuss the significance of the bloody event.

'Shotgun?' Gardner asked Brownie after nodding a cool hello to Jennifer. He was still in casual attire.

'One blast of double-O buckshot,' Brownie said sombrely. 'Right through the screen as he opened the inner door.'

Gardner shook his head, and winced. 'When?'

'Within the last five hours,' Brownie continued. 'Shot cut him clean in two.'

This time, Jennifer paled. 'Still think there's no connection between him and Addie and Henry's murder?' she said to Gardner.

Gardner did not respond.

They walked to the end of the porch in time to see the black plastic bodybag being wheeled from the kitchen.

'Who knew about the Grand Jury summons?' Brownie said suddenly.

Gardner and Jennifer were both staring absently in the direction of the black bag. There were two bulky lumps. One at each end, and very little in the middle. 'Huh?' Jennifer seemed to be mesmerized by the bizarre configuration of the body.

'Whom did you tell about the summons?' Gardner repeated Brownie's question.

'Nobody.' Jennifer looked flustered, afraid she might be blamed for what had happened. 'We wanted to catch him by surprise, so he wouldn't try to run.'

'King knew about it,' Gardner said, looking at Jennifer.

Jennifer arched her brows above her glasses. 'I never said a thing to him.'

Gardner leaned against a porch column and crossed his arms. 'Well, somebody told him. He was furious.'

Jennifer looked at Gardner in silence. This was not helpful. 'Gardner, I swear I kept the lid on.'

Gardner walked over and put his arm round her shoulder. It was their first real contact for days. 'It's OK, Jen,' he said gently. 'I'm sure King didn't hear it from you.'

Brownie interrupted. 'How do you think he found out?' The question was directed at Gardner. It was clear to all that the State Attorney was back at the helm.

'Same way he's been scooping us for years,' Gardner said solemnly. 'There's a leak in the courthouse.'

King's uncanny ability to know what was going on behind the doors of the State Attorney's office had been a sore spot with Gardner for a long time. He had even swept the office unsuccessfully – for electronic listening devices.

'The old bug-a-boo,' Brownie said with a shake of his head. 'You still on that dusty trail?'

'You have a better explanation?' Gardner was certain that King's intelligence machine was as sophisticated as the CIA's.

'Sheriff serves the summons,' Brownie answered. 'That means a lot of hands on it between your place and the field. A lot of people in the loop.'

'King knew this morning,' Gardner answered. 'Early this morning. What time did the summons go out?' He looked at Jennifer.

'Ten-thirty, eleven o'clock.'

Gardner looked at Brownie. The information had reached King long before that.

'So what are we *really* saying here?' Brownie asked. 'Are we accusing King of something?'

Gardner rubbed his foot on the peeling porch floor and flicked off a curl of grey paint. 'King might have tipped off the killer.'

'Intentionally?' Brownie asked.

'Could be,' Gardner said. 'I wouldn't put it past him.'

'So you want me to follow up that theory?' Brownie said.

'Discreetly,' Gardner replied.

'Discreetly,' Brownie repeated.

Just then, there was a commotion at the end of the porch.

The sound of running feet, and an excited voice. 'Sergeant Brown! Sergeant Brown!'

The trio turned, and were greeted by a breathless young patrol officer who had been dispatched earlier to search for evidence in the yard. 'Got something!' he shouted. Gardner, Jennifer and Brownie gathered in a semicircle around the officer, who was fumbling with a plastic bag in his hand. 'Found this in the bush, ten feet to the right of the back door.' He opened the bag, and everyone looked inside.

'Now that looks familiar!' Brownie said, poking the object with the end of his pen.

'Out of a pump-action, or an automatic,' Gardner said.

'Like the kind that Henry sold at the store,' Brownie replied. 'But look at this.' He squeezed the shotgun shell by the plastic, and pushed it out of its enclosure. 'This one's identical to the three I got off Roscoe Miller.'

Brownie dropped the shell into the bag, and signed an evidence form accepting custody. Then he thanked the patrolman, and sent him back into the bushes. 'I'm gonna run this thing through the laser,' he told the prosecutors. 'Can't load it without touching it. There's got to be a print!'

Brownie prepared to leave, when Jennifer grabbed his arm. 'But don't *you* touch it!' she said with a smile.

Carole manoeuvred her blue station wagon around the sharp curves of Watson Road, en route to the house. Granville sat silently beside her, gazing out of the window at the passing greenery. The sky was bright, and there was little traffic on this section of the road.

She slowed for a turn, and checked Granville's seatbelt. It was secure. 'You OK?' she asked, patting his knee. He had been more relaxed when they left the therapist's, but they'd run across a streaking convoy of police cars on the way to some emergency, and his attitude had changed. She had tried to talk to him after that, but he'd spoken only in mono-syllables, with no questions or comments of his own.

They were approaching the intersection with Mountain Road, the spot where the traffic changed direction for the high country. It was also the turn-off for Bowers Corner. Carole slowed again as they came towards the stop sign at the junction. She glanced at the road ahead, saw nothing, and hit the accelerator. Their momentum carried them into the intersection. She glanced at Granville again.

'Mom!' His scream was so sudden and unexpected that it almost stopped her heart. She instinctively jammed on the brake, and whipped her head forward in time to see a giant mass of metal hurtling towards her car. A vehicle was crossing against the stop sign on the other side, slashing across her path into Mountain Road.

'Uh!' she grunted as the seatbelts took hold and jammed them both back into their seats. She had added her right hand as a back-up, to keep Granville from hitting the dashboard, but it wasn't necessary. They were both unhurt.

In an instant it was over. The other car had accelerated off around a curve. Carole never got a good look at who, or what, almost hit them. All she had seen was a big red blur. 'My baby,' she said gently, 'are you all right?'

'I'm not a baby, Mom,' Granville answered firmly.

'You saved us,' Carole said. They'd pulled through the intersection, and parked on the shoulder to catch their breath. 'You know that? You saved our lives.' Granville smiled. 'I never saw him . . .' She unstrapped them, and moved over to put her arms round her son. She was comforting him, but, at the same time, in the aftermath of the close call, he was making her feel better too.

After five minutes, Carole felt calm enough to resume driving. She re-entered the road and headed for home, steering with one hand and holding Granville's slim fingers with the other. Soon the tree-lined lane came into view, and then the silver mailbox. She eased up next to it so that she could pick up the post. They'd been out all day, and this was the first chance to collect it.

Carole popped the metal door and reached in, seizing a packet of letters and folded catalogues secured with a thick rubber band. 'Here, Granny,' she said, handing the bundle to her son for safekeeping.

The boy put the bundle on his lap, and began to remove the band. Meanwhile, Carole was closing the door of the box when she noticed a white object lying against the back of it. She reached in, and pulled out a small rectangular envelope.

115

There was no stamp, and no address. All it said on the outside, in crude ink lettering, was: GRANVILLE.

Carole's heart began racing again, as it had back at the intersection. A bulge in the sealed letter signified that there was something inside. She tore open the envelope, and a hard object dropped into her hand. Except for that, there was nothing else. When she saw it, she almost screamed. Her heart pounded, and her breath came in gasps.

Granville looked up. 'What is it, Mom?'

Carole began to answer, but she couldn't form any words. Her thoughts were focused on the object she was desperately trying to conceal in her hand: a loaded twelve-gauge shotgun shell.

Carole finally reached Gardner by phone at 8.15 p.m. The earlier calls to the townhouse had triggered the answering machine, but she'd left no message. What she had to say to her ex-husband could not be entrusted to a tape. He had to hear it live.

'What?' Gardner exploded. 'Got a what?'

'Some kind of big bullet,' Carole repeated. Her voice was trembling.

Gardner scraped his forehead with his left hand. 'Oh, God . . .' This was his nightmare come true. The killer had finally realized that Granville posed a threat, and he was issuing a warning. Or a prediction? 'Carole, is the patrol car there?' He had arranged for hourly surveillance after Granville came home from hospital.

'Yes. I've asked them to stay. They're parked out front.'

'Who are the officers?'

Carole fumbled with the phone. 'Who? Uh, I don't know. A man and a woman . . .'

'Let me talk to one of them . . .' The concern in Gardner's voice was unmistakable.

'Gardner, what is going on? Why are they doing this?' Carole was matching his tone with a few hysterical notes of her own.

Gardner didn't want to spell it out completely. 'A sick joke, Carole,' he finally said. 'Somebody is playing a sick joke.'

Carole asked the driver of the police car to come into the house and take the call.

'Hello?' The young patrolman's crackly voice did not inspire much confidence.

'This is State Attorney Lawson,' Gardner said in his official voice. 'Who'm I talkin' to?'

'Officer Reynolds, Pete Reynolds.'

Two years on the force, Gardner thought. Not much experience. 'And who is with you tonight?' Maybe the partner was longer in the tooth.

'Officer Petra, Karen Petra.'

A damn rookie! Three months out of the academy. That meant there were *two* police toddlers to guard his son! 'Did Mrs Lawson tell you what happened?'

'Yes, sir.'

'Did she show it to you?'

'Yes, sir.'

'What does it look like?' Gardner had not clearly pictured the 'bullet' from Carole's description.

'Twelve-gauge shell. Double-O load.'

Gardner gasped. Purvis Bowers had been bisected by a blast of the same shot. 'You have it secure?'

'Yes, sir. Sealed and tagged.'

'Good,' Gardner said. 'Send it down to the lab immediately. Call the station and have someone pick it up.' Maybe Brownie could lift a print.

'Right away, Mr Lawson.'

'Officer Reynolds?'

'Yes, sir?'

'Take care of my family.' Gardner found himself slipping an obsolete word into the sentence. 'Family' didn't apply any more. It no longer existed. Take care of my 'son' was what he had wanted to say, but it came out 'family' instead. Strange.

Carole came back on the phone. 'I'm scared,' she said. 'Really scared!'

'Take it easy, Carole. You've got protection,' Gardner tried to comfort her.

'And what am I supposed to do?' she whined. 'Sit here and wait for a knock on the door?'

Gardner fell silent. This was not going to work. 'Carole,' he said suddenly, 'I need to see Granville.'

The switched subject caught her off guard. 'What?'

117

'I'm coming out to the house, and I want you to have Granville ready in about twenty minutes.'

Her silence signalled her puzzlement. 'What's going on?'

Gardner took a breath. 'I need to see him, and we don't have much time.'

'What's this *really* about?' Carole asked.

'Granville knows something. He's trying to communicate. I'm certain of it.'

Carole picked up on what he was saying. 'The drawings!'

'Right. I think he's drawing a picture, but it's not clear.'

'But he already had his session,' Carole interrupted.

'He's got to have another one,' Gardner said. 'Tonight.'

'No!' That was the old Carole talking. Intransigent as ever.

'Damn it, Carole!' Gardner exploded, 'don't you understand what's going on here?'

'No, I don't! Why don't you tell me?'

'The person who killed Addie and Henry just killed their nephew! With a shotgun!' The phone went silent. 'Carole?'

'Another murder? Why didn't you tell me?'

'I just did.'

'And it's the same one? The same one who killed Addie and Henry?'

'We think so,' Gardner said softly.

'And now he's after my son!'

'*Our* son, goddamnit! *Our* son.' Even at a time like this, the possessiveness came through. 'He can help. I know he can. Just give me some time with him . . .'

'No!'

'It may be our only hope,' Gardner continued.

'You've got the police. You don't need *my* son!'

Gardner let that one pass. 'Please!' he begged.

'No!' She was sounding firmer all the time. 'You told me that Addie and Henry were killed by a robber, and he was long gone. You said not to worry. But you lied!'

'Jesus!' Gardner whispered.

'He's still here!' There was outright panic in those words.

'Carole, please!'

'I'm leaving!' she announced.

'Please!' Gardner pleaded.

'We're going away. Now!'

'Granville may be the only one who can solve the case!' Gardner yelled. 'I've *got* to see him!'

'Never!' Then she hung up.

At 9 p.m., Brownie was on a roll. He'd rushed back to the lab from the Purvis Bowers house, and begun processing the shotgun shell. The preliminary dusting came up negative, so he lasered it. While the macro-photos were developing in the dark room, he manned his computer console and keyed in a name search for Roscoe *Hiller* in the county tax records. If Miller had worked under that name in the last six months, and his employer had filed the required employee withholding information, the records should be available. Previous search attempts using Miller's known aliases had come up empty. They'd already found two social security numbers he'd used, but the weasel was suspected of having others. According to an old police report that Brownie had just dug up, he had once used the name Hiller. That was the only name they hadn't run in a financial records search. With time running out, it was worth one last try.

The inquiry was fed in, and the screen replied that a search was under way. While he was waiting, Brownie dialled the number of his contact at the telephone company. A billing clerk on permanent night shift, the man had access to the records of every phone call made and received in the jurisdiction.

After two rings, a male voice answered. 'Gavin.'

'The Brown man here,' Brownie said softly. 'Gonna need your services.'

'Hold on,' the voice whispered. 'Gotta switch phones.' There was a click as the call went on hold, and soon another click as the line reopened. 'OK, give it to me.'

'All calls made in the past twenty-four hours from 887–5000.'

'Local or L.D.?'

'Local first, then I'll decide if I need the long distance.'

'OK. Hold on.' The line came up again. 'Got quite a few here. How do you want 'em?'

'Read the list,' Brownie said, adjusting his notepad.

'You got it,' Gavin replied. Then he began reciting the forty

119

numbers that were called from Kent King's office in the past two days.

Gardner had told Brownie to check on King's possible tip-off of the killer, and Jennifer had okayed a search of his phone records. If there was a tip-off, it might have been by phone.

'Uh-huh. Uh-huh. Yep . . . Yep . . .' Brownie scribbled the rapid-fire numerals as they came across the line, noting to himself that most of them were familiar. Courthouse. Police Department. County jail. Routine numbers for a defence attorney. 'Woa!' he called suddenly. 'You said 747–3222?'

'Yes.'

Brownie circled the number. It was familiar. Then it hit him.

'Carlos' Cantina' he wrote beside it. 'Gav, when did that last one go out?'

There was a pause as the time was checked on the computer screen. 'Eight forty-five last night.'

Brownie wrote 8.45 p.m. beside his other note, and underlined it. 'OK, keep going.'

The list continued, but there was nothing else of note, so Brownie thanked his friend and hung up. He'd heard enough. King had called Carlos' last night, after the decision was made to subpoena Purvis before the Grand Jury. If Miller was the shooter, that might have been the tip-off call.

Just then, the computer buzzed an announcement that the data search Brownie had requested earlier was complete. He walked to the console and scanned the information on the screen. There *was* a Roscoe Hiller listed. His employer had turned in his Social Security number on intermittent dates since December. Wages were paid in the total amount of $6080.45. And withholding was duly recorded.

Brownie scanned past the individual payment schedule, and screened ahead to the next page in search of the employer's name. 'All right!' He whistled. There was the name of the employer, at the top of the glowing green monitor. The place where Roscoe *Hiller* had been secretly hanging out over the past half year. Brownie traced the words with his pen, and then wrote them down in giant letters at the top of his pad:

ROSCOE HILLER
GROUNDS CREW
PRENTICE ACADEMY.

A pair of eyes nervously watched from the woods as Carole packed her bags. She was rushing from room to room, gathering belongings. He could see her figure as it flashed across the windows. The cops were parked in front, watching the entrance road. They were too stupid to look in this direction.

The lights went out upstairs and, for a moment, the lady disappeared. The man shifted his position to get a better angle on the front door. Something was happening, that was for sure. The lady was spooked. Freaked out. The man smiled, and thought to himself: they must have got the message.

Suddenly there was movement out front. The lady ran to her car, dragging the kid with her. She threw some suitcases in the back, and started to open her door, The male cop came over and tried to talk to her, but she shrugged him off and opened her car door. The cop said something else, but she wasn't having any of it. Again, the man smiled as he adjusted the binoculars to focus better on the lady's ashen face. She's really sweating, he thought to himself.

Just then, another car pulled in and a middle-aged man jumped out. The State Attorney! He looked more upset than the lady. By now she had started her engine and had backed up a few feet to get away from the cops. The prosecutor ran towards the car. It looked like he was shouting. The lady backed up a few more feet, then swerved, and roared towards the road. The prosecutor screamed and tried to block the car, but it changed course again, went over a low hill and disappeared into the trees.

The prosecutor ran back to the cops and started yelling at them. They stood there and took it, then got in their cruiser, and left. They did not look happy.

The prosecutor stood in front of the house after the cops pulled out. For five minutes he was immobile, staring at the building. Then he walked to his car, leaned against it with his elbows, and buried his face in his hands.

The man rolled over in the darkness and looked up at the

summer sky. The tree canopies were spread enough for a few of the stars to shine through. It was peaceful and quiet, the way it was supposed to be. No more screw-ups. No more loose ends. From now on everything was gonna run smooth.

He pushed up to his knees, then stood and stretched. From the looks of things, he would not have to come back here. The little punk was no longer a problem. His mom would see to that. No way would she let him testify, even if he could. She was scared shitless. He began to trot along his secret trail out of the woods. The kid was no problem, his thought repeated, noooo problem at all.

But what if . . . A sudden doubt seized his mind. What if . . . What if mom changed her mind? His pace slowed for a second. OK. It was gonna be OK. If that happened, he'd just have to return one more time and finish the job himself.

Brownie was hunched over his magnifier in the lab when the door opened and Gardner ran in. It was 11 p.m., and Brownie squinted at the apparition that had just ruined his concentration. 'Gard! What the hell happened?' The prosecutor looked terrible.

'Carole's taken Granville. Got spooked and ran . . .'

Brownie adjusted the giant lens that was poised over two parallel fingerprint cards, and stood up. 'She got what?'

'Scared. The shotgun shell in the mailbox . . . She panicked and took off.'

Brownie's face registered total confusion. 'Back up a second, boss. You're losing me.'

Gardner scanned the lab table for an envelope and a shell, but they were not in sight. 'Did you get the evidence package from my house?'

Brownie shook his head. 'No.'

Gardner's face contorted. 'Those idiots! I told them to send it over to you immediately. Around 8 p.m.'

Brownie looked puzzled. 'Been here the whole shift, and then some. Nothin's come in.'

Gardner pulled a chair over to the lab table and motioned Brownie to sit. Then he sat, and took several deep breaths to calm himself. 'They're after Granville,' he began, then went on to explain the shell in the mailbox, his call to Carole, and

122

the escape scene at the Watson Road house. 'She's probably headed for Baltimore. To her mother's.'

Brownie patted his friend on the back. 'The boy's gonna be OK with his mom . . .'

'But I need him *here!*' Gardner moaned. 'He's trying to remember! A little more time, and I think he can do it!'

'Take it easy, Gard,' Brownie said reassuringly. 'Might not be necessary. I'm *that* close to shutting this case down.' He pinched his fingers to within a quarter of an inch of each other. 'Got a partial print off the Purvis Bowers shell, and I'm matching it up now.' He moved the magnifier back into place.

Gardner looked over his shoulder. 'Who are you comparing with?'

Brownie flashed him an annoyed look. 'Who do you think?'

'Miller?'

'The one and only,' Brownie said as he aimed a sharp metal pointer at the known print of Roscoe Miller. 'Look here. Got one . . . two . . . three points of comparison.' He waved the wand back and forth between the two fingerprint images, touching identical ridge markings on either side.

Gardner frowned. 'Three points on a partial print? Is that enough?' Case law did not require a fixed number of points of comparison to make a positive identification of a fingerprint. All the examiner had to do was rule out the possibility that there was a non-conforming pattern somewhere in either print. But if there were any non-conforming patterns in the missing segment, it could mean there was no match.

'Don't think we've got a lot of choice in the matter,' Brownie said, peering fish-eyed through the magnifying glass. 'Only got a fingertip, but there's no doubt in my mind it belongs to Miller.'

Gardner confirmed that the three points of comparison were, in fact, identical. 'So, assuming the print is Miller's, what else do we have tying him in to Addie and Henry?' The print alone was not sufficient to close the book on the case.

'Possible ID by a girl in the school bus. Possession of twelve-gauge shells. Possible tie-in to Purvis Bowers – he said he knew Miller – weird behaviour ever since this thing went down, and a phone call from Kent King yesterday evening.'

Gardner stirred. 'You ran King's phone records?'

'Yeah. Jennifer said it was OK. King called Carlos' Cantina last night. It's Roscoe's hangout.'

'That proves nothing. King could have been ordering a pizza . . .'

Brownie shook his head. 'I disagree. King called the cantina last night, the summons for Purvis went out this morning, and "Bang", Bowers is subdivided. There has to be a connection!'

Gardner ran his hand through his dishevelled hair. 'OK, you think we have enough to pick up Miller?'

'Yeah,' Brownie replied.

Gardner nodded. It was time to do something. Arrest now, and worry about conviction later. Get the bastard into custody as soon as possible.

Just then the door opened, and Jennifer rushed in. 'Gard!' She looked frazzled.

Gardner and Brownie got to their feet. 'You got my note?' Gardner asked.

'Yes,' she said breathlessly. 'Hi, Brownie.'

'Ma'am,' the officer replied politely.

'What happened?' She looked at Gardner.

'Bad scene. Carole grabbed Granville, and ran. I couldn't stop her.'

Jennifer grimaced. 'Where did they go?'

'Baltimore, probably.'

'So what now?'

'We nail Miller!' Gardner said with resolve. 'Brownie's got a print. Maybe with that and the other bits and pieces we can justify an arrest.'

'What about this?' Jennifer asked suddenly, pulling a sheaf of papers out of her bag. She unfolded them and placed four sheets on the table.

'You got the drawings!' Gardner said excitedly. He'd sent Jennifer out earlier to pick up Granville's scribbled pages from the therapist.

'Wouldn't let me have the originals, only copies.'

Brownie bent over the table. 'What's this?'

Gardner separated the pages, and put them in order of the dates they'd been drawn. On each page, the clarity of the strange atomic symbol seemed to become more refined, more detailed. 'Granville's subconscious,' Gardner replied. 'It's a clue. I'm convinced.'

Brownie studied the first three, then picked up the last drawing, the one done just that afternoon. His face registered recognition.

'Brownie, what is it?' Gardner sensed that he was on to something.

The officer did not reply. He was too much into his examination of the paper. Suddenly he turned the page sideways, and placed it under his magnifier. 'Son-of-a bitch!'

'What is it?' Gardner and Jennifer both spoke at once, caught up in the excitement Brownie was generating.

'Hold on!' Brownie shouted. 'Hold on!' Then he ran to his file cabinet, removed a file and pulled out a stack of photographs, hurriedly sorting through them until he found the one he was looking for. In an instant, he was back at the magnifier, and he placed the photo next to the sideways drawing.

Gardner and Jennifer rushed close to peer over each shoulder, while Brownie gently realigned each page.

'Jesus,' Gardner whispered. 'I don't believe it!'

'That's it!' Jennifer added.

Under the magnifier, at a certain angle, an image appeared beneath the encircling scribbles. It was clearly defined, and unmistakable, even though it was not readily apparent from an upright view.

'*Now* we got something!' Brownie said triumphantly.

'Issue an arrest warrant immediately,' Gardner ordered.

'Yes, sir,' Brownie replied. He got up to start the paperwork, and pushed past him.

Gardner stood still, staring at the image under the magnifier. There it was. What Granville had been trying to say. The vision he'd seen at Bowers before his face had been smashed with the barrel of a gun. It was a death's head. A hideous, grotesque caricature of a death's head. And it was identical to the one tattooed on the back of Roscoe Miller's left hand.

CHAPTER 9

Prentice Academy was ready for commencement. A battalion of white chairs had been laid out in the grass quadrangle between the stone administration building and the ball field. Shaded by maple trees, the area would soon be filled with proud parents, squirming brothers and sisters and the men of the hour: the black-robed graduates. At 8 a.m. it was quiet and cool but, by noon, the ceremony would be underway.

Gardner and Jennifer parked in the lower lot, and walked briskly towards the headmaster's office on the far side of the speaker's wooden platform. It had been a hell of a night. Brownie had filled the Prosecutors in on Miller's connection with the exclusive prep school as he typed up the arrest warrant. There had to be some fire beneath the smoke, he said. The Addie-Henry killing was a two-man job. He was absolutely convinced. Miller and another person. All the work on Miller so far was inconclusive. He was a loner and a recluse, and he had no cronies to fit the profile of the second man. But now they had a line on where he'd been spending a lot of time lately. Maybe the missing piece of the puzzle lay somewhere at the school.

'You think Brownie can do it?' Jennifer puffed as her feet rushed to keep pace with Gardner. While they interrogated the headmaster, Brownie was going to try to pick up Miller.

'He'd better,' Gardner said solemnly. His anger had been building since they'd connected Granville's drawing to the tattoo. Roscoe Miller had hurt his son once, and was out to do it again. He had to be stopped, and Gardner secretly wished that Miller would try to resist arrest so that Brownie would have an excuse to shoot him.

127

They arrived at the office as the headmaster, Edwin Charles, was returning from breakfast in the main dining hall. He was dressed for commencement in a dark blue suit, with a white boutonnière pinned to the lapel. The prosecutors had arrived unannounced, and Charles seemed flustered as he encountered them in the alcove outside his door. He had a lot of details to attend to before the ceremony.

'Mr Charles? I'm State Attorney Gardner Lawson.' They shook hands, and Gardner noticed that the man's palms were wet. 'This is my assistant, Jennifer Munday.' Jennifer put out her hand, and got the same clammy response. 'We need to discuss something with you,' Gardner continued. 'It's very important.'

Charles eyed his visitors nervously. 'I'm quite busy at the moment, uh, got to get my eagles ready to fly . . .' He smiled, but the humour was forced.

'Please!' Gardner retorted. 'We're conducting a murder investigation, and we need your help.'

The word *murder* froze Charles in his tracks. He scanned the hall for wandering parents, and ushered the prosecutors into the privacy of his office. His expression had turned grave.

Gardner and Jennifer sat in straight-backed chairs opposite a black inlaid desk. Charles twitched in his leather seat on the other side.

'Have you ever seen this man before?' Gardner asked suddenly, handing a mug-shot photo of Roscoe Miller across the desk.

Charles leaned forward and adjusted his glasses, gingerly seizing the picture between his thumb and index finger. Gardner and Jennifer waited as the headmaster studied the photo for an inordinately long time, his eyes hidden behind the glossy print.

'Do you know him?' Gardner finally prompted.

Charles put the photo down and removed a handkerchief from his pocket. 'Believe he worked for us,' he said softly.

'*Worked*, as in past tense?' Gardner asked.

'Maintenance. Part time. Came and went as we needed.'

'Is he still under that arrangement?'

Charles' eyes began dancing again, the way they'd done in

the hall. 'Don't think so. Hasn't been here for several weeks.'

'What name was he using?' Gardner opened a file that Brownie had given him.

Charles wiped his hands with the handkerchief. 'Name?'

'On the payroll. How was he listed?'

Charles went to a file cabinet, and returned with a folder of his own. As he did this, Jennifer moved away from the desk, towards a side wall.

'Hiller. R. Hiller,' the headmaster said.

'Did you get any ID from him when you signed him on?' Gardner asked, turning his head to see where Jennifer had gone.

The man's face darkened. 'I don't get involved in those things. Our business manager handles maintenance personnel, things like that. I would assume everything was in order, or he wouldn't have been hired.'

Just then, Jennifer returned and tapped Gardner on the arm. He looked up, and she directed his attention to a photograph on the wall.

Gardner stood, and approached the picture. It showed a group of men standing in front of a skeet tower, wearing baseball caps. Third from the left, in the front row, was none other than Roscoe Miller.

'Mr Charles?' Gardner pointed accusingly at the picture.

The headmaster rose, and approached the photo. 'What?'

'Who are these people?' Gardner asked.

'Skeet team. This year's shooters.'

Gardner looked at Jennifer in puzzlement, then returned to Charles. 'What's *he* doing in there?' Gardner pointed to the third man.

The headmaster leaned close to get a better look. 'He's a team member.'

Gardner frowned. 'You let your employees play in your sports teams?'

'Sir?'

'Miller! Or *Hiller*,' Gardner said loudly. 'You allowed him to shoot skeet with the kids?'

Charles' eyes widened. 'What?'

Gardner was still pointing at the man in the photo.

'Oh!' the headmaster said, suddenly understanding the

129

confusion. 'That's not him. That's one of our students.'

Gardner and Jennifer pressed in for a closer look. The cap cast a shadow across his face, and Miller's wild hair was hidden, but the basic facial construction was similar, and the eyes burned the same clear blue flame. Gardner shook his head. On closer inspection, he could see that it was not Miller. There was a lot more refinement and grooming evident.

'Amazing,' Jennifer said. 'When I first saw it, he jumped right out.'

The chief prosecutor was still staring at the image. He looked enough like Miller to be his twin, and that similarity gave Gardner a nauseous sensation in the pit of his stomach. His mind suddenly pictured Granville staring up at a pair of cold blue eyes. Mesmerized and immobile. Unable to move as the gun barrel was lowered towards his forehead . . .

'Gard.' Jennifer saw his eyes glaze over, and she knew she had to bring him back. 'What are we going to do?'

Gardner snapped out of it instantly. He turned and glared at the headmaster. 'We're going to get some answers from Mr Charles,' he said angrily.

'Need back-up!' Brownie yelled into the radio of his cruiser. 'Headin' down Mountain, 'bout to turn on to Meadow Lane.'

He'd encountered Miller in his old red truck coming out of the Everheart coalfield access road. Flashing emergency lights, Brownie had tried to pull him over, but Miller hit the pedal and took off. Now he had an arrest warrant in his pocket and Miller in his sights, he was not about to let him get away.

The truck fish-tailed as it slipped from pavement to gravel apron and back to the road, sending up puffs of dust and spitting pebbles against Brownie's windscreen. The traffic was sparse, and several locals scrambled out of the way as the chase flew by them.

'Send a car down to Thomas Junction!' Brownie shouted as he took a sharp turn on two wheels, and banged down on all four on the other side. 'Set up a block at Meadow and Thomas! He's runnin'!' Miller was heading for the interstate to the north that would lead out of the county, and out of the State.

'Shit!' The truck suddenly changed course. 'Looks like he's short-cuttin' Thomas Road!' Brownie barked into his mike.

The truck made a sudden ninety-degree turn on to a dirt road, and Brownie went into a four-wheel skid to keep pace, narrowly missing a tree, leaping a small gully and finally settling into the dusty straight section at eighty miles an hour. The ground was very dry, and the dust flapped like a carpet behind the speeding truck, coating the front of the cruiser. Brownie hit the washer switch and racked his brain to recall if he'd ever explored the road they were on. The direction at least would bring them to the interstate below Thomas. And that meant there was no place for a roadblock before the county line.

'OK you motherfucker!' Brownie grunted as he jammed on the accelerator. He'd just made a decision. There was no time to get the back-up into position. No time to reposition a roadblock. He'd have to make the stop here and now.

The cruiser's two hundred horsepower engine was overtaking Roscoe's ageing six-cylinder. In an instant, Brownie was at the tailgate, a foot off the line. 'Stop now!' he ordered over the loudspeaker. 'Stop your truck, now!'

Miller's lips mouthed 'Fuck you' in the rearview mirror, and there was no hint of a reduction of speed.

'OK,' Brownie whispered softly, throwing the microphone on the seat, and gripping the wheel with both hands. 'Have it your way!' He manoeuvred the police car so that it angled off on the driver's side and slammed the pedal all the way to the floor. The cruiser leaped ahead and wedged against the truck, hustling it off the road to the right.

Miller screamed, and tried to fight the momentum, but the force was too strong. He bounced through a mass of thorny bushes and smashed headlong into a row of saplings. The truck crunched to a stop.

Brownie raced to the door, and pointed his nine-millimetre at Miller's face. 'This is for you,' he growled.

Miller gasped and looked into the little black hole. He held his breath, and waited for the blast.

Just then, Brownie laughed, and laid a paper over the lip of the open window. 'Not *this*! *This*!' It was the arrest warrant.

Miller blinked, and in seconds Brownie had him spread-

131

eagled and cuffed on the ground. 'You're under arrest for three counts of murder, and one count of attempted murder,' he said. 'Now lie there like a good boy while I read you your rights . . .'

Things were heating up in the headmaster's office. Edwin Charles was being evasive.

'What's his name?' Gardner asked for a second time. They were still gathered around the skeet-team photo featuring the Miller look-alike.

Charles shifted nervously on his feet. 'He's just a student.'

'But what's his name?' Gardner insisted.

The headmaster returned to his desk and sat down, pulling out his handkerchief again. 'You've got to tell me what this is about before I give you any more information. We have a policy of confidentiality here.'

Gardner stood and leaned across the desk. 'Sure I'll tell you, in case you didn't know. Three people are dead, and another is under a death threat. Hiller's real name is Miller, and he's being arrested this morning for the murders. We have reason to believe that his accomplice may have come from this school.'

The headmaster looked as if Gardner had just whacked him with a stick. 'That's impossible!' he said, his voice lowered.

Gardner pushed in closer. 'The hell it is! You'd better think about it. We can have you in front of the Grand Jury this afternoon! Now, are you going to cooperate?'

Charles rose. 'How dare you threaten me!'

Jennifer tugged on Gardner's arm, fearful that he might go over the desk and engage the man physically. 'Maybe we should sit down,' she said softly, 'and start again.' Gardner and Charles glared at each other in silence, then, in deference to Jennifer, sat down.

'I'm sorry,' Gardner said sullenly. 'My son was almost killed by these people. He was hit on the head. Knocked out. Now they're coming after him again . . .'

Charles' face was blank, as if he were thinking about something else. 'That's very sad,' he finally said, 'but I really do not see where the school is involved.'

Gardner continued, 'We need to know Miller's contacts while he was here. Who did he hang around with, talk to, associate with?'

Charles shook his head. 'I wouldn't know these things. This is the administration centre. We only deal with student matters.'

'Well, who *would* know?' Gardner asked. Charles hesitated again. 'How about the business manager? Can he tell us?' Gardner could see that this was getting nowhere. Charles had clammed up.

'He's busy right now. With the commencement.'

'It won't take long,' Gardner insisted. 'Where can I find him?' Charles swallowed, and waved his hand towards the window. 'I see,' Gardner said sarcastically. 'Somewhere in the great outdoors.' He stood up, motioning Jennifer to join him. 'So you're not going to tell us anything further?' The headmaster shook his head. 'No.'

Gardner took a deep breath. 'And why not?'

'Because I don't *know* anything.'

Gardner stared at the man in silence, then took Jennifer by the arm and led her from the room, slamming the door.

Charles remained immobile behind his desk for a moment after the door closed. Then he wiped his face, and re-wiped his hands with the handkerchief. Finally, he picked up his phone and dialled a number. A recording answered, and he looked at his clock. Half-past eight – too early for contact. When the beep sounded, he spoke. 'This is Ed Charles. I have a major problem here. Please call as soon as you get in. It is extremely urgent!' Then he hung up, and walked to the window in time to see Gardner and Jennifer walking towards the maintenance shed on the far side of the running track.

'He's hiding something,' Gardner said as they shuffled down an embankment towards a group of green-suited workers loading a stack of chairs on to a flatbed truck.

'What could it be?' Jennifer asked, once again scurrying to keep up with her boss.

'Don't know,' Gardner answered as they reached level ground. 'He's either involved or he's trying to protect someone. Did you see how he reacted?'

'Didn't want to tell us anything,' Jennifer answered. 'Not even a name.'

After several steps, they arrived at the truck. 'Morning,' Gardner said to a burly man who seemed to be directing the action. 'Can you point me to the crew chief?'

The man eyed both of them warily. Gardner flashed his State Attorney's badge, and Jennifer followed suit.

'Need to speak with the chief. Official business,' Gardner said in his 'jury' voice. 'Murder investigation.'

The man moved away from the work crew so they wouldn't hear. 'You're talkin' to him,' he said in a lowered voice, glancing nervously towards the administration building as he spoke.

'I'm Gardner Lawson. This is Jennifer Munday.'

'Ralph Lambert.'

'OK, Mr Lambert. I need to ask you some questions about this guy.' Gardner handed the man the mug shot. When Lambert saw who it was, he glanced at the administration building again.

These people are spooked, Gardner thought. 'He worked for you.'

'Uh-huh.'

'Off and on for the past six months.'

'Uh-huh.' Lambert was getting more and more uncomfortable.

'Who did he hang out with on the work crew?'

'On the crew?' Gardner nodded. 'Uh, nobody. Always kept to himself.'

Gardner kept probing. 'He must have spent more time with some. More than others.'

'On the crew? No. Just did his job. Never said a word.'

Gardner sighed. This was going nowhere. 'In six months he never spoke a word to a living soul?'

'No. Not on the crew.' The chief sounded hesitant.

'How about elsewhere?' Gardner asked. 'Maybe you saw him with someone outside the work crew.'

Lambert glanced up the hill again, then looked at Gardner with a resigned expression. 'There was a kid I seen him with . . .'

Gardner's senses sharpened. 'Kid?'

'Uh-huh. Student . . .' Gardner's eyes prompted Lambert to continue. 'Down at the skeet range. We done a lot of work down there over the winter. Gettin' it ready for the season.'

'Yeah . . .'

'Seems like this kid was always down there while we was workin'.'

'Yeah?'

'Well, Ross an' him seemed to hit it off.'

'Ross?' That was a new one.

'Ross Hiller. The guy in your picture. That's who we're talkin' about, right?'

Gardner nodded. 'Right.' Ross Hiller. Roscoe Miller. Clever play on words for a backwoods punk.

'Anyway, they was always together when the boys took a break.' Lambert's eyes shifted towards the sky as he thought back. 'An' one time . . .' His voice faded as he glanced over his shoulder. 'Uh, one time the kid even let Ross shoot his gun,' Lambert whispered.

'What was the student's name?' Gardner asked urgently.

'Name?' Lambert was hesitating, maybe to play for time.

'Yeah,' Gardner urged. 'What was his name?'

The headmaster suddenly appeared, almost at a full run. His eyes were on his crew chief.

'Don't know none of the kids' names. We jus' work here, but . . .'

'Mr Lambert!' the headmaster called.

'There was somethin' strange,' Lambert's voice dropped very low. Gardner's stomach tensed. 'He looked a lot like Ross. Yep. No question about it. Them two could'a been brothers.'

Just then, the headmaster arrived. 'Mr Lambert, you're needed at the podium,' he said breathlessly. 'The wiring needs to be checked.' The crew chief nodded and rushed off.

Gardner glared at Charles. 'For the last time,' he said angrily, 'I want the name of the student in the skeet picture. You give it to me now, or I must charge you with obstruction of justice.'

Charles' face blenched. 'OK,' he said. 'OK.'

Gardner waited. 'OK, what?'

'I'll give it to you,' the headmaster said, 'as soon as my lawyer gets here.'

'Lawyer? Now why would *you*,' he glanced at Charles, 'need a lawyer?'

The headmaster crossed his arms. 'To protect the school.'

Gardner suddenly grabbed Jennifer's hand and pulled her towards the commencement area. The headmaster was caught by surprise and left behind. Soon the prosecutors were sprinting towards a stand that had been set up by the podium. Several students were milling around it, carrying boxes. They halted in front of the stand. 'How much for a book?' Gardner asked, trying to catch his breath.

'Twenty-five dollars,' a student answered, laying a square black volume on the counter.

Gardner dug in his pocket, retrieved several bills, and handed them over.

'Silver Linings' was the title of the yearbook for Prentice Academy. He flipped open to the index, and ran his finger through until he found the 'skeet' reference. Then he fanned the pages. Jennifer pressed close as the photo came to light. It was the same as the one in Charles' office. Gardner skimmed his finger along the names until he came to the third one from the end. 'Starke the fourth,' he said aloud.

Just then, Jennifer nudged him and pointed towards the parking lot, where a familiar burgundy Jaguar was pulling in. 'King,' she announced.

'I might have guessed,' Gardner said sarcastically. 'Let's get out of here.' He tucked the book under his arm, and they walked to his car.

King was getting out when they arrived. 'Heard you wanted some questions answered,' he said.

Gardner ignored him and opened his car door.

'So. Do you want to talk, or not?' King persisted.

Gardner shrugged, and entered his car while Jennifer got in on the other side.

King stood there in silence, and by then the headmaster had caught up, and run to him like a lost calf. He whispered a few words to Charles, then motioned for Gardner to lower his window.

Gardner backed out, and hit the power button, pulling to within a few feet of King.

The defence attorney smiled. 'My client is ready to talk now. In case you're interested.'

Gardner scowled. 'What's it going to cost me?'

King smirked. 'The usual. Full transactional immunity.'

Gardner smiled coldly. 'You'd better be sure your insurance is paid up.' Charles frowned. 'The last time Mr King made an offer like that, his client wound up dead.'

King grimaced, and began to speak, but Gardner raised the window and cut him off. Then he spun his wheels and left the headmaster and his lawyer in the dust.

Brownie and Roscoe Miller were in the interrogation room at police headquarters. It was a small cubicle with a table, two chairs and a mirror on the side wall. Behind the mirror, in an adjoining room, the scene was being videotaped through the two-way glass. Brownie had hung his blue uniform jacket on the back of his chair. Roscoe, in hand- and legcuffs, sat sullen and silent. He had a small bandage on his forehead covering a minor cut sustained in the crash.

'I'm gonna ask you again, Roscoe,' Brownie said firmly. 'Who was with you on the Bowers hustle? And I'm talkin' about the first one. The one at the store.'

Miller's eyes stared defiantly, their pale, pale, blue cold and sinister in the harsh light. He said nothing.

'OK,' Brownie said sarcastically. 'I see. Well, don't worry about me askin' you questions about the Purvis Bowers shooting. We've got you nailed six ways to Sunday on that one . . .'

Miller cocked his head, but remained silent. They'd told him nothing so far about the evidence against him. Only the charges. Murder. Murder. Murder. And attempted murder. His only comment so far: 'Fuck you!'

'Oh, yeah,' Brownie continued. 'We've got you cold on the Purvis murder. Fingerprints. Hair samples. Witnesses.' He was lying, trying to push Miller to talk by showing him the hopelessness of the situation. And it was perfectly legal. The US Supreme Court had ruled long ago that police could use deception to elicit a statement. If the suspect was too dense

137

to realize he was being tricked, too bad. Stupidity was no defence.

'Oh, yeah? You're going down hard this time,' Brownie continued. 'Real, real hard.'

'Didn't kill nobody!' Miller said suddenly.

Brownie smiled. The tactic was working. 'Well, I say you did, and the State Attorney says you did, and the evidence says you did, and pretty soon, the jury's gonna say you did.'

Miller pushed his shoulders against the back of the uncomfortable metal chair. 'I didn't do nuthin'!'

'Don't bullshit me. Roscoe! This time we got you by the balls!'

Miller's face turned defiant. 'Like hell you do! You're lyin'!'

Brownie's smile tried to cover his disappointment. Miller knew exactly what was happening. He knew the game, and he wasn't going to incriminate himself. Brownie shifted to plan B. 'You're wrong, buddy-boy,' he said, 'but let's not worry about that now. We've got another problem . . .'

Miller's expression reverted to studied nonchalance. 'You see, at this point, you are the only fish we got in the frying-pan . . .' Roscoe didn't even blink. 'We know we have another one swimmin' around out there, but we haven't caught him yet.'

There was a hint of movement around Miller's eyes. The last comment had him thinking.

'So all we have is you! Just little old you to do time for both bad fish. A lotta time, Roscoe. Whole lotta time down at the Penitentiary . . .'

Roscoe shifted his body again, but remained silent. His ears were open, his brain in gear.

'Oh yeah!' Brownie laughed. 'The brothers down there are gonna love gettin' a shot at you! White butts go for a pre-mium down at the Pen. You're gonna hav'ta order in the K-Y jelly by the case!'

'Shut the fuck up!' Roscoe barked.

'Yes, sir!' Brownie continued. 'You're gonna be the one's gotta shut up. Gonna have your mouth so full'a black dick!'

'Stop it!' Roscoe screamed.

'No!' Brownie screamed back. 'I'm *not* gonna stop it!' He then put his hands on the table and pushed his face into

Miller's. 'You've got no idea how bad it is down there. Makes our jail look like Disneyland.' Miller's jaw was set, and he was trying to pull away from the wide-bodied monster who was crowding closer and closer into his space. 'And you're gonna do it all alone!' Brownie continued. 'Butt-fuck after butt-fuck while that other fish, your buddy, the one that was with you up at the store, is free! Laughin' and jivin' and havin' a ball while you get stuffed downtown . . .'

Miller suddenly straightened up. 'Are you offerin' me a deal?'

Brownie leaned back, and let out his breath. Miller was not going to reveal the accomplice unless the State made him a concession. Brownie's mind began to consider possible offers.

'So you *do* know something,' he responded.

Miller hesitated. Admission that he knew *something* was as close to a confession as you could get. 'I never said that. I just asked you if you was plannin' to give me sumpthin'.'

Brownie froze. He was attempting to manoeuvre Miller into making an incriminating statement, but Miller was manoeuvring *him* instead. If a promise is made in return for a statement, anything said thereafter is inadmissible in court. The bastard must have learned that trick from King.

Brownie swallowed, and sat back in his chair. He'd just come within a hair of making an offer for Miller's statement. And it was all on videotape.

'I'm not offering you anything,' Brownie finally said.

'Are you gonna?' Roscoe persisted.

Brownie stood up. 'If you want to tell me who the other fish is, that's up to you. I'm not giving a thing in return.' He raised his voice for the video recorder. 'Just remember, he's out there and you're in here. And a couple'a months from now, he'll still be out there, and you'll be a nigger pincushion. Better think about it.'

Miller suddenly smiled. 'You don't have shit on me!' This time Brownie went silent. 'If you did, you wouldn't try to jack me up for a statement. You wouldn't need it!' Brownie remained immobile. 'I want my lawyer, and I want him now!'

That was it. When a lawyer is requested, all questioning

must cease. It's the law of the land.

'You'll get your call,' Brownie said wearily. At first, when Miller had been told his rights, Brownie thought it strange that he'd not requested King. But now, in retrospect, the motive was becoming clear. King had already told him what to do. Tipped him off about the impending arrest, and advised him *not* to request counsel. Told him to play dumb and try to bluff the State into making an offer that would set up a guaranteed suppression of evidence. King was diabolical with that kind of tactic. And the scary thing was, it had almost worked.

'You can still waive counsel, and give me a statement,' Brownie said, trying one last time to get him to talk.

'Gonna cut me a deal?' Miller had now taken charge of the entire proceedings.

'Can't do it,' Brownie said solemnly.

'Then, fuck you!' Miller quipped.

Brownie turned and left the room. There was nothing more he could do with Miller at this point. Thanks to the Constitution, his hands were tied.

As Brownie left the interrogation room, he ran into Gardner and Jennifer. They looked excited.

'You got him!' Gardner exclaimed.

Brownie ushered them back to the lab, where they sat around the table. 'Tried to run, but I jammed him.'

'Did you have to bust him up?' Gardner's voice sounded hopeful.

Brownie grimaced. 'Nope. He let me put the cuffs on, no problem.'

Gardner shook his head. 'To be expected.' Criminals ran like hell when the heat approached, but once they were caught, they usually submitted.

'You interrogated him,' Jennifer said.

Brownie laughed ironically. 'Sort of. More like the other way round.' He then filled them in on the details of the questioning, ending with his supposition that the whole thing had been engineered by Kent King. When he had finished, he looked at Gardner. 'King's in this thing. Up over his head.'

The State Attorney nodded. 'Seems to be . . .'

'He's connected to Purvis Bowers and Roscoe,' Brownie continued. 'And then, there's the money. The unaccounted-for cash. I tell you, King's pulling some strings out there.'

'Are we really suggesting that he's involved in the killings,' Jennifer asked suddenly, 'or just the clean-up?'

That had been Gardner's question at the Purvis Bowers crime scene. Had King really gone the way of his clients? Had he finally turned into an actual criminal?

'I don't think we can rule anything out at this point,' Gardner said gravely. 'Brownie's right. there's too much going on here, and King's always in the middle of the action.'

'So what are you saying?' Jennifer asked. 'We bring King in?' The hatred between Gardner and King was legendary, but the playing field had always been the courtroom. They were soldiers in the system, each on his own side. This would take the battle to a new level.

'We keep working the case, and see what happens,' Gardner answered. 'Run the evidence all the way out to the end of the line. If King is criminally involved, we charge him too.'

'There's still a missing link,' Brownie interjected. 'Another fish on the loose. And Roscoe won't lead us to him.'

Gardner placed the yearbook on the table. 'Maybe he already has.'

They then reviewed the information they'd dug up at the school, and showed Brownie the picture.

'Holy mother!' Brownie exclaimed when he saw IV Starke.

'Shotguns,' Gardner said. 'Miller and this Starke guy seem to have an affinity for shotguns.'

'And one could spit out of the other's mouth,' Brownie interrupted, 'they look so much alike!' Then he stood up suddenly, as if he'd been hit on the head by a club. 'Jenneane Dorey!'

'Huh?' Gardner and Jennifer said in unison.

'Jenneane Dorey!' Brownie repeated. 'The girl on the school bus. My witness! She saw someone in the *back* of Roscoe's truck on the day Addie and Henry got killed. Description fitted Roscoe, but maybe it was really . . .'

Three sets of eyes flashed to the yearbook picture. 'Set her up for a photo line-up!' Gardner exclaimed.

'No problem,' Brownie replied. He'd pull some photos out

of his mug-shot book, transpose Starke's picture into a five-by-seven enlargement and head over to the Doreys immediately.

'Jennifer, let's get to work on a search-warrant application for Starke's room,' Gardner said, his excitement rising. 'We'll key it in to the ID. If the girl identifies him, we'll shoot the warrant out there and serve it . . .'

'Right.'

The prosecutors stood and prepared to leave. Brownie had already removed the photo from the book and was inserting it in the copier. Things were finally moving. After weeks of chasing their tails, they were finally on their way. One suspect in custody, and another identified. With any luck at all, they should have the case tied up by nightfall.

PART 4

Dealing with the Devil

CHAPTER 10

'Time for lunch, Granny!' Carole called.

The boy stirred on the couch in the TV room of his grandmother's house, but didn't answer. The room was dark, the curtains drawn. A cartoon was on the screen.

'Granny!' Carole repeated. 'Come in here now.'

'Not hungry.' The boy's voice barely reached the door.

'What?' She was still bustling around in the kitchen.

'Not hungry!' Granville said, louder.

Carole came to the door of the darkened room and looked in. The child was lying on the couch with his knees up. 'You've got to eat something,' she said softly. 'You hardly touched your breakfast.'

'Not hungry,' Granville said for the third time.

Carole walked over and sat beside her son. 'What's wrong?' she asked, as if she didn't know. Let him vent, the therapist had said.

'Nothin',' Granville answered, locking his arms round his raised legs. First he'd hurt his head, and now mom and dad were having a fight. He just didn't want to eat.

'I'm sorry about what happened,' Carole said softly, 'but your father did something bad. I couldn't allow it to go on . . .' Granville listened quietly. 'That's why we had to leave. So you wouldn't be hurt.'

'Dad wouldn't hurt me,' Granville suddenly said.

Carole stroked his face. 'What he was doing was wrong . . .'

The boy gripped his legs tighter, and forced his head down into the soft cushion. Carole stopped talking. It was obvious that her son didn't want to hear another word.

A line of cumulo-nimbus clouds had already begun to build

beyond the mountain ridge. It was 11 a.m. and, at the rate the white giants were billowing, a thunderstorm would form and invade the town by mid-afternoon. That was the usual summertime pattern. Cool clear nights, followed by humid days. And by 4 p.m., the clouds burst, and the process started all over again.

Brownie bounced his lab van down the road that led to Jenneane Dorey's house. He was in a hurry. The wheels of the investigation were finally grinding out solutions to the mystery, and now another question could be answered. When Jenneane had hit him with the Miller look-alike in the back of the red truck, it had not made sense. Why would he be riding in the bed and not in the cab? He didn't have many possessions, but what he did own was jealously guarded. No way he'd ever let another hand guide his personal chariot. No way.

Brownie chugged to a halt at the Doreys' house, and rang the bell. Jenneane answered. Her hair had been combed out and straightened, and she wore a bright red jumpsuit. Her face beamed when she saw him. 'He's here!' she yelled over her shoulder.

Mrs Dorey appeared behind her daughter, and assisted in pushing open the door. 'Thanks for getting here so soon, Sergeant Brown,' she said. 'We do have plans for this afternoon.' The mother was wearing a dark green outfit that clung to her shapely body. Her hair was gathered up in a topknot, and her makeup was fresh and glowing.

Brownie beamed a warm smile. 'Thank you, Mrs Dorey, for seeing me at such short notice.' He turned to the child. 'How's the little lady doing today?'

Jenneane cast her eyes down shyly. 'Fine,' she said in a coquettish voice. It was obvious she was happy to see him again. The three of them walked to the kitchen and sat at the table.

'You said you had some pictures,' Mrs Dorey said.

'Yes, ma'am,' Brownie answered. 'This is what we call a photo line-up. I'm going to show Jenneane a set of eight photographs. She can look at them as long as she wants. What I need to know is if she recognizes anybody . . .'

'From the day the people got killed,' Jenneane said.

146

Brownie looked at the mother, then back at the little girl. 'That is the day we're talking about. You told me you saw a boy in the back of a red truck.'

'Randy Sands,' Jenneane interrupted.

'Yeah,' Brownie said. 'Like Randy Sands, the actor. That's what you told me last time.'

'Uh-huh.' Jenneane nodded.

'Do you think you might recognize him if you ever saw him again?' Brownie fiddled with the manila envelope he was holding, but he did not open it.

'Yes,' Jenneane said, 'I think so.'

Brownie opened the envelope, and laid the eight photos face down on the table, arranging them in a line in front of the girl. 'I'm gonna turn these pictures over one by one, but I do not want you to say anything until you see them all.'

'Uh-huh.' Jenneane's eyes were roving the photo backs, as if she couldn't wait to get at them.

Brownie reached for the first photo, then hesitated. This whole thing was crazy. Really crazy. An eight-year-old girl in a school bus got a glimpse at a guy in the back of a truck. She was talking to a friend, casually glancing out of the window when the truck passed. A fraction of a second. No more. That's all the time she had, and now, weeks later, she was being asked to make an ID. Adult crime victims had problems with IDs every day. Often, they couldn't remember a thing, not even eye colour.

He held his breath, and began to turn the photos over. One by one, the faces appeared. All white males with dark features and clear eyes. A fair array under the constitutional guidelines laid down by the Supreme Court. No one's appearance stood out above the rest.

Jenneane focused on the pictures from left to right. Her mother watched from the other side of the table, following the movement of her daughter's head.

Suddenly the girl picked up a photo, and stopped. Brownie tensed, but said nothing. It was the Roscoe Miller mug shot, taped over and sanitized to obliterate the police markings. Brownie *had* to include it. With the look-alike issue unavoidable as it was, to keep Miller out of the array would have been legal suicide. Starke had to go one-on-one with Miller in the line-up to avoid the charge of a set-up. With only one Randy Sands look-alike in the array, the results would look like they were rigged. With two, the charge could not be made. The ID had to come from recollection, not manipulation, and including both photos was the only way to make it fair.

Jenneane studied Miller's photo. It was his scowling self – ratty hair and piercing blue-eyed stare. She started to say something, but Brownie tapped her arm. 'Don't say anything until you've looked at them all, OK?'

She reluctantly put down the picture, and Brownie turned up the next and the next. There was only one to go. All of the faces were upended except IV Starke's. Brownie had put him last to avoid any implication of favouritism. He reached down slowly, and flipped the corner of the photo. It rose up on edge and flopped over.

'That's him!' Jenneane exclaimed. 'That's him!' she repeated. There was no hesitation. No pause for reflection as she'd done over Miller's mug shot. The blow-up of the skeet team picture lay under her pointing finger, and she was jabbing him in the nose.

'You're sure?' In all his years, Brownie had never seen such an instantaneous, explosive, identification.

'That's him!' Jenneane said for the third time. 'I'm sure. Thought it was this one at first,' she continued, picking up Miller, 'but he looks mean ... *That's* the boy I saw.' She touched the picture in Brownie's hand. 'He looks nice. Like Randy.'

'Was he wearing a hat?' Brownie asked.

Jenneane reflected for a moment. 'No.'

'What about his hair? Was it long or short?' Brownie had to be sure she had picked the right one.

'Short. Real short.'

Brownie smiled. That definitely ruled out Miller. He turned the photo over and wrote the date, the time, and 100 per cent ID, Jenneane Dorey, at the top. Then he stood up and patted Jenneane on the back. 'You did good, girl,' he said. 'Real, real, good.'

'So that's one of the killers, huh?' Mrs Dorey said.

'We think so,' Brownie replied. 'Already got the other one

locked up. Shouldn't be long before we know for sure that this guy was with him. They were seen together out at the private school, and now,' he looked at Jenneane, 'on the way to the crime.'

'Will she have to testify?' Mrs Dorey asked, a worried expression crossing her face.

'Don't know yet. Depends on how far this thing goes.'

'When will you know?' Mrs Dorey continued.

Jenneane had moved so that she could hug Brownie round the waist. He lifted his arm, and hugged her back. 'Gotta see the State Attorney first, then we'll contact you.'

Jenneane was still hugging, looking up at Brownie as though he was her idol.

'Maybe you could come over for dinner? We could talk about it.' Mrs Dorey was giving Brownie the same type of look as her daughter.

Brownie smiled. 'Sounds nice. If I can get some time . . . Real nice.' He gently detached Jenneane's arm. 'I'll give you a call this week,' he told her mother. 'Right now I have to get back to town.'

Brownie said good-bye and rushed to his van. IV Starke was man number two; sidekick to his evil twin. He radioed the station, and patched into the phone lines.

Gardner answered when the call came into the State Attorney's office.

'Positive ID,' Brownie said.

Gardner sighed. 'All set here. Application's done. All we need is a judge's signature, and we're on our way.'

'Next step?' Brownie had started driving, and needed to know which direction to head.

'Call the stop squad, and go out to the school. We'll bring the paperwork. Find Starke, and detain him until we get there.'

'Roger!'

'And, Brownie . . .' Gardner's voice sounded expectant, 'take it easy on him . . .'

They'd already pegged Starke as Miller's tag-along. Miller was the violent bastard who'd hurt Granville and wiped out the Bowers. Maybe they could get a confession from Starke that could ice Miller for good. No deals or promises. Just an incriminating statement from a schoolboy who hooked up with bad company. If they played it right, Starke would crack, and bury Miller for good.

'No sweat, Gard,' Brownie replied. 'I'll be polite.'

'OK. Just hold him till we get there.'

Brownie agreed, and clicked off the mike. Suspect number two was in the bag.

Gardner and Jennifer stood in the outer sanctum of Judge Carla Hanks' chambers. She had been appointed to the bench six months before, and assigned paperwork duties until her courtroom certification came through. The other judges were in court, languishing through the civil docket. With court in session, they could not easily be approached.

'She's busy now,' the judge's grey-haired secretary said. 'Might be able to fit you in late this afternoon.'

Gardner put both hands on her desk. 'We've got a warrant application. It can't wait.'

The secretary smiled uncomfortably, and looked at her hands.

'It won't take long!' Jennifer interjected.

'Let me tell her you're here,' the secretary said.

Gardner flashed Jennifer a wordless thank-you. In the protocol department, judges' secretaries were goddesses. They controlled access to the black robes.

The secretary announced the prosecutors on the intercom. There was a hesitation, followed by an audible sigh. 'Book them in for 5.15,' the judge said. It was clear she did not want to be disturbed.

'Tell her it's an emergency,' Jennifer urged.

The message was conveyed, and the judge sighed again. 'Can't they get another judge?'

'They're all busy,' Gardner said in a voice loud enough to pierce the closed door. 'We have to get this thing signed now!'

The secretary's expression shifted to annoyance. 'Mr Lawson. . . .'

But Gardner rushed past her and entered the inner chamber. 'Sorry, Judge, I know you're busy, but we have a bad situation here . . .'

Judge Hanks was practically invisible behind the paper-

150

work on her desk, buried in her files, catching up with the county judiciary's backlog.

'Mr Lawson!' She did not appreciate the intrusion.

'I said I'm sorry!' Gardner repeated. 'Please look over this warrant application, and we'll get out of here.' Jennifer had silently joined him, and was standing by his side. The judge acknowledged her with a glance.

Gardner handed over the three-page document, and the judge snatched it out of his hand. Like it or not, it *was* her job to review and sign search warrants. And if no one else was available, she'd have to do it, despite the inconvenience. Carla Hanks was a chubby dark-haired woman in her late forties. A former civil law practitioner, she was not comfortable in the criminal arena. From what Gardner had heard, she'd never handled a criminal case in her life.

'Who's the affiant?' she barked suddenly, looking up from the documents.

'Sergeant Joe Brown, and myself. Co-affiants,' Gardner said, reaching across the desk and pointing to Brownie's signature at the bottom of the last page, with his own higher up on the preceding page.

'Why's there such a gap between the text and the signatures?'

Gardner gulped. They'd had Brownie sign the page in blank before he went out to see Jenneane Dorey, and he and Jennifer had filled it in later. The only contact Brownie had had with the page was to sign it. Technically, that was a no-no.

'Standard format,' Jennifer piped up. 'Signatures do not have to coincide.' She knew that Hanks had seen very few of these documents. The judge nodded, and went back to the text.

Gardner let out his breath, and thanked Jennifer again with his eyes. An admission as to how the papers had been prepared might have invalidated them on the spot. No way were they going to tell Carla Hanks that the application was possibly defective.

Hanks bought it and administered the oath to Gardner, making him swear that everything in the application was true, based upon his own personal knowledge and belief.

'I do,' he said solemnly when she had finished.

There was another pause as the judge's eyes returned to the application. She was still having trouble with something. 'Identification near the scene. Association with another suspect prior to the incident . . . What else do you have to support probable cause?'

Gardner told her, 'We're still investigating . . .' That was the whole purpose of the warrant in the first place. Find more evidence to tie Starke to the crime. 'You have enough facts there to support the search, your honour.'

Judge Hanks put the paper down. 'This investigation is incomplete. You just said so.'

Gardner's face heated up. She was hesitating, flailing about in ignorance. Maybe she wouldn't sign.

'The level of proof one needs at this stage is minimal,' Jennifer said softly. 'More than mere suspicion, but far less than certainty.'

The judge looked at Jennifer with surprise. 'Are you requesting I sign this, Miss Munday?'

Jennifer nodded. 'The facts cited establish an adequate level of probable cause, your honour.'

Gardner held his breath again.

Judge Hanks picked up her pen, scribbled her signature and tossed the papers at Gardner. Then she looked at Jennifer, and smiled. 'You are very persuasive. More so than your colleague.' Then she lowered her head and disappeared behind the stack of files.

Gardner mumbled 'Thank you', and they headed for the door. Outside, he gave Jennifer a kiss.

'What was that for?' she asked with a smile.

'Working your feminine wiles in there. Hanks wouldn't give me the time of day!'

Jennifer squeezed his arm. 'What now?'

Gardner fell silent for a moment. 'We nail Starke, and extract a statement. And then . . .' His voice faded.

'Then what?' Jennifer prodded.

Gardner's expression turned resolute. 'Then we go after Granville!'

The clouds had built into majestic thunderheads that sat on

the horizon like unwanted guests. Commencement activities at the Prentice Academy were in progress, and the quadrangle was filled with the families and friends of the graduates. The parking lot was clogged with cars. Brownie stood, arms folded, on the edge of the grass, unsmiling and agitated, waiting for Gardner.

The State Attorney zig-zagged through the maze of vehicles and came to a stop beside the officer. The window was down, and he brandished the warrant triumphantly in the air.

Brownie shook his head. 'He's not here.'

Gardner and Jennifer quickly got out of the car. 'What'd you say?' he asked hurriedly.

'Said he's not here,' Brownie repeated. 'Left early this morning.'

Gardner glanced at the graduation gathering. 'What about that?'

Brownie shook his head again, 'He's not gonna graduate this time.'

Gardner was flabbergasted. Starke was listed as a senior in the yearbook, and he was an *old* senior at that. They had counted on grabbing him as he came down the platform, but now he'd apparently run. 'Where's the squad?' he asked, noting that the other officers he'd ordered earlier were nowhere in sight.

'Went up to the room,' Brownie said. 'We got it sealed off.'

'But no entry,' Gardner interjected.

'Nope, no entry.' Without the warrant in hand, the police could not conduct a search. The best they could do was blockade the premises until the warrant arrived.

'And what about Starke?' This time Jennifer spoke.

Brownie looked at her, then turned to Gardner. 'I put a call out to the State cops. He's driving a red BMW convertible. Vanity tags BOOM. Shouldn't be too hard to find.'

'Just our State?' Gardner asked.

Brownie always had the bases covered. 'West Virginia. Ohio. Pennsylvania. Delaware. New Jersey. Every State between here and New York.'

'That's where he's heading?' Jennifer asked.

'Don't know for sure,' Brownie answered. 'He's from up

153

there, and best info we got was he just packed up and left. No hurry. No worry. Just clearing out at the end of the school year.'

Gardner rubbed his cheek. 'So he wasn't running?' Evidence of flight could always be used in court to prove the guilt of a defendant. He was fleeing to escape capture and punishment. That was the theory, but if the exit was nonchalant and routine, they might have trouble with that argument at trial.

'Didn't seem to be spooked,' Brownie answered. 'At least, that's what the folks we talked to said.'

'OK,' Gardner said, 'we can't worry about that now. Let's hit the room.'

They pushed past the ceremony towards a vine-covered dormitory at the far end of the campus. Gardner caught the headmaster's eye as they passed. He was busy handing out diplomas, certifying his 'eagles' for flight. He stared at them nervously, wondering what they were doing. But he was trapped on the dais, and couldn't cry out for King.

The dorm was a two-storey stone building in the same gothic tradition as the rest of the campus. There was a main stairwell in the centre, and corridors leading off on each side, at each level. IV Starke's room was at the far end of the second storey south wing.

Three uniformed officers guarded the closed door. They were part of the department's 'stop' squad, a special team which served search warrants and arrested fugitives. Trained in the legal and physical aspects of their special job, the men were experts at busting doors, sniffing out evidence and bringing down felons.

'Any activity?' Brownie asked the team leader.

'Nothing,' the bulky officer replied.

'OK,' Gardner said, pushing to the front of the team, and handing him the warrant. 'Let's do it.'

The team leader nodded, and tried the doorknob with his hand. 'Locked,' he said, looking at Brownie.

Brownie nodded, and swept his hand towards the door. In an instant, another squad member produced a thick battering-ram, and the three of them powered it into the wooden door. 'Wham!' The door crashed off its hinges, and fell into

154

the room. When the dust cleared, they entered.

'Holy shit!' Brownie whispered. The electronic gear was still there. Top-of-the-line stereos, recorders, TVs, telephones. The best that money could buy. 'Rich kid,' he said wistfully.

'Most students here can't complain,' Gardner answered. He'd attended a similar school closer to Baltimore. Another all-male prep, packed with privileged sons.

Brownie pulled open a desk drawer, then another. 'School papers'. Gardner looked over his shoulder as he riffled through the stack of lined composition sheets. Nothing incriminating.

'Sarge!' a team member cried out. The others had fanned out in the room, picking through the student's possessions in search of any clue that he was tied to Roscoe Miller or any of the shootings. 'Take a look!'

They gathered at a slide-door closet, and stared in. 'Jeez!' Brownie exclaimed. 'I see what you mean by not complaining!' Inside the closet was a large industrial-strength safe, bolted to the side wall and the floor. It was large and heavily reinforced, more suitable for a bank than a dorm room. Brownie signalled to the officer, and he tried the handle. It was locked. The officer gave Brownie a 'What do I do now?' look. Brownie passed the same expression on to Gardner.

'Can you drill it?' Gardner asked.

The officer shrugged. 'Never had one this big.'

'OK,' Gardner sighed. 'Call for reinforcements, and get this thing open.'

Brownie nodded, and waved one of the team out to make the call. Then they all resumed the search. 'Check this,' he said to Gardner a few moments later. He was standing next to the window, pointing down.

Gardner approached, and saw the fire-escape platform below the sill. A spiral stairway curled down to the ground, and just feet from the bottom was a parking lot. Behind the lot was a dense growth of foliage and trees.

'Guess what's over there,' Brownie said, pointing towards the trees. Gardner's eyebrows rose. ''Bout two miles that way is Bowers Corner.' Brownie had studied some aerial photos, and discovered that there was a straight line between the school and the store. It was miles and miles by road, but across country, through some very heavy and uncharted bush, lay the scene of the crime.

Gardner looked at the fire-escape, and beyond, at the woods. 'Convenient,' he said solemnly.

'Looking better all the time,' Brownie said in the same tone of voice.

'So you think he left his room this way and cased out Bowers, before the crime?' Jennifer said. She'd been eavesdropping.

Gardner turned to face her. He was pale and serious, thinking about the Bowers, Granville and the gun. 'Can't rule it out,' he said. 'Might explain how they disappeared. Miller took the truck, and Starke came back here.'

'Sergeant!' Another officer had found something. They gathered by the bed as he unloaded an armful of magazines on to the spread. 'They were in the closet, behind some clothes.'

Gardner picked up one of the books. *Mercenary Soldier* its glossy cover proclaimed. Jennifer picked up another one. It was a copy of *Gang Bikers*. They fanned through the lot. More of the same. Guns, outlaws, and glorified violence.

Brownie walked over to the night table and picked up the telephone. There was no inscribed number. He hit the 'operator' button, and a voice answered. 'May I help you'

'Yeah. Can you tell me the number I'm callin' from?'

There was a pause. 'You don't know, sir?'

Brownie took a breath. 'No, ma'am. That's why I'm asking.'

There was another pause. 'I'm afraid it's unlisted.'

Brownie silently counted to ten. 'You're not gonna give it to me?'

'Sorry, sir. I can't.'

Brownie hung up and cut her off, then dialled 911. 'Emergency operator.'

'This is Sergeant Joe Brown, County Police. What number are you painting?'

'887–6543. What's your problem?'

'No problem,' Brownie said. 'Just a phone check. Police business.' Then he hung up and wrote on his pad. By tomorrow he should have every number IV Starke ever dialled.

'Sergeant Brown!' This voice was coming from outside the room. The officer they'd left downstairs to guard the perimeter rushed in and handed Brownie a piece of paper. 'Pennsylvania State Police just called! They picked up your suspect!'

Gardner clenched his fist, and waved it in the air. They had Starke.

Brownie thanked the officer and turned to the prosecutors. 'Out-of-State arrest. What do you want to do with it?'

Gardner's feeling of triumph quickly faded. An out-of-State arrest meant trouble if the defendant refused to waive extradition and voluntarily return to Maryland. If he fought the warrant, it could be months before they got him back. And if Pennsylvania set a bond on the extradition proceeding, Starke could be released before they ever touched him.

'Where is he?' Gardner asked, craning his head to see the paper.

'East of Breezewood, on the turnpike,' Brownie answered.

Three hours by car, Gardner thought. 'Call the chopper, Brownie. We can be there in an hour.'

'And head off an extradition problem,' Brownie cut in.

Gardner smiled and looked at Jennifer. 'Feel like taking a ride?'

'Do I have a choice?'

'Sure,' he said. 'You can stay here and watch them open the safe.'

Jennifer grabbed his hand. 'I'd rather fly!'

Brownie led the way, and they hurried down the stairs. If the helicopter was free, they could be out of there in minutes, and maybe surprise Starke before he had a chance to assert his constitutional rights.

Joel Jacobs lounged on the patio of his Parkside East penthouse. It had been a heavy week of negotiating and scrapping in the corridors of the City courthouse, and he was tired. He lay back on the chaise and lifted his glass of iced tea, admiring a cloud of pigeons that was swooping low over the puffed green trees of Central Park. At that moment of peaceful reflection, the phone rang. 'Hello?' He was off duty.

157

No calls or interruptions expected.

'Mr Jacobs, it's Wendell.' He was an associate at the firm who worked round the clock. In four years there, it was doubtful he'd ever seen the sun.

'What is it?' Joel's voice edged into the irritated range.

'A call, sir. Urgent, they said. Mr Starke the fourth. In trouble. In Pennsylvania.'

Jacobs sat up, and shielded his eyes. The pigeons swooped into the leaf cover and disappeared. The mood was shattered. 'When did the call come in?'

'A few minutes ago, sir. I knew you didn't want to be disturbed, so I took the call. Then I thought I'd better let you know . . .'

Jacobs toed around for his slippers under the chaise, and stood up. 'Relax, Wendell. You did the right thing.' The associate was typical of his breed: sycophantic to a fault, and terrified of displeasing the master.

Jacobs walked to the kitchen and picked up a notepad, clamping the portable phone between his chin and neck. 'You got a number, of course,' he said.

'Yes, sir. Area code 717. 323–1111. Pennsylvania State Police Barracks.'

'OK. You wait there for my return call. We may have some strings to pull before the day is done, and I want you to stand by.'

'Yes, sir!' Wendell sounded as though he would follow Jacobs off a cliff. Jacobs clicked off, then dialled the Pennsylvania number.

'Barrack C, State Police.' The voice was female, and very official.

'Who am I speaking with, please?' Jacob's voice was as smooth as clover honey.

'Corporal Zane.'

'Corporal, my name is Joel Jacobs. I'm an attorney, calling from New York City.' His tone was melodic, mesmerizing. As if he were trying to woo her. 'I understand you've got a young man in custody, is that correct?'

'Yes, sir. We've got several young men in the lock-up.'

'Does one of them happen to be a Mr Starke?'

There was a short pause as the corporal checked her prisoner manifest, 'Yes, sir. A Mr Wellington Starke the fourth.'

'OK. Now, can you tell me what charges he's being held on?'

There was another pause. 'It's a fugitive warrant out of Maryland. Looks like two counts of murder, and one count of attempted murder.'

Jacobs grimaced, but kept quiet. 'May I speak to the commanding officer, please?'

'Yes, sir. That would be Captain Henderson.'

There was a click, and a male voice answered, 'Henderson.'

Jacobs repeated the same introduction he'd given the other officer. His voice was polite. Courteous. Deferential.

'OK,' the captain replied. 'What can I do for you?'

'I want you to listen carefully,' Jacobs said. 'And I want you to take down these instructions verbatim.' The voice was still soft, but each word carried the aura of a threat.

'Do what?' the captain did not follow.

'I'm Mr Starke's attorney. I'm recording this conversation so there will be no mistake later as to the instructions I'm about to give you . . .' He keyed a beeper on the console to acknowledge that a recording was being made. 'I suggest you write down each word. Do you understand?'

'Uhhh . . .' The captain was speechless. He was a road trooper, used to pulling over drunk drivers and clearing accidents off the interstate. He'd never heard anything like this before.

'First, I'm instructing you not to allow anyone, and I repeat *anyone*, to question my client until I am able to be present. Do you acknowledge what I have just said?'

'Uh-huh . . .' The captain still sounded dumbstruck.

'Second. My client does not, and again, I repeat, does *not* waive extradition to Maryland. You are forbidden to present him with any waiver forms or even to discuss the matter with him until I arrive. Do you have that?'

'No waiver. Uh-huh. I heard you.'

'Third. You are to fax a complete set of charging documents to the following number immediately. Area code 212 445–6700. Do you copy that?'

'445–6700. Yeah.'

'Area code 212.'

'Yeah. 212.'

The phone beeped as the recording continued. 'Captain . . .'

'Yeah?'

'I expect these instructions to be obeyed.' The voice had lost its sugar coating. Its tone was ominous.

'Yeah. Whatever you say,' the captain replied. The point was made. 'Do you wish to speak with your client?'

'No,' Jacobs replied firmly. 'I'll see him when I get there. In the meantime, keep him on ice.'

The captain mumbled an answer, and Jacobs hung up. Then he rapidly dialled another number. 'Let me speak to Mr Starke,' he told the servant who answered. 'Joel Jacobs calling.'

'Joel?' Wellington Starke sounded surprised.

'Problem, Wel,' Jacobs said gravely.

'My son?'

'Yes, I'm afraid.'

Wellington seemed to choke on his own breath. 'How bad?'

'He's been charged with murder.'

'Ohhh!' It was a father's wail of pain.

'Take it easy!' Jacobs said calmly.

'But, but . . .' Wellington was groping for words.

'Just tell me how far I can go.'

The blubbering stopped. 'How bad is it?'

Jacobs blew a hissing sound through his lips. 'We can assume it's very bad. I just need to know how much authority I have.'

'You're gonna take care of it?'

'Yes, if you authorize it.'

Wellington went silent for a moment, then came back on the line. 'No limit, Joel,' he said sombrely.

'No limit?' Jacobs asked.

'Whatever it takes. Just help him.'

'Thank you,' Jacobs said. 'I'll keep you posted. Don't do or say a thing until you hear from me.'

He hung up, walked to his bedroom and pulled a suitcase out of his closet. There was no time to waste.

The Maryland State Police helicopter lifted off at 3.15 p.m.

160

with its turbine engine whining and its rotor blades thwop-thwop-thwopping against the humid air. The craft made a lazy turn over the town, then dipped its nose and picked up speed as it raced towards the east.

Gardner sat up front in the co-pilot's seat, with Brownie and Jennifer on jump-seats behind. Each had on a headset so they could communicate above the vibrating roar of the engine.

'OK back there?' the State Attorney asked his colleagues.

There had been very little planning before they had called in the helicopter. No strategy session. No discussion. Gardner had made another spur-of-the-moment decision, like he did so often. Acting on impulse, propelled by his intuition, he was not one for lying back and allowing events to overtake him.

'School,' the pilot said, banking right so that his passengers could get a better look.

Below, the geometric lines of Prentice Academy suddenly appeared, trimmed and symmetrical as an English garden. Gardner had asked for a fly-by on the way to Pennsylvania. He wanted to see the bee-line that Brownie had described earlier. 'Over there,' he told the pilot, pointing to the square block of stone on the edge of the campus that was IV Starke's dormitory. The helicopter banked again, and aligned with the building, passing over the thinning crowd of commencement celebrants as it adjusted course. The ceremony was over. Many of the cars had left the parking lot, and the gathering was now down to a handful of family groups. They passed over the quadrangle and descended to rooftop level.

Gardner glimpsed several police cars beside the dorm as they roared over the structure and crossed into the treeline. 'Keep it low,' he ordered.

'Roger,' the pilot replied, easing forward on the stick, so the metal skids were almost touching the leafy treetops.

'Path's in there somewhere,' Brownie said from behind. He'd moved forward to get a better view, and Jennifer had joined him.

The vegetation was thick. Too thick to see beneath the canopy of oaks, maples, evergreens and a blanket of vines.

161

From above, at least, it did not look as if anything could get through.

'Bowers Corner,' the pilot reported.

Gardner had been looking down, so the gabled roof bursting out of the foliage on the horizon caught him by surprise. The helicopter picked up speed, and leaped over the store with a sudden burst of speed.

'Jeez!' he exclaimed. The G-forces constricted his stomach as the aircraft climbed, but that was not what had made him cry out. It was so close. The school where Miller worked. Where he and Starke played with shotguns. Where a student's room backed up to the woods, and the student read magazines that praised violence. So close to the woods. So close to the store. So close to Addie and Henry.

'You get the picture?' Brownie said.

'Yeah,' Gardner replied. They were on the right track. Finally, after false starts and miscues, they were getting somewhere. The simple robbery theory was starting to fade. Brownie and Jennifer were probably right. In some bizarre way, the missing money, Purvis, King, Miller and IV Starke were tied together. There was a pattern here, but, like the obscured path in the woods, it wasn't yet apparent.

'Uh-huh!' The pilot's voice suddenly interrupted his thoughts. Gardner looked through the windscreen into a massive black cloud ahead. 'Storm,' the pilot said, jerking the stick left, and canting into a dizzying high-speed bank. The daily 4 o'clock visitor had arrived early, and in minutes the valley would be inundated with rain, lightning and high winds. The helicopter turned eastward, threading through several bumpy curtains of rain, rising and descending above and below the boiling storm.

'Sorry, folks. Looks like we're gonna have a rough ride ahead,' the pilot announced grimly.

Gardner silently agreed. On all counts, the man was probably right.

CHAPTER 11

The helicopter landed beside the Pennsylvania Police Barracks at 4.30 p.m. It had been buffeted through the edges of several storms, but had come out unscathed. Gardner, Jennifer and Brownie ducked below the rotor blades and ran for the squat brick building. They were glad to be on solid ground.

A uniformed officer allowed them past the outer waiting area after they showed their badges and a copy of IV Starke's arrest warrant. They were then directed down a long green-tiled hall to Captain Henderson's office. Gardner knocked, and a voice told him to enter.

Gardner led his entourage into the room, and Henderson stood up. 'Afternoon, Captain,' Gardner said, showing his badge. 'We're here to see IV Starke – the guy you picked up on the Maryland warrant.' He handed a copy of the charging document across the officer's grey metal desk.

Henderson's square face went serious as he took the papers. He was a prototype State trooper. He sat down, and motioned the trio into a semicircle of chairs around the desk.

Gardner could sense something was wrong. 'What's the problem?'

Henderson looked as though he were trying to swallow a raw egg. 'Got a call from the man's attorney,' he said. 'New York hot-shot.' There was an edge of contempt to his words. In criminal justice, prosecutors and police were on one side, defence attorneys on the other. The captain's allegiance was obvious. 'Gave instructions not to allow anyone near his client.'

Gardner looked at Jennifer, then back at Henderson. 'When was this?'

'About two hours ago. We let Starke use the phone when he came in. Think he called New York. Ten minutes later the lawyer called.' Henderson's face set as if he was going to say more, but his voice trailed off. 'Weird . . .'

Gardner caught the trooper's eye and urged him to continue. 'Jacobs,' Henderson said. 'That was his name. A real arrogant son-of-a-bitch.' Gardner's mind suddenly focused on Kent King. 'Didn't *ask* me. *Ordered* me. And recorded the conversation!'

Gardner stirred in his seat. This did not sound good. Starke already had a lawyer, and the lawyer was up and running with counter moves. 'Recorded?' He had never heard that one before.

Henderson nodded. 'Yep. Said if I didn't follow his instructions, he'd use the tape in court . . .'

'Damn!' Brownie exclaimed. 'Looks like we got another live one!'

Gardner looked at his friend. His face was grim.

'Did *Starke* ask for an attorney?' Jennifer suddenly interjected.

Gardner jerked his head in her direction. The lawyer had called on his client's behalf, but that was not the crucial issue. Did the client ask for his lawyer? That was the key. If Starke had not yet asked for his lawyer, they still might have a chance to talk to him.

Henderson smiled, as if he suddenly saw the same opening. 'No, I don't believe he did. Jacobs called me and gave the instructions, but Starke never specifically said that he wanted an attorney . . .'

'Did you read him his rights?' Gardner asked hopefully. They might be on to something. Only the defendant can make the lawyer request. No one else can do it for him.

Henderson's smile widened. 'Yep. He was Mirandized in the field, and again back here at the barracks.'

'Was he questioned?' Gardner asked.

'Why, no,' the captain answered. 'It wasn't our case. We would not really know what to ask.'

Gardner smiled. 'So he's been told his rights, has not asked for a lawyer, and has not been interrogated?'

'Correct,' Henderson answered.

'So it looks like we're OK,' Jennifer said.

Gardner whispered. 'Uh-huh', then leaned forward and looked at Henderson. 'Can you let us talk to him?'

'You know I've been ordered not to.'

'I know,' Gardner answered, 'but the rights belong to the client, not the lawyer. We're not violating any *law* by talking to him.'

Henderson hesitated. Jacobs sounded as if he could make a lot of trouble for anyone who crossed him. 'He's on his way down here,' he said.

'Who?' Gardner asked.

'Jacobs. Said he was coming down immediately.'

Gardner got to his feet. 'Then we don't have a lot of time.'

Henderson remained seated, still contemplating his dilemma. 'He said something else . . . No extradition waivers allowed.'

Gardner put his hands on his hips. '*He* said. The *lawyer*. Did you ask Starke?'

'No.' Henderson was still on the fence.

'Then that's an open issue too,' Gardner said.

'Captain.' This time Brownie spoke. 'Starke was in some heavy shit. Was with a guy who blew the heads off two old folks and cracked the skull of this man's little boy . . .' He put his hand on Gardner's back. 'It's not the strongest case in the world, and we think Starke can fill in the gaps.'

Henderson stood up. 'You're gonna need this,' he said, handing a printed form to Gardner.

Gardner took it and read the caption at the top: WAIVER OF EXTRADITION. 'So you're letting us in,' he said softly.

'Correct,' Henderson replied. 'You'd better get moving. Jacobs could be here any time. And if you're not done and out of here by then, we might all get the firing squad.'

Joel Jacobs was in the corporate jet hangar at La Guardia airport waiting for his plane to be fuelled. As chief counsel to the Landau Chemical Company, he was given access to the corporation's Learjet whenever he requested it. A phone call to the on-duty pilot had secured its availability, and now all they had to do was gas up and he'd be on his way.

The attorney sat in the lounge, and opened his briefcase.

The charges against IV Starke had been faxed as promised, and he reviewed them word by word. 'Accompanied.' 'Aided and Abetted.' 'Accomplice.' The operative phrases echoed the same theme. Starke was a participant in the crimes, but not the moving force. The shooter was a man named Roscoe Miller. Jacobs circled Miller's name, and reached for the telephone on the table beside him.

After several rings, a man answered. 'Udek.'

'Drew, this is Joel.'

'Yes, sir!' Drew Udek was Jacob's private investigator.

'Got a job for you,' Jacobs said, 'in Maryland. How soon can you leave?'

'Is right away soon enough?'

Jacobs smiled. The guy always came through. 'That would be fine. I need in-depth backgrounds on some people down there. Wendell Stein has the list. You can pick it up at the office before you leave.'

'I'm on my way, sir.'

'And, Drew, I want it *all* on these people. The complete picture. Strengths, weaknesses, a full bio.'

'No problem, Mr Jacobs. I *am* somewhat familiar with that State.'

'Good. Now I'm on my way down to Pennsylvania, then on to Maryland. Wendell will have my location, so check in with him, and he'll guide you through to me.'

'No problem,' Udek echoed. He'd got the message the first time.

As Jacobs hung up, he saw the pilot waving to him through the window. The plane was ready. He closed his briefcase and stood up. From the tenor of the charging documents, they'd barely snagged IV Starke by his toenail. There was so little information to connect him to any crime that it was almost laughable. The man named Roscoe Miller was obviously the killer, and he had somehow drawn Starke in for the ride.

Jacobs walked to the plane, and entered. Soon he was strapped in, and they were taxiing for take-off. The phone call to Captain Henderson suddenly returned to his mind. 'Do you want to talk to your client?' the officer had asked. At the time, Jacobs had declined. Police officers had a way of

166

overhearing conversations 'accidentally on purpose'. In an uncontrolled environment, Starke could have blurted something incriminating, and the cops could have picked it up. If the phone was in the squad room, and he spoke with the officers in hearing range, the eavesdropping would have been legal.

The jet accelerated to rotation speed, and the sharp nose lifted steeply in the air. Jacobs looked out of the window as the ground dropped away precipitously. The scene was like a rocket launch, the ascent was so steep. Soon they were in the clouds, and then above, into a clear azure sky. Jacobs returned to his thoughts. Starke would know what to do. He'd be able to hold out until help arrived. He was a smart kid. But a doubt persisted. He looked out of the window again as earth and clouds reeled by. Maybe he'd made a mistake. Maybe he should have talked to his client and told him to clam up.

Gardner, Jennifer and Brownie stood outside the cell-block area of the barracks. A steel door separated them from the narrow cage that held IV Starke.

'OK, We're here,' Brownie said. 'Now what do we do?'

Gardner ran his hand through his hair. So far, they'd been lucky. They'd hitched a ride to Pennsylvania, and talked the captain into giving them a shot at Starke. From this point on, every move was crucial. They had to walk the constitutional line, or risk losing whatever evidence they got from Starke. Gardner's mind was grinding out a plan. 'We all can't go in,' he said.

'Only one,' Jennifer said.

'Yeah,' Gardner replied. 'Only one.'

The three fell silent as the needle in Gardner's mind spun towards his choice. 'Don't think I should do it,' he said, looking at Jennifer. 'And you probably shouldn't either.'

'So I'm elected,' Brownie said.

Gardner handed him the waiver form. 'You'd better do the honours.'

'What's our tack?' Brownie whispered.

A trooper walked down the hall, and the trio huddled together as he passed. 'Lie and cheat. Whatever you have to do,' Gardner said. 'Just get him to waive extradition. And get a statement. If you can.'

Brownie nodded. Again, deception was the name of the game. If they could trick Starke into cooperating without threatening or coercing him, it was perfectly legal. The Supreme Court said so. 'Do my damn best,' Brownie said, seizing the door handle.

'Just make it quick,' Gardner admonished. Jacobs was en route.

Brownie said OK, and went through the door. Gardner and Jennifer peered through the spyhole.

Starke stood up when Brownie entered the cell. Both Gardner and Jennifer got a look at him at the same time. In person, he was a far cry from Roscoe Miller. In fact the resemblance did not leap out in the way it had in the picture. Maybe it was the close-cut hair, or the fashionable clothes, or the way he moved his body. There was no slouching shuffle. No go-to-hell expression. Starke moved smoothly, gracefully, towards the officer, as if he were approaching a shot on the tennis court. His features were serene, his expression passive. Just then his eyes went past Brownie to the faces framed in the door's tiny opening. Gardner and Jennifer froze for an instant as they found themselves locked into a pale-blue-eyed stare. The eyes turned icy for a millisecond, then warmed. But, in that moment, the resemblance to Miller came through. There was mystery in his pale eyes. And a hint of hostility.

Gardner pulled Jennifer away. 'Let's back off, and let Brownie work.'

Jennifer nodded. 'He's definitely . . .' Her words faded.

Gardner waited, but she didn't continue. 'Definitely what?'

'Scary . . .'

'Yeah,' Gardner said, as an image suddenly flashed into his mind. Miller, Starke, the gun and Granville. Evil blue eyes all round, focused on his son. 'Get him, Brownie,' he whispered as they walked from the cell. 'Nail him!'

Brownie met Starke at the bars. 'Mr Starke, I'm Joe Brown, County Police.'

Starke looked him over cautiously. 'What's this all about?

Cops stopped me on the turnpike. Said I've been charged with murder.' His face twitched as he said the last word.

'We put a warrant out,' Brownie said. 'Fella named Roscoe Miller said you were with him when he killed Addie and Henry Bowers. That makes you an accessory.' Brownie's lies were up and running, as he tried to provoke a response.

Starke didn't flinch. 'I don't know anything about it.'

'There's other evidence too. Fingerprints. Body hairs. A real good case against you, but Miller might get off . . .' He was using the same ploy against Starke that he'd used against Miller.

Again, there was no response. Starke was calm, nonreactive. 'I really don't understand.'

'OK,' Brownie said casually, 'we can discuss that later. Back home. First, you have to sign this form.' He slipped the extradition paper through the narrow opening in the bars.

Starke studied it carefully. 'I need to check with my lawyer about this first.'

Brownie smiled. 'Mr Jacobs.' Starke nodded. 'We just talked to him,' Brownie said. 'Made arrangements for you to return to Maryland. He'll meet you there. Said to go ahead and sign the waiver.' As long as Brownie was lying, he might as well go all the way.

Starke frowned. 'He said what?'

'Said for you to come back with us,' Brownie replied. 'Since this is a Maryland case, it was decided it would be best to go back there to get things straightened out, rather than stay here. He said to go ahead and sign the waiver, and he'll meet you back in the county.'

Starke looked sceptical. 'When did you talk to him?'

'Few minutes ago. Before coming in to see you. He okayed everything.'

The scepticism lingered. That did not sound like something Joel Jacobs would do. 'I think I'd better call and check on it first.'

Brownie smiled bravely. Starke was calling his bluff. 'OK with me.' If Jacobs could be contacted, they were dead.

The lock-up trooper was called, and Starke was provided with a cordless telephone. In a moment, he had Wendell

169

Stein on the line. Brownie stood by, and held his breath.

'Uh, yes, Mr Starke,' Wendell said. 'Mr Jacobs is on his way.'

What about the plans to go to Maryland? Starke asked.

Wendell paused. He didn't know anything about that. He did know that Mr Jacobs *was* going to Maryland eventually, but as to meeting Starke there, he'd heard nothing about that.

'Shall I sign the waiver paper?' Starke asked.

Wendell was on the spot. If Joel Jacobs *had* arranged to meet his client in Maryland, and Wendell vetoed it, his boss would crucify him. But if it was *not* planned, and Wendell okayed it, he'd be flogged. Either way, he'd suffer. He put Starke on hold, and tried to contact Jacobs at the airport, but the call would not go through.

'You can reach me in Maryland tomorrow,' Jacobs had said. Wendell decided to take a chance. 'Sign the papers,' he instructed his boss's client.

Starke hung up, and took the pen from Brownie's hand.

Prentice Academy was abuzz. The storm had roared across campus, blowing over commencement chairs, uprooting the refreshment tent and sending the celebrants screaming for cover. And, in the midst of that chaos, there was a procession of police flowing in and out of IV Starke's dorm.

Edwin Charles, the headmaster had finally managed to pull away from a group of parents on the pretext of fleeing the storm. Racing to Starke's room, he found the 'stop' team digging through the student's possessions like madmen. He called Kent King from the student's phone, and minutes later King arrived. The attorney reached the room as two hefty police officers wheeled in a set of acetylene torch bottles.

'How can they do this?' Charles asked worriedly.

King spoke to one of the officers and procured a copy of the warrant. He scanned it and handed the paper to the headmaster. 'They think your boy Starke has some evidence hidden away,' King announced.

Charles reviewed the document, and glanced up at King, 'Oh, God!'

'Step out of the room, please!' The team leader suddenly approached the intruders, and pushed them towards the door with his massive frame. In the background, the torch was being lit, and a masked figure crouched by the safe.

'OK, OK,' King said, backing towards the door.

The huge officer kept advancing until the attorney and the headmaster were outside the room. Then he stationed two of his men to block the entrance.

Charles was working overtime on the handkerchief in his sweaty hands. 'This isn't right,' he whispered to King.

The attorney had risen to his tiptoes in an effort to see over the shoulders of the guards. The torchman was etching the safe door with a dagger of flame, and there was an acrid smell of burning in the air. King lowered himself, and seized Charles by the lapel, leading him out of earshot of the officers in the room. 'What are you so nervous about?' he asked. 'Is there anything in there that you should be afraid of?'

Charles continued mopping his hands. 'Don't think so . . .' he said, 'but . . .'

King casually folded his arms. 'But what?'

'If anything does come out, they'll close down the school! Our reputation . . . the finances . . .' His words were almost hysterical.

King smiled. 'You're forgetting something.' Charles stopped fidgeting. 'You hired me to make sure it doesn't,' King said smugly.

The headmaster took off his glasses and rubbed his eyes. 'But the police think Starke and Miller killed the Bowers. They're both connected to the school. This is a disaster . . .'

King put his hand on Charles' shoulder and squeezed the nerve. The headmaster winced. 'You'd better calm down,' he said. 'Nothing is going to happen. The whole case is bogus. Against Miller. Against Starke.' His face twisted into a sneer. 'Lawson doesn't have a thing he can use in court! He's so upset his boy got hurt that he's making mistakes all over the place. *Nobody* has a thing to worry about.'

Just then, a cheer went up in the room. King rushed to the door, and looked over a shoulder. The safe was open, and the cops were busy extracting its contents. He shifted to get a better view. They were piling documents on the table, labelling them and placing them in plastic bags.

The headmaster pushed against King's spine. 'What do you see?' he whispered excitedly.

King turned suddenly. 'Go back to your office, and wait for me there.' Charles retreated slowly, then picked up his pace until he was almost running. King smiled. 'Damn worry-guts!' he whispered to himself. Then he stretched up on his toes again.

The safe was empty now, and all the items inside were neatly stacked on the desk, each in the protective cover of an evidence bag. King scanned the faces of the officers in the room. Most were familiar – officers he'd run across in court. He caught the eye of a stop team member, and signalled a greeting. The officer, an older member of the group, issued a subtle acknowledgment with his eyes. King cocked his head slightly, and sent a message: meet me outside. The officer's eyes barely flickered: OK.

A short time later, King was in the quadrangle. The grounds crew was busy rounding up the scattered chairs, and the 'burrr' of a chainsaw suddenly erupted in the distance. He surveyed the damage. The winds had snapped some tree limbs and wreaked havoc with the furniture, but the structures were intact. The sun was out again, dipping towards the ridge line, and the humidity was starting to creep back.

'Kent,' a deep voice said from behind.

King turned as officer Barry Light walked towards him, his arms stacked with envelopes. 'Hi, Barry.' King smiled warmly. 'What'd you get?'

The policeman scanned the area and signalled 'walk with me' with his chin. King fell in beside him. 'Records, mostly. Family histories. Birth certificates. Death certificates. Stuff like that.'

'What else?' King whispered. He was sauntering casually, as if they were simply sharing the sidewalk.

'Bunch of cash bands. Hundreds. Thousands . . .'

'Any cash?' King's mouth barely moved.

'Not a penny.'

King glanced at the stack of folders. 'Anything else?'

The officer slowed his pace. They were nearing the parking

lot. 'Yeah. Some weird shit.' King slowed to keep abreast, his ears tuned. 'Tattoos . . . Temporary tattoos.'

King stopped suddenly, and the officer halted with him. 'You got 'em with you, Barry?'

The officer glanced around nervously, then sifted through the pile in his arms. In the meanwhile, he'd resumed walking. 'Uh-huh,' he whispered.

'Let me see 'em,' King said.

'How?' They were almost at the police car.

'Drop the bag, and I'll pick it up,' King whispered.

They reached the car, and Light suddenly got clumsy. The evidence bags squeezed out of his arms, and scattered on the gravel. King bent down to help, and picked up one of them. He lingered for a moment in a crouched position, studying a set of multicoloured decals through the clear cover. Then he stood up and handed the envelope to the officer.

'Thanks, Kent,' Light said.

'No, Barry,' King replied with a smile. 'Thank *you*.' Then he turned and walked nonchalantly away, pondering what he'd just seen. Starke had a thing about tattoos, that was clear. But his choice of designs was interesting. Some of the grotesque images looked *damn* familiar. A lot like the markings that ran the length of Roscoe Miller's arms.

Granville sat by the window of his grandmother's house and looked out. It was dusk, and the fireflies were swarming.

'Lightning bugs,' he called to his mother. 'Can I go out and catch some?' It was a once-a-year treat. A chance to trap stars in a bottle, put them beside the bed, and get twinkled to sleep.

'Come away,' Carole called. 'Come away from the window.' She was still keeping her son sequestered.

'Can I?' The boy begged, his face drooping.

'No!' Carole said sternly. 'Not now. Not tonight.'

'When?' Granville asked.

Carole looked at him in silence. 'When' was a good question. Gardner had phoned earlier and spoken to her mother. He was calling from Pennsylvania to say the coast was clear. They had two men in custody, and the danger was over. Please tell Carole to come home, he'd said. Please!

Carole looked at her son. He was so small. So vulnerable. He wanted to go outside and play, but if she had her way, he'd never go out. There were too many things she could not control out there.

'When can I go out?' Granville repeated. The imprisonment was taking its toll. He was getting restless.

Carole stroked his blond hair. 'Maybe tomorrow.' Then she thought about what she had just said. Tomorrow. What was going to happen tomorrow? If they went home, Gardner was just going to start again, getting Granville stirred up, getting him involved in the case.

Granville sneaked back to the window and looked at the dancing lights.

No! Carole thought. She was not going to let it happen again. One way or another, she was going to protect her son. Even if it meant keeping him away from his own father. Just then, she noticed that Granville had strayed back to the forbidden zone.

'Granny!' she said sternly. 'I told you to get away from the window.'

And when the boy didn't move, she took him by the arm and led him back to the centre of the room.

The helicopter was aloft again, heading back to Maryland. Inside was the prosecution crew, Gardner, Jennifer and Brownie, and their prisoner, cuffed hands and feet, strapped into the jumpseat in the rear of the cockpit. The sun was below the horizon, and the knobby West Pennsylvania hills were turning purple beneath them. The engine was at max power, and they vibrated and shook with the scream of the turbine.

A coup, Gardner thought. They'd pulled off a coup. Swooping down out of the sky, they'd snatched their man and escaped. A couple of well-placed lies had smoothed the way, but now they had Starke in custody, and there was no way he was going to wriggle out. He smiled to himself. The law was strange sometimes. If you could get a criminal defendant into the jurisdiction where he was charged, you could always prosecute him. The courts didn't care *how* he got there. You could do almost anything, legal or illegal, and it didn't matter. In the county, he was fair game.

The aircraft burbled in an updraught, and Gardner's head tapped against the window. His thoughts suddenly jumped to Granville. Carole had no reason to stay away now. He'd begged her mother to send them home as soon as the crisis was over, calling from Henderson's office before they'd even left the barracks. Carole was at the house, he was sure, but she wouldn't come to the phone. She was still holding out. He visualized Granville's face in the window of Carole's fleeing car, dazed and confused, and his stomach ached. She had no right to do this – to keep Granville away. The boy needed to be with his father, now more than ever.

'Look at him.' Brownie's voice suddenly cracked into the earphones.

Gardner twisted his neck and peered back. IV Starke was slumped against the rear of the cabin with his eyes shut. His face was serene, and he was asleep.

'Doesn't seem to have a care in the world,' Brownie said. Without a headset, Starke couldn't hear.

'Yeah,' Gardner replied. 'He doesn't seem to be sweating it.' After signing the waiver form, Brownie had gone back for another try at interrogating, but Starke had balked at saying anything. As long as they were going to meet his lawyer, he might as well wait.

'We still have a problem,' Jennifer whispered into her mike, sneaking a look at Starke to make sure he was still dozing.

'Yeah,' Gardner replied. 'They don't want to turn against each other.' Miller was not acknowledging Starke, and Starke was not acknowledging Miller. Honour among thieves.

'So we try again on the forensics,' Brownie said. 'Get some positive proof of them at the scene. And . . .'

'And Granville . . .' Gardner interjected. 'He can help too.' The copter bounced again, and he sucked in his breath. 'Just got to get him back.'

Jennifer looked at Starke. His head lay against the fuselage, and his mouth was open slightly. She tried to imagine him at Bowers, face-to-face with Addie and Henry as Miller pulled the trigger.

175

'State line!' the pilot announced, pointing down. In seconds they'd crossed over, and IV Starke opened his eyes.

'You're in Maryland!' Brownie shouted to him. Starke nodded groggily.

'Welcome home,' Gardner said sarcastically.

Joel Jacobs stood in the cell block area of the Pennsylvania State Police Barracks and looked at the empty space where his client had been. Captain Henderson waited beside him in silence. The man had to see for himself. The orders were disobeyed, and Starke was gone, but the lawyer had to see for himself. Jacobs put down his briefcase, and folded his arms. Henderson still waited in silence, wondering what kind of explosion was going to erupt from the well-dressed out-of-towner.

Jacobs turned slowly and looked at the trooper. His face was relaxed, and his eyes betrayed no sense at all of what was going on behind them. 'Do you have a copy of the waiver?' he asked. There was no hint of anger.

Henderson said Yes, and opened a file he had been carrying under his arm. He handed the paper to the attorney. 'Here.'

Jacobs took it, pulled a pair of reading glasses from his breast pocket, and slipped them into place. 'Thank you.'

Captain Henderson remained silent and at attention by his side. This was not at all what he had expected. The man had sounded like a sabre-toothed tiger on the telephone. But the real-life creature was a pussycat.

'Did you have the signature witnessed?' Jacobs suddenly asked, raising his glasses so he could see the trooper.

Henderson balked. 'Uh, no. No, we didn't.' He was not aware that the form required it.

'I see,' Jacobs said softly. 'And can you tell me if anyone on your staff actually observed my client execute the waiver?'

Again, Henderson was stymied. The form had been signed, duplicated and filed before they had allowed Starke to leave with the Marylanders. There was no rule that said the signing had to be done under surveillance. They received a signed waiver, and that was it. 'Don't think so,' the captain said.

'I see,' Jacobs repeated. 'May I keep this copy?'

Henderson checked his file for a duplicate, and nodded yes.

Jacobs picked up his briefcase, and walked to the door. Henderson followed him out of the cell block, and then down towards the front exit. The lawyer's gait was slow and even, but the pace was not the product of age. The man was clearly in shape. His walk echoed his manner. Each step, like each word, was measured and deliberate. He didn't waste energy. But inside the lanky body lay an untapped reserve of power. Henderson followed Jacobs to the front door, and turned to retreat back to his office.

'Captain!' Jacobs was at the exit, but he hadn't gone through. Henderson turned. 'I told you not to let my client go.' The words were soft, but there was a foreboding in the way they were uttered.

Henderson shrugged his shoulders as if to say Sorry, and waited for a follow-up.

But Jacobs said nothing. He stared coldly for a moment, then set his shoulders and marched out of the door.

It was well past midnight, and Gardner and Jennifer were just getting to bed. They had secured IV Starke at the detention centre, checked their messages at the office, picked up a bite to eat and finally dragged themselves back home. It had been a long twenty-four hours, and they were both exhausted.

Jennifer slipped on her blue silk nightie and crawled in beside Gardner. He cranked his arm round her neck, and let her settle against his ribcage. She could feel the throb of his heart as she pressed her ear to his chest. The pulse was rapid.

'It's just beginning,' he said softly, nuzzling her hair with his lips. She held him tight. 'Tomorrow the gloves come off.'

Jennifer kept gripping, listening to his pounding heart. The easy part was over, and tomorrow the real struggle would begin. Bond hearings. Motions. Discovery. The labyrinth they had to traverse before they could convict. One psycho defence attorney was in town, and another was on his way. And their case was as weak as a cobweb. 'We'll get through,' she whispered.

'Yeah,' Gardner mumbled sleepily. 'We'll get through.'

Soon they were both asleep.

CHAPTER 12

It was 8.45 a.m., and bond hearing for Roscoe Miller and IV Starke had been added to the morning docket at the courthouse, but there was no sitting judge available to hear them. Two civil cases had carried over from the day before, and the juries were waiting to resume deliberations. That left only the chambers judge, Carla Hanks, to preside over the hearings. It was to be her honour's first appearance in court.

Gardner and Jennifer marched into courtroom three, and took their places behind the counsel table. Gardner sported the trademark navy blue pinstripe suit and a red tie he always wore on the first day of a big trial. His face was fresh, but his eyes showed fatigue.

Jennifer was also wearing her number one court outfit: a red linen blazer flared neatly at the waist, and a black cotton skirt. Her hair was pulled back, and her eyes were alert behind her spectacles.

The defence attorneys were already in the room when the prosecutors entered. Kent King and Joel Jacobs sat side by side like Roman centurions. As Gardner passed, King whispered in Jacob's ear, and the New York lawyer shifted his gaze to the State Attorney. This was the flip-side of the prosecutor–police alliance. Defence attorneys had their own secret society. In the presence of a prosecutor, it was 'us' versus 'them', and they conspired constantly against the State.

Gardner put down his file, and Jacobs walked over to the prosecution table. 'Mr Lawson?' He extended his hand. 'Joel Jacobs.' He was nattily turned out in a grey double-breasted suit.

'Glad to meet you,' Gardner said, crushing his adversary's hand as tightly as he could. 'This is Jennifer Munday, my assistant.'

Jacobs released Gardner's hand with a strong snap of his wrist, and extended his hand to Jennifer. 'It's a pleasure,' he said with a twinkle in his eye. King had obviously told him the attractive female was more than an 'assistant'. She exchanged pleasantries, and allowed Jacobs to refocus on Gardner.

'I hear we had a conversation yesterday,' Jacobs said. Gardner knit his brow, but didn't answer. 'Tell me, was I *that* cooperative?' he continued. The sarcasm was thick.

Gardner glimpsed King smirking over his shoulder. These two were going to make quite a pair. 'Yeah,' he said flippantly, 'you were *real* cooperative.'

Jacobs smiled. 'I'm not always that way. Sometimes I can be downright un-cooperative.'

'All rise!' The clerk's announcement interrupted the face-off. 'Her honour's court is now in session. The Honourable Carla Hanks presiding.'

Jacobs nodded to Jennifer, and bowed to Gardner before joining King at the other table. King whispered in his ear, and both men smiled.

'Be seated!' Judge Hanks declared, giving the gavel stand a tentative whack with her mallet. She then settled into the high-backed leather chair, and looked out from behind the bench.

'Call the case, Mr State Attorney,' she barked to Gardner.

The prosecutor stood up. 'We call State *v.* Miller and State *v.* Starke for bond hearings, your honour.'

Judge Hanks shifted her attention to King and Jacobs at the defence table. They immediately stood.

'Please identify yourselves for the record,' her honour said.

'Kent King for Roscoe Miller.'

'Joel Jacobs, 215 Park Avenue South, New York City, appearing on behalf of Mr Wellington Starke the fourth.'

'Are we ready to proceed, gentlemen?' the judge asked. The defence attorneys nodded, and she turned to Gardner. 'Any preliminary remarks, Mr Lawson?'

'Yes, Judge,' Gardner replied. 'As soon as the defendants get here . . .'

'Where are they?' Judge Hanks asked.

'On their way up from detention,' the clerk answered.

In a moment, the defendants entered. Miller was first, and Starke followed. They were dressed in blue denim detention centre uniforms, their hands and feet cuffed, chained together at the waist. Even with those encumbrances, Miller still managed a foot-dragging saunter down the aisle. In contrast, Starke walked with a preppy's gait. Next to Miller, he seemed out of place. Their facial features showed a resemblance, but that was as far as it went.

'The defendants are present in court,' Gardner said loudly as the two prisoners sat down. It was time to get his own show on the road. 'May I be heard, your honour?' Judge Hanks nodded. 'Thank you, your honour. Mr Joel Jacobs entered his appearance on behalf of defendant Starke and listed his address as New York. May we then assume that he is *not* a member of the Maryland bar?'

Judge Hanks had been digging through paperwork when she got the call to sit on this case. No one had said anything about qualifying foreign attorneys to practise. She looked at Jacobs.

He got up. 'I'm a member of five State bars, your honour, but Maryland is not one of them.'

'Object to his appearance in this case, Judge,' Gardner argued. 'He's not a member of our bar, and he's therefore unqualified to practise here.'

King rose to his feet. 'I'll sponsor him, Judge. An out-of-State attorney can practise on a per-case basis, if a member of the bar sponsors him and moves his admittance for that particular case.'

'Conflict of interest,' Gardner interjected. 'This is a two-defendant murder case. For the attorneys to have any formal relationship with each other is improper, according to the Canons of Ethics.'

Judge Hanks was sinking into confusion. 'Does anyone have any specific law on this point?'

Joel Jacobs stood up. He'd been listening, but it was now time to cut in. 'That won't be necessary, your honour.' He pulled a sheet of paper from his briefcase, and showed it to King.

'Withdraw my offer of sponsorship,' King said with a grin.

Jacobs approached the bench, and handed the document to Judge Hanks.

She studied it, and waved Gardner up. 'I believe this resolves any question you may have as to Mr Jacob's qualifications.' Her voice was mildly sarcastic.

Gardner took the paper. The letterhead said: 'Maryland Court of Appeals.' And below it: 'VIA TELEFAX.' He read the text.

> To whom it may concern:
> Please accord Mr Joel Jacobs of the State of New York, and member of the New York bar, all of the privileges and rights of a Maryland attorney. He is hereby duly admitted to practise in all proceedings, criminal and otherwise, involving Mr Wellington Starke IV. He is granted this admission without reservation, and without the need for individual sponsorship.
> Signed: John J. Biddington, Chief Judge,
> Maryland Court of Appeals.

Gardner whistled inwardly. Jacobs was connected. Big time. Here was a personal endorsement by the highest-ranking judge in the State. The case had barely begun, and already strings were being pulled. He dropped the paper on the bench. 'Objection withdrawn,' he said. And on the way back to the counsel table he wondered just how deep Jacob's connections actually ran.

While the bond hearing was going on, Brownie was hard at work in the crime lab. He had been up late the previous night, processing IV Starke and getting him bedded down at the detention centre. Then he'd gone back to the police department and checked the return on the search warrant, the document that listed the items that had been seized in the search. The contents of the safe were grouped together under the headings: personal papers, receipts and tattoos. Unfortunately the items themselves were locked in the evidence vault, and the custodian had gone home. Brownie had to wait until morning to get his hands on the actual items.

He opened the top envelope and pulled out a sheaf of

papers. The first was a photocopy of IV Starke's birth certificate. He scanned it, and locked in on the date. 'Huh?' he said aloud, making a quick calculation in his head. According to the date of birth, IV Starke was twenty years old, still in high school, and not even graduated! The kid seemed bright. There had to be a reason why he was taking so long to get his diploma. Maybe it had something to do with the case.

Brownie put down the certificate, and moved to the next documents. More birth certificates. One for Wellington Starke the third, the father of the fourth. Born 1946. Another for the grandfather, Wellington Starke Jr, born 1910. Beneath that was a 'Certificate of Death', certifying the grandfather's demise in 1978. A copy of his will was attached.

Brownie ran through the wherefores and the whereases and got to the meat of the bequests. 'Whew!' he whistled. Millions and millions and millions. He'd never seen so many zeros behind a dollar sign. Grandfather was loaded to the hilt. He read on to the bottom line. A substantial part of the family fortune had been left in trust to Wellington Starke the fourth; when he turned twenty-five years of age the trust was due to terminate, and he was entitled to draw the proceeds. Brownie whistled again. In a few years, IV Starke was going to be the richest man in his cell block. Hell, he was going to be one of the richest men on earth!

Brownie shook off his surprise, and moved to the next set of documents. They were school records, yellowed and creased, obviously quite old. They belonged to IV Starke's father: Wellington Starke the third. The school logo on the father's records was that of Prentice Academy. This was a new revelation, but no shock. Families often trod the same academic turf. He scratched his chin. Maybe this accounted for the headmaster's nervous attitude and the hiring of Kent King. The Starkes were deeply invested in the school; not just one generation, but two. No wonder Edwin Charles was acting up. He had a major investment to protect.

Brownie sifted through the evidence pile until he came to the tattoos. Of all the things in the safe, these were the most puzzling. Temporary tattoos. Inked images that adhered to the skin. Kids wore them to look cool, but they were just playing. The things washed off without a trace. He laid the four sheets out on his table. Each contained three flesh decals. Daggers. Sexy sirens. Screaming eagles. The same pictures that Miller liked, but there was no death's head. IV Starke obviously idolized Miller. He was a rich kid who wanted to play tough, but not go all the way. That's what it had to be. He was trying to emulate Miller's wildness. The aristocrat had a secret fantasy, and he was acting it out. IV Starke had no reason to kill anyone. He had all the money in the world, and certainly didn't need Henry's stash. But maybe in his misguided fervour to mimic Miller's lifestyle, he had gone along for the ride. And got in way over his head.

Carla Hanks was still presiding over the bond hearing. After the qualification of Jacobs to appear in her court, she read the defendants the charges against them. Now it was time to cut to the chase. 'What is the State's bond recommendation as to defendant Miller?' she asked Gardner.

Gardner stood up, 'No bond, your honour.'

'No bond?' Hanks looked confused, as if she didn't know such a category existed.

'That is correct, Judge,' Gardner replied. 'Under the Maryland code, you have the authority to deny bond in certain cases.' Hanks nodded. 'Here we have a person of no fixed address,' he continued. 'He ran when police attempted to arrest him, and he has been charged with not one, but *three* murders.' The prosecutor glanced at King, 'and that's grounds in itself to deny bond.'

King stood up. 'That's assuming they can prove the case, but they have *no* evidence. Absolutely nothing that places my client at the scene of the crime.'

Gardner folded his arms. 'Evidentiary matters are not relevant in a bond hearing, your honour. That's the law.'

'OK, OK,' Judge Hanks answered. 'I understand your positions. Mr King, what amount of bond would you recommend?'

'Under ten thousand with ten per cent acceptable,' King replied.

Gardner grimaced. That figure was absurd. It meant that Miller could walk by posting a mere thousand dollars. 'On a

184

triple murder?' he said aloud. His expression warned Judge Hanks not to do it.

'All right,' Hanks replied. 'I have the recommendations. No bond on one side, and ten thousand on the other . . .' She leaned back in her chair, and closed her eyes. A decision was about to be made.

Jennifer suddenly stood up. 'May I be heard, your honour?'

Hanks opened her eyes, and leaned forward.

'Objection!' King sneered. 'They've already had their say . . .'

'Two against two seems fair, Judge,' Jennifer answered softly.

Hanks gave King an annoyed look. 'Are you afraid of what she might have to say, Mr King?' King was speechless. 'I'm going to allow her to speak,' Hanks said.

'Thank you, Judge,' Jennifer replied. 'I only wanted to point out that Mr Miller has, in fact, failed to appear in court before.' She unfolded a sheet of paper. 'On six occasions he has neglected to answer summonses.' She showed the paper to King, and walked up to the bench.

'His driving record,' King snorted. 'That's hardly relevant here.'

'It shows his propensity to be irresponsible,' Jennifer said.

'Baloney,' King retorted. 'My client always went to court on his criminal cases. Ignoring a few traffic tickets doesn't mean he's a risk to flee.'

Hanks turned to Jennifer. 'Did he always appear at his criminal trials?'

'Yes, but he had no choice. He never made bond on any of those cases. He was held in detention until the trial.'

Hanks shifted back to King. 'Still think the traffic cases aren't relevant?' That sounded like a challenge.

'Yes,' King answered without hesitation. 'They were minor matters.'

'If he couldn't be responsible on a *minor* matter, he's not going to be responsible on a murder charge,' Jennifer replied.

Hanks nodded. She was convinced. 'Mr Miller's bond is set at five hundred thousand dollars!'

King remained calm. 'How about ten per cent acceptable, Judge?'

Hanks did a rapid calculation in her head, 'All right, Mr King, that's probably reasonable. Five hundred thousand with ten per cent posted.'

Gardner jumped to his feet. 'But, your honour!'

The judge shook her head. It was too late. 'That's my ruling, Mr Lawson.' She was not going to change her mind.

Gardner clenched his jaw and sat down. 'Thanks for the help,' he whispered to Jennifer. He'd overlooked the traffic ticket argument, but there was still a major problem. If Miller could somehow come up with $50,000, he'd be back on the street.

'Let's move to Mr Starke,' Judge Hanks said. They were finished with Miller, and it was time to set IV Starke's bond. 'What is your recommendation on this one, Mr Lawson?'

Gardner pushed to his feet. 'No bond, your honour.'

Hanks gave him a quizzical look. 'You're putting him in the same category as Mr Miller?'

'The comparison is appropriate,' Gardner said. 'He's from out of State. Has no roots here whatsoever. And would be a substantial risk to flee if given the chance.'

'Has he ever failed to appear for court?' Hanks looked at Jennifer.

'Not that I'm aware of, your honour,' Gardner said as Jennifer shook her head.

'I see,' Hanks replied. 'But you're still insisting on a no bond status?'

Gardner felt his jaw tighten again. 'If he's released, we have no guarantee he'll ever come back. He's got nothing to keep him here. Nothing whatsoever.'

Judge Hanks adjusted her glasses and picked up Starke's charging document. Then she looked at the defendant. 'What's your bond recommendation, Mr Jacobs?'

The attorney smiled and stood up. 'Well, your honour, the bond should be at least as low as Mr Miller's. Certainly not higher.'

'He'll run!' Gardner blurted out. 'Any bond you set but "no bond" is going to be a mistake. He'll flee!'

Hanks glared at him. 'You have proof of that?'

Jennifer stood. 'His lawyer advised him to fight extradition.'

Jacobs frowned. 'You can't punish my client for asserting his rights, your honour,' he argued. 'He was under no obligation to waive extradition, and my advice not to do so cannot be used as proof that he's a threat to abscond.'

Hanks removed her glasses and rubbed her eyes. 'OK. Everyone has made their point.' She was ready to rule.

Gardner gave it one last shot. 'The Maryland code permits you to add restrictions to pretrial release. Please, I beg you, don't make it unconditional!' If Starke did run, they'd never get Miller. It was crucial to keep him in the jurisdiction.

'OK!' Judge Hanks snapped. She was getting tired. 'Bond is set in the amount of $500,000, ten per cent acceptable, with a restriction to the State of Maryland as a specific condition of release.'

Gardner wrote the figure on his pad and circled it with disgust. Starke had that kind of cash in his pocket. He'd be out within the hour. 'Request an arm monitor, Judge.' He leaped to his feet.

'What?' Hanks had never heard of it. 'Arm what?'

'Monitor.' Gardner said. 'A device that tracks the location of released prisoners. Electronic beeper.'

Hanks looked at Jacobs for his reaction.

He frowned. 'You're kidding, of course.'

'No,' she answered, 'I think it's a reasonable request. Monitors are to be installed on *both* Roscoe Miller and Wellington Starke in the event that either makes bond ... We stand adjourned!' Then she hit the bench with a resounding blow of the gavel and left the courtroom.

Gardner glanced over at the counsel table. Jacobs and King had their heads together, conferring. When King noticed him, he stopped. 'Do you mind?' he asked in a sarcastic voice.

Gardner smirked. 'If it bothers you, go somewhere else.'

King ignored the remark and went back to his conversation. They were really into it now. Whispering and chuckling, hatching a plot for round two.

'Starke's going to get out,' Jennifer said, nodding towards the defendants who were being led away by the sheriffs.

'Yeah,' Gardner replied sullenly.

'For sure.'

'I guess it was expected.' Gardner stood, and tucked the file under his arm.

'At least we'll know where he is,' Jennifer said.

'Yeah.' Gardner looked at Jacobs and King. 'At least we'll know that. And if he comes within five miles of my son . . .' he raised his voice '. . . he won't need a lawyer. Because I swear to God I'll *kill* him!'

Brownie had finished examining the evidence retrieved from IV Starke's safe. He'd analysed and catalogued everything, making notes as he went along as to the significance of each piece. Then he'd drawn up a list of follow-up inquiries.

He took a manila envelope from his 'in' box. There was no return address, but he recognized the scrawly handwriting as Greg Gavin's, his man at the phone company. This was the answer to the request for Starke's phone calls for the past half-year. The envelope was thick, and he ripped it open with his lab knife. 'Whoa!' There was a sheaf of computer paper inside, filled with numbers, four columns to a page, fifty numbers to a column. There were about a hundred pages in all, documenting thousands of calls. From the notations for the key, 'O' meant the number was outgoing from Starke, 'I' that the number was incoming. Brownie flipped through the pages, noting that there were about as many 'I' as 'O's. The phone lines were buzzing in both directions. Returning to the first page, he ran down the columns of numbers looking for patterns or familiar exchanges. NY. NY. NY. NY. Dozens of outgoing New York calls. Two, in particular, repeated again and again as he backtracked towards, and then beyond, the date of the shootings at Bowers Corner. Having noted on his pad, 212 775–3222 and 212 543–8000, he picked up his phone and dialled the first number. After several rings, an accented female voice answered, 'Starke residence'.

Brownie cleared his throat. 'Is this the home of Wellington Starke the fourth?'

'Yes, sir, it is. Who is calling, please?'

'Phone company, ma'am,' Brownie answered. 'Thanks for your time.' He hung up and wrote 'home no.' below the digits. The second number answered immediately. 'Udek investigations.'

'This is 543–8000?' Brownie asked.

'Yes, it is.' The voice sounded irritated.

Brownie thought fast. A ruse would not work this time. 'I need an investigator,' he said, lowering his voice.

'What type of case?'

Brownie took a shot in the dark. 'Need to locate a missing person.'

'OK. Can you tell me how you were referred to us?'

Brownie sucked in his breath. 'Mr Starke sent me.'

'Mr Starke?' The voice sounded surprised.

'Uh-huh. Wellington Starke the fourth. Said you people did good work.'

There was a hush on the line for a long moment, then the voice came back. 'We don't know anyone named Starke.'

'Oh,' Brownie mused. 'Maybe I got that wrong.' There was silence on the other end. 'Could you give me your address? I'd still like you to help me out.'

'Who is this?' the voice demanded angrily.

'Just told you,' Brownie answered. 'A man who needs some help.'

'Can't help you!' the voice snapped. Then the line went dead.

Brownie wrote 'investigator' below the number, and put a giant question mark beside it. This was odd. IV Starke had contacted a New York investigator about something. He'd called dozens of times from the school, but now they disavowed any knowledge of him. He flipped the pages and checked the dates when the investigator's number had been called. The first came three months before the Bowers Corner murders. Then there were a lot of 'O's and a few 'I's for two months. Then the calls stopped, and there was none in either direction from that point on. Brownie went back to the beginning of the printout, and re-checked. He scanned page after page without a reference to the number. He was right. There was no contact with 'Udek Investigations' until three months before Addie and Henry were killed.

Returning to the first date the number appeared, he prepared to make a notation when an 'I' call caught his eye. It had come in at exactly 11.35 p.m. and lasted seven minutes. '727–3355,' he said out loud. The number awoke a dim memory. '727–3355,' he repeated, struggling to put a name

189

to the numbers. He repeated it again, and pulled out a phone book. 'That can't be right . . .' he said to himself. 'No way it could be right.' He turned to the B section and ran his finger down a page. 'No way,' he mumbled to himself absently as he searched. 'Jesus Christ and Mother Mary!' His finger had hit the reference he was looking for. '727–3355.' He jumped to the printout and confirmed the number: 727–3355. It was identical. 'No way,' Brownie said with disbelief.

But there it was. A phone call had been made from that number to IV Starke's private phone at 11.35 p.m., exactly three months and one day prior to the murders.

'Got to be a mistake,' Brownie mumbled. The number was listed to BOWERS, H. It was the upstairs phone at Bowers Corner. The private line of Addie and Henry.

PART 5

Stratagem

CHAPTER 13

Gardner was gripping the office telephone so tightly that his fingers ached. 'I *know* she's there,' he told his mother-in-law.

'I said before that I haven't seen them,' Kathryn Andrews replied, her voice quaking slightly. It was obvious that she didn't like being in the middle. 'Please stop phoning here.'

'Did you give Carole my message?' Gardner persisted. 'We picked up the suspects.'

'She knows,' Kathryn answered.

'She *is* there! *Please* let me speak with her!'

There was a muffled sound as Kathryn covered the mouthpiece. A delay so she could ask Carole once more to take care of her own problems and leave the parents out. 'I'm sorry, Gardner, there's really nothing I can do.' Her voice was filled with sad resignation. 'Please don't ring again.'

'Kathryn . . .' Gardner stuttered, but it was too late. She'd already hung up. 'Damn it!' he snarled, slamming the phone so hard against the cradle that it bounced back and skittered off the desk. He watched it jerk back and forth on the end of its twisted cord.

That was him. In reality. A yo-yo on the end of a string. Since the divorce, his role in life had been to go wherever Carole tugged him. She had custody of Granville, and that left her in control. He was helpless. Unable to defend himself because he might hurt his son in the process.

Gardner loosened his necktie and unbuttoned his shirt collar. Carole was not bringing Granville back soon, that was obvious. He'd seen this type of behaviour before. When she ran, she stayed away a long time. Two months, when they separated. Two months without seeing Granville. Two months of not knowing where they were. He could keep phoning, begging her to come back, but he knew it wouldn't do any good. When Carole decided to act, there was no stopping her, no reasoning with her. It was time to consider more drastic action.

From his bookshelf he took down the Court Proceedings Article of the Maryland code. After running the index, he opened to the Material Witness page. The words of the statute were clear. A State Attorney had the right to take a material witness to a crime into custody, and it was unlawful for *anyone* to interfere. He rubbed his chin and re-read the page. A summons could be issued for the witness, and the sheriff could pick him up. It was that simple, and no one could stop it. Gardner stood by the shelf and read the page four more times. The power to secure a witness was absolute. There were no exceptions and no exemptions. If the State Attorney ordered it, it could be done.

He slowly walked to his desk and laid out the statute. Then he picked up his pen and began to draft a summons. When he got to the section where the witness's name was to be inserted, he hesitated. If he went through with this, the war with Carole would be escalated to a level he could not even contemplate. Knowing her, there would be massive retaliation. And what about Granville? What would it do to him? He skipped the name and went on to the next line.

Having completed the form, he sat staring at the blank space for the witness's name. Granville, he thought. Granville Alcott Lawson. Such a big name for such a little boy. 'Gran-what?' people had asked when they saw the tiny infant and asked for a name. 'Gran-ville,' Gardner always replied patiently. 'It's a family name.' It had come from a great-great grandmother, Emily Granville, who'd married Thaddeus Lawson the third. Later generations changed it to a first name for their eldest males. And although Gardner himself had missed out, he revived the name and bestowed it on his son.

Gardner suddenly had a vision of Granville in the stern of the old boat on Valley Lake. They had rowed out to the middle to try for deep-water bass. Granville was about three, and he was trussed up in way-too-big life-preserver. His arms and legs were as thin as pencils, and he was holding on to the seat. The boat was drifting as Gardner tried to put an uncooperative worm on the boy's hook.

'Dad?' His voice was soft, like a breeze. Gardner looked up. 'Who's Grand Bill?'

'Huh?' Gardner was still struggling with the worm.

'Who's Grand Bill?'

Gardner put down the hook. 'Grand Bill?' He didn't understand.

'You and Mom say it a lot.'

'Grand Bill,' Gardner said to himself. Then it hit him. He called the boy Gran, or Son. And Carole always used the obnoxious Granny. But neither of them ever called him by his full name. The only time they used it was when they were talking to each other about him. 'Granville,' he said. 'That's you. That's your full name.'

The boy smiled. 'Grand Bill.'

'No. Gran-ville.'

'Grand Bill,' the boy repeated.

Gardner smiled and patted him on the head. 'Close enough,' he said. Then they got the hook baited and caught a three-pound bass.

His heart was aching as the memory faded. The Material Witness summons was still waiting for the addition of a name. He had the pen ready to write GRANVILLE ALCOTT LAWSON in the space, but he stopped short. This was too drastic a move to make in his usual spur-of-the-moment style. The consequences were too extreme.

Gardner put the pen down. Before he completed the form, he needed a second opinion.

Joel Jacobs stood at the window of his suite in the Anderson Mountain Inn and looked out at the valley. The lush green of summer spread from horizon to horizon like an avocado dip. Orchards, meadows and fields of clover. It was a far cry from New York, where the only respite from concrete and asphalt was Central Park. But, in its own quaint little way, it was charming.

He turned to survey his room. It wasn't the Plaza, but it would do. He'd requested the best accommodation in town and the best room in it, and they'd turned over the keys to the Lincoln Suite: a place where the president had allegedly stayed after Gettysburg, but which historians had never documented. Furnished in period antiques, it was regal enough for a chief executive or a Joel Jacobs. Suddenly there was a knock at the door.

'Who is it?' Jacobs called.

'Me,' a voice answered.

Jacobs opened the door to Drew Udek's narrow face. 'Come in, Drew.'

Udek was a tall thin man in his fifties, emaciated as a skeleton. He entered, and looked around appreciatively. 'Niiice,' he said.

'Glad you like it,' Jacobs replied.

They sat at a round mahogany table in the bay window alcove.

'Got your data here,' Udek said, pulling a stack of papers from a beat-up leather case.

Jacobs put on his reading glasses and thumbed quickly through the pile. 'This is going to be very helpful.'

Udek smiled. Over the last twenty years he had turned over a lot of rocks for the old man, uncovering little secrets that had enabled Jacobs to be one up on his opponents with a vengeance. In that department, Udek had never let him down. 'Information was tight,' he said. 'I can tell you that. I had trouble getting this much.'

Jacobs frowned. 'That doesn't sound like you, Drew.'

'This is a small town.' People notice when someone's poking around. They're suspicious. I had the same trouble last time I was down here.' Jacobs suddenly flashed an angry look, as if the investigator had broached a forbidden subject. Udek caught the stare, and reddened. 'I mean, it's tough to root things out in this pigtown.'

Jacobs went back to the file, and Udek stood. 'Thanks again, Drew,' the lawyer said without looking up.

'Welcome,' Udek replied on the way out of the door.

After Udek had gone, Jacobs walked to the telephone beside the four-poster bed. Seconds later, his call to Annapolis had gone through.

'Court of Appeals.'

'Chief Judge Biddington, please.'

'May I say who's calling?'

'Jiff Jacobs.' He lapsed into his law school nickname: Jiff. Like the peanut butter, smooth and sweet. But hard to digest.

'One moment, sir.'

There was a click, a pause, and a familiar bass voice came on the line. 'Jiff! You made it down!'

'Hi, Bid,' Jacobs answered softly. 'I'm here.'

'How long do you expect to stay?'

Jacob's paused. 'Not really sure. May have to go to trial.'

'Can't work it out, huh?'

'Not so far. Listen, Bid. I wonder if you could do something for me.'

'What is it?'

'Can you arrange a trial assignment up here?'

There was a brief silence. 'Assignment?'

'Can you arrange for a particular judge to hear a particular case?'

Again there was a short silence. 'They're not exactly under my jurisdiction. Assignments are up to the local administrative judge.'

'But if you made a suggestion, they'd listen.'

'Yes,' Biddington answered. 'They usually follow my advice.'

'OK. Can you make a recommendation in the Starke case?'

'I suppose I could. Judge Danforth and I are pretty close.'

'Good. We just had a bond hearing, and I found the judge to be top notch. An excellent jurist.'

'That's quite a compliment,' Biddington replied. 'And you want that judge to hear your case?'

'Yes, if it can be arranged.'

'We can swing that. What's the judge's name?'

'Hanks,' Jacobs said sweetly. 'Judge Carla Hanks.'

Gardner was at the therapist's office in Veil Valley. He was still struggling with his decision to issue the Material Witness summons because of the effect it might have on Granville. He wanted the boy home, and it looked as though the summons was the only way to make it happen.

'There could be problems,' Nancy Meyers told Gardner in

the privacy of the therapy room. Toys were still strewn on the floor from a previous session, and the smell of paint and glue lingered in the air. 'Forceful removal could really set him back.'

'But isn't that what already happened?' Gardner cut in. 'His mother took him. What's the difference?'

Meyers groped for a response. 'Carole is not the sheriff. It might confuse him,' she continued. 'He won't know who to listen to. Who to trust.'

'He'll listen to me,' Gardner said.

'Don't be so sure. You take him from his mother, and he may turn on you. He's very attached to her.'

'But he's close to me, too. He loves me.'

'This isn't about love.'

Gardner looked her in the eye. 'I think it is.'

'No. It's about trust and being in a safe place. Tell me, Mr Lawson, can you provide a safe place for him after the sheriff takes him away? Do you really think he'll feel safe?'

He closed his eyes for a second. Meyers was not making the decision any easier. 'He'll be safe with me.'

'But he won't necessarily "feel" safe.'

'So what choice do I have? Leave him where he is?'

'It might be best,' Meyers replied.

'But what about his treatment – his sessions with you? He's been making progress. Shouldn't he continue?'

'In time . . .' Meyers answered.

'But we don't have any more time!'

'As long as he's in a stable environment, he'll be OK. Therapy can resume later.'

Gardner stood up. 'Are you telling me *not* to issue the summons?'

Meyers pushed her glasses up against her nose. 'I have no right to do that. I'm just telling you the possible consequences.'

' "Possible," ' Gardner said.

Meyers nodded. 'You asked, I told you.'

'I'm going to do it,' he said resolutely. 'I have to. Granville is a strong boy. He'll be all right with me. We have to prepare for the case.'

Meyers shook her head slightly. 'That may be, but this is

not about a *case*, Mr Lawson. It's about his *life*.'

'Thanks for your time,' Gardner said. He had to get back to the office to finish the paperwork. The decision had finally been made. If they didn't win the *case*, Granville might not have a *life*.

Although bond had been set that morning, IV Starke and Roscoe Miller were still locked in the detention centre at 6 p.m. They occupied separate cells on the B wing, a section that held the most dangerous of the county's pretrial detainees. On Gardner's orders, the warden had kept the two men apart, so they were placed in staggered cells on the block, with another indicted murder defendant occupying the space between their narrow steel enclosures.

'Roscoe!'

Miller got up from his bunk and shuffled to the bars. The voice was coming from the cell next door.

'Roscoe!' It was a loud whisper, not intended to attract the attention of the guards.

Miller edged his cheek against the cold steel. 'Yeah?'

'Heard you got a bond.'

Miller smiled. His neighbour was not so lucky. Hank Smatt killed his ex-girlfriend and her new lover, and threatened to kill the rest of her family. His status was 'no bond'. 'Yeah, they put one on me,' he whistled through his teeth. 'Gave me the armband, too.'

On the other side, IV Starke was listening. He had quietly slipped close to the bars so he could eavesdrop on the conversation. He was going to be released first thing in the morning when the bank certified the funds in the $50,000 cheque that Joel Jacobs had posted after court. The delay had angered him, but Jacobs told him to shut up, so he bit his tongue. Just a few more hours, and he'd be free.

'I had that bitch one time,' Smatt continued. He was talking about the electronic tracking device that the sheriff bolted to the wrists of released defendants. Its signal was displayed on the locator map, and every movement was tracked.

'Yeah? What's it like?' Miller had never been given the honour of wearing one.

'Sucks!' Smatt hissed. 'Can't do shit without them knowin'.'

Starke leaned against the bars and canted his ear towards Smatt's cell.

'But I heard that you kin beat it,' Smatt went on.

'Huh?' Miller whispered.

Starke held his breath and pricked up his ears.

'Heard that Tommy Pascoe done beat it.' Another notorious county tough guy, well versed in every conceivable punishment. 'That's what I heard. He found a way to knock the damn thing out.'

Miller grabbed the bars with both hands, and squeezed. 'What'd he do?'

Starke slowly let out his breath, took another, and held it.

'Microwaved the son 'bitch. That's what I heard. Somehow got the fucker in the damn microwave and blew out the signal.'

Miller clutched the bars tighter. 'In the microwave? What about his hands?'

The sound of a clanging door at the end of the long corridor interrupted the answer. A guard was approaching.

'His hands!' Miller repeated. 'What'd he do with his hands?'

'Gloves,' Smatt rasped. 'Wore some kind'a gloves.'

The guard's footsteps were echoing down the corridor. Miller and Smatt silently retreated to their bunks, and IV Starke remained standing with a curious smile on his face.

Carole and her mother were seated at the dining-room table of the Andrews home in suburban Baltimore. Kathryn Andrews was angry, her well-preserved face creased with worry. She was a grey version of the dark-haired Carole. Attractive, feisty, and just as sharp with her tongue. The Gardner-Carole impasse was getting old fast.

'You cannot keep doing this!' she said sternly. 'You *must* work out your problems!'

Carole glared at her mother. 'I'm only trying to protect my son!'

'But you can't keep him away for ever!'

'God, Mother!' Someone had tried to kill Granville. Didn't the woman understand that?

'And what about Gardner?' Kathryn was trying her best to keep the situation under control.

'What about him?' Carole screamed. 'Do you *know* what he did? He tried to get Granny to talk about the case.'

'So what? He's the father. He's entitled . . .'

'But he promised not to!' Carole hit the antique cherry dining-table with her hand. That was her memory from their conversation at the hospital. Gardner was *not* going to use Granny as a witness.

Kathryn winced. She had always liked Gardner. Even after the divorce, she had tried to maintain cordial relations, although Carole had regarded it as betrayal. Gardner was a good man. He had his flaws, like anyone else, but his love for Granville made up for his inability to hold her daughter's affection. 'So what do you plan to do?'

'Don't worry, Mother,' Carole said grimly. 'I'm not going to involve *you* any more.'

'What are you going to do?' Kathryn repeated.

'I've got a friend in Switzerland with a chalet on Lake Lucerne. We can stay there.'

'Europe?' Kathryn's face registered shock.

'I've already booked the flight. We're leaving the day after tomorrow. Then you won't have to be involved.'

'What's Gardner going to say?'

'Nothing he *can* say!' Carole snapped. 'All he cares about is his case. He couldn't care less what happens to Granny!'

'That's not true, dear,' Kathryn said gently, trying to touch her daughter's arm.

Carole pulled away, and stood up. 'I can't go back.'

During the argument, Granville had been in the upstairs den trying to watch TV. The loud voices had rung out over the sound of the show, and he'd got scared. Quietly he'd descended the stairs, and stood outside the dining-room door.

'But, dear . . .' Kathryn persisted.

'No!' Carole screamed. 'We're going away, and that's final!' Suddenly she noticed the small figure in the doorway. 'Granny!' she called.

But the boy turned, and ran back upstairs. 'We're going away!' rang in his ears like a forgotten refrain. He ran back

201

to the TV room and curled up on the couch. 'We're going away! Going away!'

His memory seemed to have begun with that phrase. Mom looking down into his bed one night and telling him 'We're going away.' The words were bad. They went away, and Dad didn't come with them. Mom cried all the time, and he had nothing to do but watch TV. And when they came home, Dad wasn't there any more.

Carole ran to the upstairs room, and lifted Granville to a seated position. 'Granny . . .' she said softly.

It was the same words, the same look. And it was all bad. 'I don't want to, Mom,' he said.

'What?'

'I said I don't want to.'

'Granny.' She hugged him without responding.

'No, Mom!' He tried to wriggle out of her grasp.

'Stop it, Granny,' she said sharply.

'No!' He kept wriggling.

'Granny!' Carole finally got his small body still, and she hugged him with a powerful grip.

'Mom,' he moaned, his voice cracking into a whine.

Carole's eyes filled with tears. This was going to be tough, but there was no other way. They had to 'go away' as far as they could. Away from the killers, and Gardner, and the *case*.

After a while, Granville calmed down and Carole went downstairs. Granville rolled over, snuggled his face against the couch, and whispered a single word: 'Dad.'

Joel Jacobs was in Kent King's private office. It was late in the evening, and the two men were alone. King leaned back in his chair and put his feet up on the desk. He was dressed in shorts and a knitted shirt. Jacobs was casual also, in a lime-green golf ensemble.

'We're gonna do this together, or we're gonna have trouble,' King said. 'Coordinate and cooperate.'

Jacobs smiled. 'What makes you think I can't handle my case alone?'

King sat forward and placed his elbows where his feet had been. 'They're gonna try to tie our guys together. Whatever your guy did is gonna be attributed to mine, and vice versa.'

'So we split the trials and take them one at a time,' Jacobs replied.

'Or we hold them together and knock the bottom out with one blow,' King countered.

Jacobs looked his fellow defence attorney in the eye. The report on King that Udek had shown him was glowing. The man was a maniac in the courtroom. A history of devious procedural manoeuvrings had marked King as a master of deception. Jacobs knew he had to be careful. 'Give me your client's version, and I'll consider it,' he finally said.

King smiled. 'OK, but you give me yours first.' In truth, as Gardner had said in the bond hearing, it was a conflict of interest for the men even to talk. As co-defendants in a murder case, either could turn against the other at any time, and make a deal for leniency with the State. If that was done, the other would go down for the count. Any information passing between them could sow the seeds of their own destruction.

Jacobs returned King's cynical smile. 'Maybe it's better if we keep our respective clients' business to ourselves and find some common ground to plough.'

King nodded. Neither man was going to tell the other any lawyer-client secrets. 'Looks like a one-witness case all the way.'

'The kid,' Jacobs replied.

King nodded again. 'Uh-huh.'

'What do you have on him?' Jacobs asked.

King broke into a smile. 'I don't think he's gonna be here for trial.' He knew that the boy was in Baltimore with his mother.

'Sure about that?' Jacobs inquired.

'That's how it's shapin' up. Without his testimony, they don't have a case against anyone!'

Jacobs crossed his legs at the knee. 'You got any contingency plans if your prediction fails to materialize?'

King reached into his desk and pulled out a stack of legal papers. 'In a case involving juvenile witnesses, it's a good idea to have them tested by a shrink.' He handed the papers to Jacobs. 'This set of motions has knocked more than one rug-rat out of the box.'

Jacobs scanned the motions. 'So we get him examined? What does that do?' He knew the answer, but he was playing dumb. Working on King's ego. Softening him up.

'By the time the shrink is done, we'll have five conflicting versions of the story. He'll never even get to the jury.'

'That sounds promising. What other little gems do you have hidden in there?' Jacobs jerked his chin towards the desk drawer.

King pulled out another set of papers. 'Motions to suppress. Discovery. Qualification of juvenile witnesses. Enough paperwork to choke Lawson to death.'

Jacobs took the second set of papers and examined them. 'Do you mind?'

'Be my guest,' King said cordially. 'You can give me something later, if you have a chance.'

Jacobs frowned. 'Such as?'

'Dunno,' King replied. 'Maybe if your snoop finds something that's helpful.'

Jacobs tried to smile, but it didn't come. King knew about Udek. It was supposed to be a secret, but King knew. Jacobs wondered what else the crafty attorney was hiding.

It was 10 a.m, and the prosecution team was in conference in the library of the State Attorney's office. Gardner presided at the blackboard in shirt-sleeves. There were dark purple circles under his eyes. Jennifer and Brownie sat at the large oak table in the centre of the room. She looked tired also, but her glasses screened the redness under her eyelids.

Only Brownie looked fresh. In a crisp dark blue uniform, he was alert and restless. They had a lot of ground to cover, and he was anxious to get to it. 'Have you read my reports?' he asked, assembling a stack of police files in front of him.

Gardner picked up a piece of chalk. 'Everything you've submitted so far.' He turned to the blackboard and wrote the name MILLER on the left side, at the top.

'What do you think?' Brownie continued.

Gardner walked to the other side of the board and wrote STARKE. 'What am I supposed to think?' he said wearily. 'You've got a lot of facts, but they don't fit together.'

Brownie could sense the frustration in Gardner's voice.

The detective had worked the case to the core, and stirred up only unconnected pieces.

'I have to admit I was wrong about the botched robbery theory,' Gardner went on. 'There's no question in my mind now that this thing revolves around money. Big money.' He moved to the centre of the blackboard and wrote ADDIE BOWERS, HENRY BOWERS, and PURVIS BOWERS at the top. Then he drew a line and wrote MONEY underneath. 'This thing was triggered by greed. Somebody had it. Somebody wanted it. And somebody took it. It's that simple.'

Jennifer smiled. Gardner was fashioning his 'theme'. To him, every case had a theme, and that produced a plot to lay before the jury like the story-line in a thriller. Jurors needed to know that events happened as the result of some master plan. If you never told them the 'why' behind the evidence, they got confused. And jury confusion was tantamount to reasonable doubt.

'So we need to know those facts,' Gardner reiterated. 'Who had it? Who wanted it? And who took it?'

'Number one is simple,' Brownie said. 'Henry Bowers. He had it in the safe-deposit boxes.'

Gardner nodded and wrote DEPOSIT BOXES under Henry's name.

'And then it went to Purvis after Henry died,' Jennifer added.

Gardner drew a line from the word BOXES to the space under Purvis Bowers' name. 'OK, where do I go from here?' he said, his chalk poised. He looked at Brownie.

The detective shrugged. 'Don't know yet,' he said softly.

'It would be nice if I could get from *here* to *here*,' Gardner said, dragging the chalk over to the MILLER side. 'Or here.' He wrote the name KING beside MILLER, and looked at Brownie again. 'I *have* to know where the money went if we're going to prove a plot.'

'I'm working on it,' Brownie answered. 'But you've got to remember that we've never actually put any money in the boxes in the first place. We just assumed it was there . . .' He made a note. That aspect of the case had dogged him from the beginning. Henry having big money did not make sense. He lived poor his whole life. But he sure as hell kept *some-*

thing in the boxes, and it was valuable enough to kill for.

'So we track down the money, and it doesn't lead to Miller,' Jennifer piped up. 'What then?'

Gardner turned. 'It *will* lead to him. Or someone near him. Why else would he kill three people?' The room went silent as the team pondered that question. 'OK,' Gardner said at last. 'Now that we know what we *can't* prove, let's take a look at what we *can*.' He turned back to the board and drew a line that connected MILLER and STARKE. 'We can put these two together at the school prior to the first murder.' He wrote RALPH LAMBERT under MILLER and in parentheses WORK CREW. 'We can put them together on the day of the murders, near the scene of the crime.' Under MILLER he wrote J. DOREY and in parentheses RED TRUCK. Then he wrote J. DOREY under STARKE and next to the name: ID. 'What else do we have?' He looked at Brownie, then at Jennifer.

'The tattoo,' Brownie barked. 'Identification of Roscoe's tattoo.'

Gardner's eyes saddened as the words were spoken. He winced, and wrote GRANVILLE in giant letters in the centre of the board. Then he drew a line to MILLER and wrote TATTOO ID underneath. 'What else?' he said, backing away from the board.

Again, there was silence in the room. No other evidence came to mind. There had been no confessions. No accusations by one defendant against the other. No murder weapon. No forensics at the crime scene except the dragmarks that had alerted Brownie to Miller in the first place.

'The shell at Purvis',' Brownie answered. 'Got Roscoe's print on it.'

'A partial,' Gardner said. 'It won't get to the jury.'

'What about the shell they put in the mailbox?' Jennifer asked. 'It was the same kind that killed Purvis.'

Gardner laid down his chalk. 'It was clean, right, Brownie?' The detective nodded. 'We may be able to get it into evidence, but it still doesn't prove a thing. We *have* to tie it to one of these two, and we can't thus far.'

Gardner stared at the board. This was it. Their whole case. A tenuous, speculative, circumstantial conglomeration of nothing. They'd hoped to turn Starke against Miller and learn some answers, but he'd clammed up. And Miller had been uncooperative from the beginning. He picked up his chalk again and walked to the right side of the board. Without saying anything he wrote in a vertical column:

SCHOOL

WEAPON

MONEY

MOTIVE

'Better add phone call,' Brownie said to his back.

'Huh?' Gardner asked.

'If you're listing the blanks we gotta fill,' Brownie replied, 'add in the phone call that Henry made to Starke. That's as much of a question mark as the others.'

Gardner mumbled OK, and added it to the list. Then he backed off and studied it.

'What about "shooter"?' Jennifer asked. The assumption from day one had been that Miller had been the shooter and Starke had been the tag-along. But now they had the look-alike issue to deal with. And the paste-on tattoos in IV Starke's safe now made Granville's drawings suspect. It was possible, but not probable, that Starke pulled the trigger.

Gardner nodded, and wrote SHOOTER on the board.

The room fell silent again as they contemplated the list, until slowly all eyes came to rest on the name in the middle:

GRANVILLE

Gardner turned and crossed his arms. 'We have to use him,' he said sadly. '*Have* to, or we've got no case.'

Jennifer and Brownie glanced at the board, then turned to Gardner. They could see it as clearly as the chalk lines against the black slate. Without Granville, they had nothing. Even if Brownie filled in the other blanks it was not going to be enough.

Gardner pulled a sheet of paper from his file and shot it across the table. 'This went out this afternoon.'

Jennifer gasped when she saw the Material Witness summons for Granville. Gardner had not told her about it. 'Gard,' she whispered, 'are you sure about this?'

Brownie leaned over her shoulder and read the document. This was a major development. 'Taking your own son into custody . . .' he said in a low voice. 'Man . . .'

'I've given it a lot of thought,' Gardner said gravely, 'and it has to be done.'

Brownie and Jennifer looked at each other with alarm. 'Can't you reason with Carole?' Brownie asked. 'Get her to cooperate?'

Gardner shook his head.

'Maybe we can find what we need so we won't have to use him,' Jennifer suggested.

Gardner shook his head again. 'I don't think so. If we haven't found it by now, we're not going to. Face it: Granville's the only hope.'

'But bringing him in on a warrant . . .' Jennifer persisted.

'There's no other way. God, I wish there were, but I know Carole. She's not going to let me near him.'

Brownie stood up. 'Please, Gard, don't do it. Recall the damn summons. I'll fill in the blanks. Just give me some more time.'

'No,' Gardner said. 'It's too late.'

Brownie gathered his things and prepared to leave. 'I'm gonna get what you need, I swear . . .' Then he went out, shaking his head.

After he had left, Jennifer approached Gardner. 'You know it's not worth it,' she said softly. Gardner eyed her sullenly. 'Nothing's worth putting your own family through hell.'

'Family,' Gardner said. 'That includes you.'

'Yes.'

'I've got to do it, Jen. Got to.'

'No, you don't,' Jennifer replied, putting her arms round him. Then she clamped his face against her chest and stifled his words.

At 10 that evening, Gardner and Jennifer were in bed. He was asleep, and she had nothing to do but sit beside him and stare at his back. Her knees were drawn up, and a novel rested on her sheet-covered thighs. She was at page five, where she'd been for the past half hour.

208

The summons was on its way. As they lay there, an unmarked sheriff's car was en route to Baltimore to pick up Granville. Suddenly the phone rang. Jennifer answered before it could disturb Gardner.

'Hello?'

'It's Brownie. Gard there?' He sounded excited.

'Sleeping. What's up?'

'Gotta talk to him . . .'

Jennifer nudged Gardner awake and handed him the phone. 'Huh?' he said groggily into the mouthpiece, then, 'What!' He sat upright in the bed. 'No! Goddam it! No!' He said good-bye and slammed down the phone. His face was ashen.

'What is it?' Jennifer's voice was trembling.

'They're out,' Gardner said gravely. '*Both* of them. Starke posted bond this afternoon, and Miller tonight.' He looked at Jennifer with fear in his eyes. 'We knew Starke could do it, but not Miller too. Shit! Somehow he came up with the money!'

Granville would be in the county by morning. And both suspected killers were back on the street.

CHAPTER 14

Gardner was bleary-eyed when he opened the door to his townhouse at 6.30 a.m. and greeted the deputy sheriff, Perry Pike. His sleep had been fitful after the phone call in the night, as his mind wound through twisted scenes of pursuit and terror.

'Wha' happened?' he asked. Pike was the deputy he'd chosen to serve the witness summons on Granville. A huge man with a wide friendly face, he looked like a panda bear. He had three kids of his own, one of whom was in Granville's class at school. That made him perfect for the job.

'It was bad, man,' Pike said with a grimace. 'Your ex-wife went bonkers . . .'

Gardner's heart leaped, as he looked past the deputy towards his car. Maybe he'd failed, and left the boy in Baltimore.

'Don't worry,' Pike said, 'I got him, but it wasn't easy.'

Gardner ran to the vehicle and looked inside. Granville was curled on the back seat, asleep. His knees were pulled up, his body turned at an awkward angle against the seatbelt.

'She went nuts when I showed her the summons,' Pike continued. 'Called the City cops. Threatened me. Threatened you. Got the boy upset.'

Gardner looked at his son's face. It wasn't smooth and relaxed, the way an eight-year-old's should be. There were tension lines on his forehead, and dirty streaks below his eyes. His stomach began to throb. He had been warned. 'What did you tell him?'

'Said Dad asked me to pick him up,' Pike replied.

Gardner glanced back at his son. He'd shifted into another

211

contortion, but he was still asleep. 'What'd he say?'

'He asked where you were,' Pike replied. 'Refused to come with me.'

Gardner put his hand over his eyes. 'How'd you get him into the car?'

'Had to carry him. Mom was screaming, he was crying. Struggled a little . . .'

'Oh, God!'

'Finally got him calmed down,' Pike continued. 'Got him talking about school and stuff. He was pretty OK after that.'

Gardner opened the car door and reached in to unbuckle the seatbelt. Granville stirred when the metal clasp clicked. Then he opened his eyes.

'Hi, Gran,' Gardner said.

Sleep still ruled, and Granville had to blink a few times to get his bearings. Gardner reached in, and scooped him up like a baby. 'Dad!' he yelled. 'Dad!' His eyes filled with tears, and he began to squirm.

Gardner set him on the ground. 'Gran,' he said again.

Deputy Pike cleared his throat, and motioned to Gardner that he had to leave, so he moved his son away from the car and allowed it to back out of the parking space.

Then Gardner put his arms out. It was the 'hug' signal, the sign that Granville always reacted to instantly. But the boy gave his father a petulant look and stood his ground. Gardner kept his arms open, then lowered them slowly. 'Not going to give me a hug?' His voice quavered. Granville shook his head. 'Why not?'

The boy lowered his eyes. 'Don't want to.'

Gardner took Granville's arm and led him inside. 'Let's get some breakfast.' Maybe food could break the ice.

They entered the kitchen, and Gardner took a wax carton from the refrigerator and filled a glass. 'How about some milk?' Granville again shook his head. Gardner's temper flared, but he held it in. He picked Granville up, and placed him in a chair at the kitchen table. Then he sat down on the other side.

'Gran, we have to have a talk,' he said softly.

The boy eyed him sullenly, and remained silent.

'I'm sure you're confused about what happened last night.'

Granville did not answer.

'You know Dad puts bad people in jail. You know it's my job. When someone hurts another person, I take the bad person to court, and put him in jail.'

Granville stared blankly while his father talked.

'I want you to be a witness in court,' Gardner said.

Granville's face paled.

'I want you to help me put some *very* bad people in jail.'

Tears were beginning to form in the boy's eyes.

'The people who killed Addie and Henry are going to court soon, and I need your help.'

Granville began to shake his head violently from side to side.

'Gran!' Gardner reached across the table and grabbed his son's shoulder. 'Listen to me!' His voice was loud. 'It hurts! I know. But we have to do it. You and me! Together.'

'But Mom . . .' Granville blubbered.

'Mom doesn't want you to, I know. But Mom just doesn't understand! That's why the sheriff went to get you. So you could come back here and help Dad. I *need* you, Gran. I *need* you to help me!' Gardner walked to the other side of the table. Permission or not, he was going to hug his child. There was another cold response, then the boy went passive and allowed his father to hold him. Gardner fought back his own tears as he clutched Granville like a rag doll in his arms.

Gardner held tight, and closed his eyes. Granville could do it, he was certain. Together they'd solve the case and end the nightmare.

'Want to play some ball later?' Gardner finally asked.

Granville stirred, and looked up. 'When?' His voice was weak.

'After breakfast.' Gardner grabbed a box of cereal. 'Right after breakfast.' He poured some cornflakes into a bowl and set it on the table.

Granville slowly picked up his spoon. 'Can I hit a few?' he asked.

Brownie's shift did not begin until 10 a.m., but he was already at the lab by 7, well into his tasks for the day. MILLER and MONEY topped his notepad and, beneath those words, a list of items he still had to check. The first item was 'teletype'. He'd put out an alert on Miller to local police departments weeks ago, but received no response. Last night he'd decided to extend the range of his search. He'd faxed a photo of Miller with a description of his truck to all the surrounding States. The man was not only a loner, but a wanderer. Maybe he had dropped a clue across the border.

The teletype beeped to signify an incoming message. Brownie watched the paper slide up as the type-keys jittered out the words. Another beep signified that the transmission was complete.

He ripped out the paper and laid it on his table.

'TO SGT. JOE BROWN, COUNTY POLICE. FROM LT. DARRELL AVIS, PENNSYLVANIA STATE POLICE.' The message followed. 'ROSCOE (NMN) MILLER WAS ARRESTED OUR JURISDICTION ON JUNE 15 OF THIS YEAR AND CHARGED WITH ASSAULT. INSPECTION OF HIS PERSONAL BELONGINGS REVEALED HE WAS CARRYING $8000 US CURRENCY . . .' Brownie blinked and re-read the last three words: '$8000 US currency,' he said aloud. He adjusted the paper, and read on: 'THE ASSAULT WAS PERPETRATED AGAINST A LOCAL MINER IN THE "DRIVE INN" BAR ON THE EVENING OF JUNE 14. BOND WAS SET AT $5000 ON THE 15TH, MILLER POSTED BOND IN THAT AMOUNT, AND WAS RELEASED. A TRIAL DATE WAS SET, BUT THE CHARGES WERE LATER DROPPED BY THE COMPLAIN-ANT. AN ATTEMPT WAS MADE TO NOTIFY MILLER AT THE ADDRESS GIVEN, BUT THE LETTER WAS RETURNED. THE BOND MONEY IS STILL BEING HELD BY THE COURT. END OF MESSAGE.'

Brownie flicked the corner of the paper with his finger. A connection! Miller had a pocketful of cash within weeks of the murder. He imagined Gardner's face lighting up when he heard the news. He dialled the number for the Pennsylvania State Police. When it answered, he asked for Lieutenant Avis.

'Avis.' The man's voice was rough, as though he'd been screaming at criminals all his life.

'Sergeant Brown, county police, Maryland. Sent you that teletype on Miller.'

'Yeah,' the gravel voice responded. 'Did you get our answer?'

'Just came in,' Brownie replied. 'Got one question, though.'

'Shoot.'

'What address did Miller give you at intake?'

'Hold on a minute,' the lieutenant replied. Brownie grabbed his pen and arranged his notepad. In a second, the trooper was back. 'Here it is.' Brownie poised his pen. '426 Cedar Road . . .'

'Huh?' Brownie thought he'd heard it wrong.

'426 Cedar Road,' Avis repeated. 'In your home town.'

Brownie wrote it down, and underlined it with a hard stroke of his pen. 'Jesus,' he said under his breath.

'What's wrong?' the lieutenant asked.

'You're sure he gave you *that* address?'

Avis hesitated, then replied, 'Positive!'

Brownie shook his head and looked at his note. The address provided by Roscoe was the home of Purvis Bowers!

Roscoe Miller slouched in the leather chair opposite Kent King's desk. He was dressed in his usual ensemble of jeans, tee-shirt and boots. He was tempted to put his feet up on the desk, but knew better. King would probably bust his kneecap if he did it.

The lawyer was wearing his trademark double-breasted pinstripe. Unlike Gardner Lawson, he looked relaxed and rested. 'Are you gonna thank me?' he asked Miller sarcastically.

Miller fluffed his hair. 'For what?'

'It's customary to show appreciation to the person who arranges bail,' King said.

'Oh, I get it. Thanks a lot, Mr King.'

The lawyer smiled. 'You can really thank the other guy – Starke. He put up the cash.'

'He did?'

'Uh-huh,' King replied. 'Pretty generous, don't you think?' Miller nodded blankly. 'Seems like he wants to pay you back for something. Care to tell me about it?'

Miller's face was impassive. He began to fiddle with the black shiny plastic tightly encircling his wrist. 'He don't owe me nuthin',' he said.

King stared across the desk with a disapproving glare. 'No?'

Miller shook his head. 'Nuthin',' he repeated.

'Well, why would he want to put up $50,000 of his own money, then?'

'Maybe he's got nuthin' better to do with it,' Miller answered.

'What the hell happened out there, Roscoe?'

Miller tried to turn the monitor round on his wrist, but it wouldn't budge. 'Nuthin',' he repeated. 'Nobody done nuthin'.'

'What are you so afraid of?'

'I'm not afraid!' Miller snapped.

King leaned forward. 'He's gonna try to burn you . . .' Miller looked up. 'Why else would he want you out on the street?' King went on. 'He's got something planned, and you're part of it.'

Miller squirmed, and rubbed the monitor again. 'What if this thing quit working,' he said suddenly, 'and the county shits couldn't track me?'

King crossed his arms. His client was changing the subject. 'We're not talking about that, Roscoe! We're talking about Starke.'

'What would they do if the signal quit?' Miller persisted. His mind was fixated on the monitor.

King gave up trying to hold him to the discussion. 'They'd probably come after you.'

Miller smiled, and let go of the bracelet. 'But they wouldn't know where to find me.'

King nodded condescendingly. 'Right.'

'Would it be a violation of my release conditions?'

King glanced at the monitor. 'If it quit working?'

'Yeah,' Miller said.

King shook his head. 'No, I'd say not. It's *their* damn equipment. If it goes wrong, they can't really blame you.' Miller smiled again, but he did not say a word. 'Can we get back to some case prep now?' King was irritated at the diversion.

Miller sat up. 'Whatever you say.'

The main post office was located on Court Avenue in the downtown section. It was a granite building, hewn from the quarry-stone of the mountains, and assembled a hundred years ago. Although there were several small branches scattered across the remote rural sections, the main post office was the hub of all mail operations in the county. Every letter entered and exited at that point.

At 11.45 a.m. Brownie pushed his way through the revolving door and into the central hall. Its vaulted ceiling echoed with the voices of the mail-handlers behind a wooden partition that ran the length of the room. Purvis Bowers' address turning up on Roscoe Miller's arrest report was an unexpected jolt, as strange as Henry calling IV Starke on the phone. It had to be checked.

He entered the postmaster's office and asked to see 'Mr Jim'. If there was a certified 'character' in all of the county, eighty-year-old James 'Mr Jim' Johnson certainly qualified. He had worked for the post office for over sixty years and 'never missed a day on the job', so the legend went. He was well past retirement age, but his mind still had the snap of a teenager's. He'd been able to obtain a waiver that kept him employed, but his real claim to fame was his hobby. He was an amateur genealogist, and it was said that he could recite the ancestry of every man, woman and child in the county.

He greeted Brownie warmly. 'Sergeant Joseph Brown. Son of Althea and Joseph senior. Grandson of Robert and Emmaline . . .'

Brownie smiled. 'Hello, Mr Jim.' The man was a trip. Wizened and skinny, his clothes hung on him like a scarecrow. But he had a thick head of silver hair, and bright, attentive eyes.

'Doing all right for a man of my age,' the postmaster replied with a grin that showed all his natural teeth still in place. 'What brings you to my humble place of employment?' He motioned Brownie into an antique chair beside his roll-top desk.

Brownie sat down and handed Mr Jim a piece of notepaper. The names ROSCOE MILLER and PURVIS BOWERS were written above the address 426 CEDAR ROAD. The postmaster's genealogical genius was not his only talent. He had a photographic memory to boot. 'Recognize these names?' Brownie asked.

Mr Jim skipped Miller and went to Purvis. 'Purvis R. Bowers, son of Purvis senior and Rosalind,' he said. 'Nephew of Henry and Addie . . .' His voice dropped an octave when the last two names came out. 'Lived at 426 Cedar Road. That's where he lived . . .' He emphasized the past tense.

'Ever seen the other name sent through to that address?' Brownie said, prodding the postmaster out of the reverie he'd slipped into.

'Miller . . .' Mr Jim said. 'Roscoe Miller, 426 Cedar Road.' He was trying it on for size. Brownie waited while the ancient computer in the postmaster's skull began to whirr. 'Roscoe Miller, 426 Cedar Road,' the old man repeated. 'Roscoe Miller . . .' He was searching his memory banks for the ancestry. Brownie leaned forward and rested his thick arms on his knees. 'Roscoe Miller, son of . . .' It was starting to focus. Brownie took a deep breath. 'Son of Cletus and Anna Miller!' Mr Jim exclaimed, his eyes flashing with triumph. Suddenly, the excitement dampened. 'Addie Bowers,' he said absently.

'Huh?' Brownie didn't follow the name shift.

'Addie Bowers,' Mr Jim repeated. 'Daughter of Andrew and Sarah *Miller*.' Brownie's chin jerked up. 'Aunt of Purvis Bowers,' he continued. 'Aunt of Cletus Miller . . .'

'Great-aunt of Roscoe Miller!' Brownie burst out. Another connection! And this one was more bizarre than the last. 'Roscoe Miller and Addie Bowers were related,' he said.

'Sure were,' Mr Jim said. 'Didn't think of it at first, but when you trace it out, it comes clear.'

'So Purvis Bowers was related to Roscoe too. He was Roscoe's . . .' Brownie was groping for the correct genealogical term.

'First cousin once removed,' the postmaster said sadly. 'Never made the connection till now. That Miller boy was related to the Bowers clan!'

Gardner and Jennifer sat at the table in the conference room at the State Attorney's office. The evidence outline that Gardner had drawn earlier was still there, below a 'DO NOT ERASE' sign. Nothing had been added since the diagram had gone up. With Granville in Gardner's private office, plied with books and games, they were discussing the Grand Jury presentation on State *v.* Miller and Starke. Both defendants were on the loose, so the boy could not be left at home.

'Got to convene the Grand Jury on Friday,' Gardner said. His face looked as though it had been in a wine press. 'Got to try to get another bond after indictment.' He scribbled notes on a yellow legal pad. 'Maybe we can get a new judge. One who'll up the ante.'

The release of *both* prisoners had been a shock, but once the Grand Jury issued formal charges, another bond would be set by the court.

'Rumour has it that Carla Hanks is going all the way on this one,' Jennifer said.

Gardner looked up. 'Rumour?'

'Betty in the clerk's office said that Danforth got a call from Annapolis. She was told to put Hanks in on all motions.'

Gardner shook his head. 'Judge-shoppers,' he muttered. It had to be the Jacobs-Biddington connection again. Inexperienced and unfamiliar with criminal law, Hanks was sure to wreak havoc with the rules of evidence. And that could only help Miller and Starke. 'Let's get to it,' he said solemnly. 'We must put this indictment together.'

'But what about the evidence?' Jennifer asked, waving her fingers at the blackboard. 'Do we have enough to indict?'

Gardner walked over. 'What we offer to the Grand Jury does not have to meet in-court standards of admissibility,' he said, circling the PARTIAL PRINT notation under ROSCOE MILLER's name. 'We do not have to tell the Grand Jury that it's only a "partial". We can say we have Roscoe's print.'

Jennifer frowned. 'Withhold information?'

'No. We say here's a print with X number of comparisons to the print of Roscoe Miller.'

'But we don't say it's only a partial,' Jennifer replied.

'Right. If anyone in the Grand Jury asks, of course, we tell the whole story, and admit it's only a partial . . .'

'But we don't tell them up front,' Jennifer said.

'Right. We have no obligation to impeach our own evidence. We're going to *offer* that fingerprint in court. That's our plan . . .'

Jennifer ruffled the smooth line of her dark hair. 'But

that's intellectually dishonest! You *know* that the print won't be admitted in court.'

'I do not. We shall submit the print as part of our case. It might get in . . .'

Jennifer went silent. Gardner was back to square one with his attitude. He'd been restless at night, unreasonable by day. And now that Granville was here, he was getting worse.

Suddenly there was a knock at the door.

'Yeah?' Gardner had left orders not to be disturbed, unless Granville needed something.

'Deputy Pike,' a voice from the other side replied.

Gardner flipped the latch and opened the door.

'Perry,' Gardner said. 'What's up?'

The deputy entered. 'I'm sorry,' he said haltingly, as he fingered a paper in his hands. 'I was the only one at the station when this came in. They made me do it. I didn't want to . . .'

Gardner was puzzled as Pike handed him the elongated sheet. 'Christ!' he sputtered suddenly. 'Jesus Christ!' He threw the paper on the table, and ran his hand through his hair.

'I'm sorry . . .' Deputy Pike mumbled.

Jennifer grabbed the paper and began to read: 'Summons,' it said. 'Emergency Custody Hearing re: The parental rights of Gardner Lawson to the minor Granville Alcott Lawson . . .'

She shuddered. Carole had counter attacked! She had hired an attorney and filed a civil custody suit. Jennifer looked at the date the hearing was set: this coming Friday. Grand Jury day.

At 8.30 that night Gardner sat by Granville's bed and tried to read him to sleep. They were in Granville's 'weekend' room, decorated with baseball-player wallpaper and cowboy prints. He tried to concentrate on the words he was reading from *Treasure Island*, one of his own favourite books as a boy. 'From the side of the hill,' he read, 'which was here steep and stony, a spout of gravel was dislodged, and fell rattling and bounding through the trees . . .'

Granville stirred, and opened his eyes. Gardner stopped. 'What's "bounding", Dad?' the boy asked. He'd finally calmed down from this morning. Unresponsive and almost hostile at first, he was now softening.

'Bounding,' Gardner said. 'Uh, it's like bouncing. The stone went bouncing through the trees.'

'Oh,' Granville said.

'My eyes turned instinctively in that direction,' Gardner continued reading, 'and I saw a figure leap with great rapidity behind the trunk of a pine. What it was, whether bear or monkey, I could in no wise tell. It seemed dark and shaggy; more I knew not. But the terror of this new apparition brought me to a stand.' He stopped reading as his mind visualized the scene. A young boy on a lonely isle, pursued and terrorized by criminals. When he was a child, the words had been fantasy, an adventure that made him want to be at the boy's side as he ran from the pirates. But, now, the adventure had lost its appeal. Real children were being pursued by real criminals in jungles of asphalt and steel.

Gardner looked at Granville. His eyes were closed, and had not opened since he stopped reading. Maybe he'd finally fallen asleep.

Suddenly the boy's eyes popped open. 'Dad?'

Gardner looked back at the book to pick up his place.

'When am I gonna see Mom?'

Gardner's neck warmed at the sound of the word 'Mom'. 'Soon, Gran,' he said as calmly as he could. 'You'll see her real soon.'

'Is she still gonna be mad?'

'Probably.'

Granville rolled on his side and looked at his dad. 'Do you want me to ask her to stop?' Innocence shone in his eyes. There was nothing the boy wanted more than harmony between his parents.

Gardner smiled. 'You could tell her that Dad's not such a bad guy,' he said as his mind flew ahead to the custody hearing. He had used the criminal code to seize his son. Carole had countered with civil domestic law. A prosecutor had a right to free access with a key witness. And a mother had a right to custody of her son. There was no predicting where Solomon's knife would come down.

'I'll tell her,' Granville said, his eyes aglow.

'Go to sleep now, son,' Gardner said, kissing his cheek. 'We have a big day tomorrow.'

Granville didn't answer. His breathing had turned heavy, and his face was serene. He'd finally drifted off.

At 11.45 p.m. the pretrial release monitor section of the sheriff's office was manned by only two people. Deputy Peter Smawley was ending his shift, and Deputy Sam Ellen was about to begin his. After midnight, there would be only one deputy on duty for the rest of the night. The unit had been made possible by a federal grant the county had received in the late eighties. With prison overcrowding an issue nation-wide, the lawmakers had determined that the most cost-effective way to deal with the situation was to release as many prisoners as they could. The result was the develop-ment of the arm monitor and the base-station tracking equipment that went with it. Letting prisoners roam free on an electronic tether seemed like a good idea at the time.

Deputy Ellen sat at the console and began arranging for the start of his shift. He was another member of the sheriff's beef trust, heavy-set and muscular. He picked up the clip-board and began to run down the list of the monitorees, checking the names against the numbers displayed on his screen. He was scanning the screen, when suddenly he stopped. 'Hey, Pete,' he yelled. 'Come here a minute!'

Deputy Smawley was a contradiction to his name. He, too, was gigantic. Ellen had caught him just as he was about to hit the door. 'What's the matter?' he asked, leaning his head over Ellen's shoulder.

'How many sheep did you count last?'

Smawley grabbed the clipboard, and scanned to the last line. 'Twelve. That's what they gave me. Twelve.'

Ellen turned to look at Smawley. 'Twelve? I can only find ten.'

Smawley pushed closer to get a better look at the screen, counting out loud as he went. '. . . eight, nine, ten. Shit!'

'Looks like we got two sheep unaccounted for,' Ellen said gravely.

They quickly matched up the numbers with the names. 'Miller,' Smawley said. 'Roscoe Miller's one.'

Ellen had to go to the bottom of the alphabetical list before he found the other. 'And Starke. Mr Wellington Starke the fourth.'

Ellen looked at Smawley. 'What do we do?' He was new to this duty and had not encountered such a situation.

Smawley shrugged. 'Nothing to do. They were both on the screen five minutes ago, so we know they didn't skip. Equipment malfunction, most likely . . .'

'On two codefendants at the same time?' It was too much of a coincidence for Deputy Ellen.

Smawley shrugged again. 'It happens. Make a note and report it when the morning shift gets here. I gotta get goin'.'

After the other deputy left, Ellen wrote down the names and penned a reminder to make the report in the morning. Two monitors down. At the same time. On two defendants charged with multiple murder. Ellen shuddered at the thought, and prayed that nothing happened before they got the monitors repaired.

CHAPTER 15

It was Thursday, the day before the Grand Jury and the emergency custody hearing were to be convened. Gardner was in his office, struggling with the schedule. Both proceedings were set to begin at 9.30 a.m. If the assignment clerk didn't move one of them to another docket, Gardner would be fatally double-booked and would have to delegate the Grand Jury to Jennifer.

Chief clerk Ellie Richards was on the phone. She was in charge of all courthouse scheduling. 'Sorry, Mr Lawson,' she said sadly. 'I have orders to keep it the way it is.'

'But you've got me in two places at once!' Gardner argued. 'Why can't you move the custody hearing to 2 p.m.?'

'No. Judge Cramer has a full divorce docket in the afternoon. That time is firm.'

Gardner swivelled his chair. 'OK. What about moving the Grand Jury to the afternoon? We can surely do that?'

'The summonses have already been served,' Ellie replied. 'Those folks are going to be here at nine. They've had to rearrange their own lives just to come in as it is.'

'They can be notified to switch the report time to the afternoon.'

'No,' the clerk answered, 'we're shorthanded today. Got three people out, and the filing's backlogged.'

'For God's sake, Ellie! I can make the calls myself!'

'Sorry, Mr Lawson. That's *our* responsibility. We can't let you do it.'

The intercom buzzed. Gardner put the clerk on hold, and answered the call. 'Kent King is here to see you, sir,' his secretary announced.

'King?' Gardner was surprised. King never came to their

office. He patrolled the waters around the courthouse like a shark, but he never ventured into the harbour of the State Attorney's office. 'Find out what he wants.'

There was a pause, then the secretary was back. 'Says it's *very* important that he sees you. A private matter, he says.'

Gardner looked at the blinking light where Ellie waited. Two conflicting cases tomorrow, and neither was going to budge. And now he had King at the door. He told Ellie he'd call back later, then he gave the OK to send King in.

Kent King strutted into the room wearing a silk suit, matching red tie and pocket square. He surveyed the office with a cynical glance. The antiques were a stark contrast to his own modern headquarters.

Gardner motioned him to sit. 'What's so important, King? Thought you vowed never to set foot in here.'

King flopped in a chair. 'Untrue,' he sneered.

'You've always avoided this place,' Gardner said. 'Must be some reason.'

'No reason, until now.'

Defence attorneys came to the prosecutor's office for one purpose only: to make a deal. But King had never, in five years, attempted to deal. He always went to court, and battled it out.

'This one's different,' he continued. 'We've got a problem.'

King's use of the word 'we' almost knocked Gardner sideways. It was always 'us' versus 'them'. King was always on one side and he was always on the other. 'We' never applied.

'This Starke kid is a maniac,' King went on. 'I'd like to help you nail him.'

Gardner was stunned. Not only had King ventured into prosecution land for the first time and used the word 'we', now he wanted to 'help'. It didn't make sense. King was the ultimate warrior. He never 'helped'. He eyed him cautiously. 'Continue,' he said.

'I want to deal Miller for Starke,' King answered.

Gardner smiled ironically. 'You've got to be kidding!'

King's jaw went slack. 'Absolutely not. Starke is *bad news*. Real bad news. He almost killed your boy.'

Gardner's smile vanished. 'So Miller is going to help put Starke down?'

King's voice dropped. 'He doesn't even know I'm here. If I can get a commitment from you, I'll see to it that he helps.'

'What's this bullshit, King?' Gardner said angrily. 'You're tendering a deal, and your client doesn't even know about it?' In criminal law, that was unheard of. An attorney always needed his client's permission to make a plea offer. His anti-King instincts began resurfacing.

'He'll cooperate,' King replied. 'I just need a commitment from you.'

Gardner crossed his arms. 'What are you looking for?' he asked. In deal-making, each 'quid' had a 'pro quo'.

'Lower the stakes,' King said with a straight face. 'Drop the murder charge down to accessory.'

'You're out'a your mind!'

King remained immobile. 'You need Miller to get Starke. I don't have to tell you that.'

Gardner was still reeling. King wanted Gardner to cut Miller's charges down to a misdemeanour. That was almost like letting him off the hook completely: freedom for cooperation against the co-defendant. King was right about one thing – the Starke case was slim. Testimony from Miller would help, but Miller was the number one suspect. 'Give me something, Kent,' Gardner finally said. 'Give me a fact: one fact that I don't already know. Give me a reason even to consider your absurd offer.'

King's expression had not altered since he'd entered the room. 'I can't,' he said.

'Can't as in "cannot",' Gardner said loudly, 'or can't as in "will not"?'

'*Cannot* at this time,' King answered. 'But if you take the deal, I'll get what you need.'

'That's ridiculous!' Gardner snapped. 'I've never done that in my life.'

'Maybe it's time to start.' King still looked halfway sincere. 'Starke is dangerous as shit.'

'Don't play games with me, Kent!' Gardner screamed. 'You give me something up front, or get out of my office! I don't have time for your bullshit.'

King stood up. 'I'm not playing a game here, Gardner. I am making a serious offer . . .'

'But you *know* I can't accept it. Not without something concrete on the table. You knew it before you even came in here!' The two men stared at each other in silence for a moment, then Gardner picked up his file. 'I know why you're really here, man.' His mind had been working overtime to figure out why King had finally crept over to his office. Now, suddenly, it came clear. 'You're scared,' he said.

'Huh?' King was not prepared for that one.

'We're working the money angle on the case,' Gardner continued. 'Turns out Roscoe Miller was actually related to the Bowers: Addie's long-lost cousin. There's a lot of missing money. And an attorney who represented *both* parties . . .' He gave King an accusing stare. 'We're getting close, pal. The money trail is leading in your direction.'

King smiled nervously. 'You're off base on that one, buddy boy!'

'Yeah?' Gardner put his hands on his hips. 'Then why all of a sudden do you want to plead Miller and focus the case on Starke? Getting a little too hot for you? Want to divert the heat? Lead us away from the *real* mastermind?'

King placed his hands on his hips in a reverse-image of the prosecutor. 'If you're accusing me, you'd better spell it out.'

'Getting too hot for you, King?' Gardner taunted.

'I told you one time, and I'm telling you again, the money's got nothing to do with these crimes. All financial transactions were absolutely legit. Cut my man a deal, and I'll prove it!'

'No way!' Gardner said. 'Give me the facts, and I'll consider a deal.'

King shook his head. 'No can do.'

'Then I guess there's nothing more to say.' Gardner sat down at his desk and picked up the file.

King stood silent for a moment, then pushed the door open. After he'd left, Gardner broke into another smile. They had to be getting close. King was squirming like an insect on a pin, trying to deal his client. Maybe, finally, they were on the right track.

Brownie was in the catacombs of the courthouse, the basement file-room where the vital records were stored. Births. Deaths. Wills. The ebb and flow of humanity had been docketed on blue paper and folded into the darkness of the vault. Brownie disliked going there, much like he hated the morgue. Life was reduced to spots of ink on a page, statistics and numbers slowly crumbling into dust.

The Miller–Bowers connection had given the investigation a major boost. He'd called Gardner immediately and given him the news: the money trail began with Henry and ended with Roscoe Miller. But so far they'd located only $8000 in Miller's possession. His bond had been posted by Starke, so that didn't count. It was time to find out what had happened to the rest of the money.

Brownie pulled copies of Henry and Addie's wills and laid them beside Purvis Bowers' will which he'd obtained earlier. All three had been drafted by Kent King. Upon the death of both Henry and Addie, everything they owned passed to their heirs.

He opened the pages to Purvis Bowers' will. He had no wife, no children. His estate, at death, if he were still unmarried, was slated to go to his trusted counsellor: Kent King. He did a double-take. King was named in Purvis' will as the sole beneficiary. 'My God,' he said aloud. 'The man actually wrote himself in!'

Brownie laid the papers aside and drew a diagram on his pad. HENRY – ADDIE – PURVIS – KING. Then he paused for a moment and added ROSCOE. He was a relative, too, but he was not listed in any of the wills. This was very odd. Miller was related through Addie, so he should have had a claim to the estate. Maybe Purvis hired Miller to kill Addie and Henry but didn't tell him about the secret money, and paid him $8000 for the job. But, later, Miller found out what Purvis had done, and killed *him*. That might be it. Miller was just reclaiming his rightful share of the estate.

Brownie went back to the statistics file again. Addie was the pivotal figure. Her relationship to Miller linked him to the money. He pulled her vital stats and studied them for additional clues: 'Born: 1908. Married: 1941. One child born: October 1946.' Brownie re-read the last item: 'One child.' He'd always thought she was childless. Scanning ahead, he found another reference: 'Robert Thompkins Bowers, male child born to Addie and Henry Bowers, Died November 1946.'

This was a surprise. In all the years that he'd known the Bowers, they'd never mentioned a child. It was assumed that Addie 'couldn't have children'. Brownie recollected that phrase being used by the stove at Bowers Corner. A gentle, barren, old lady. That was her image. But, like everything else in the case, the image was false.

On Friday morning at 9.15 Gardner reported to the court-room of Judge William Cramer. He had decided to represent himself, so he was alone. Carole was already on the plain-tiff's seat, conferring with her attorney. She was dressed in black, and wore little makeup. She glared at Gardner as he entered, but said nothing.

Gardner motioned to her attorney, and the man walked over. He was the Kent King of the domestic trade, Gardner had heard, the hottest child-custody lawyer in Baltimore. He extended his hand. 'Gardner Lawson,' he said.

The man shook hands quickly. 'Stuart Bieman.'

'Listen, Stuart,' Gardner said in his best negotiating voice, 'can't we work this thing out?'

Bieman shrugged. 'What's to work out? Return the child, and you might get your visitation back some day.'

'He's a witness,' Gardner whispered. Carole had craned her head to see what was happening. 'Under summons to testify in a murder trial. That's the only reason he was picked up. After the case, he goes back to his mother.'

'That's bull, and you know it,' Bieman said. 'He cannot testify.'

'All rise!' The entry of Judge Cramer interrupted Gard-ner's attempt to head off a hearing, but it was already clear that an agreement was out of the question. Carole and her hot-shot were not going to budge.

Judge Cramer swept up to the bench and sat down. In his late fifties, the grey-haired gnome-like jurist had been a family law specialist for his entire career. Some said he got the cases by default, as the other judges wanted nothing to do with divorce. But, whatever the reason, he was the only choice. Most of the time he was fair.

'Call the case,' Cramer instructed his clerk.

'Lawson *v.* Lawson, your honour. Emergency custody hearing.'

'Identify yourselves for the record, counsel,' Cramer said.

Biemen went first, and Gardner followed.

Cramer scanned the near-empty courtroom. 'Where's the child?' he asked Gardner.

'In my office, Judge.'

'I want him available,' Cramer said, 'in case I need to question him.'

Gardner nodded. 'Just say the word, your honour, and I'll have him here in ten minutes.'

'Very well,' Cramer said. 'Now I'd appreciate it if someone would tell me what this is about.'

Gardner began to speak, but the judge waved him off. 'Maybe the petitioner should have the first word.' Gardner sat down. 'You'll get your say, Mr Lawson. Proceed, Mr Bieman.'

Carole's attorney opened his file. 'We have a case of child abuse here, your honour. Simple and clear cut.'

Gardner began to rise to object to the terminology, but Cramer directed him back down with another wave.

'Mr Lawson claims his son is a witness in a case, when in point of fact, the boy is a *silent witness* . . .'

The judge frowned. 'Silent witness?'

'That's right, Judge,' Bieman continued. 'The boy was at the scene of a crime, but he has never given a statement as to what he saw. He has a mental block. He's been in therapy, and it has been advised that he not be *forced* to confront the incident. Mr Lawson is trying to *force* the boy to remember, against the advice of medical authority. And he has further traumatized the child by physically removing him from his mother and placing him in the custody of the sheriff. All of this amounts to nothing less than child abuse.' Carole nodded agreement as her attorney spoke. 'We ask the court to pass an immediate order,' Bieman continued, 'restoring custody to the mother, Carole Lawson, and enjoining the father, Gardner Lawson, from *any* contact with the boy for the foreseeable future.'

While the custody case held Gardner in the domestic

231

relations courtroom, Jennifer was down the corridor with the Grand Jury. She and Gardner had been up most of the night, finalizing this presentation. The proposed charges were listed on the indictment form. Roscoe Miller was charged with three counts of first degree murder (Addie, Henry and Purvis), one count of attempted murder (Granville), robbery, assault and battery. Starke was charged with two counts of first degree murder (Addie and Henry), one count of attempted murder (Granville), two counts of accessory to murder (Addie and Henry), robbery, assault and battery. The accessory charges against Starke had been added in as a back-up. If the Grand Jury felt that the evidence against him was too weak to prove actual participation in the crimes, they could compromise and hold him in as an accessory.

Brownie had done the presentation of facts, and now Jennifer was ready to answer the jurors' legal questions.

'OK,' Jennifer said. 'There you have it.' She motioned to the blackboard where Brownie had sketched out the evidence. There was a money trail from Henry to Miller. The relationship to Purvis. The $8000 cash in Pennsylvania. The empty safe-deposit boxes. The conclusion by the medical examiner that the murders were executions. The contact between Miller and Starke at the school. Their fondness for shotguns. The shotgun shell in Granville's mailbox. The drag-mark in the dirt at Bowers Corner.

Every conceivable fact was laid out, whether they could get it admitted in court or not. Gardner had finally convinced Jennifer to blast it all at the Grand Jury; it was their only chance to get a formal charge. They'd included the ID of Starke in the truck, Granville's ID of the tattoo and the 'partial' print on the shell that killed Purvis Bowers. It was all there. Everything they had so far.

'Miss Munday, I have a question.' A female juror in the back row raised her hand. She was a housewife who watched too many TV cop shows. She knew just enough to cause problems.

'Yes, ma'am?' Jennifer said cautiously.

'I think I understand how you say this happened,' she said,

'but can you tell us who actually shot the people at the store? Which one of the two suspects?'

Jennifer swallowed. That was the sixty-four-dollar question, the one that not even the prosecutors had the answer to. 'In a joint venture,' she said, 'the person who actually, physically, commits the act that constitutes the crime is no more culpable than the one who doesn't. They are both principals, and are chargeable with the highest degree of the crime. In a bank robbery, for example, the getaway driver is as guilty of robbery as the man who enters the bank. And if someone is killed inside, the driver is as guilty as the person who pulled the trigger.'

The back-row lady frowned. Jennifer's answer had not helped. 'But where's the proof of what the Starke suspect did?' she asked. 'Did he go inside or did he wait outside?'

Jennifer took a breath. She hated this kind of half-baked logic. 'Ma'am,' she said deliberately, 'I just told you it does not matter if he was inside or outside. The guilt, and the charge, are equal.'

'But what if he didn't know what was happening? Maybe he didn't know what the Miller guy was doing?'

Jennifer folded her arms. Several other jurors were shaking their heads in agreement, as if the inquiring mind were on to something. 'You have to look at what happened before, during and after the crime to be able to assess that. Starke never reported anything to the police. He had ample opportunity to dissociate himself from the crime, and he did not do it. One would have to assume, therefore, that he was part of it.'

That seemed to shut the lady up, but the expression on her face said she was still troubled.

'Any other questions?' Jennifer asked, praying there were none. The jurors were quiet. 'Very well, then. You know the procedure. Sergeant Brown and I are going to leave the room, and you will vote on each count in each indictment. When you have concluded, please have the foreman sign the indictments, and come outside to find us.'

Jennifer and Brownie turned to leave, when a voice rang out. 'Miss Munday!' It was the back-row lady again. 'What if we can't agree?'

Jennifer looked her in the eye. 'If you all take reasonable positions, I'm sure that you can.' Then she walked out and left the jurors alone, crossing her fingers tightly as she shut the door.

At the custody hearing, Carole's attorney had called Nancy Meyers to the witness stand. As petitioners, they had the burden of establishing that it was in the best interests of the child to remove Granville from his father. Meyers was a so-called 'neutral' party. Her only allegiance, presumably, was to her young 'client'.

She was on direct examination by Bieman. 'Miss Meyers, how many meetings did you have with Granville Lawson prior to today?'

'I met with him five times,' Meyers said.

'And during that time did you have occasion to form an opinion as to his physical . . . uh, check that, as to his mental condition?' Bieman was looking at his notes as he spoke.

Meyers smiled. 'Yes, I did.'

'And can you tell his honour, Judge Cramer, what that opinion is?'

'Yes, sir . . .'

'Objection!' Gardner jumped to his feet. 'This witness is not a medical doctor, a psychiatrist or even a certified psychologist. She's not qualified to give an opinion.' Nancy Meyers was merely a certified social worker with a degree in psychology. She'd never taken the examinations to become a qualified psychologist.

Bieman smiled coldly. 'She's got the experience to give an opinion, Judge. Counsel has already stipulated that she's been a therapist for ten years. That alone qualifies her.'

'But not to give a formal diagnosis!' Gardner argued. Anyone who had seen Granville since the shootings could say he was withdrawn and moody. But Nancy Meyers should not be permitted to give his condition a clinical name.

Judge Cramer squeaked forward in his chair. 'If she's got no other credentials, Mr Bieman, I'd be inclined to agree with Mr Lawson.'

'We're not going into some complex evaluation here, Judge,' Bieman said calmly. 'We just want her to acquaint the court with his general condition.'

'I think we can permit that,' Cramer replied. 'Just a general overview. But no specific diagnosis.'

'But, your honour . . .' Gardner protested.

It was too late. Cramer had ruled, and that was it.

'Tell the court the nature of the boy's problem,' Bieman said.

Meyers nodded. 'Dissociative behaviour, due to severe trauma.'

'Object!' Gardner yelled, springing back to his feet. 'How much more clinical can you get?'

Cramer looked annoyed, as if his directive had been disobeyed. 'Sustained! Ask another question, counsel.'

Bieman looked nonplussed. 'Miss Meyers, you may not characterize Granville's condition in clinical terms. The judge has ruled that. Please simply *describe* his demeanour during the times you saw him.'

Cramer nodded as if to say that question was OK.

'Very turned in on himself,' Meyers said. 'Non-communicative. Withdrawn. *Very* reluctant to participate in any interrogative aspects of therapy.'

'And did there come a time that you prescribed a course of treatment for this condition?' Bieman continued.

'Yes, sir.'

'And what was that?'

Meyers glanced at Carole, and then at Gardner. 'I decided that play therapy was the best course. Allow him to communicate through play and art if he wanted to, but no direct questioning, and *no pressure*.' She flashed another glance at Gardner when she said the last part.

'And did you discuss this course of treatment with the parents?'

'Yes, sir.' Meyers looked at Gardner again.

'And what reaction did you receive from the parents?'

'The mother, Carole Lawson, was totally cooperative.'

Now Bieman stared at Gardner accusingly. 'And the father?'

'I had no problem with him either, at first . . .' Her voice trailed off.

'But later?'

'Later he disregarded my advice. Tried to force his son to answer questions about the crime.'

'Objection!' Gardner said. 'She doesn't know that.'

Cramer twisted his seat towards Gardner. 'What's the basis of your objection, Mr Lawson?'

'Hearsay, your honour. She has no personal knowledge of that fact.'

'Did you actually see him do this?' Cramer asked the witness.

'Uh, no, sir.'

'Then how do you know it happened?'

Meyers looked at Carole. 'Mrs Lawson.'

'Hearsay,' Gardner repeated.

'Objection sustained,' said the judge.

Bieman went on with the therapist's questioning for another half hour, emphasizing the fact that Granville's appearance as a witness would cause irreparable damage to his psyche. Gardner knew that, it was said. He'd been told of the consequences, but he forged ahead anyway.

Finally, Gardner was permitted to cross-examine. He rose, and walked to the witness stand. 'Just a few preliminary questions, your honour.' Judge Cramer nodded OK. 'Miss Meyers, are you familiar with the murder case against Roscoe Miller and Starke?'

'Object!' Now Bieman was standing. 'Beyond the scope of my direct.'

'Background, Judge,' Gardner countered.

'I think she can answer,' Cramer replied.

Bieman sat down.

'I've heard about the case. Yes, sir,' Meyers said.

'And then you must know, as it has been reported, that Granville has already communicated some important facts about the case.'

'The drawings.' Meyers said.

'Right. Contrary to your testimony that the boy is reluctant to communicate, he *has* in fact communicated an important clue as to the identity of one of the murderers.'

Before she could answer, the door to the courtroom opened, and two men walked in and sat in the back row.

Gardner shot a furtive glance in that direction, Kent King

and Joel Jacobs, together! He tried to get his mind back to the task at hand, but seeing King and Jacobs momentarily sent him into a spin. King had tried to stab Jacobs in the back, and the old bastard didn't even know it! And now they were cheek to jowl on a joint spy mission. They took seats on Carole's side, like family at a wedding. Gardner stepped back from the witness stand for a moment to gather his thoughts. King and Jacobs had a vested interest in unnerving him. If he faltered in his presentation, the ruling could go against him. The judge could take Granville away and forbid any contact, and the murder case would be over.

'Uh, can I have a moment, please, your honour?' Gardner asked.

'Very well, counsel,' Cramer replied.

Gardner walked to the rear of the courtroom, and leaned over the seated attorneys. Without acknowledging Jacobs, he looked directly at King. 'I've been thinking about your *offer*,' he whispered. If they wanted to play games, so could he. This one was divide and conquer.

King smiled wanly, and Jacobs didn't stir. 'Good,' King whispered.

Gardner gave Jacobs a wink. 'Real loyal partner you've got here.'

Jacobs remained immobile. Either he didn't get the innuendo, or the whole thing was a set-up from the start, cooked up to torment the prosecution. 'I'm surprised you can sit in the same room, after what *he* just did.' Gardner cocked his head towards King.

A thin smile crossed Jacobs' lips. 'I have no problem with Mr King,' he said casually. There was still no sign he understood what Gardner was trying to communicate.

'You don't?' Gardner said through his teeth. It was time to give it a name. 'He just tried to sell your man out!'

Jacobs didn't flinch. 'There's nothing to sell,' he said calmly.

Gardner glared at King. The defence attorney grinned sheepishly, and shrugged his shoulders. He'd obviously covered his tracks with Jacobs. Warned him that the prosecutor would try to split them with false accusations. King was already a step ahead.

237

'Mr Lawson!' Judge Cramer called from the bench. 'Can we please get back to business?' The witness was still on the stand.

King and Jacobs looked like Tweedledee and Tweedledum. Gardner's attempt to shatter the alliance had failed.

'Don't turn your back on him,' Gardner told Jacobs. Then he spun round and headed towards the stand.

'Miss Meyers,' he said, trying to refocus, 'did you not tell me at one point that it was therapeutic for my son to confront, actually *confront*, what happened to him?'

The witness pushed her grey hair to the side. 'No.'

Gardner's eyes widened. 'No? Was the play therapy not designed to give him the opportunity to express himself? To get it out, as it were?'

Meyers had to think about that one. Her prior testimony contradicted the answer. 'That could be a result, but it was not *designed* for that purpose.'

'What was it designed for?' Gardner glanced at the judge, who was hanging over the bench, listening attentively.

'Play therapy is a non-adversarial treatment course that allows the child to proceed at his own pace . . .'

Gardner looked at Cramer again. 'That answer is not a response to the question. What is the ultimate goal of play therapy?'

'To make the child comfortable,' Meyers replied.

'In order for the child to be able to do *what*?'

'She's already answered the question!' Bieman shouted, leaping to his feet. 'Objection!'

'She has not given an answer!' Gardner argued.

'Answer his question, Miss Meyers,' the judge instructed.

'What was the question again?' Meyers asked.

'What is the ultimate *purpose* of the play therapy?' Gardner said.

She hesitated. She was supposed to be neutral, but her bias was starting to show through. 'To release tension. To provide a calming atmosphere . . .' Her voice trailed off.

'In order to enable the child to do *what*?' Gardner was running out of patience.

'Objection!' Bieman yelled angrily.

'Overruled!' Cramer said firmly. 'Please answer the question, Miss Meyers.'

She fell silent, as if she knew the answer, but could not bring herself to utter the words.

'I'll answer it for her,' Gardner said. 'Play therapy sets the stage for remembering. That's what it's all about. Let the child relax, so that he can remember!'

'That's not a question!' Bieman yelled from the other counsel table.

'Isn't that right, Miss Meyers? You let them play to stimulate their memory?' Gardner continued.

Meyers looked down. 'Uh-huh,' she said under her breath.

'You'll have to speak up,' the judge said.

She raised her chin. 'Yes, that is correct.'

Gardner smiled and turned towards the rear of the courtroom. King and Jacobs were gone.

Jennifer paced nervously outside the Grand Jury room. It had been over an hour since they'd made the presentation, and the jurors still had not agreed on indictments. What was taking them so long? The usual procedure was a three-minute rubber-stamping of the State Attorney's proposed list of charges, but today, they were hung up. Brownie had been sent on his way. There was nothing more he could do there but wait, so she had released him. He was anxious to get back out to Prentice Academy.

She checked her watch. Another five minutes had passed, and the door was still locked. What on earth could they be doing? Suddenly she noticed two men approaching from the other end of the corridor. In an instant, their features clarified into King and Jacobs. They were laughing. She was trapped until the Grand Jury let her back into the room, and there was no place to hide.

'Waiting for a bus?' King said sarcastically. He knew their case was on the Grand Jury docket, and that any delay in returning the indictments spelled trouble for the State.

'Funny, King,' Jennifer said.

King tried to switch from sarcastic to sincere. 'Really, Jennifer, how long have they been out?'

'A while,' she replied. There was no reason to say exactly how long. And, in front of King, it was never wise to show concern.

'How long?' King persisted.

Jennifer folded her arms. 'Couple of minutes.'

King looked at Jacobs. 'Over an hour,' he said.

Jennifer winced internally. As usual, King knew everything.

'They must be having trouble in coming to a decision,' Jacobs said.

'It's a complex case,' Jennifer countered. 'Not unusual for them to consider it carefully.'

'They're hung up,' King said. 'That's obvious.'

Jennifer prayed that the door would open at that moment and the jury would come back with the full slate of charges, but it didn't.

'Your case or mine?' Jacobs asked King.

'Huh?' King had seemed to sense Jennifer's anticipation about the door opening, and he had turned in that direction.

'Do you think it's Mr Miller or Mr Starke who's giving them trouble?' Jacobs asked.

King glanced at Jennifer. 'What's your view?'

Jennifer levelled an unflinching stare at King. 'I'd say that my view is none of your business.'

King smiled again and motioned for Jacobs to leave. 'Guess we're not wanted here. Let us know if you hear anything by midnight.'

Jennifer stood silently while they left. The smugness was knee-deep, and she had an urge to run over and rake King's face with her nails. She looked at her watch again. Ten more minutes had passed, and the door was still sealed shut. Her eyes wandered down the long passage towards the domestic relations court. This was starting out to be a bad day. She only hoped that Gardner was faring better than she was.

Brownie parked his lab van in the gravel lot at Prentice Academy. The school year was officially over, and the campus was deserted. The green lawn in the quadrangle had been recently cut, and the hedges along the walkway trimmed. He closed the door to the truck and looked around. A soft breeze off the mountains shook the maple leaves overhead. He leaned on his vehicle and let his mind drift.

The Bowers–Roscoe Miller connection had given the crimes a twisted kind of logic. The killings were deliberate

240

and planned. But the underlying question remained unanswered. Who was behind it all? Miller? King? Starke? Starke's tie-in was puzzling. He, too, was connected to the Bowers in some bizarre way. But his tie-in was more mysterious, more illogical. He was a privileged kid with a billion bucks. Why would he want to hang around with Miller? The macho 'rebel with a tattoo' played OK on TV, but Starke had too much going for him to settle for 'wanna-be' status. And then there was the phone call: Henry, or Addie, calling him from the store.

Brownie's reverie was snapped when he detected motion and saw a figure scampering across the far end of the athletic field. He shouted, and raised his arm. The figure stopped, then ran over a crest and disappeared.

Brownie went from stop to full speed in three seconds. Something was wrong. Whoever it was did not want to talk, and that made him all the more curious. He raced across the grass, towards the hill and the woods beyond. The shadowy figure he'd called out to was not stopping. Like a spooked animal, he was running away, fleeing towards the underbrush.

'Stop!' Brownie yelled. 'County police!'

The man kept running, entering the overgrown thicket on the threshold of the woods without breaking stride, and then he was gone. Brownie took six more steps, and came to a halt. There was too much of a lead, and the vegetation was too thick. He'd never be able to catch up.

He unsnapped his radio and called the police station. 'Patch me to the sheriff's office,' he told the dispatcher. The call was transferred, and a deputy answered. 'Detainee surveillance,' Brownie said.

Again, there was a transfer. 'Deputy Smawley.'

'Pete, Joe Brown,' Brownie gasped into the mike. He was still breathing hard from the run. 'Give me the current locations on Miller and Starke.' From the size, shape and hair colour of the mystery man, it could be either one.

'Uh . . .' Smawley sounded frustrated.

'Hurry up!' Brownie growled. If he could get a read-out, maybe he could swing around the woods and intercept.

'Didn't you get the word?' Smawley asked.

241

'Word?' Brownie didn't like the sound of his voice.

'We lost them three days ago. Equipment failure.'

'What?' this was the first Brownie had heard.

'Sam Ellen reported it,' Smawley said.

'They never told me!' Brownie yelled. Two dangerous defendants loose without a leash, and the sheriff had never informed the prosecutors. Gardner was going to explode when he found out! 'So you're showing nothing on either of them?'

'Right. Thought you-all knew.'

Brownie stopped his slow drift towards the woods. By now Miller, or Starke, or whoever it was, had found an escape path out.

'Brownie?' Smawley was still connected to the radio patch-in.

'Yeah,' the officer said disgustedly.

'What' you want me to do?'

'Nuthing,' Brownie said coldly. 'You've done enough already.' Then he clicked the mike button and shut off the receiver.

He stood in the open field and put his hands on his hips, angry enough to throw a punch. But there was no one to hit. A few moments later, he walked slowly back towards the van, his mind still churning with anger. Suddenly his eye caught an open door on a shed at the east end of the field. If he retraced the path of the fleeing man, it would lead back to that area.

He ran over to the shed and looked in. It was a small, tin-roofed storage building, large enough to house two riding mowers, a stack of fertilizer bags, shovels, rakes and trimming implements. The lock on the door had been cut by a hacksaw. Brownie unsnapped his flashlight and probed the interior with the beam. The construction was crude: dirt floor, slatted wooden strips nailed across support posts, and open rafters. He scanned the floor for footprints, but the clay was dry and hard. There were some heel indentations, but none was defined enough for an identification. He then swept the walls with the light, but nothing seemed amiss.

Suddenly Brownie's beam caught a slat on the far wall that was not flush with the others: it stood out slightly. He rushed over and knelt down. There was a mark on the end of the slat. With his penknife he prised the slat loose, and shone his light into the hole. He could see a space between the inner and outer wall. Six or seven inches deep, it made an ideal hiding place. Angling off so he could shine his light down, he couldn't see the bottom. He grabbed the next slat down and pulled it off. Then he pulled off another slat. Then another. There was only a foot left above the floor.

Brownie pointed the light into the gap, but it was empty. He was about to pull away when he noticed something. As the beam shifted in his hands, a faint outline seemed to appear on the clay floor. There must have been some water seepage under the edge of the building, because the clay seemed softer, susceptible to impressions. He tore the slats all the way down to the floor and shone his light into the gap. 'Uh-huh! Uh-huh!' he exclaimed to himself.

The distinct outline of a handgun was neatly etched in the soil, defined enough to cast in plaster.

PART 6

Confrontation

CHAPTER 16

The custody hearing was still dragging on. Gardner had cross-examined the therapist as rigorously as he could, but she insisted that an outright interrogation of Granville was wrong, and that the boy might suffer emotional damage because of it. Gardner finally stopped questioning.

Carole then took the stand. With her dark hair piled on top of her head, she still looked quite alluring, despite the circumstances.

'Tell the court why you should have exclusive custody of Granville,' Bieman said.

She glanced at Gardner. 'Because his father doesn't know how to take care of him.' Gardner stirred in his seat. 'Granville is a special boy, very sensitive. He needs to be treated gently . . .'

Judge Cramer looked at the witness over his glasses. There was a sympathetic expression on his face.

'His father doesn't understand that. He pushes him. He's always pushing him.'

Gardner looked down at the desk, as a vision of a baseball field and a crying son flashed into his head. 'Get up!' he had yelled.

'Granville is a little boy. Just a little boy. He's not big. He's not strong. He's just a child . . .'

Gardner's heart began to throb as the words came out. He'd always felt the same way. He'd always believed that Granville was special, a big-eyed innocent, untainted and pure in spirit. But he couldn't be sheltered for ever; he had to be shown the realities. Thoughtfully, and gently, of course, but it had to be done. The world was real. The bullets were not imaginary. Some day, he'd have to learn that.

'He was hurt at the store,' Carole continued. 'His head was hit, and he was unconscious . . .' Tears began to roll down her cheeks. 'And, right away, his father comes in. The prosecutor. The almighty prosecutor! The boy is lying there knocked out, and *he* . . .' she pointed accusingly at Gardner . . . '*He* comes in! Not as a father! No! He has to make his own child a witness . . .' Carole was starting to lose it.

'Your honour!' Gardner stood up shakily. The words were hitting too close to home. 'This isn't proper testimony . . .'

The judge looked at Gardner sternly. 'Sit down, Mr Lawson, you'll have your turn to speak.'

'But she's giving her *opinion*!' Gardner spluttered, 'not fact . . .'

Cramer was unswayed. 'Opinion is what this case is all about, Mr Lawson. Opinion as to what's best for the child. Now sit down!'

Gardner slumped into his chair.

'Granville doesn't *want* to do this!' Carole continued. 'Judge, you heard the therapist. He doesn't remember! God! He doesn't *want* to remember! He cries at night. He curls up like a baby. He jumps at loud noises.'

'Mrs Lawson.' Attorney Bieman decided it was time to bring it back under control. 'Do you have a plan for the child in the event that the judge awards you exclusive custody in this case?'

Carole rubbed her cheek with the back of her hand, and took several deep breaths. 'Yes, I do. We plan to go away, to Switzerland.'

Gardner almost fell out of his chair. Europe? She was going to Europe? Jesus Christ, no! No way the judge could allow that!

'And why the drastic change of locale?' Bieman asked.

Carole's eyes clouded with tears again, 'Because we, uh, I mean, *he*'ll go crazy if he has to stay here. He's practically psychotic now.'

'Object!' Gardner shouted. 'She cannot give that kind of opinion, Judge. That's a medical conclusion.' He recoiled at his own words. It was his son they were talking about, 'Grand Bill', not some nondescript witness in some nondescript case. His emotions were running in one direction and his legal instincts in the other, and they were crashing in the centre.

'I'll accept it for what it's worth,' the judge said curtly, his eyes urging Gardner to sit down.

Gardner was boiling. 'I'm not going to ask you again, Mr Lawson,' Cramer warned. 'Sit down!'

Gardner remained standing. 'Please don't do this!' he said to Carole. There was a look of desperation in his eyes.

'Mr Lawson!' the judge boomed.

'Object!' Bieman followed up.

'Please, Carole!' Gardner had lost his dignity. He'd decided to skip protocol and go straight to the source. 'You don't know what you're doing!'

Carole stood up in the witness chair. 'No! *You* don't! You're going to kill him!' The word 'kill' reverberated in the empty courtroom like a scream.

'*Mrs* Lawson, uh, *Mr* Lawson!' The judge had lost control.

'Judge!' Bieman shouted.

'Carole, please!' Gardner yelled.

Everyone was standing except the judge, so he, too, rose and slammed his gavel so hard it almost snapped in two. 'Quiet, everyone!'

The parties fell silent but held their ground.

'I realize this is a *very* emotional issue,' Cramer said with forced composure, 'but we're not going to resolve *anything* if we act like this. Please!' He looked at Gardner and then at Carole. 'Please let's try to remain calm. I'm going to take a ten-minute recess so that you can get yourselves under control. When I come back, I expect civility to be restored.' He slammed his gavel again, and swept off the bench.

Gardner and Carole remained standing, glaring at each other through their tears.

Jennifer had almost worn a rut in the marble floor in front of the Grand Jury room. Over three hours now without a knock at the door; this had to be some kind of record. Grand Juries were supposed to be rubber stamps. Whatever the prosecutor asked for, he usually got. But, today, they had a mind of their own.

Finally, it happened. A barely audible knock-knock on the

massive oak door. Jennifer opened it and ran in. The place looked as though a bomb had hit it. The men were in shirt-sleeves, and there was the odour of perspiration in the air. Two women in the back row were red-faced and sullen.

The foreman looked as if he'd just lost a heavyweight bout. He handed Jennifer the indictment sheets with a frown. 'Sorry,' he said. He was a fiftyish businessman with lightly salted brown hair. 'I pushed as hard as I could.'

Jennifer tore through the documents. On the third page, six charges had been crossed out in ink. She glanced at the top of the page. It read: State *v.* Starke.

'There was a concern about the degree of proof necessary to charge him with the actual crimes,' the foreman said wearily. Then he jerked his chin in the direction of the trouble-making housewife.

Jennifer looked at the dragon lady. 'Participation at the scene in any degree, coupled with flight, is evidence of complicity,' she said. 'I told you that before I left the room.'

The woman shook her head. 'But you never told us exactly what Starke did! How could we decide?'

Jennifer went silent. Starke *was* involved in the crimes. Up to his neck. They all knew that. And every honey-coated word out of Joel Jacobs' mouth underscored his guilt. But they had no hard facts. And it was obvious that, until they did, Starke would get off easy. She put the indictments down on the desk, and went back to page one. They'd had no problem with Miller. Murder. Murder. Murder. Attempted murder. Robbery. Assault. Battery. Roscoe Miller had been charged with all proposed counts.

But back to page three, and it was a different story. On Starke, hardly anything had been left. No murder. No attempted murder. Not even assault or battery. The only charge they'd agreed on was the count of accessory before the fact, a misdemeanour that carried a maximum of five years in jail.

Jennifer thanked the jury and dismissed them. It only took a few minutes for the room to clear.

The foreman lingered outside the door, and came back in when the others had faded to murmurs down the hall. 'Ms Munday, I really *am* sorry,' he said. 'You don't know how hard I tried.'

Jennifer managed a wan smile. 'I'm sure you did.'

'We knew he was guilty of something,' the foreman continued, 'but without evidence, we couldn't in good conscience
endorse the charges. I hope you understand?'

'You did the best you could,' Jennifer replied.

'I hope you can get him . . .'

'Huh?' Jennifer's mind was trying to come up with a way
to break the news to Gardner.

'I hope you find some more evidence on that guy before you
go to trial.'

Jennifer nodded listlessly. 'Me, too,' she said. They'd got
the Miller indictments by painting his evidence in the most
favourable light, but it wasn't that good. Most of it was sure
to unravel in court. If Starke had been hit with the full list of
charges, there was still a chance he could be turned against
Miller, offered a lesser charge in return for his testimony.
But now that couldn't be. Starke's maximum exposure was
five years, and there was no way they could deal that down.
With Miller overcharged and Starke undercharged, their
dilemma continued. It was the worst of all possible
outcomes.

Gardner was seated at the counsel table when Judge Cramer
returned from the recess. Sullen and silent, he looked like an
English schoolboy who'd just been caned for misbehaviour.

Carole had stepped down from the witness stand and
joined her attorney. Her expression was as bitter as her ex-
husband's. The tears had dried, but the pain remained.

Cramer looked at Bieman. 'Any more testimony, counsel?'

The Baltimore lawyer whispered to his client, then stood
to address the court. 'No, your honour.' He had decided to
pull her off the stand before she went to pieces again and
destroyed her motherly image.

'Any other witnesses, then?' Cramer asked.

'No, your honour, but we would like to be heard in
argument.'

'Very well,' the judge said. 'After Mr Lawson presents his
case.' He turned to Gardner. 'Any witnesses, counsel?'

Gardner stood up, his face still red. 'Just me, your honour.'
He walked to the witness stand, and raised his hand. The
oath was given, and he sat down.

'What do you have to tell me?' Cramer asked.

Gardner leaned forward and placed his mouth near the black goose-neck microphone. 'This case isn't about custody. It's about survival.' He looked at Carole, and she avoided his eyes. 'I love my son, Judge,' he continued. 'Uh, maybe *love* is not a strong enough word for how I feel. He's my only child. The one thing that Carole and I did right . . .'

'Objection!' Bieman yelled. 'He's doing the same thing he accused my client of.'

'Noted, Mr Bieman,' Cramer replied. 'Overruled.'

'I'd never do anything to hurt him,' Gardner continued. 'Never!'

'So why are you pushing him so hard?' the judge asked.

'Objection!' Bieman was back on his feet.

The judge glared at Carole's lawyer. 'You have a problem with my question?'

'Not the question, Judge. The *questioning*.'

Cramer smiled. 'The man has no lawyer, so I'm going to fill in.'

'That's not fair, your honour!' Bieman was getting frustrated.

The judge's smile turned sardonic. 'Nothing's fair, Mr Bieman.' He turned back to Gardner. 'Why are you forcing the boy?'

'I'm not.'

'Miss Meyers and your wife, uh, I mean your ex-wife, say you are.' He was being patient with Gardner, almost parental.

Gardner looked into Cramer's eyes. 'He's got to deal with it some day . . .'

'No, he doesn't!' Carole yelled, jumping up from her chair.

'Mrs Lawson!' Cramer did not want to repeat the earlier scene. '*Please*! Please sit down and let me handle this!'

Carole sat down and grabbed her counsel roughly by the arm, whispering angrily in his ear.

'Please!' Cramer begged. 'Let's try to relax and get through this.' He looked at Gardner again. 'You *are* pushing him, aren't you, Mr Lawson?'

Gardner didn't respond. The answer was 'Yes, with an explanation', but no one seemed to care what the reason was.

If he pushed Granville to learn the truth, he was a bad father. And if he didn't, and that allowed two murderers to go free, that made him worse.

'Mr Lawson?' The judge was waiting for his answer.

'He's my witness, Judge,' Gardner said forcefully. 'My *only* witness. As State Attorney I'm entitled, no, *required* by law to ensure that a witness appears at trial and testifies. If anyone,' he glanced around the room, 'I mean *anyone* interferes with that process, it is a crime. Witness tampering. Or obstruction of justice . . .'

'Objection!' Bieman sensed that Gardner was about to score a hit.

'Overruled.' Cramer was listening intently.

'I am the boy's father, that is true,' Gardner continued, 'and, as his father, I do not want any harm to come to him. Physical. Psychological. *Any* kind of harm. But I'm also the elected Prosecutor of this jurisdiction. I can't shirk that responsibility just because it touches me and my family personally.'

'Your honour!' Bieman sounded almost hysterical. 'This is out of order!'

Cramer looked at the attorney calmly. 'As I said before, Mr Lawson is entitled to present his point of view.'

'But he's trying to hide behind his so-called prosecutorial privilege. He's already admitted to forcing the child against his will . . .'

A light seemed to flash behind Cramer's eyes. He turned to Gardner. 'What about that Mr Lawson? By what authority do you suggest that the Prosecutor's rights supersede parental responsibilities?'

Gardner had researched this point, and found the precedent. 'The common law says that the right of a State Attorney to proceed with a prosecution is unrestricted. Not even a writ of mandamus can interfere. If I wanted to, I could keep my witness locked up until trial and deny access to him by *anyone*.'

'This is outrageous!' Bieman was up again.

'But, Mr Lawson,' Judge Cramer interjected, 'do you really *want* to do that? Put your own child under that kind of pressure?'

Gardner glared at him. 'No! Of course I don't *want* to do it. I'd do anything not to have to. But I have no choice!'

The judge nodded and folded his hands. This was a tough one. The law the Prosecutor had cited was good law. A State Attorney *could* guard a witness like a mother hen, and no one could interfere. On the other hand, a father could not psychologically abuse his child. That was grounds for loss of custody. But what happened when the father and the prosecutor were one and the same? Which law took precedence?

'Anything further, Mr Lawson?' Cramer asked.

'No, your honour,' Gardner said sadly, then stood up and left the stand.

Judge Cramer took another short recess to consider his options. In a sense, he was in the same position as Gardner. A ruling in either direction was bound to hurt someone. The bottom line was, which would do the least damage, not which would do the most good.

When he returned, he'd made his decision. He mounted the stand with a bounding leap, and banged the gavel. 'I want to hear from the boy.'

Gardner and Carole stared at each other in shock. This was unexpected.

'Is it really necessary?' Carole queried.

'Afraid so,' Cramer answered, 'if you want a ruling on your petition.' Carole went pale, and nodded listlessly. He turned to Gardner. 'Can you bring him down?'

'If you order me to,' Gardner was not happy about this either.

'I do,' Cramer replied. 'Please bring him in now, and do not discuss the case with him on the way. That's an order, too.'

The prosecutor excused himself, and left the courtroom. He ran back to the State Attorney's office and retrieved his son, leading him quickly along by the hand.

'What's goin' on, Dad?' Granville puffed, trying to keep up.

'Judge wants to talk to you,' Gardner replied as they reached the courtroom door.

'Why?'

'He'll tell you,' Gardner said as they went in. 'Just be good and answer his questions.'

254

Granville saw his mother, smiled, and waved. She smiled tearfully, and waved back. Gardner guided him up to the witness stand, and lifted his right hand for the oath.

'That's OK,' Judge Cramer said gently. 'We'll do this informally. I don't need him under oath.'

Gardner released his son's arm and stepped off the stand.

'You can sit down,' Cramer said. His voice was grandfatherly, soothing.

Granville sat in the leather chair and all but disappeared behind the witness-box rail. His blond head was the only thing showing above the carved wood.

'There's nothing to be scared about,' Cramer said. 'I just want to ask you some questions, that's all.'

Granville fidgeted nervously in the large seat. He had no idea what was going on. He only knew that his mom and dad were having an argument, but he really didn't understand why.

'How are you today?' Cramer asked.

'OK,' Granville said, his voice hardly a whisper.

'If you talk into that gizmo there, I can hear you better,' Cramer said, pointing to the microphone.

Granville moved forward and put his mouth against the muzzle. 'OK,' he repeated. This time the words echoed in the speakers overhead.

'I understand you've been staying with your dad the last few days,' the judge continued.

'Uh-huh.'

'Everything been OK?' Cramer was leaning over the side of the bench, practically into the witness box itself.

Granville glanced over at Gardner, as if he wasn't sure what to say, 'Uh-huh,' he finally answered.

'And before that, you were staying with your mom. Right?'

'Uh-huh.' Granville was getting into the rhythm.

'Now, I guess you know that your mom would like you to come back and stay with her.'

'Uh-huh.'

'What do you think about that?'

Granville stretched up so he could see Carole, then he moved his mouth back to the mike. 'OK.'

'You would like to do that?' The judge was leading

somewhere, but no one in the courtroom knew where.

'If you say I have to,' Granville answered.

'But do you want to? Do you want to go back and stay with your mom?'

'Uh-huh . . .' Granville said. 'After . . .' He fell silent.

'After what?' Cramer was trying to draw him out as gently as he could.

'After I help Dad.'

Judge Cramer looked over at the counsel tables. Both Gardner and Carole were as immobile as sculptures. There was no pain or triumph on either face, only emotional shell-shock.

'Do you know what Dad wants you to do?' Cramer continued.

'Uh-huh.'

'And what is that? What does Dad want you to do?'

'Remember.' Granville said, his voice dropping to a barely audible range despite the boost of the speakers.

'And do you know what he wants you to remember?'

Granville bit his lip, and for a second it looked like he was going to cry. 'Sumpthin' bad.'

Carole was beginning to stir. Cramer knew he'd have to wrap it up soon. 'OK,' he said. 'I just have one last question. You know that your dad wants you to remember something. How do *you* feel about that? Do you *want* to try to remember?'

Granville's lip started to tremble, and tears were approaching rapidly, 'Don't know,' he whispered, his lip twitching.

'OK. OK,' Cramer said, reaching down and patting the boy on the shoulder. 'You did just fine. I don't have any more questions. You can go back with your dad now.'

Granville stood up, and ran over to Gardner. They embraced. Carole put her head down and sobbed quietly as Gardner took Granville out of the room.

When he returned a few moments later, the look on Judge Cramer's face signified he'd made a final decision. 'First, let me say that this is one of the toughest cases that's ever come before me,' Cramer began. 'There's no clear-cut right or wrong here. No illicit or improper motivations.' He looked at Carole, then at Gardner. 'On *either* side. Both parents obviously care for this child. And both parents obviously

256

want him to be safe and secure. The problem I'm having is how to accomplish what *both* parents want to provide, seeing as how they have conflicting viewpoints . . .'

Gardner pushed his hands against the table. Cramer certainly wasn't telegraphing which way he was going to rule.

'The prosecutorial prerogative is, as Mr Lawson points out, practically absolute. He has the power, I believe, to do what he's doing. The State *has* an unfettered right to a witness. I have decided therefore . . .' Gardner held his breath . . . 'To temporarily grant custody to the father, pending further psychological evidence that the child will be irreparably harmed by participation as a witness in the criminal trial.' Carole gasped aloud. 'In the meantime, I will order supervised visitation by the mother on a schedule convenient to both parties, and I will further order that the underlying custody *will* revert to the mother at the conclusion of the criminal trial, in any event. So ordered!'

Cramer slammed his gavel, and beat a hasty retreat off the bench.

Brownie had rushed back to the van to pick up some plaster, then he poured the casting material into the gap he'd torn in the shed wall. Viscous and white, it congealed like pudding on the clay floor. Ten minutes' drying time should do the trick.

'What the hell are you doin'?' a gruff voice behind him suddenly screeched. The officer turned round. 'I said, what are you doin?' An old man in overalls pushed the door wide to let in the afternoon light.

'County police,' Brownie said. 'Afraid somebody's been usin' your shed to hide a gun.' He'd already pegged the old man as a custodian.

'Say what?' The man squinted in the semi-darkness and moved closer.

'Someone stuck a handgun down in the wall here,' Brownie answered. 'Take a look.' He shone the light on the hardening white mass. 'You see anyone around here today?'

The custodian shuffled his feet into the edge of the beam. 'No, sir. Just you. That's why I come down here. Saw you runnin' across the field.'

'But you didn't see anyone else?'

'No, sir.'

Brownie stood up and extended his hand. 'Joe Brown. Sergeant.'

The man took it. 'Clarence Conley. Guard.'

'Nice meetin' you, Mr Conley,' Brownie said. 'Where were you earlier?'

'In my trailer behind the main buildin'. That's where I stay most of the time. It's usually quiet round here in summer. No need to patrol . . .' He looked into the hole, then back at Brownie. 'What's this about? That Bowers, uh, Bowers . . .'

'Yeah,' Brownie cut in, 'The Bowers case.'

'My, my,' Conley said. 'Henry Bowers.'

Brownie picked up on a personal note. 'You knew the man?'

Conley looked at Brownie apologetically, 'I knew him, sort of, when he used to come down here.'

'When was this?' Henry visiting the school might mean something.

Conley scratched his head. 'Long time ago. Twenty, twenty-five years. Maybe more than that.'

'You been here that long?'

The old man smiled, displaying a row of false teeth, 'Forty-two years. Seen more than six head men come and go.'

'Headmasters?'

'Uh-huh. Lot of changes out here since then . . .'

'OK,' Brownie said impatiently. 'Can we go back to Henry? Tell me about him coming to the school. Do you know why?'

'Liked to watch the football games. That's what I remember. Came to every game for a couple'a years. Every game.'

Brownie had pulled out his pad, and began taking notes. 'Do you recall a date? A year?'

Conley scratched his head again. 'Uh, let's see. It was headmaster Wilkins here then . . . No, it was Slater. That's right. Slater. He came in fifty-three and left in sixty-four. Had to be durin' that time.'

Brownie noted 'mid-50s to mid-60s on his pad. 'Do you remember how often he came out to watch the games during that period?'

Conley went back to his head for a third time. By now his thinning hair was thoroughly rumpled. 'Every game for several years.'

'How many years?'

'It was more than one, I remember that. More than two, even. I'd say three, maybe four years.'

Brownie noted '3 to 4'. 'And what happened after that?'

'Nothin',' Conley said. 'He just stopped comin'. Far as I remember, he never came back.'

Brownie wrote 'ceased visits' on the pad. 'Tell me, Mr Conley, how is it that you remember this man so well?'

Conley smiled. 'It was the money.'

'Money?' Brownie asked cautiously.

'I wuz workin' in the grounds crew back then. On game days they had us parkin' cars and handin' out programmes. The first time I ever seen Henry Bowers, he got a game programme from me. They wuz free . . .' The old man's eyes drooped for a second as his mind searched out the image.

'Yeah?' Brownie could sense a major breakthrough just ahead. 'Got a programme . . .'

'Programme for the game. Names of the players. All that stuff . . .'

Brownie was getting restless. 'Uh-huh . . .'

'Give me a twenty-dollar bill. New twenty-dollar bill. They wuz free, I told him, didn't have to pay nuthin'. But he just smiled. Told me to keep it . . .' The eyes drooped again. 'And then, the next week, the next time they had a game, he done the same thing. Always got a programme from me. Always give me a twenty-dollar bill. Every time . . .' Brownie was writing furiously. 'That's how come I remember Henry Bowers, Sarge. How could I forget? Over them years the man done give me over five hundred dollars.'

CHAPTER 17

Jennifer met Gardner in the courthouse corridor. She was leaving her disaster, and he was crawling away from his. They could see the results of their respective proceedings in each other's eyes.

'Tell me something good,' Gardner said wearily, glancing at the sheaf of signed indictments in his assistant's hand.

Jennifer put her arm round him as they walked. 'What happened with the custody?' She was in no hurry to tell him about Starke.

'Granville stays with me,' Gardner answered softly. 'What charges did we get?'

Jennifer was still gripping the indictments like a steel clamp. 'Everything on Miller,' she said. 'Three first degree murder and all lesser includeds.'

When she didn't continue, Gardner turned suddenly. 'What about Starke?'

She handed him the documents. 'Accessory before the fact . . .' Gardner grabbed the papers and tore through to Starke's indictments. 'They didn't think they had enough evidence,' Jennifer said sadly.

Gardner stared at the crossed-out page in disbelief. 'What happened? Didn't you give them the accomplice rule?'

'I did, but they didn't buy it. I gave them everything, the way you wanted. All of the facts. None of the contradictions.'

'So what do you think happened?'

'A know-it-all bitch,' Jennifer answered. 'Hung it up for three hours.'

Gardner shook his head. 'They just don't get it. You explain the law, and they just don't get it.' Jennifer kept silent. 'I know you did your best, Jen,' he said gently.

'I did. I'm just sorry the way it came out.'

Gardner's expression turned more serious. 'We can't worry about that now. We have work to do . . .'

'With Granville?'

Gardner nodded. The biggest challenge was yet to come.

Granville was sitting in Gardner's big leather chair in the inner fortress. Several puzzle books lay on the desk, and an electronic game-boy was in his hands.

'Dad!' His eyes widened when he saw Gardner. The courtroom scene had confused him. He had told the judge how he felt, and the judge had said OK and sent him back to Dad's room. Now he wanted to know what was going to happen next.

Gardner walked over and patted his son's head. 'I was very proud of you in the courtroom. *Very, very* proud.'

Granville looked up. His father loomed over him like a mountain. 'Am I going to see Mom?' he asked.

Gardner squatted down to eye-level. 'Yes, you're going to see Mom.'

'Am I going back to stay with her?' His expression was expectant.

'No. Not quite yet.'

'So am I going to stay with you?'

'Yes. For a while.'

Granville's eyes closed briefly. 'Are you going to talk to me about it?' Gardner felt a tightness in his stomach. He was free to interrogate his witness, to try to unlock the memory. 'Are you . . . Dad?' Granville was still waiting for his answer.

Gardner looked him in the eye. 'I don't know, Gran. It really depends on you.'

The boy was confused. 'Huh?'

Gardner touched Granville's shoulder and gently squeezed. 'If you can be strong. Real, real, strong.'

Granville put his arms round his father's neck. 'I can do it, Dad.'

Gardner lowered his head and prayed that he was doing the right thing.

Brownie was excited. He had lifted the plaster cast from the hole in the shed and found a neat, finely-etched impression of a handgun underneath, complete in its dimensions. Unlike the partial fingerprint, the entire outline of the weapon was defined. But there was a problem. As he studied it in the dim light of the shed, he noticed something peculiar. It was not a standard-issue firearm. Clearly not nine-millimetre. Not thirty-eight calibre. Not even forty-five calibre. It was huge. An oversized pistol with a barrel that could carry a massive slug. Brownie had never seen anything like it.

He raced to the van, and gently laid the cast in a cardboard box. Then, as he was about to leave, an idea suddenly popped into his mind. After locking the van, he ran to Clarence Conley's trailer. He could see the old man through the window, feet propped on a table, watching television. After two knocks, Conley came to the door.

'Thought you was leavin',' the caretaker said.

'I was about to, but I need to ask a favour.'

Conley nodded agreeably. 'OK.'

'Can you let me into the school library?'

There was a hesitant blink before Conley said, 'Sure.' Then he grabbed a massive set of keys, slipped on his shoes and led Brownie to the deserted administration building.

Inside, there was a short walk down the unlit passage, and then they were in a large book-filled room. Brownie scanned the shelves for yearbooks. He found them, and began pulling volumes out. 'Just letting you know,' Brownie said to Conley. 'I'm borrowing these, and I'm gonna bring them back.' He handed the old man five books and took ten for himself.

They walked out of the building and back to the van. 'I'm going to need to speak to you again later—' Brownie said as he took the books from Conley and put them into a box beside the plaster cast— 'about Henry Bowers and the money he was giving away.'

Conley wasn't listening. He'd spotted the outline of the handgun, and was riveted by it.

Brownie noticed his interest, so he lifted the box. 'Ever see anything like that before?'

Conley scoured the impression with his watery eyes. 'No, sir. Cain't say as I have.'

263

'How 'bout anyone with *any* kind of handgun or pistol? Ever see *anyone* on campus with one of those?'

Conley reared back and looked at Brownie. 'That boy Hiller had one, I think.'

Brownie's heart leaped. Hiller was Miller. 'You think? Did you *see* it?' Putting a gun in Miller's hand at this point would just about do it.

'Naw,' Conley said with disgust, '*I* didn't. Heard some of the crew talkin'. They said he was packin' a gun.'

'Who said it?' Brownie asked.

Conley closed his eyes, then opened them abruptly. 'Don' remember.'

Brownie switched tracks. 'How many crew members you got?'

'Ten. Fifteen. Depends on time of year. Right now, only got three.'

'Do you have any idea who talked about Hiller havin' a gun?'

Conley's memory was selective. A twenty-dollar bill three decades ago stood out, but a gun yesterday did not. The old man was trying, but it just was not there. 'Sorry,' he finally said. 'Cain't bring it to mind.'

'That's OK, Mr Conley, I can take it from here. Just do me a favour and write me out the names of all the crew members.' It would take time, but maybe Brownie could track down the witness himself. Conley's face flushed, and he looked away. 'What's the problem?' Brownie asked.

'Cain't do it,' the caretaker said. 'Cain't read. Cain't write.'

Brownie sighed. Each step forward laid the groundwork for three steps back. He didn't have time to fool with this now. He had to get back to the lab, and work on a trace of the gun. That was a lot more practical than chasing a possible hearsay witness. 'Don't worry about it, Mr Conley,' he finally said. 'I'll get the names later.'

He then closed the door to the van, started the engine, and headed down the road, trying to figure out just when 'later' was going to be.

Brownie placed the plaster cast under the optical scanner as soon as he returned to headquarters. Immediately, its

264

computer image was recorded and sent on an electronic journey to the FBI and ATF labs in Washington D.C., where it would be run against thousands of weapon profiles until it found a match.

As he waited for the computers to compare notes, he went over to the table where he'd stacked the yearbooks, one volume for each year between 1955 and 1970. He opened the 1955 and thumbed through it. Henry had come to see football games. Regularly, Conley had said. Never missed a game. And he was upbeat, in a good mood, happily dispensing cash. But the question was: who did he come to watch?

The first volume was no help. Nothing in the football category stood out. The same with 1956, 1957, 1958 and 1959. But, in 1960, a familiar name appeared. Then again in 1961, 1962 and 1963. A player on the varsity football team. A running back with a phenomenal record of touchdowns. Team captain starting in his sophomore year. A gifted player and revered leader. The person Henry Bowers must have come to see. The only one in the books that made any sense. A superstar from a wealthy family in New York State: WELLINGTON STARKE THE THIRD.

It was 9 p.m., and Gardner was getting ready for bed. He was totally wrung out. Despite the fact he'd 'won' the custody battle, he felt no elation.

Granville was already bedded down in his room. He had accepted the news about the court ruling stoically, and vowed to help his dad. But there was still fear in his eyes. He, too, was exhausted by the day's events, and he had fallen asleep immediately.

Jennifer had gone back to the office to untangle the indictment problem. The arraignments were the next morning, and they had to prepare, so she had volunteered.

Gardner had just turned off the light when the phone rang. 'Hello?'

'I hope you're happy!' a voice said sarcastically. It was Carole.

Jeez! Gardner thought. Not again. 'What do *you* want?'

'Visitation. Like the judge ordered.'

Gardner sat up. 'We'll make the arrangements tomorrow.

Get your lawyer to call my office, and we'll set up a schedule.' Carole went silent. 'Is that OK?' Gardner asked. 'Tomorrow we'll hammer it all out. You can see him as much as you want.' Carole did not answer. 'Please let's come to an understanding?' Gardner said. 'Gran needs to feel that we're *both* behind him. Our fight is hurting him more than the case.' Carole seemed to be listening. 'Let's try to get along until this thing is over. For Gran's sake, how about a truce?'

Carole hesitated. 'I don't know if I can . . .'

'Fake it, then.'

'I'll . . . I'll try,' Carole said hesitantly.

'Good. The less dissension the better.'

'But when it's over . . .' Her voice turned cold.

'Shoot me if you want,' Gardner interjected, 'but for now let's keep it civil.'

'You can count on it,' Carole replied.

'OK. It's a deal. No more arguing.'

'Agreed.'

The players were all in court. Gardner and Jennifer on one side, and the four horsemen across the room: Kent King, Joel Jacobs, Roscoe Miller and Wellington Starke the fourth. Each one seemingly confident, ready for battle.

The arraignments in State *v.* Miller and Starke were to be heard this morning, one day after the indictments had come down. The cases had been expedited, and Judge Carla Hanks was ready to roll.

'All rise!' The bailiff announced the entry of her honour.

'Good morning, counsel,' Judge Hanks announced. 'We have arraignments and scheduling matters to attend to today. Mr King, Mr Jacobs, have your clients received copies of the indictments?'

Before either attorney could answer, Gardner stood up. 'Excuse me, your honour . . .' He was dressed in a charcoal suit and a burgundy tie. Despite his exhaustion, he still cut a sharp figure.

'What is it, Mr Lawson?' Hanks asked in an irritated voice.

'Before you proceed with the arraignments, there's a matter that needs to be addressed.' Hanks nodded a 'go ahead' signal. 'The tracking devices on both defendants have

266

failed, and they have been virtually unsupervised for the past week. I request that you permit an immediate inspection of the devices by the sheriff to determine if any tampering has taken place.'

King and Jacobs both bounded to their feet. 'Objection!'

Hanks glared at Gardner. 'This is an arraignment, Mr Lawson! We can't do that now.'

'The armbands have gone off the air,' Gardner argued.

'You ordered the defendants to wear them, Judge,' King said arrogantly. 'You did not specify that they had to function properly.'

'That's ridiculous!' Gardner cut in. 'There's no point in using them if they don't work.'

'My point exactly,' King retorted. 'If the monitors are defective, they shouldn't be used at all!'

'All right, gentlemen!' Hanks interrupted. 'This is not the time or place for tinkering with those — those things. You'll have to arrange for that to be done later, Mr Lawson.'

Gardner's face began to burn. 'You don't understand, Judge. I need your authority to unhook the monitors and check them out . . .' She fired a nasty look at him. 'No, sir, *you* don't understand. We're not turning this courtroom into a radio shack. Let the sheriffs do it later.'

King and Jacobs both waived the formal reading of the charges against their clients. They each had copies of the indictments. How did the defendants plead, the judge asked. Guilty or not guilty?

'Not guilty,' King said on behalf of Roscoe Miller.

'Not guilty,' Jacobs echoed on behalf of IV Starke.

'How do you elect to be tried?' Judge Hanks asked.

'Trial by jury,' King said.

'Jury trial,' Jacobs said.

'Are the cases to be consolidated or tried separately?' Hanks asked.

Gardner stood up. 'Your honour, we move to consolidate the cases. They involve the same set of incidents, the same witnesses, the same legal theories . . .'

Jacobs rose to his feet. 'Excuse me, Judge, I'm not seeking a separate trial.' He glanced at King, who gave him a signal. 'And neither is Mr King.'

Hanks turned to Gardner. 'You heard him. They don't want separate trials.'

Gardner was surprised. An ideal defence strategy would be to split the cases and wear out the prosecution.

'All right,' Hanks said. 'The cases will be tried jointly. Now that that's out of the way, let's move on. I have here a defence motion for the witness Granville Lawson to be examined by a psychiatrist. I am inclined to grant the motion.'

Gardner said nothing. He was already under orders by the domestic court to have Granville evaluated. It was going to come to pass one way or another, so why fight it?

'I have determined that Dr Glenmore Grady should carry out the examination and I have scheduled an appointment for the child tomorrow afternoon at 3. Any problem with that Mr Lawson?'

Gardner rose to his feet. 'No, Judge.' Dr Grady was a local psychiatrist who specialized in child trauma. He'd appeared against the State a few times as a defence witness in abuse cases, but he wasn't a paid lackey. He would be as fair as any.

'Good,' Hanks said, writing on her pad. 'That's settled. Now, motions and trial date . . .'

Gardner propped his arm under his chin. Give me some time, he prayed.

'Motions set for Wednesday, July 6 . . .' OK, Gardner thought. 'And trial to follow immediately, July 7.'

Gardner jumped up. That was only two weeks away. Here was a complicated, consolidated murder trial, without evidence, without a witness, without preparation. It couldn't be done. 'We need more time, Judge. At least ninety days.' He tried to keep his voice steady.

'I'm under a *mandate* to move these cases without delay,' Hanks replied, 'and the trial date is *the* trial date. Is that clear?'

Gardner was fighting a battle within. There was no way he could be ready on time. Granville wasn't ready. Brownie wasn't ready. He wasn't ready. They needed more time. And that was precisely why they were not going to get it.

'Trial date is set, and we stand adjourned!' Hanks barked, slamming the gavel without giving Gardner a chance to respond.

Gardner looked at Jennifer after the judge left the bench, his face a deep red.

'Take it easy,' she whispered.

'I *am*,' Gardner said in a forced voice. 'But we're being railroaded. The word's come down not to cut us a break.'

'That's why the rush,' Jennifer said.

'They *know* we can't be ready.'

'So maybe we surprise them?' Jennifer smiled bravely.

'Yeah. We do three months' work in the next two weeks.'

There was noise in the rear of the courtroom, as King, Jacobs and their clients walked out, gloating as if they'd just kicked the State's ass.

The arraignment had concluded by 11 o'clock, and there was nothing further on the docket for the day. Gardner had hung round the State Attorney's office until 11.30, then grabbed Granville and headed out. The trial would begin in fourteen days. Ready or not, the State was going to trial, and Granville was still the key. He had what they needed inside his head, and Gardner could not wait a second longer to try to get it out.

They drove out along Mountain Road, towards the ridge line. The air was warm, yet dry. A cool front had rolled in and deposited a dome of high pressure over their heads that gave the entire valley the shimmering clarity of October.

'Where we goin', Dad?' Gardner had snatched him by the hand without fanfare and rushed him to the car. There was no discussion of purpose or destination.

'Going for a drive. It's such a beautiful day. Too nice to sit up in the office.' He tried to sound upbeat and happy. There was a plan, but he didn't want to spring it on Granville too soon. It had to be done gradually. 'How are you comin' along with that Ray-Man?' The boy had brought along his electronic alien zapper, which he fiddled with as they drove.

'OK,' Granville replied as a 'bing!' and a 'zyzz!' erupted from the small grey box.

'Those things are really cool,' Gardner said. 'Wish we'd had something like that when *I* was little.'

Granville was still engrossed in the liquid crystal figures zigging and zagging across the tiny screen. 'What did you

269

have, Dad?' he asked without looking up.

Gardner had to think about that. He was so engrossed in his adult problems that his thoughts hardly ever drifted back to his own childhood. There seemed to be a wall deep in his brain that blocked any attempt to retreat to his youth. 'Little dinosaurs,' he finally said with a smile.

Granville looked up from his game. 'You had your finger bitten by your stegasaurus.'

'Thanks for remembering,' Gardner answered. His strategy was working.

The sign ahead read 'CRYSTAL GROTTO – 15 MILES'. Gardner stole a glance at his son, but the boy's eyes were back with the aliens. He slowed for the turn and guided the vehicle off the main highway. His heart began to pick up tempo as the miles unrolled. Pastures and woodlands flew past as they neared the spot where the tragedy had begun. He glanced at Granville again. The aliens were still jumping. The boy still didn't know what was happening. Suddenly there was another sign: 'CRYSTAL GROTTO – NEXT RIGHT'.

The car slowed again and, this time, Granville looked up. He saw the sign, and looked at the surrounding scenery. 'Dad . . .' His eyes widened with surprise.

'Take it easy, son,' Gardner said calmly. 'You're all right. I'm here.'

Granville put down the game and looked out of the window. He was studying the landscape nervously.

Gardner put his hand on Granville's knee. 'It's OK, Gran. Nothing's going to happen. You just stick with Dad.'

Granville was starting to squirm against the seatbelt. Why had his father brought him to this place?

Gardner pulled into the parking area and shut off the engine. 'Listen to me, Gran.'

The boy was still looking out of the window. He was now subdued, his legs pulled under him on the seat.

'I want to take you inside. We'll go and take a look, and then we'll come out. OK?'

Granville turned to face his father, the smile from the dinosaur joke long gone. He was very pale. 'Do we have to?' He could sense that if he got out of the car, he'd have to start remembering. And that was something he really did not *want* to do.

Gardner rubbed his flaxen hair. 'We have to start some-where, son. You came here on the day you got hurt . . . You and your classmates. You all came up here and had a fine time. It was only later that the bad things happened. Nothing happened up here.' There was a slight relaxation in the boy's face. 'Shall we get out and walk around, and if you can remember anything, maybe you can tell me. What do you say? Can we try that?'

Granville nodded weakly. He didn't want to get out of the car, but he did want to try to help his dad.

Gardner unbuckled Granville's seatbelt and opened his door. 'Let's go.'

As soon as they were out of the car, Granville gripped Gardner's hand like a two-year-old. They paid the entrance fee at the gate and headed for the opening to the cave which was set in rippling rock against the bottom of a five-hundred-foot cliff. As they reached the entrance, Granville began to drag his feet, so Gardner stopped. 'We're just going to pop inside, then come out.'

Granville looked like a toddler about to be forced into a funfair. The therapist had said he'd probably blocked out the entire day of the shootings. That covered anything that happened before, as well as after the savagery, including the cave. But, Gardner thought, maybe if he recalled something here, it might crack the door a little. With time running out, he had to give it a try. 'Ready?' he said, giving Granville's hand a squeeze.

Granville gave a nod. Then he closed his eyes and accompanied his father into the shadows.

Carla Hanks sat at the desk in her chambers, reviewing the case file on a civil matter that was overdue for a ruling. She was under pressure to finish her other work in a hurry, to make ready for Miller and Starke. She had given her secretary orders that she was not to be disturbed, but her phone rang.

'Yes?' She was irritated at the interruption.

'Chief Judge Biddington on line one,' her secretary said.

Hanks put down the file. 'Thank you,' she said. 'I'll take it.'

'Judge Biddington, this is an honour.' It was rare for the number one judge in the State to contact a circuit court member, especially one as low in the ranks as she.

'Judge Hanks, the pleasure is mine. I've heard a lot of good things about you.'

'I appreciate that, sir.'

'Well, uh, good.' His voice sounded strange.

Hanks waited for him to continue, but there was an embarrassing pause. 'Sir?'

'Uh, yes, Judge Hanks,' Biddington said. 'Just called to check in with you. Everything OK?'

'Yes, sir.'

'Anything you need? Anything at all? Extra law clerk? Secretarial help? Anything like that?'

'No, sir.' She was overworked, but not to that extent.

'Well, if you need something, just let me know.'

Hanks drew a breath. 'Yes, sir. I'll do that.'

'OK, then. Nice talking to you.'

'Nice talking to you, too, sir.'

'OK, then. Good-bye.'

'Bye, sir.'

Hanks hung up and leaned back in her chair. That had to be one of the weirdest phone calls of her life. The senior judge in Maryland was suddenly interested in her welfare. But he didn't say why.

Jennifer walked up to the door of the county police laboratory and knocked. She had seen Gardner and Granville zoom out earlier, but she had no idea where they were going. After the set-backs of the last few days, she needed a dose of optimism. And the place for that was Dr Brownie's lab.

'Come in!' Brownie called.

Jennifer opened the door and found him hunched over the lab table. As she entered, he didn't turn round. 'It's me,' she said from behind.

'Hi, Jennifer.' He was still engrossed in his work.

Jennifer looked over his shoulder. Brownie was peering through a giant magnifier at a plaster cast. 'What have you found?' she whispered.

Brownie eventually looked up. 'Got an ID on the gun. ATF had it in their archives . . .' He picked up a computer print-out and handed it to her.

Jennifer examined the strange-looking gun depicted on the page. 'What is it?'

'Prototype for a new sidearm the USA was developing in World War Two,' Brownie said. 'Bigger than a forty-five, with a whole lot of knock-down power . . .'

'Can you trace it?'

Brownie shook his head. 'That's a problem. These things were scattered to the winds after the war. It was too heavy for combat use, so the government abandoned the project. Only a couple of hundred were made, and they all became souvenirs or collectors' items. Pretty hard to trace.'

'So where would Miller have got it?' Jennifer asked.

'He could have stolen it, or picked it up off a gun-runner workin' the interstate. Only one thing's for certain: this gun fires massive slugs. And that's what killed the Bowers.'

'But who fired it?' Jennifer picked up the print-out again.

'I'm workin' on that,' Brownie said. 'And if I can run down where it came from, we'll have the answer.'

Gardner and Granville followed the curving path through the damp cavern hand-in-hand. There was a hollow resounding sound as their feet crunched on the gravel floor, and an occasional melodic 'ping' as drips of water fell in the darkness.

Gardner had forgotten how beautiful this place was. An underground river had cut away the limestone under the earth and left a maze of honey-glazed rock. Suddenly his own memories began to creep back. He'd been a lot like Granville as a child. Sensitive. Insecure. Lonely at times. He'd got along with his father, but there was a distance between them. It was the old style of raising children: kids were to be seen but not heard. Gardner felt a pang of sadness. When he had visited the cave long ago, his father hadn't held his hand.

'Look, Gran!' They had just entered the main chamber – a high-ceilinged room filled with glistening stalagmites and stalactites. It was spectacular, and the owners had back-lit the stone with dramatic effect, like a grand cathedral.

'Gran!' Gardner repeated.

The boy had kept his eyes shut most of the time, gripping

his dad's hand with a strength that surprised him. But he kept moving and didn't whimper. Now, finally, he opened his eyes.

'Beautiful, isn't it?' Gardner said, waving his finger around like a pointer.

Granville kept his eyes open. 'Uh-huh.' The hand still gripped tightly.

'Took millions of years to form. Did you know that?'

Granville was still studying the dazzling display. 'Uh-huh.'

'They told you about that?' Gardner held his breath as he broached the subject of the school visit.

The boy began to respond, but suddenly shook his head and shut his eyes. The grip on Gardner's hand was tighter than ever.

They started moving again, on the path that wound through another twisting corridor, and then back to the entrance. Almost there, now. Just a few more turns, and they'd be back in the sunlight. Granville was still silent. As they neared the final curve, Granville suddenly pulled Gardner to a stop. 'Dad!' he said urgently.

Gardner looked at his son. Something was going on. 'What is it, Gran?'

The boy's eyes were wide now, and they seemed to look past Gardner into the shadows of the path ahead. Gardner turned round, but could see nothing. 'What is it, son?' he repeated.

Granville pulled free of his father's grip and put his hands together in front of him as if he were praying. Gardner grabbed his hand, and they raced round the corner. Fifty steps down the trail they turned the bend and arrived beside a lit-up rock alcove. There was a sign spiked in the stone: THE ANGEL OF CRYSTAL GROTTO.

'She's beautiful,' Gardner told his son.

'Uh-huh,' said Granville.

And the two of them marvelled at the rock formation that a million years had moulded into being: a glossy ten-foot stalagmite in the exact shape of a praying angel.

CHAPTER 18

Dr Glenmore Grady's rooms were in the centre of town, near the courthouse. He had been at that location for over thirty years, and he wasn't about to move out to Veil Valley.

Granville sat in the elderly psychiatrist's consultation room in a soft leather chair. Dr Grady was beside him, on the couch. He wore a plaid shirt and cotton pants. Gardner was out in the waiting area. The court order forbade him from observing.

'Heard you got a knock on the head?' Grady said, looking at a folder containing the boy's medical files. 'How're you feeling now?'

'OK,' Granville said tentatively. Dad had told him to co-operate, that Dr Grady was a pretty good old guy.

'Still having headaches?' Granville stirred, but didn't answer. 'It's all right, son,' Grady said. 'You can talk to me. I talk to young fellas like you all the time. Haven't eaten one yet . . .' Granville relaxed slightly. 'Have you been getting any more headaches?' The medical reports said there was no organic brain damage.

'No,' Granville said.

'That's good.' Grady made a note on his pad. 'How about nightmares? Your mom said you'd had some bad dreams.' Granville shrugged his shoulders. 'Have you had any bad dreams?' Granville shrugged again.

Grady got up and opened the drawer of the cabinet against the wall. 'Want a piece of candy?'

'OK,' Granville said. He was always ready for sweets.

Grady brought a handful of lollipops and presented them to the boy. Granville surveyed the selection, then grabbed a lemon pop, and pulled off the paper. 'Go ahead,' Grady said, pulling the paper off a red one of his own. Granville put it in his mouth.

Grady sat down and picked up his notepad. 'Mmmmm!' he said through his teeth. 'Tastes good!'

Granville nodded, his face relaxed.

Grady made another note on his pad, watching his patient as he wrote. The lollipops were a special order, brought in that morning just for Granville.

The prosecution team was assembled at the State Attorney's office, reviewing the case. Earlier, Gardner had spent two hours at the psychiatrist's rooms, waiting for Granville. 'The report will be ready in three days,' Dr Grady had said. Then he had given Gardner an off-the record run-down on his son's condition, including a few observations that he was *not* going to write in the report.

Gardner stood at the blackboard, dressed in shorts and a tee-shirt. The previous diagrams were still up, delineating the progress they'd made in proving the guilt of Miller and Starke.

'This is how it goes,' Gardner said. Brownie and Jennifer were seated at the table, also casually dressed. Granville was next door in Gardner's private office, laden with video games, happy to have some playtime after this morning. 'Henry Bowers was a rich man. Somehow he'd amassed a fortune, and he kept it in a set of safe-deposit boxes in the bank. He never spent the money. He hoarded it, and only occasionally gave it away.' Gardner wrote SCHOOL, CLARENCE CONLEY and FOOTBALL PROGRAMMES on the board. 'Meanwhile, nephew Purvis, ostensibly the only living relative, was allowed access to the safe-deposit boxes by Henry to help dispense the money to Addie, if he became incapacitated.'

Jennifer and Brownie listened intently as Gardner spoke. This was the first time that anyone had officially painted the big picture, and so far, it was making sense.

'But it has to be noted,' Gardner said, 'that by putting Purvis' name on the boxes, Henry was not making a gift of the money. Purvis was only to be the caretaker if Henry got sick.' Gardner wrote KNOWLEDGE OF MONEY under Purvis' name. 'Now we come to Roscoe Miller. Good old *cousin*

Roscoe, the black sheep of the family. We know that Roscoe and Purvis were connected.' He wrote COUSIN, ADDRESS and ADMISSION on the board. 'He admitted to you, Brownie, that he'd seen Roscoe around.'

'Uh-huh,' said Brownie.

'And that confirms that they knew each other, in addition to the fact that Roscoe used Purvis' address on the Pennsylvania State Police arrest form.'

Gardner turned towards them. 'So Purvis Bowers is languishing in this town. An accountant with a two-bit practice. Unknown, and very *unrich*. He's going nowhere fast, while his old uncle is sitting on a pile of money that *he*, Purvis, has access to but cannot touch. It begins to eat at him. Each day passes, and his uncle gets older and older and doesn't get sick and doesn't die. So Purvis decides to help it along a little. He formulates a plan to get the money. He can legitimately withdraw the funds. All he needs is for Henry and Addie to be dead.'

'And that's where Roscoe comes in,' Jennifer interjected.

'Right,' Gardner said. 'A murder in the course of a robbery would do nicely. Purvis makes a deal with Roscoe to hit the store and wipe out his aunt and uncle. Purvis agrees to pay Roscoe a major sum of cash to do the deed.' He wrote CONTRACT on the board and drew a line connecting Purvis and Roscoe. Then he circled $8000, a figure already written under Roscoe's name.

'While this is going on,' Gardner continued, 'Roscoe is working at the school, and he comes in contact with IV Starke, a man who bears a strange resemblance to him. Roscoe Miller and Starke become friends, and start sharing common interests like guns and disdain for authority. One thing leads to another, and Roscoe decides to bring Starke in on the deal. Not for money, just for the thrill. And, of course, Starke, who's rich, and bored, *likes* to point guns at people.' He wrote SHOTGUN INCIDENT under Starke's name. 'Starke is more than happy to oblige.' He then underlined ID and JENNEANE DOREY. 'There's no doubt he's with Miller when the crime takes place.' Gardner stopped and took a breath. 'Then, something goes wrong.' He picked up the pace again.

'Granville,' Jennifer replied softly.

Gardner frowned. 'No. I'll get to that later.' Jennifer gave an apologetic nod. 'Something goes wrong between Miller and Purvis Bowers. Could have been money. Who knows? Maybe Miller was supposed to get more from Purvis, and he reneged. Maybe Miller found out about the full amount . . . Whatever the reason, now Miller comes in and blows away Purvis Bowers.' Gardner circled the FINGERPRINT notation. 'And now the money could all end up *here!*' He angrily circled the word KING. 'Right, Brownie? Give us the run-down on that again.'

The officer stood up and walked to the board, gently removing the chalk from Gardner's hand. 'Like I told you,' he said, 'Kent King is the only man with legal title to the money. He's in the will. Put himself in there, and unless Roscoe makes a claim against the estate, King could get all the cash.' He looked at Gardner. 'That's it.'

'But, in the meantime, where's the money?' Gardner asked.

Brownie shook his head. 'Wish I knew.'

Across town, Roscoe Miller was meeting with Kent King in his law office. They had not accomplished much in the past hour.

'I'm getting tired of repeating it, Roscoe,' King said. 'You gotta give me something I can use against Starke!' Miller was playing with the new monitor the sheriffs had strapped on him. 'Look at me, please,' King said. 'I don't like talking to the top of your head.'

Miller's face slowly came up and his blue eyes met King's.

'They are tryin' to *burn* your ass,' King said. 'Don't you understand that?'

Miller fluffed his hair. 'That's why I hired you,' he said casually, 'to keep 'em from doin' it.'

'How much money did you get?'

'Dunno,' Miller said, lowering his attention back to the bracelet. This one was a new model. More durable, the cops said.

King pushed Miller's wrist down to his side. 'Give me your full attention, Roscoe. Stop playing with that thing.'

The blue eyes came up again. 'OK, sorry.'

278

King put his hands on the desk. 'How many times have we been over this now, Roscoe? Thirty? And every time it's the same. You didn't do a thing. And you don't know a thing. But you had a fistful of cash after the first shooting, a fingerprint on a shotgun shell, and Starke lays out your bond . . .' Miller stayed silent. 'What are you afraid of?'

Miller's expression wavered for an instant, then returned to his personal version of normal. 'I ain't afraid of nuthin',' he finally said. 'Just don't have nuthin' to say.'

'I think I could get you a deal with Lawson,' King said. 'Maybe get him to drop everything down to accessory. I've already talked to him about it . . .'

Miller suddenly looked alarmed. 'You made a deal?'

'No. Just suggested the possibility. I need your authority to work it out. And I need you to provide some information.'

The alarm had changed to fear. 'Told you I ain't got any information!'

King opened a folder. 'Starke is not the nice boy he appears to be.' He pulled out a set of documents. 'He's been kicked out of six prep schools for misbehaviour. Some really weird shit, too. Challenged some freshman kid to jump off a dormitory roof, and the kid did it. Now he's paralysed for life.'

'Why are you telling *me*?' Miller asked.

'To show you what this guy's all about. He may have put up your bond, but he's definitely not your friend. You've got to turn him in!'

'Thought you already had the case worked out,' Miller replied. 'Thought they didn't have good evidence, and that that kid . . .' he squinted his eyes, 'that kid can't remember . . .'

King smiled. 'That's true, but you never know about these things. Trials can sometimes bite you in the ass.'

'So the kid might testify . . .' He had a look of expectation in his eyes. 'You said he couldn't. That he was messed up . . .'

King shook his head. 'At this point, he's incapable. I'll know more in a few days, after I get the psychiatrist's report. Right *now* I'd still count him out.'

'He drew a tattoo,' Miller said suddenly.

'Don't sweat it,' King said. 'You're not the only guy in town with a tattoo.' If push came to shove, he'd convince the jury

279

it was one of Starke's stick-ons. 'Right now we have to decide which way we're going: trial or deal. You finger Starke now, give me something to back it up, and you're home free.'

'And if I don't?' Miller was thinking.

'Then we go to trial and pray that the kid doesn't take the stand.'

'But what if he does?' Miller was still thinking.

'Then pray he doesn't remember.' Miller fell silent. He was considering his options. 'Well?' King said, 'what's it going to be? Turn in Starke and cut a deal, or go to trial?'

Roscoe Miller looked his attorney in the eye. 'I'll take my chances with the kid,' he said.

At the State Attorney's office the strategy session was still in progress. Gardner was back at the blackboard, and Jennifer and Brownie were seated at the table. Granville was dozing in the next room after one-too-many alien encounters.

'So King ultimately ends up with the money,' Gardner said disgustedly, 'and, from everything I can see, it's perfectly legal. He represented both Henry and Purvis. And there was a contingency to leave the residual to him . . .'

'So maybe he engineered the whole scheme,' Jennifer suggested.

Gardner shook his head. 'No. I wanted to believe that. That King was behind it from the start, but it doesn't fly. King is a number one asshole. Devious. Unscrupulous. But he's not stupid, and he's not a murderer. Check the dates on the documents.' Jennifer glanced at Henry's and Purvis' wills. 'They were drawn *long* ago. The connection is too clear. Too obvious. The logical suspect would be King if everyone wound up dead.'

'So maybe that's what he wanted you to think,' Jennifer replied. 'That he'd never do something that could be traced to him so easily.'

'No,' Gardner said firmly, 'I don't think King has anything to do with any of this. At least not with the murders. What do you say, Brownie?'

Brownie had been uncharacteristically quiet all day. He'd responded when spoken to, but, except for his brief presentation, he'd hardly offered a thing. 'What do I think?' he asked. 'About the money, and King, and all that stuff?' Gardner nodded. 'I don't think *any* of it is relevant!' Brownie stood up and walked to the blackboard. Without warning, he began to draw diagonal lines across the evidence.

'Brownie!' Gardner was taken by surprise.

'Take it easy!' Brownie said. 'I'm just trying somethin' out.' Most of the words were now crossed through. The only ones remaining were HENRY, PRENTICE ACADEMY, WELLINGTON STARKE THE THIRD, TELEPHONE CALL and HANDGUN. 'Your scenario sounds pretty good, and it'll probably do OK in court, but that line of thinking doesn't begin to explain this.'

Gardner leaned against the wall. 'What's the point?'

Brownie gestured with the chalk. 'Point is, that maybe everything started from another direction. Maybe Starke had some reason to take out the Bowers, and maybe *he* dragged Roscoe along with *him*.'

Gardner crossed his arms. 'Got anything to substantiate that?'

Brownie smiled. 'Other than a hunch? No, I do not.'

'So what am I supposed to do with it?' Gardner asked. 'Tell the jury one version, then say: wait a minute, we may have another theory? Jesus, Brownie, the trial starts next week!'

The officer walked over to Gardner. 'I got some ideas. Maybe they're crazy. Maybe got nothing to do with the case at all. But I'm putting together an alternative theory, and I've got to check it out.'

Gardner closed his eyes. 'And what am I supposed to do in the meantime?' They were in the final stages of laying out the theme that would be played to the jury. Purvis, Miller and greed were the main storyline. A last-minute switch to Starke as the villain could undermine the entire presentation.

'Stick with what you got now,' Brownie said. 'If my hunch pans out, none of that's gonna make any difference anyhow.'

Gardner jerked his head toward the inner office. 'What about Granville?' His testimony was still the ultimate key. 'I'm still going to work with him.'

'That's up to you,' Brownie replied. 'But if I find what I'm looking for, you can send the boy home to his mom.'

Gardner and Granville were eating a late lunch in the kitchen of the townhouse. The strategy meeting had lasted most of the afternoon, straight through. Jennifer had gone out to talk to witnesses while Brownie had left to chase his mysterious lead.

'Want some more?' Gardner asked, pushing a plate of peanut butter sandwiches across the table.

'No,' Granville said.

'No, what?' Gardner prompted.

'No *thanks*, Dad.'

'Better,' Gardner said, reaching over with a napkin and dabbing a blob of peanut butter off the boy's bottom lip. 'So you liked Dr Grady?'

'Uh-huh.' Granville took a drink of milk, then wiped off the white moustache with his own napkin.

'He said you're a really smart boy.'

Granville's shoulders drooped. 'He asked me . . .' he said softly, the sentence incomplete.

'I know. That's his job. To find out how you're doing.'

'I cried some.'

'I know,' Gardner said. He'd heard the sounds behind the door.

'Can we go outside?' Granville asked. 'Play catch?' The electronic aliens were starting to get boring.

'Yes, in a little while. But, first, I want you to look at something.'

Granville's eyes took on an expression of dread, as his father pulled a stack of papers out of his briefcase and laid them on the table. He glanced down, then back at his dad. They were copies of the drawings he'd done for Miss Meyers.

'You used to be the best drawer I ever saw,' Gardner told him. 'You could draw the best space-ships, and cars, and trucks . . .' Granville's eyes were blank. 'But I'll be darned if I can tell what this is . . .' He picked up one of the earlier scribblings. Granville remained immobile. 'Or this one,' Gardner said.

Granville looked at the next page, then shot his eyes away.

'Or *this* one . . .' Gardner picked up the last drawing that Granville had done. The one with the hidden skull. 'I can't really make it out.' He laid the page in front of his son. Granville turned his body to the side. 'Gran,' Gardner said gently, 'take a look, and tell me what you drew.' The boy silently refused to turn his head. 'Please?' Gardner begged. 'Just one quick look.' Granville's face began to contort, but no tears had come.

Gardner scooped the papers up, and put them back into his briefcase. 'OK, no problem. No problem. Baseball. That's a much better idea.'

Granville stepped down from the chair.

'Wait a minute,' Gardner said.

Panic flickered across the boy's face.

'What do you say?'

Granville suddenly realized what his father meant. 'May I be excused?' he asked.

'Yes,' Gardner said. 'You may. Now run and get your glove.'

Brownie had decided not to lay out the particulars of his new theory for Gardner. The Purvis–Miller scenario made sense, and their evidence came close to backing it up. He had no proof at all for his hypothesis and, until he did, for the sake of the prosecutors' sanity, it was best to keep the theory under wraps.

By crossing out the other evidence on the blackboard, Brownie had left a list of three names: HENRY. WELLINGTON STARKE. PRENTICE ACADEMY. And when it came to names, there was only one man who could possibly connect them: Mr Jim Johnson, the town genealogist. Brownie drove to Mr Jim's house on Maple Avenue. The post office was closed, and Mr Jim had gone home. He parked and walked to the cream-coloured Victorian structure. The glass in the windows and doors was clean, and the paint on the shingles was fresh. It looked like a museum.

Mr Jim answered the door. 'Sergeant Brown, Sergeant Brown, Sergeant Brown . . .'

'Evenin', Mr Jim.'

'It is an honour to have you in my abode.' He directed Brownie into the foyer, then into the library.

'Whew!' Brownie exclaimed. 'See you got some books in here!' The walls were all shelves, filled to the top row with hard-covers.

'My life,' Mr Jim said. 'Studying the trek of humanity.' He motioned Brownie to sit in a tufted chair. 'What can I do for you tonight? You said it was important.'

Brownie had written the three names on a piece of paper, which he handed to Mr Jim. 'What can you tell me about these? Do you remember any kind of . . .' Brownie was groping for words. 'Uh, any reason that these three might be tied together?'

Mr Jim took the paper and read the names. 'Bowers . . . Starke . . . Prentice . . .' His eyes seemed to roll back the way they'd done at the post office. 'Bowers . . . Starke . . .' Brownie watched in amazement as the old man worked on his memory. 'Bowers . . . Starke . . .' he repeated. Then, suddenly, his eyes came open. 'Starke!' he exclaimed.

Brownie sat up straight. 'Mean anything?' he asked. There was definite recognition in Mr Jim's eyes.

'Wellington Starke . . .' the old man said, getting up from his chair, and pulling a thick book from one of the shelves. It looked like a scrapbook. 'Wellington Starke . . .' Mr Jim was leafing through a section of newspaper clippings. Yellowed and brittle, they were from a long time ago. Brownie looked on from the side as Mr Jim's fingers lifted page after page of pasted clippings. Finally he stopped, scanned the page and turned the book so that Brownie could read. 'Wellington Starke,' he said proudly.

Brownie adjusted the book on his lap, and read the headline. 'Wellington Starke, Jr. Awarded the Silver Star for bravery,' the caption read. The story was from the *New York Times*, dated September 10, 1944.

Brownie swallowed, and began reading the text:

Lieutenant Wellington Starke, Jr., son of prominent New York businessman Wellington Starke, was awarded the Silver Star on Friday September 8, for bravery in battle, the European Command announced. Lieutenant Starke, member of the 118th antitank company of the 15th Infantry Division, distinguished himself in a fierce tank and infantry battle with members of the 6th Panzer Division and supporting troops of the Nazi SS.'

Brownie slowed his reading. This was a story about Starke

IV's grandfather. He went back to the text.

The battle, which took place in France near the Belgian border, cost the lives of 455 American soldiers, but has been listed as a victory for the Allied forces. In a particularly bloody skirmish, which included a point-blank artillery duel and hand-to-hand combat, Lieutenant Starke was able to hold his position, and turn back the enemy. It was during this period of the conflict that Lieutenant Starke acted so bravely.

The story ended at that point, and was continued on the next page. Brownie turned it over.

Under blistering enemy fire, Lieutenant Starke rescued one of his men, who had been overrun by the advancing enemy. Crawling into the face of the most murderous barrage, Lieutenant Starke covered the soldier with his own body until they were both able to crawl back to friendly lines. This act of courage, it was said, inspired the other men in his company to hold their ground and repel the assault.'

Brownie stopped reading. Below the text was a grainy photo of two men in battle gear, their young faces beaming with triumph. They had their arms locked, like blood brothers. 'Miraculous Reunion' the caption said. He let his eyes drift down to the line under the photo's caption. 'Jesus Christ!' he said, looking at Mr Jim.

The old man nodded knowingly.

Under the picture was the name of the man Wellington Starke Junior had saved: a young man like himself, brave and proud, happy to be alive. A simple man from a simple background: Sergeant Henry Bowers.

'Bowers and Starke,' Mr Jim said.

Brownie smiled. There it was.

Gardner and Jennifer were readying themselves for bed. It had been a long day, and there was a lot more to do tomorrow. They had to get the witness list finalized, the legal motions

285

answered and the opening statement outlined. Even though they were splitting the workload, it was still going to be a major task.

Gardner turned from the basin and raised his toothbrush. 'You stick with the witness line-up, and I'll work on the suppression motions.'

Jennifer was drying her face. She had just removed her makeup. 'OK,' she said.

'We have to go forward with the Purvis–Miller angle of attack,' Gardner continued. 'We can't wait until the last minute to switch gears. If Brownie finds something, great. If he doesn't, at least we'll be prepared.'

Jennifer applied her moisturizing cream. 'I agree.'

They got into bed, said good-night, kissed, and rolled back-to-back. Jennifer clicked off the light.

Suddenly Gardner turned towards her. 'Do you think he's on the right track?'

'Whaa?' Jennifer was sliding rapidly towards sleep.

'Brownie thinks Starke did it,' Gardner insisted. 'What do *you* think?'

Jennifer put her face against his chest. 'He could have . . .'

'But do you really think he *did?*'

'Only two people know the answer to that one . . .' Jennifer's voice faded. Three more deep breaths, and she'd be out.

Gardner stroked her hair in the darkness as she drifted off to sleep. 'Make that *three*,' he whispered.

Brownie wasted no time in following up the Starke–Bowers link he'd discovered at Mr Jim's. He photocopied the article and phoned a Pentagon contact he'd consulted on other investigations. That got him into the military records section of the National Archives, and soon he received a faxed list of the roster of the 118th antitank company, 15th Infantry Division, US Army European Command in 1944. Then he hit a snag. The first ten men on the list were dead. The next was still alive, but he'd moved and left no forwarding address. The next was in the Alzheimer's ward of a veterans' hospital. By the time Brownie had worked down to the bottom of the list, three precious days had been used up. Now, finally, he had a name and an address: Sergeant

Raphael Romero. Active member of the Main Street chapter of the Falesville, Pennsylvania, VFW. Alive, and well.

Having obtained the man's phone number, he made a call. On the pretext of being a World War Two scholar, he asked Romero if he would consent to an interview about his war experiences. There was no sense in telling the real reason for the contact. A frontal approach might not work. Romero hesitatingly agreed. So Brownie made the two-hundred-mile drive to Falesville to see what the man had to say.

The Pennsylvania hill town was a lot like home, with Appalachian peaks, rocky valleys and old-time architecture. It was a bright, slightly hazy, summer noon. Raphael Romero was waiting for Brownie on the front steps of his brick row-house.

'Mr Romero?' Brownie extended his hand to the elderly man. 'Joe Brown.' In civilian clothes, Brownie looked quite unofficial.

Romero eyed Brownie cautiously. He wasn't expecting a black man.

'Thanks for seeing me,' Brownie said. 'I'm putting together a piece on the battles in northern France, and I need some information. I understand you were there?'

Romero looked like a well-aged Hollywood extra. White hair, and smooth pink skin. His eyes were black olives. And he smoked incessantly. 'Who told you?' he asked.

'What?' Brownie didn't comprehend.

'Who told you I was there?' Romero repeated.

'The archives. Came across your name in the personnel file. 118th antitank company . . .'

'Not many of us left,' Romero interrupted. 'Most dead now . . .' His eyes almost crossed as he took a drag on his cigarette. 'Them that the Germans didn't get . . . all cut down by time . . .'

'Mr Romero?' Brownie realized he'd awakened some deep memories.

'The 118th is history . . .'

'But you're not,' Brownie said. 'Look pretty good to me.'

Romero glanced up and removed his cigarette. 'Those were tough days, Mr Brown. Very, very tough.'

'But you never quit,' Brownie added. 'You were overrun by

the Germans, but you never quit. Thanks to your commanding officer, uh . . . Lieutenant, uh, Lieutenant . . .' Brownie
pretended not to remember the name, hoping Romero would
pick up the slack.

'Starke,' the old man said. 'Lieutenant Beef Wellington
Starke.' There was admiration in his voice, and sadness.

'Tell me about him,' Brownie said, pulling out his notepad.
If he was going to play the scholar, he had to act the part.
'You called him "Beef" Wellington?'

Romero sucked the cigarette again, then pulled it out and
smiled. 'It was a joke. Beef Wellington. Rich man. Silver
spoon. Money. All that . . .' Brownie scribbled on his pad.
'But that wasn't really him,' Romero continued. 'Not at all.
He was kind, generous . . . Bravest man I ever knew.'

'He saved a member of your company,' Brownie cut in. 'Did
you see it?'

Romero removed his cigarette and looked at Brownie. 'I
was there.' His expression darkened, as if he were remembering the most horrific scene of his life. 'Sarge got cut off.
He . . .'

'Sarge?' Brownie knew damn well who 'Sarge' was. He just
wanted to hear Romero say it.

'Henry. Sergeant Henry Bowers. He'd been sent up to a
forward listening post by Lieutenant Starke. And he was
up there when the dam broke. Everything was coming in.
Eighty-eights, burp-guns, Tigers. They had ground forces
alongside. Goddamn SS . . .' Brownie was writing furiously.
'Sarge got run over by a tank. Tracks went over top, and he
dropped in a hole. We were back at the line, and they were
coming in on all sides . . .' His voice was breathless, as if he
was reporting from the scene. 'Lieutenant Starke called in
the artillery. Right on top of us! They were overruning. And
he called in a strike from our own guns . . .' Brownie tried to
keep the notes apace with his words. 'Sarge was screaming.
He'd been hit in the leg. Two or three times. We could hear
him over the shellfire. Let him go, someone said. But the
lieutenant went out, in the middle of the shrapnel rain. With
the SS shooting and slashing and chopping all around, he
went out. And damned if he didn't bring Sarge back alive . . .'
Romero stopped talking and took another drag of his

288

cigarette, this time pulling the smoke in as deep as he could.

Brownie stopped writing. 'Why do you think he did it?' he asked.

Romero exhaled a white cloud. 'Because that's the way the man was. And . . .' he cut off his own words.

'And?' Brownie sensed something important.

'The way he felt about Sarge,' Romero answered. 'He loved the man.'

Brownie looked up. 'Do you know why?'

Romero frowned, as if that was a strange question from a scholar, but he shrugged it off. 'Don't know, really. We all liked Sarge, but the lieutenant really loved the man. Like a brother. And it went the other way round too.'

Brownie's heart began to race. 'Mind elaborating on that?'

Romero folded his hands and spoke with the cigarette still in his mouth. 'They were inseperable. Sarge and lieutenant. Lieutenant and sarge. Rich man, poor man. Mutt and Jeff. Starke loved Bowers, and Bowers worshipped Starke. Nothing either man wouldn't do for the other. Cut off his own arm . . .'

Brownie took it all down. 'Did you ever see them later? After the war?'

Romero shook his head. 'No. We all went back to our own worlds. I heard lieutenant died, quite some time ago. Don't know what ever became of sarge . . .'

Brownie opened his folder and took out the ATF photo of the handgun. He handed it over to Romero. 'Ever see this before?'

The old man's eyes leaped. 'Where'd you get this?'

'You've seen it?' Romero suddenly realized he'd been had. Brownie was no scholar.

Brownie pulled out his police ID. 'I didn't want to do it this way, Mr Romero, but I have to,' he said. 'I'm a police officer from Maryland. Henry Bowers is dead. Murdered. I'm sorry to have to tell you that. This was the murder weapon.'

Romero froze. This was too much. From the horrors of the war to the murder of a long-lost friend, all in an instant.

'Please?' Brownie asked. 'I need your help.'

Romero hesitated, and looked at the picture again. There was recognition in his eyes.

'Tell me about the gun,' Brownie said.

Romero handed the photo back, and lit another cigarette. 'Our unit was assigned to carry those things,' he said. 'Some kind of special project. Gave each man a gun, and he was supposed to report how it functioned . . .'

'So Lieutenant Starke had one?'

'Yup. Sergeant Bowers too. We all had 'em.'

Brownie swallowed hard, and almost snapped his pen. Starke to Bowers. Bowers to Starke. He'd thought he was almost there, but he wasn't. The murder weapon could have come from Bowers *or* Starke. And that didn't help at all.

PART 7

Revelations

CHAPTER 19

Trial day dawned clear and warm. The sun pierced the shadow of the valley from the northeast, and slowly made its way to the courthouse dome, where it burst in a dazzling golden flash.

Gardner and Jennifer were in the courtroom, rushing through final preparations. They had been moving non-stop for the past week, trying to get ready for the trial, and now the day was upon them.

A crowd had gathered early. Unlike the arraignment, which few had attended, this one was a sell-out. The bailiff had kept the people outside until he checked how many seats would be available. Now the spectators were coming in, their throaty babble breaking the silence that hung in the air above the counsel tables.

'All set?' Jennifer whispered to Gardner. Her hair had been pulled back and clipped with a gold clasp. She looked calm.

'No,' Gardner said. His eyelids were droopier than ever, and his skin was pallid. He'd paced the bedroom most of the night.

'All rise!' The bailiff wasn't wasting time. At precisely 9 o'clock Judge Hanks mounted the bench and struck her gavel: State *v.* Miller and Starke was under way.

There were the usual preliminary introductions, then Judge Hanks turned to the defence side. 'Gentlemen, I have a list of pretrial motions here. Which shall I consider first?'

Kent King rose and put his hand in his suit pocket. 'None of those, your honour. Mr Jacobs and I would like to add a new motion to the list at this time and ask for its immediate consideration.'

Gardner looked at Jennifer, then stood up. 'We've had

no notice of a new motion, Judge!'

Carla Hanks turned to King. 'Have you notified the State as to your intention?'

The defence attorney smiled. 'No, Judge, we haven't . . . But this issue is so central to the case that Mr Jacobs and I have decided to raise it now.'

'If they haven't told us, they can't raise it!' Gardner said firmly.

Hanks looked back at King. 'He's technically correct, counsel.'

King didn't flinch. 'I know that, Judge, but if you address this issue now, it'll save a significant amount of court time later. In fact, it might even obviate the trial altogether.'

That got Gardner's attention. King and Jacobs had done it again: they'd held back on a hot potato and dropped it in his lap at the last minute. 'Judge!' he begged. He was about to say, 'Don't allow this,' when Hanks spoke.

'Tell me about it, Mr King.'

'It's simple, really,' King said. 'In their answer to discovery the State has indicated that they intend to call a witness by the name of Granville Lawson . . .'

Gardner tensed as his son's name came out in the criminal court for the first time.

'To the best of our knowledge, this witness is the only purported eyewitness to the crime. He's eight years old, and we believe that the State is unable to make even a prima facie case without his testimony.'

Gardner was burning. He now knew where this was headed, a last-ditch effort by the defence to disqualify Granville before the trial even started. It was a nasty move. But the trouble was, if it succeeded, King was right. The case against both defendants could be over. Without Granville, the rest of their evidence might not do the job.

'Object to this, your honour,' Gardner said. He had to stop this tactic in its tracks.

'Overruled!' Hanks snapped. 'Continue, Mr King.'

'It's quite simple, Judge,' King went on. 'There are two prerequisites that must be met before the witness may testify. First, as a minor, he must be *qualified* before he's allowed to take the stand. And, second, he has to be able to

294

offer relevant testimony. I have here—' he raised Dr Glenmore Grady's report— 'a document that indicates the boy has no memory whatsoever of the events that he will purportedly testify to. It is our position, therefore, that an examination of the child's qualifications and the relevance of his testimony be made *now*, before we proceed any further.'

Hanks turned to Gardner. 'What's the State's position?'

'We object most strenuously,' Gardner managed to say. 'This is procedurally improper and premature. We have not yet called the witness,' he swallowed hard, 'so no issue of qualification is on the table.'

Hanks gave Gardner a stern look. 'Do you intend to call the child as a witness?'

Gardner recoiled. 'Ma'am?'

'Are you going to call Granville Lawson to testify?'

Gardner looked down. 'I'm not required to say at this point.'

'Your honour!' King interjected. 'If he commits to *not* using the witness, I'll withdraw the motion.'

'I can handle this, Mr King!' Hanks replied curtly. 'What about it, Mr State Attorney? Are you going to call the child as a witness or not?'

This was it. In or out. Win or lose. All at once. 'Yes,' Gardner said with resolve. 'Yes, we are.'

'Then the defence motion is granted,' Hanks said. 'We examine qualifications and relevance *now*, before we do another thing.'

Brownie was in the lab, frantically sifting through his file. With Gardner and Jennifer already in court, time was running out. He'd been chasing the gun lead non-stop since his talk with Romero, finally rustling up every member of the Prentice Academy work crew and showing them the ATF photo. None of them had seen Roscoe 'Hiller' with anything like it. In fact, none had ever seen him with a handgun at all. Only one man made reference to a gun, and he merely said that Roscoe had bragged about having one. He himself had not seen a thing.

That sent Brownie back to the drawing-board. He'd scoured the plaster cast for a serial number, but the print was too shallow. The military records section of the archives couldn't locate any reference to the experimental gun project. Brownie was not going to be able to trace who had the weapon, even if he found the serial number. At this point the gun trail was cold. He'd have to find another lead.

He pulled the birth records that had been found when the police executed the search warrant and blow-torched the safe in Starke IV's closet and laid them on his table. Adjusting the magnifier, he began to study the pages. Wellington Starke Jr. Wellington Starke the third. Wellington Starke the fourth. Each document was authenticated by a certification seal, and each had a file number imprinted at the top. Family records, Brownie thought. Why would Starke be so interested in family records? And what was so valuable about them that they had to be kept in the safe?

He put grandfather's certificate under the lens. Lieutenant Starke. 'Beef' Wellington. The man who saved Henry's life. Under heavy magnification, Brownie studied the page. NYSDVS 4728512 was handwritten in the upper right corner and, underneath, the indented certification. New York State Department of Vital Statistics, with a picture of the State seal.

Brownie put that document aside and picked up the next one in the pile. It was Starke IV's birth record. NYSDVS 21134699. The numbers were partially printed on the seal, but it was still readable: New York State Department of Vital Statistics.

The next certificate was the father's: Wellington Starke the third. Brownie ran his eyes down the page, then back to the top. NYSBVS 4576833. New York State Department of Vital Statistics. He blinked, and raised the page closer to the magnifier. N-Y-S-**B**-V-S. He angled the page to be sure he'd not misread it. N-Y-S-B-V-S. The letter was clearly a *B*, not a *D*. He snapped his fingers. Someone had made a mistake!

A child witness, unlike an adult, was not presumed to be competent to testify. Because of immaturity, an eight-year-old had to answer a set of preliminary questions before he could give proof at a trial. The issues were simple. Did he understand what was going on? Did he know what an oath was? Did he understand that he had to tell the truth? Did he know what would happen if he didn't? They were simple enough issues, but there was a major problem: Gardner hadn't gone through a dry run with Granville first. He'd planned to do it later, during the trial. But now, the boy was coming in cold.

Granville was ushered into the courtroom and up on the witness stand. King began with a blast. 'Request that *I* be allowed to qualify the witness,' he said.

'Objection!' Gardner snapped to his feet.

Granville's eyes jumped to his dad. Gardner moved over to block his son's line of vision to Miller and Starke. There was no telling what might happen if he had a sudden resurgence of memory now.

'What is it?' Judge Hanks asked.

'It is customary for the court, and I emphasize *court*, to ask the qualifications questions,' Gardner argued. There was no way he wanted to give King a free one-on-one shot against Granville. He could have the boy disavowing his own name in ten seconds.

Hanks frowned. Again, she was in virgin territory. She had never done a child qualification in her life. 'Uh, do you have any authority on that, Mr Lawson?' When caught short on legal knowledge, throw it back to the lawyers.

Gardner tensed. He had not anticipated this: a qualifications battle right out of the blue. 'Authority?' He was playing for time, searching his memory for a ruling.

'It's always done in this jurisdiction,' Jennifer suddenly said, rising to the rescue. 'In the Donner case before Judge Simmons, and the Haskins case before Judge Danforth, that's how it was done.'

Gardner's eyes said thank you.

'But what is the underlying authority?' Hanks persisted. 'Where is it written that I can't allow counsel to ask the questions?'

Gardner and Jennifer hesitated. There was no such ruling. Like many legal traditions, it had just evolved through custom. The judge was not handcuffed by precedent, and could do anything she pleased.

'I am prepared to run through the qualifications questions,

297

Judge,' King said. 'Just give the word.'

Hanks nodded, but said nothing.

Damn! Gardner thought. She's not prepared, so she's going to let King do the work. He looked at Granville. The boy was nervously twitching in his chair, oblivious of what was happening. 'I most strenuously object!' he said.

Hanks looked at the prosecutor. 'I understand your position,' she said apologetically, 'but we have to move this case along. Mr King is ready to proceed, and so am I. Objection overruled. Ask your first question, counsel.'

Gardner slumped into his chair as a nightmare flashed across his mind. He was safe at the top of a wall, and a terrified innocent was about to be devoured by dogs.

King rose from his seat, strolled to the witness stand and peered down at the face that greeted him from the oversized chair. Behind, Gardner stirred restlessly at his post.

'How're you doin'?' King asked.

Granville eyed him cautiously, but did not reply.

'My name is Kent King,' the attorney said. His voice was low, almost gentle. 'I'm a lawyer. Do you know what that is?'

Gardner's heart was racing, and acid rose in his throat. King was taking the high road. The soft approach.

Granville nodded his head to King's inquiry.

'You need to answer out loud,' King said, 'so the reporter, uh, that lady over there—' he pointed to the stenographer seated in front of the bench —'The lady needs to hear you on her earphones.'

'Ask your question again, counsel,' Hanks prompted.

'Right,' King replied. 'Do you know what a lawyer is, son?'

Gardner choked on the word 'son' coming out of King's mouth. He started to rise, but Jennifer grabbed his arm.

Granville looked King in the eye. 'My dad's a lawyer.'

King smiled. 'And do you know what he does?'

'Uh-huh,' Granville replied. 'He puts bad people in jail.'

King folded his arms. 'What else does a lawyer do?' Granville's eyes searched for his father. 'What else does a lawyer do?' King repeated.

Granville's eyes turned back to King. 'Some of them try to hurt my dad . . .'

King hadn't expected that. 'I see,' he said, trying to cut off the answer.

298

'They get bad people out of jail.'

Gardner's heart surged. He's never discussed the details of his profession with the boy. It was always good guys and bad guys, good deeds and bad deeds. But Granville had absorbed the deeper meaning, and he had sorted out the players.

King smiled again, giving no hint that he'd just been bested by a kid. 'OK. So you know what lawyers do. Do you know what a trial is?'

Granville wrinkled his forehead. 'Think so,' he said softly.

'What is it?' King asked.

'Where the judge says who's guilty.'

'Your *dad* teach you about that?'

Granville shook his head. 'Uh-huh.'

'You have to answer yes or no,' Judge Hanks said, leaning down from the bench. Granville looked up at her. 'Do you understand?' Hanks said. 'You have to answer the questions yes or no. OK?'

Granville nodded. 'Uh-huh. Uh, yes.'

'Good. Let's move on,' Hanks said.

King turned to the witness box. 'Do you believe in Santa Claus?' he asked.

'Objection!' Gardner was back on his feet.

'Grounds, counsel?' Hanks asked.

'The question is irrelevant,' Gardner argued. Granville was sure to say yes.

Hanks looked at King.

'State of mind, Judge,' King said nonchalantly.

'Witness can answer,' the judge ruled.

'But your honour . . .' Gardner protested.

'That's my ruling, Mr Lawson.'

Gardner gripped the counsel table with both hands.

Hanks looked down at Granville. 'Mr King asked if you believe in Santa Claus. How about that? Do you believe in Santa Claus?'

Granville looked up at her. 'Uh-huh' he answered softly.

'Remember to say "Yes",' she prodded gently.

'Uh, yes.'

'And how about the Easter Bunny?' King picked up the tempo again. 'Do you believe in him?'

Granville tried to look at his father, but King blocked the view. 'Yes.'

'And the tooth fairy?' King was beginning to roll. 'When you lose a tooth, does the tooth fairy leave money under your pillow?'

'Uh-huh, uh, yes.'

Gardner was dying inside. King was soft-pedalling Granville down the fantasy trail. The boy couldn't sort fact from fiction, the argument would go, and the proof was from his own mouth.

'And cartoons,' King continued. 'You watch cartoons on TV?'

Granville nodded.

'Remember,' Hanks said, 'Yes, or no.' In her own way, she was trying to help.

'Yes,' Granville replied.

King glanced at Gardner, then back at the witness. 'If you told me that Santa Claus came to your house last Christmas and left some toys, would that be the truth or a lie?'

Gardner couldn't allow this to continue. 'Objection! The question is compounded. There is no way *anyone* could give a correct answer! Not even an adult!'

For the first time that day, Judge Hanks hesitated. Gardner's comment sounded kind of right. 'Can you elaborate, Mr Lawson?'

'It's a compound question. If toys were received, a Yes answer would be the truth, but counsel is trying to discredit the witness. To combine his perception of truth with his belief in Santa Claus, and insinuate that he doesn't know the difference. There's really no correlation.' Gardner was drawing on legal instinct.

'Wrong!' King said when Judge Hanks looked at him for a response. 'He's already admitted to believing in Santa Claus. That lays the foundation for a follow-up question.'

'But the question you asked *is* compound,' she replied. 'Rephrase it.'

King smirked at Gardner. He was about to resume questioning, when he spotted Jacobs motioning to him from the defence table. 'May I have a moment, please, your honour?' he said.

The judge said OK, and King huddled with Jacobs. After a few words, King looked over at the witness stand.

Gardner followed King's eyes back to Granville. Something was wrong.

'Your honour,' King said, 'We'd like to request an immediate recess.'

Gardner looked at his son. Until now, the boy's attention had been bouncing between Gardner, King and the judge. His eyes had maintained that track all morning. Or so he thought.

'Please Judge!' King repeated. 'We need to recess now!'

'Very well, counsel,' she answered. 'Ten-minute recess.' Carla Hanks banged her gavel, and left the bench.

King and Jacobs wasted no time in hustling their clients out of the room. In an instant, they were gone.

Gardner rushed to the stand. 'What is it, Gran?'

The boy seemed to be in a hypnotic state. 'Huh?'

'Tell Dad what's wrong,' Gardner insisted. Jennifer pressed in close behind, anxious to hear the answer.

'Nuthin', Dad,' Granville finally said, his expression still distant.

But something *had* happened. Jacobs had seen it. Granville had finally focused on the two defendants side by side at the counsel table, Roscoe Miller and IV Starke. And, suddenly, something had clicked.

'Are you OK?' Gardner asked his son again. Maybe he had experienced a flashback, a recollection, prompted by the men across the room.

Granville nodded, but his mind was still way, way off. There was no question about it. The memory was stirring.

Brownie paced the floor of the lab, waiting for his fax to come in from New York. After finding the discrepancy in the filing number of Stark IV's father's birth certificate, he'd decided to check further. He'd phoned the New York State Department of Vital Statistics, and ordered the records that had been filed just before, and just after, that certificate. The clerk had said OK. It would take a few minutes, but he'd send them.

Stopping beside the fax machine, he scratched his head. A

301

certain answer from New York would revitalize his theory. The machine beeped, and Brownie watched as the paper slowly crept out of the vent. One page, then another. Then a beep to signal that the transmission was complete.

Brownie put the first page under his magnifier. Wellington Starke the third's control number was 4576833. This one's number was 4576832. Brownie checked the notation preceding the number: NYSDVS. He turned to the second fax, number 4576834. This was the certificate filed immediately *after* Starke's. NYSDVS, it read. He put Starke's certificate with the two he'd just received. Each had a date and time stamp on the bottom of the page. He compared them under the lens. All three were the same date, and all three had been filed within two hours of each other. That meant that they should have been identical, in sequence, all should have had the same stamped notation of the New York State Department of Vital Statistics. But they were not the same. Wellington Starke the third's was different. The substitution of a 'B' for a 'D' in the NYSDVS notation was not the mistake of a file clerk. It must have been done by someone outside the department!

Brownie hurried to the phone, and dialled the State Police Aviation Section. 'Joe Brown here,' he said, 'How're you-all doin' today? Listen, I need a favour real bad. I need to go to New York.'

At the courthouse, King and Jacobs had sequestered their clients in a witness room and requested a private conference with Judge Hanks. Granville had been whisked back to the State Attorney's office under sheriff's guard. Now the two sides eyed each other in silence as they waited to be called in by the judge.

'She will see you now,' the judge's secretary announced.

Gardner and Jennifer let King and Jacobs go first.

'We have a problem,' King announced as soon as the door closed. 'Our clients would like to absent themselves from the remainder of this hearing.'

Hanks leaned back in her chair. 'This is a critical stage of trial; they're required to be there.'

'They can waive it,' King said. 'Any right is subject to

'waiver.' Jacobs nodded agreement. Until now he'd been content to let King do all the talking.

'Why the change of heart?' Hanks asked.

King looked at Jacobs. They dared not show weakness here, not in front of the prosecutors. 'Convenience,' King said. 'Their time can better be utilized outside the courtroom.'

'Are they both willing to waive their right to be present?' the judge asked.

'Yes, ma'am,' the defence lawyers said in unison.

Hanks turned to Gardner. 'What's your position?'

'I fear we're being set up for an appellate attack on the right to be present at trial.' Gardner was shooting from the hip, but intentionally aiming off-centre. He knew exactly why they didn't want Miller and Starke in the courtroom. 'Unless the waiver is perfect, we're going to hear about it on appeal.'

'Nonsense!' King said.

Gardner smiled. It *was* nonsense, but King was squirming.

'Appeal only follows *conviction*,' King continued, 'and there's not gonna be a *conviction* in this case!'

Gardner maintained his smile. 'Don't be so sure,' he said to King. The tide was about to turn. He could feel it. The defence had just fallen victim to their own hand. They had insisted on a psychiatric report and they'd got a humdinger from Dr Glenmore Grady. The boy had no memory, it said. No memory of the event at all. And King and Jacobs had believed it.

'So we go in and have the defendants waive their rights?' Hanks said, standing up.

'Correct,' King replied.

'Then we bring the witness back and get on with the qualification hearing,' she continued.

'Fine by me,' Gardner answered.

At 4.15 p.m. the helicopter lifted off from the State Police helipad and turned east. They had a stop to make in Baltimore, and then they could head north.

'What's the big deal, Brownie?' the pilot asked over the headset. 'Big date in the Big Apple?'

303

Brownie tightened his seatbelt and fought the dizzying sensation of the rapid ascent. 'Checkin' on some medical records,' he said.

'And for that, you gotta fly?' The pilot sounded surprised.

'No time for anything else. Can't get them sent down. Got to pull them myself.'

'The Bowers case?' The pilot had flown Gardner to shock-trauma on the first day.

'Yeah,' Brownie said.

'How's the little boy?'

Brownie closed his eyes and saw Granville's face. 'Doin' OK.'

'And the case? Heard it started today. What's the word?'

Brownie felt embarrassed. He was so caught up in his own investigation that he hadn't checked on the prosecutors. 'Don't know,' he mumbled.

The pilot stopped talking, so Brownie settled in for the flight. Three hours to New York. After the stops, that's how long it was going to take. Three hours in a shaky tin can. But if Brownie's suspicions were correct, what lay deep in the files of Manhattan's Sacred Heart Hospital would make it all worthwhile.

The recess was over, and Granville was back on the witness stand. The defendants had been told by their lawyers to leave the courthouse. They didn't want the two men sitting in front of Granville Lawson any longer. The boy seemed to be getting restless, and that was a bad sign.

Starke IV walked out first, down the steps of the granite building. At the bottom, he lingered. Roscoe Miller was about a minute behind. Starke waited. Soon, Miller was beside him. They both acted nonchalant, intentionally avoiding a face-to-face look. Starke nervously fingered the new wrist monitor that the sheriffs had bolted on. 'Gonna try again?' he whispered.

Miller looked across the street and kicked his boot on the pavement. 'Already did. Damn thing still works.'

Starke gripped his bracelet. 'Know any other way?'

Just then, several people bounded down the steps towards them. Miller glanced around, then turned back towards the street. 'Naaa!' he said. Then he raced away, crossing in front of an oncoming car that had to slam on its brakes to avoid running him down.

Starke held his ground for a moment as the people passed, and Miller disappeared on the other side of the street. He twisted the monitor again, feeling it chafe his skin. The first one had been a breeze. Ten seconds on high in a microwave was all it took. He'd busted out the glass so he could close the door, put on a pair of asbestos gloves, and wham! the beeper went down. But this one was going to be tougher to beat. Starke looked both ways before crossing, then walked away from the courthouse. He'd just have to try something else.

In the courtroom, Joel Jacobs rose and walked toward the witness stand.

Gardner leaped to his feet. 'Your honour . . .'

'I defer my questions to Mr Jacobs,' Kent King told the court.

'Procedurally improper,' Gardner argued. 'Direct examination cannot be bifurcated.'

'My client is part of this case too,' Jacobs said. 'And since there's only one qualification for this witness, who is going to presumably testify against *my* client as well as Mr King's, I'm entitled to participate.'

The answer scored a hit. 'That sounds reasonable, counsel,' Hanks said.

'But, Judge . . .' Gardner insisted.

'Sorry, Mr Lawson,' Hanks replied. 'You charged both men, and joined the trials. They each get a say. Objection overruled.'

Gardner sat down. No sense labouring the point. One way or the other, Jacobs was going to get his shot.

'Hello, young man,' Jacobs said to Granville.

'Hi,' Granville replied. His eyes were alert.

'How are you today?'

'Fine.' Granville was relaxing, as the grandfatherly voice flowed.

'That's good. You look like a smart young man. Are you smart?'

'Uh,' Granville replied. It wasn't a 'Yes' or a 'No'.

305

'Remember what I told you before,' Hanks said with a smile. 'You have to say Yes, or No.'

Granville nodded.

'I have a grandson about your age,' Jacobs said. 'He's smart, but sometimes he tells fibs. Do you know what a fib is?'

'Yes,' Granville whispered.

'What is it?'

Granville looked the lawyer in the eye. 'When somethin' didn't happen.'

'Right,' Jacobs replied. 'Something didn't happen, but you said that it *did*. Have you ever done that?'

Gardner froze. Every eight-year-old in the world told fibs. It was part of life. Part of growing up. 'The dog ate my homework.' 'There's a monster in my closet.' The list went on and on. But Jacobs had set a trap. If Granville said 'No', he'd lose credibility. And if he said 'Yes', he'd brand himself a liar. There was no way to win this one. 'Objection!' he said. 'The question is too general. He has to lay a foundation by asking about a specific instance. Then he can proceed.'

Hanks turned to Gardner. 'Overruled. This proceeding involves the witness's credibility, and the inquiry goes straight to the point.'

'But the question . . . The question is . . .' Gardner was flailing. He wanted to say 'a trap', but there was no such ground.

'Overruled, Mr Lawson,' Hanks said.

'Son,' Jacobs continued, 'do you ever tell fibs?'

Gardner's stomach twisted.

'Sometimes,' Granville answered.

'So you *do* tell fibs,' Jacobs repeated.

'Uh-huh, uh, yes.' Granville replied. He'd finally learned the drill.

'What was one of your fibs?' Jacobs asked, folding his arms. This was heading right where he wanted it to go.

Gardner lowered his eyes.

'Sometimes me and Dad play ball . . .' Granville said.

'Right . . .' Jacobs acknowledged.

'And maybe I fall down, or get hit, or something . . .'

'Right . . .' Jacobs was still waiting for the punch line.

306

'And Dad asks me how I am, and I say "Fine".

Jacobs frowned. This time he didn't say 'right'.

Granville stopped talking.

'So what's the fib?' Jacobs asked.

Gardner held his breath.

'Dad asks if it hurt, and I say "No",' Granville said softly. 'But it does . . .'

Jacobs dropped his arms. This was not what he'd expected. 'OK,' he said disgustedly.

'But it does hurt,' Granville repeated.

Jacobs excused himself and walked over to conference with King. This little nut was going to be harder to crack than they'd thought.

Granville searched over the rail for his dad, but Gardner's head was lowered. He'd spotted Jacobs coming and didn't want the lawyer to see the tear in the corner of his eye.

CHAPTER 20

Joel Jacobs and Kent King discussed their strategy at the defence table while the courtroom waited.

'Gentlemen, can we resume?' Judge Hanks called impatiently from the bench.

'Ready,' King said.

Gardner stood up. 'Another switch?' King was taking back the reins.

'I relinquish my questions to Mr King,' Jacobs said.

'They can't do this,' Gardner argued. 'Back-and-forth another time!'

Hanks closed her eyes for a second. 'I'm going to allow it,' she said. 'Proceed, Mr King.'

King flashed Gardner a 'got'cha' smile, and returned to the witness stand. 'Who are you living with?' he asked Granville. His voice was formal and cold.

'Objection!' Gardner yelled. 'What possible relevance does that have to witness qualification?'

'Overruled,' Hanks said.

'Who are you living with right now?' King repeated.

'My dad,' Granville replied.

'And when did you go to stay with your dad?' King asked.

'While ago.'

'This is outrageous!' Gardner was losing it. 'Truth or falsity and knowledge of consequences is the only issue, not who he lives with!'

'Overruled, Mr Lawson,' Hanks repeated. 'Counsel has a good deal of latitude, and I'm going to let him take it.'

Gardner bit his tongue. How the hell did she know what latitude was? He clasped his hands in front of him and fixed his jaw.

'Your dad has been mean to you, hasn't he?' King went on.

Granville cocked his head.

'He's been making you very unhappy.'

Gardner started to rise, but Jennifer held him down.

'Your dad has been trying to get you to tell him something,' King continued. 'Isn't that right?'

Granville nodded. 'Yes,' he said, barely audible.

'Day and night he's been after you,' King continued. 'Pushing you. Trying to make you tell him something. Isn't that right?'

Gardner was boiling. His hands were sweating, and he wanted to leap at King. Jennifer kept her fingers securely clamped on his arm.

Granville lowered his eyes. 'Yes.'

'But it hurts when you try to remember, and you *can't* tell him. Isn't that right?'

Gardner clutched and unclutched his hands.

'Uh-huh,' Granville said.

'That is a "Yes" for the record,' King announced triumphantly. '*Yes*, he does not remember.' He turned back to the boy. 'And it hurts when you try, doesn't it?' Granville's eyes were welling with tears. 'Doesn't it?' King said loudly.

'That's enough!' Gardner pulled out of Jennifer's grasp and stood up. He was trembling with rage.

Judge Hanks slammed her gavel again. 'Mr Lawson!'

Gardner stared her down. 'Judge, stop this now, or I'm going to!'

King crossed his arms defiantly.

Granville blubbered quietly on the stand.

Gardner took a step towards King.

'OK,' Hanks said. Things had gone too far. 'Let's take a break. Everyone take fifteen minutes and try to relax! Court's in recess.'

During the recess Gardner approached the witness stand.

'Can't talk to him now,' King said, stepping across his path.

'Out of the way!' Gardner ordered.

The attorney stayed put. 'You're not supposed to ex-parte a witness.'

'I'm going to see my son!' Gardner said, pushing past King with a thrust of his elbow.

King stepped aside. 'Don't discuss testimony,' he warned.

Gardner bent down, and raised Granville's chin. 'You OK?'

The boy tried to smile. 'Uh-huh. Uh, yes, Dad.'

'I told you to be strong,' Gardner said, 'and you were. I'm real proud.'

'He said you're mean,' Granville whispered, 'but you're not. *He's* mean . . .'

Gardner smiled. 'Just stay strong. Real, real strong.'

'I *will*, Dad,' Granville pledged.

And Gardner knew that he would.

When court resumed, King tried to pick up where he left off. 'So you don't remember anything. Isn't that right?'

'We've been over that, counsel,' Judge Hanks said. 'Let's move to something else.'

King collected his thoughts and went back to work. 'You admitted that you tell fibs, right?'

'Sometimes,' Granville replied.

'And you believe in Santa Claus, the Easter Bunny, the tooth fairy, and all that.'

'Yes.'

'But you know they don't exist.' Granville's face went blank. 'You know they're not real. They're just make-believe.'

Granville remained silent.

'What's the question, counsel?' Hanks asked.

'Does he know the difference between truth and fantasy?' King asked.

'Rephrase it,' Hanks ordered.

King looked down at the boy. 'If I said it's dark in here, would that be the truth or a lie?'

Granville raised his eyes to the lit chandelier overhead. 'Lie.'

'And if I said this is a knife,' King raised his pen, 'would that be the truth or a lie?'

'Lie,' Granville replied.

'So you think you can tell the difference between the truth and a lie?'

'Yes,' Granville answered.

'So if I said that you *did* remember the thing that your dad has been asking you about, would that be the truth or a lie?'

'Objection!' Gardner said. 'There's already been testimony on that point.'

Hanks leaned forward in her chair. 'I think he can answer. Overruled.'

'If I said you *did* remember what happened to you at the Bowers Corner store,' King repeated, 'would that be the truth or a lie?'

Granville closed his eyes as if he were trying to understand the question. It was confusing enough, even for a grown-up. 'Truth!' he finally said.

King widened his eyes, and took a step back. 'It's the truth that you remember what happened at the store? The truth, not a lie?'

Granville nodded, and Gardner looked at Jennifer. This didn't make sense.

'Judge, ask that the last answer be stricken from the record,' King said. It was definitely not the one he was looking for.

'But *you* asked the question, Mr King,' Hanks told him. 'I'm afraid *you're* stuck with the answer.'

'But *I* want it stricken!' King demanded. He was clearly shaken.

'Too late!' Hanks said. 'The testimony stands.'

King scowled. It was time for another conference with Jacobs. 'A moment, please, Judge.'

'Make it fast,' Hanks replied.

'What's going on?' Jennifer whispered.

Gardner looked at his son in the witness chair. The faraway eyes evoked by Starke and Miller were back. The boy's mind was obviously on the move.

At the other table, King and Jacobs were talking excitedly. Maybe Granville had not made a mistake. Maybe when he said *truth*, he meant it. Maybe he did remember.

Granville looked at Gardner, and smiled weakly. He was trying his best to help his dad, just like he promised. It really hurt, but he had to keep going. Dad was counting on it.

Gardner and Jennifer were sprawled on the couch at the townhouse. It had been a hell of a day. The battle over Granville's witness qualification had filled the entire trial time-slot. The boy had been on the stand for five hours, and

312

after the King–Jacobs team had finished with him, Gardner cross-examined. Yes, Granville said. He did understand the difference between the truth and a lie. Yes, he knew it was wrong to tell a lie. Yes, he knew he could be punished if he told a lie in court. Yes, he knew what the oath was: promising to tell the truth. Yes, if he took the oath, he *would* tell the truth. That was it. All the key questions answered in the affirmative. The boy had stuck it out, and the judge had ruled he was a competent witness. The defence had decided not to press their other issue: that Granville's memory loss disqualified him. After Granville implied that he *did* remember, King and Jacobs left it alone. So Granville *could* testify. And the only question now was: would he have anything to say?

'Tired?' Jennifer asked.

Gardner shifted a pillow behind him. 'Totally,' he said, then he looked at Jennifer. 'I almost went over the edge, didn't I?'

'Yes.'

'Not very professional.'

Jennifer shook her head. 'You can't lose it like that in front of the jury.'

'I know,' Gardner said. 'So I've been thinking . . .'

Jennifer blinked her eyes. 'What?'

'You do the honours . . .'

'As to what?'

'The direct examination of Granville. *You* handle it.'

Jennifer frowned. 'Are you sure?'

'Yes. You take it. I'll sit side-saddle.'

'When did you decide that?'

Gardner sat up. 'This afternoon, while we were in court. And I've changed the order of witnesses. I want Granville to lead off.'

'What?' Jennifer was astounded. 'The first witness?'

Gardner stood and began to pace in front of the couch. 'He's on the verge. I can feel it. He recognized something in there today. Just a little push – that's all it will take. Dr Grady said that once the dam breaks it will all come out. There's a crack now. It won't take much more to bring it down completely.'

'Are you sure? That's a real gamble. What if he can't do it?'

313

Gardner stopped pacing. 'He will. I have a plan to make it happen . . .'

Suddenly the phone rang.

Jennifer answered. 'Brownie!' she exclaimed, then handed the phone to Gardner.

'Gard, I hope you're not mad,' Brownie said, 'but I had to get away this afternoon. I'm in New York.'

'New York?' Gardner sputtered, 'God, Brownie, I need you down here, in case something comes up. Things are moving fast at the trial.'

'I'm on to something,' Brownie said. 'My theory . . .'

'Still on that?' Gardner asked. 'Thought you'd given up.'

Brownie chuckled. 'I never give up.'

'Yeah. Tell me about it.'

'Like I said before, Gard, there might be another side to this thing. I almost got it sorted out.'

Gardner let out his breath. 'We start testimony tomorrow, Brownie, and I'm putting Granville on the stand.' There was silence on the other end. 'Brownie?'

'I heard you.' He sounded disappointed. 'You do what you gotta do, but just . . .' His voice faded.

'What?'

'Keep an open mind. If I'm right about this, you might have to make some adjustments.'

'We're committed,' Gardner said.

'So am I,' Brownie answered.

CHAPTER 21

The morning after Granville's qualification hearing, the trial officially began. Gardner and Jennifer were present and ready, and the defendants were at the defence table with their lawyers. Miller was stiff and sullen, Starke more relaxed. Granville was sequestered in Gardner's office. The courtroom was packed with potential jurors, talking quietly as they waited for something to happen.

Judge Hanks entered, and wasted no time in starting the clock. 'We can select the jury this morning, go to opening statements after lunch and be ready for the first witness late this afternoon. Let's get moving.'

So the jury selection began, and in an hour and a half the overtly biased people had been weeded out. That left a group from which the final twelve could be selected. A cluster of farmers, retailers, housewives and pensioners. Gardner scanned the array, and came to a conclusion: one juror was as good as any other in this case. Addie and Henry could have been grandmother and grandfather to the entire bunch, and Granville the son. These people were going to convict if the evidence was there. The final roster would make very little difference.

For the next hour the parties took their 'strikes', each side dismissing jurors with prejudices, each side keeping jurors they thought might vote their way. And, for the most part, the selection was smooth. As the lunch hour approached, the jury box was full.

'Is the jury as now constituted acceptable to the State?' Hanks asked.

Gardner checked the two rows of serious faces. It was

315

a snapshot of a church picnic, law and order all the way. 'Acceptable, Judge,' he replied.

'Mr King? Mr Jacobs? Is the jury acceptable?'

They looked at their jury rosters. Each had remaining strikes. If they used them now, the procedure could go another two hours. 'Acceptable,' they finally said.

Jennifer nudged Gardner's arm. 'Why didn't they use all their strikes?' she whispered.

Gardner shook his head. 'They didn't need to use *any*, King and Jacobs are banking on the fact that Granville can't do it. Who's on the jury won't make any difference.'

Jennifer focused on Gardner's sombre expression. 'And you're sure he *can*?'

Gardner closed his eyes. 'He has to.'

The lunch break flew by, and court reconvened at 2 p.m. Under Hanks' blitzkreig schedule, opening statements were to begin immediately. That put Gardner in a dilemma. If he told the jury he was going to prove a fact, and during trial he didn't deliver the goods, the case was dead. At this point he was caught between conflicting theories: the Miller version and Brownie's Starke hypothesis. And then there was Granville. His testimony was still an unknown.

Gardner was not in a position to tell the jury anything specific about the State's case. How could he? He didn't know himself. So he decided to make a generic opening statement. He introduced himself and Jennifer to the jury and gave a procedural rundown of how the case would proceed. He told them to listen to the evidence, to be fair and to pay attention throughout the trial. And he predicted that they would reach a verdict that would do justice to the memories of Addie, Henry and Purvis Bowers. Then he sat down.

King went next, and gave his own generic response. The State didn't have any evidence. The State never had any evidence. There was no case at all against his client. The whole thing was a sham. A disgrace. A travesty. 'If they had anything, they would have told you about it in opening statement. But they don't, and they didn't!' End of story. 'You will acquit!' King predicted, then he sat down.

Hanks turned to Jacobs. 'You now have the right to make an opening statement.'

Jacobs stood up and smiled. 'I'd incorporate the comments of Mr King and apply them to my client.'

'Anything else?' she asked.

'No, your honour.' The message clear: my man has nothing to worry about.

'Very well,' Hanks said, then turned to Gardner. 'Call your first witness, Mr Prosecutor.'

Gardner swallowed and stood up. This was it. The moment of truth. 'I have a motion, Judge. With respect to the witness, Granville Lawson.'

Hanks leaned forward. 'What is it, counsel?'

'I move that we transfer the trial to Bowers Corner and take the witness' testimony there.' Gardner had concluded that there was only one way to be sure Granville's memory would come back: he had to return to the scene of the crime.

Brownie was upset. His appointment at the hospital had not panned out. He had arranged to meet a lady named Anna Gleason in the records section, but she'd not turned up for work and no one knew where she was. 'Can you ring her?' Brownie asked.

The red-haired receptionist gave him a blank look. 'We've rung her already.'

'And?' Brownie didn't have time for a run-around.

'And she didn't answer.'

'Give me her home address.' She shook her curls. 'Can't do that, sir.'

Brownie pulled out his police ID and slapped it on the counter. 'I'm a cop!'

The girl studied the badge. 'Do you have a summons?'

Brownie tried to hold his temper, but it was slipping away. 'No, I do not have a summons.'

'Then we can't give out any information.'

'Thanks a lot,' he said sarcastically, then ran to the pay-phone. He didn't have time for this. He'd hoped to get the truth from Anna Gleason, a records custodian at the Sacred Heart Hospital for the past forty years. Brownie had worked his charm on the phone, and convinced her that the privacy rule could be bent a little to solve a murder case. But that avenue was closed, it seemed. Ms Gleason was AWOL. He'd have to shift to plan B. Rather than going for the document-ation, he'd have to go to the source. Right now, there was no other choice.

He dialled a number that he'd been saving. This was not what he'd envisioned, a direct confrontation, but maybe, if they were lucky, it might work.

'Starke residence,' a voice answered.

'I need to speak to Mrs Starke,' Brownie said.

'May I say who's calling?'

'This is Sergeant Joseph Brown, county police in Mary-land. It's *very urgent* that I speak with her.'

'Just a moment, sir,' the voice replied. There was a hush as the line went quiet, and the servant went off to find the lady of the house. She was an eighty-five-year-old widow who lived in lonely opulence. Florence Eggers Starke, wife of the late Lieutenant Wellington Starke, Jr, and IV Starke's grandmother. Perhaps she was keeper of the family secret.

Gardner's request to move the trial to the crime scene had taken King and Jacobs by surprise. They conferred hur-riedly, then King stood up. 'No way,' he said.

'Are you objecting?' Judge Hanks asked.

'Yes,' King answered. 'Most vigorously, and Mr Jacobs, as well.'

Hanks seemed nonplussed. 'Do you have any legal author-ity as to why it *cannot* be allowed?'

King stared at Gardner. This guy was crazy. Forcing his own son back to the murder zone, he was obviously ready to do *anything* to win the case. 'It would prejudice our clients,' King finally said.

'But do we have any case citations that forbid it?' King shook his head. 'Your objection is noted, Mr King,' Hanks said. 'What about you, Mr Jacobs? Do you have anything to add?'

Jacobs stood up. 'As Mr King has said, going to the scene would be very detrimental to our clients' position, not to mention a logistical nightmare. *Please* do not permit it.'

Hanks turned back to Gardner. 'Any response, Mr Prosecutor?'

'It is permissible under the law,' Gardner replied. 'And I'm sure the move can be made with a minimum of upset.'

Hanks nodded. 'Under the circumstances, I would be inclined to grant the State's motion.' She looked at the clock on the far wall. 'It's 3.45 now, too late to get things set up. Let's suspend the proceedings, and meet out at Bowers Corner at 9 tomorrow morning.'

Gardner had not expected it to be so easy, with King and Jacobs almost speechless, and Judge Hanks so accommodating. They were actually going to give him a chance to pull it off!

Judge Hanks banged her gavel and was about to leave the bench, when King spoke up. 'Not so fast, Judge!' Hanks paused. 'We have to discuss logistics. Mr Jacobs and I have some concerns about the witness's contact with our clients.'

Hanks sat down again. 'What do you mean, Mr King?'

'I mean that we do not want the thing set up so that there will be unfair influence,' King replied. 'The whole case hinges on identification. If the boy comes in and sees a traditional set-up, defendants up front, *et cetera*, he'll be tipped off as to whom to pick . . .' He looked at Gardner. 'Mr Lawson may try to pull something. I move that my client be allowed to mingle with the audience. I don't want him isolated up front, sticking out like a sore thumb.'

'I ditto the request for my client,' Jacobs said.

'That sounds reasonable,' Hanks replied. 'What's the State's position?'

Gardner crossed his arms. He'd manoeuvred well, but the defence had countered brilliantly. Maryland law allowed defendants to hide in a crowd so that the witness could not assume that the person next to the lawyer was the one to choose. 'Object,' he said weakly. There was no legal way to stop it.

'Overruled,' Hanks said. 'The procedure will be permitted.'

She was about to rise when King spoke again. 'One more thing, Judge . . .'

Hanks settled down in her chair. 'What?'

'I would like to substitute another person at the counsel table for my client.'

Gardner groaned inwardly. It was bad enough to move the defendant away, but to substitute another person doubled the chances of a misidentification, especially if the substitute looked anything at all like the defendant himself. Again, the counter-move was deadly.

'I join that request,' Jacobs said.

Hanks looked at Gardner. He was at a loss for words. Upon request, a look-alike *could* be seated at the counsel table prior to a witness's entry into the courtroom. 'Objection,' Gardner repeated.

'Overruled,' Hanks said. 'Council will be permitted to seat non-participants at the counsel table. Now I want to meet the bailiff and the sheriff in chambers to discuss the physical arrangements for tomorrow. We'll need tables and folding chairs. I want the place set up and ready for trial by 9 a.m. Court's adjourned.'

King and Jacobs left the courtroom.

After they'd gone, Gardner slumped in his chair. 'I think I screwed up,' he said to Jennifer. 'Granville's not going to be able to do it. Not in these circumstances.'

Jennifer touched his arm. 'Why don't you wait, then? You can still change the order of witnesses.'

'I could . . .' Gardner mumbled, 'but . . .'

'Maybe Brownie will come good,' Jennifer interrupted. 'He's convinced he's on the right track.'

'What track? He's never filled us in as to what he's looking for. Instead, he's off to New York, and we're no closer on that end than we were before. And now we're committed . . .'

'We?' Jennifer touched his chin, and raised it.

'We. Me. Granville. This is the end of the line. He's either going to do it, or he's not. The more we wait, the worse it gets.'

It was 9 p.m., and Gardner had tucked Granville up in bed. The boy's head stuck out of the fold in the sheet, and Gardner sat beside him. He had on a pair of 'space raider' pyjamas, and his baseball glove lay on the night table. 'Try to get some sleep,' his father said.

'Not sleepy.' Granville had been told what was going to happen in the morning, and he was scared and restless.

'Try closing your eyes,' Gardner said. Granville kept them open. 'Don't fight me, Gran.' Gardner needed him rested. A bleary look at the mixed-up courtroom would be disastrous. 'You have to go to sleep.'

There was no movement in the eye department. 'Dad . . .'

'What, son?' Gardner could sense another 'do I have to?' question.

'What's gonna happen?'

Gardner smoothed the blond hair back from his son's forehead. 'You mean tomorrow?'

'Uh-huh.'

'I told you,' Gardner said softly. 'We're going to go out to Bowers.' Granville blinked. 'And we're going inside . . .' The eyes blinked again, then clamped shut. 'And Miss Jennifer is going to ask about the day when you got hurt . . .' The eyes squeezed tighter.

'And if you remember anything . . . or if you recognize anything or *anybody*, then you tell the judge. That's it. I'll be right there.'

Granville opened his eyes. 'But what if I can't?'

Gardner stroked his son's head. 'That's OK. If you can't, you can't.'

'Will you be mad?'

Gardner smiled down into Granville's widened eyes. 'No, of course not. You do the best you can do. That's all. I'll not be mad, no matter what.'

'But the bad guy,' Granville whispered. 'Will he get away?'

Gardner's pulse began to race. Granville had never said anything about a 'bad guy' before. 'What do you mean, Gran?'

The boy shut his eyes again. 'If I don't remember, then the judge can't put the bad guy in jail.'

Was it a question or a statement? Gardner didn't know, but the context was correct. If Granville could not make an ID, the killer would walk free. 'Oh, no,' he lied. 'The judge will hear from some other people. They'll help, too.'

'So why do I have to do it?' Granville was back to the eternal why. The best question of all. If the bad guy was going to be punished anyway, why did Granville have to go back to Bowers?

'Because *I* want you to. You have to try to remember, so you can forget.' That was the clinical prescription. Dredge it up. Get it out. And, then, forget it.

'Huh?' It was too advanced a concept for the boy.

'The bad dreams. The scared feelings you've had. Once you remember, they'll all start to go away.'

321

'But . . .' Granville was still fighting it. 'I'm still gonna be scared.'

'Maybe, but not so much. And, slowly, it'll all go away. And then you won't be scared any more.'

Granville closed his eyes again, and this time there was a more peaceful cast to his face.

'Ready to go to sleep?' Gardner asked.

'Can you tell me a story?' That was a sign that the answer was 'Yes'.

'I suppose so. Which one do you want?' There were plenty to choose from.

'The ant,' Granville said.

'You mean the ant and the flower?'

'Uh-huh.'

'OK.' It was one of the boy's favourites. 'Once upon a time there was a little worker ant who lived in an ant colony in a big, big, garden. The ant's name was . . .'

'Ralph,' Granville said. He was sinking deeper into his pillow now.

'Right,' Gardner said, 'and Ralph the ant became attracted to a beautiful red flower that grew just above the entrance to the colony. The flower's name was . . .'

'Alice,' Granville whispered sleepily.

'Correct,' said Gardner. 'Anyway, each day the ants went in and out of their ant hole, and only one ant stopped to speak to Alice. "Good morning, Alice," Ralph would say. "Good morning, Ralph," Alice would answer. And this went on and on all summer . . .'

Granville was breathing heavily now.

'Well, there was a terrible drought. No rain for weeks. And Alice began to droop. She was thirsty. Sooo very thirsty . . .'

'So Ralph brought water,' Granville said. He was still listening.

'Right. Bucket after tiny bucket of water from an underground stream he brought. And finally Alice began to perk up . . . Until one day she was brighter than any other flower in the garden. This attracted the attention of the owner of the garden, a lonely old woman who lived in the house. She came over to investigate this strange bright flower, and, when she did, she found the ants. "Oh, my goodness," she

322

exclaimed. "Nasty little ants." She ran back to the house to get her ant poison, and when she did, Alice began to cry. The old woman was going to hurt Ralph, the nice little ant who had saved her. She cried, and cried. So hard and so much, that she dried herself out. Now she looked as droopy as all the other flowers, and the old woman couldn't find her again. So . . .' Gardner waited for Granville to say 'So Ralph and the ant colony were saved!' but he had gone over the edge. Deeply, and peacefully, it appeared, asleep.

'And so Ralph saved the flower, and the flower saved Ralph,' Gardner said, 'and they all lived happily ever after.' God, if it could only be like that, he thought, as he kissed his son on the forehead and turned out the bedside light. Tomorrow was Armageddon. The old woman was coming with the poison, and all the tears in the world couldn't keep her away.

CHAPTER 22

The night was over, and the day dawned warm. A crew of sheriff's deputies and court clerks had worked round the clock to convert Bowers Corner into a makeshift courtroom. Shelves were moved out, tables and chairs moved in. By the time the sun had found its way to the base of the ridge line, the job was complete. The scene was set, and all they needed now were the players.

Gardner arrived at 8.30 to meet with the judge and review the deceptive manipulations of the defence attorneys. A crowd had already gathered outside the gabled building when he got there. Word had spread through town as to what was to happen, and there was a rush to queue up. The jurors were being held in a bus outside the store, but there was no hurry to get them inside. Their seats were reserved.

Judge Hanks came in through the rear door, and took her place at a desk on a raised platform that they'd rigged as a bench. King, Jacobs and their clients were already seated silently at the folding counsel table. Gardner nervously took up a position on the prosecution side. He hadn't slept a wink, and it showed. His face was puffy and his eyes were bloodshot.

'How do you propose to situate your clients?' Judge Hanks asked.

King and Jacobs stood up. 'We have to bring in the spectators, Judge,' King said. 'Then we can make the substitution.'

Gardner said nothing. The procedure was preordained. There was no way he could stop it.

'Very well,' Hanks said, motioning to the bailiff at the door. 'Bring in the public.'

There was a commotion as a crowd entered and picked through the folding chairs that had been set up as a gallery.

'Mr King?' Hanks turned to him for the next move.

'Please allow my client to be seated in the crowd,' he said, walking to the front, 'and allow *this* person to take his place at the counsel table.' King led a young man in at the door and brought him towards the bench. He had dark unkempt hair and light eyes, and was dressed in jeans and boots. His bare arms were emblazoned with tattoos.

Jesus, Gardner thought. A ringer from King's gallery of rogue clients. There was no facial resemblance to Roscoe Miller, but the other characteristics were almost a perfect match. He swallowed against the lump in his throat.

'Take a seat there,' Hanks told the substitute. 'And *you*,' she pointed to Miller. 'You may be seated among the public.'

Gardner tensed as Miller took a seat in the third row of the spectators. By contrast, King had scrubbed him up, cut his hair and put him in a suit. He looked like a college student, here to learn the workings of the law.

'Mr Jacobs?' It was the New Yorker's turn to make a substitution, and his ringer was at least as effective as King's. Another clean-cut, pale-eyed, dark-haired man in his late teens or early twenties, calm and poised. Dressed in a coat and tie, as refined in appearance as Starke himself. He took his place next to Jacobs as Starke hid far back in the fourth row.

Gardner tried to calm himself, but he couldn't slow his heart-rate or stop the flow of perspiration. If Granville could come even close to making an ID, it would be a miracle.

'Are we ready now, gentlemen?' Hanks asked.

King and Jacobs checked the set-up. Their clients were neatly camouflaged, and the decoys were in place. 'Ready,' they said.

'Very well. Bring in the jury.' Hanks made a few last-minute adjustments to her notepad and gavel, the jurors marched in and took their seats to the side of the witness stand, and then they were ready.

'Call your witness, counsel,' Hanks told Gardner.

He stood. 'Call Gr— Granville Lawson to the stand.' He barely got it out.

The bailiff went outside. Jennifer and Granville had

followed in the other car with orders to wait until sent for. Then they could come in.

A hush fell over the room as the door opened, and Jennifer slowly entered, gently pulling Granville behind her by the hand. The boy's face was white, his eyes clearly frightened. He was dressed in his Sunday best: blue blazer, grey pants, white shirt and tie. He looked like a country gentleman. Gardner swallowed again. His heart felt as though it would burst out of his chest. Somehow, they made it up to the witness chair. Jennifer told him to raise his right hand.

'Do you swear or affirm under penalties of perjury that the testimony you are about to give is the truth, the whole truth, and nothing but the truth?' the clerk asked.

Granville glanced at Jennifer, then at Gardner. Each gave him an encouraging 'Go ahead' with their eyes.

'Uh, yes,' Granville answered.

'Very well,' Hanks said. 'Be seated, and state your name and address for the record.'

Granville sat down, but said nothing.

Jennifer walked over to the witness stand. She was wearing a red cotton suit and a string of pearls. As usual, she looked both professional and beautiful at the same time. 'What is your name?' she asked softly.

'Granville.'

'Your complete name, First and last name.'

'Granville Alcott Lawson.' There was a hint of pride in the response.

'Good. And where do you live?' Jennifer was standing close, shielding him from the rest of the room.

'With my mom. I'm with Dad now, but I'm gonna go back to my mom's tonight.'

'OK,' Jennifer said. 'And how old are you?' Take it slow and easy at first was the plan. Non-threatening, irrelevant background. Slowly and gently get him acclimatized, then move to the hard stuff.

'Eight years old.'

'OK, and . . .'

'Your honour!' King was up, and he had fire in his eyes. 'I would like to voir dire the witness on what he's been told about today's procedure!'

Gardner rose to his feet. This was a challenge to his

integrity. 'Approach the bench, Judge?' he asked.

'I fear that Mr Lawson may have instructed the witness about the special arrangements we've made today,' King continued.

'Your honour!' Gardner was angry now. King was playing to the jury.

'To the bench, Mr King!' Hanks roared. The attorneys hustled up on the platform. 'Keep your voices down!' she ordered. 'What's your problem, Mr King?'

King looked at Gardner. 'I have reason to believe that Mr Lawson may have tipped off his son as to the substitutions we've made here today. Told the boy to look in the crowd . . .'

'That's a lie!' Gardner said, clenching his fist.

'Keep your voice down!' Hanks admonished. 'What do you propose we do, Mr King?'

'Let me question the boy,' the attorney said.

'No way!' Gardner snapped.

'Gentlemen, please! No more by-play. *I'll* ask the questions. Now return to your seats!'

Gardner glared at King, and King glared back. Then they turned to their respective sides.

'Jury, please return to the bus for a few moments,' the judge said. This procedure was not for their ears. When they had all left, Hanks looked at Granville. 'I need to ask you a few questions.'

'OK,' Granville replied.

Gardner clutched his hands in front of him and stared down at the table.

'Did you talk to your dad about what was going to happen here today?' the judge asked.

'Uh-huh,' Granville said. 'Uh, yes.' He remembered.

'And what did you dad say?'

Gardner held his breath. That was a loaded, open-ended question.

'To do my best.'

Gardner let out his breath.

'And did he tell you who would be here or where they might sit?'

Granville frowned. He didn't understand.

328

'Did your dad tell you to look in a certain spot when you came into the courtroom?'

Granville stared at the judge, and a light came into his eyes, 'Yes,' he said.

Gardner's heart sank. This was it.

King smirked on the other side. He smelled blood.

'And where did he say to look?' Hanks continued. If the answer was 'in the back of the room', it was all over. Gardner's heart froze.

'At Miss Jennifer,' Granville replied. 'Only at Miss Jennifer.'

King stopped smiling, and Gardner took a deep breath. That was the right answer. The *only* answer.

'Anywhere else?' Hanks asked. 'Did he ask you to look anywhere else?'

Granville didn't hesitate. 'No.'

Hanks looked at King. 'I find no tampering, Mr King. No tampering whatsoever. Now let's get on with the case!'

Brownie was in the co-pilot's seat of the State Police chopper. He'd been moving at racing speed since the day before, and now he was in the home stretch. His stomach jiggled against the seatbelt as they hit a downdraught. The weather was touch and go en route, with rainstorms and cumulus clouds across Pennsylvania. It was going to be rough, no matter what.

It was amazing, really, what he'd learned. The old lady had actually agreed to talk to him. She'd invited him into the mansion, sat him in a luxurious wing chair and even served him tea. He'd come out hard with the allegations, and his suspicions. He laid out the evidence he'd gathered so far, and, despite the fact that her own grandson was on the hook, she'd kept talking. There was no admission, no smoking gun, no actual evidence, but he got his answer, the bizarre connection that tied the whole thing together. She didn't come out and say it, but it was there, in the deep, deep sadness of her dark brown eyes.

Brownie conferred with the pilot, and a call was placed to police headquarters through a radio link-up with air traffic control. He'd telephoned his lab partner, Sam Jenkins, earlier, and instructed him to get a cellular phone out to Bowers Corner ASAP. In the rush since yesterday, he'd been unable to reach Gardner, and now they needed to talk. Even if Gardner was in court.

'Sam?' Brownie tried to confirm that the call had gone through.

'Yeah, Brownie.' It was Sam.

'Where are you?' The connection was broken by static, but the words came through clearly.

'At Bowers Corner. Like you said.'

Brownie put the mike to his lips. 'Trial goin' on?'

'Yeah. They're all inside.'

Brownie clicked the mike again. 'Take the phone in to Lawson. Put him on.'

There was a hesitation. 'OK,' Jenkins said. There was another pause, as background noise and mumbles came through the speaker. Finally there was an answer.

'Brownie?' Gardner's voice was hushed and excited. 'Where are you?'

'In the air. I know you're in court, so I'll make this fast.' There were more mumbles in the background.

'Granville's testifying!' Gardner whispered, his voice clearly pained.

'How's he doin'?'

'Just getting started. I can't stay on long.'

'OK,' Brownie said. 'Here it is. I'm on my way back home. Got one more stop to make before I report in. But I need your authority to do something.'

'What?' Gardner gasped hurriedly.

'Dig up a body.' The line seemed to go dead. 'Gard? Did you get that?' There were more mumbles in the background. 'Gard?'

'Jesus,' Gardner said. He'd got the message.

'Just say it's OK, that's all. I need permission from the State Attorney, and that's you . . .'

'Brownie . . .' Gardner was mixing in with the mumbles. 'What . . . Who . . .' The transmission was breaking up.

'No time for that now,' Brownie snapped. 'Just say it. Yes or no!'

The line cleared again for an instant. 'Do it,' Gardner said, 'but you'd better have a good explanation!'

'Don't worry. It'll blow your mind . . .' He stopped talking. The connection was drowned by static, now, and the call was lost.

Brownie clicked off the mike and hung it on the hook. The hills of western Pennsylvania were rising below, with the Maryland border fading under the fuselage. They'd be down soon, and the painful truth would finally be laid bare in the sun.

Jennifer stood next to the witness stand and looked into Granville's eyes. 'I'm going to ask you some questions, about the day you went to the cave. Do you remember that day?'

'Objection!' King said. 'Leading!'

'It's permissible to lead a child witness, Judge,' Jennifer said.

'I agree,' replied Hanks. 'Overruled. Proceed, counsel.'

'Do you remember going out to the cave with your classmates?' Jennifer repeated.

'Yes,' Granville said tentatively. The visit with Gardner had revived at least that much memory.

'And do you remember how you got there?'

'Bus,' Granville said.

Gardner tried to listen, but Brownie's call had broken his concentration. Dig up a body? What the hell had Brownie found? He looked at Granville, so small and vulnerable, trying hard to be strong. In a few moments it would all be over. Brownie was racing at them from one end, Granville was crawling from the other, and their fate would meet somewhere in the middle.

'What did you see in the cave?' Jennifer asked.

'An angel,' Granville said. That part was clear.

'The Angel of Crystal Grotto,' Jennifer said.

'Object,' King said. '*She's* testifying, not the boy.'

Hanks shot an annoyed look at the defence attorney. 'Overruled!'

'OK,' Jennifer said. 'After the visit to the cave, where did the bus go?' A dark cloud passed over Granville's head. His skin seemed to go paler, and he began to shift nervously in his chair. 'Do you remember where the bus went after it left the cave?' Jennifer repeated.

Granville did not answer. The cave was as far as he'd been

willing to go in his mind. Now he was being asked to travel further, and it was taking its toll.

Gardner felt a sweat line forming on his brow. This was agony.

'You went down the road . . .' Jennifer prompted in an expectant voice. 'Down the road to visit . . .' She was leading heavily now, trying to get her witness to fill in the rest of the sentence.

'Judge!' King barked. 'This is too much! Now she's taken over the questions *and* the answers!'

'Quiet, Mr King!' Hanks snapped. 'Let her proceed.'

'After you left the cave,' Jennifer continued, 'your teacher said you could make a stop before going home. Do you remember that?'

Granville was fighting a battle within. 'Yes,' he finally said.

'And do you remember *where* the teacher said you could stop?'

Granville was biting his lip to keep from crying. The memory was eating through the barrier. 'Bowers,' he said sadly.

Jennifer shot a look at Gardner. His face was as white as his son's. There was fear, and anger and shame, all mixed in. This was *his* idea. To put the boy through the wringer and squeeze out the past. He'd insisted on it, almost from the beginning, and now that it was happening, there was a feeling of regret. Gardner had got what he wanted, but now, at the eleventh hour, he was wondering if it was worth this much pain.

'So the bus made a stop here,' Jennifer said, 'at Bowers Corner.'

Granville was holding on. 'Yes,' he said, the word pushed out of his mouth by a convulsion in his chest.

'Now, I want you to come down here,' Jennifer said, pointing to a spot by her side.

Granville opened his eyes wide, and stood up.

That brought King to his feet, and Jacobs right behind him. 'Object!' they said. This was an obvious ploy to get the boy out in the audience.

'What are your intentions, Miss Munday?' Hanks asked. She, too, had been caught off guard by the manoeuvre.

'I'd like him to go to the front door with me, and then retrace the steps he took on the day of the incident,' Jennifer said.

Hanks looked at King and Jacobs. 'That's permissible.'

King scowled. 'Object,' he repeated. Jacobs shook his head.

'Overruled,' Hanks answered. 'Go ahead, counsel.'

Jennifer walked Granville to the door. With her hand on his narrow shoulder, she kept him in a straight line that took him directly to the starting point. When the arrived, Jennifer gave Granville a gentle tap to turn him round. Gardner looked over to his son. The boy looked as though he might faint. He was beginning to shake, and his face was as colourless as death.

'Now I want you to think back,' Jennifer said softly. 'To the time after you went to the cave. When your teacher brought you here to Bowers Corner.'

Granville's eyes were spinning now, and he seemed like he was about to go into a spasm. Gardner had seen enough. He stood up and walked towards his son.

'What do you think you're doin'?' King said nastily as Gardner passed by.

'Go to hell!' he snarled.

'Mr Lawson?' Hanks had no idea what was happening.

Gardner didn't answer. He walked over to Granville and took his hand. This had gone far enough; he was going to take the boy out. Out of the door. Out of the case. Gardner pulled on the boy's hand, but Granville resisted. 'No, Dad,' he said with a sob.

There was terror in Granville's eyes, but also resolve. He did not want to give up. 'We can leave now,' Gardner whispered, a quiver in his own voice.

'No,' Granville repeated. 'I want to stay!' The dam was about to break.

When Brownie arrived at the Maple View Memorial Park, the digger was already in position. He'd called and arranged it with the caretaker, then scrambled from the helicopter to a waiting car. Now he was in the field of marble monuments, ready to unearth the final piece of the puzzle.

The sun was hot, but the shade trees in this secluded

corner shielded the grave from the burning rays. Brownie waved the digger operator into position, and gave him the thumbs-up. The whirr of the engine rattled through the air as the machine took its first bite of earth. Another roar was followed by another gulp of root-infested soil. In a few minutes, the operator stopped and signalled OK with his thumb and forefinger.

Brownie looked into the hole, where the top of a burial vault had been exposed. He nodded, and the man hooked a cable to it. In another second, the heavy metal lid had been lifted free. Brownie peered into the shadows.

'Want me to pull that out too?' the operator asked.

Brownie signalled No, and jumped down into the vault. Then he loosened the bolts in the coffin, held his breath, and raised the lid.

CHAPTER 23

'Are we proceeding or not?' Judge Hanks demanded. Gardner, Jennifer and Granville were still at the door, and it was not clear whether they were going to stay in or go out.

'We're ready, your honour,' Jennifer said.

Granville gave his dad's hand a mighty squeeze.

'Can you ask Mr Lawson to sit down?' King inquired. There was still a nasty twang in his voice.

Gardner turned to the court. 'I'm here for support, Judge. Miss Munday will continue to ask the questions.'

Hanks nodded. That sounded OK to her. 'Fine.' King threw his pen down on his table in disgust. 'Let's move on,' the judge said.

'Thank you, your honour,' Jennifer replied, turning to Granville. 'Now I want you to think back to the day you visited the cave. You saw the angel, then the bus brought you all down here. The other kids had lined up outside, but you ran ahead, in at the door . . .'

'Objection!' King was up again. 'There's no evidence of that! She's adding in details that aren't even in the record!'

Hanks gave King a stern cold-eyed stare. 'She can lead, Mr King! I've already ruled that! Now please keep quiet!'

King uttered 'Huph!' and crossed his arms.

'Go on, Miss Munday,' the judge said.

Jennifer bent down and looked Granville in the face. 'You ran inside the door, didn't you?'

Granville shuffled his feet and squeezed Gardner's hand so hard that his fingernails almost broke the skin. 'Uh-huh,' he said.

'Show me where you went,' Jennifer said.

The room hushed. Granville glanced at the door to get his

bearings, then began to take a few tentative steps to the side, at an angle away from the entrance.

'Is this the way you went?' Jennifer asked.

Gardner matched his son's strides, giving his hand a reassuring squeeze.

'Ye . . . Yes,' Granville stuttered.

The room was frozen. Every eye was on the boy, every heart pounding.

'OK,' Jennifer said. They were still moving forward, towards the spot where the bodies had been found. The markings were no longer there, but the prosecutors knew the lay-out by heart. Granville was on the right track. 'OK,' she said. 'You were going in this direction. Now, do you remember what you saw?'

That was it. The thrust of Granville's head through the door of time. He squeezed Gardner's hand in an unbelievably strong grip and looked down at the floor. Then he let out a scream. 'Aahhhhhhh!' It was a scream of grief; a wail that came from the very roots of his soul.

Gardner and Jennifer froze in place. The sound was horrible, gripping. It echoed from the walls like a siren. And then, suddenly it died.

Jennifer caught her breath. 'What . . . What did you see?' she asked shakily.

Granville had shut his eyes tightly during the scream, but now he opened them. A line of tears rolled down each cheek. Gardner rubbed the boy's back with his free hand, and held on tightly with the other.

'Unca Henry,' Granville answered softly. The demon had finally been released.

'And where was he?' Jennifer had concluded that they could go on. Granville pointed to the floor. 'Let the record show that the witness designated the floor,' Jennifer said.

'So noted,' Hanks responded.

'Can you tell the judge about Uncle Henry?' Jennifer pressed on. 'What did he look like?'

A sob began to ripple through Granville, but he managed to stifle it. 'All bloody,' he said.

'Was anyone else in the room?' Jennifer asked.

'Objection!' King and Jacobs couldn't allow this – an invitation to an ID.

336

'Overruled! Witness can answer.' Hanks was going to let this go as far as it could.

'Anyone else in the room?' Jennifer repeated.

'Aunt Addie,' Granville said, as a few more tears rolled out.

'And what happened to her?' Jennifer asked.

Granville closed his eyes again and squeezed his father's hand. 'She got all bloody too.'

Jennifer sneaked a glance round the room. The people were immobile, like headstones. 'And where was she?'

Granville pointed to another spot on the floor, and Jennifer read its coordinates into the record. Again, it was correct. The exact location of Addie Bowers body.

'Now, then,' Jennifer said, clearing her throat nervously, 'was there anyone *else* in the room? Other than you, Addie and Henry?' If the prior questions were lead-ins, this was truly it. *The* moment of truth.

'Objection!' King and Jacobs had decided to give it one more try.

'Overruled!' Hanks didn't even look at them.

Granville looked into Jennifer's face. His tears were drying, and he seemed calmer.

'Was there anyone *else* in the room?' Jennifer repeated.

'Uh-huh,' Granville said.

'That's a "yes",' Jennifer declared.

Gardner felt his son's grip loosen. Granville had gone into the woods and come out on the other side. Now he was ready to keep moving on his own. He removed his hands from his father's grasp.

'I want you to look around the room,' Jennifer said. 'Look around the room, and see if you recognize anybody. Anybody else who might have been in this room on the day you visited the cave.'

King upended his chair, clambering to his feet. 'This is out of order!' he yelled. 'She's deliberately circumventing proper identification procedures!' The witness was nowhere near the decoys. He was standing directly opposite Roscoe Miller, manoeuvred there by the State. And it was perfectly legal.

'The question is proper!' Judge Hanks said.

'But . . .' King stuttered. He, the master, had finally been outflanked.

'Shut up, Mr King!' Hanks snapped. She was tired of his interruptions.

'Look around the room and see if you recognize anybody,' Jennifer said again.

Gardner held his breath.

The boy searched the crowd, and immediately locked on Roscoe Miller. He was cleaned up and trimmed, but he still had the gleam of a rebel in his blue eyes. There was no hesitation on Granville's part. He took a step closer, and the room hushed again.

Miller looked like a rat in a trap, caught only by a snag of flesh. He was trying to play it cool, to look nonchalant, but his eyes couldn't stay away. He looked into the boy's face.

'Now, take your time,' Jennifer cautioned. No need to rush it. The ID had to be perfect.

Granville took another step towards Miller, and by now they were in a stare-down. And then, slowly, the boy lowered his own eyes. Down to Miller's hands, folded on his lap. Down to the back of his wrist. Down to the tattooed face of death.

'He . . . He . . .' Granville stammered, pointing directly at Miller.

Miller moved his head away as the finger came closer.

'He . . . He . . .' Granville couldn't seem to get it out.

And then, suddenly, Gardner lost it. The months of pain. The grief over Addie and Henry. The savagery of the crime. The senselessness. The suffering of Granville and himself. It all hit at once. 'You animal!' Gardner screamed, drawing back his arm. 'You goddamned animal!'

Gardner's rage caught everyone by surprise. They were too mesmerized by the scene to be prepared for this. The prosecutor was on the verge of battering the defendant to death, and no one was near enough to stop it. The sword of vengeance was about to come down.

'No, Dad!' Granville cried suddenly, blocking his father's arm with his own.

Gardner stopped. What the hell was happening? He looked at his son.

'Don't hurt *him*,' Granville stuttered. 'He . . . He *helped* me!'

Gardner dropped his arm, and the courtroom exploded

into bedlam. Chairs fell over. People scattered, and everyone started talking at once. And Gardner and Jennifer stood wordlessly in the middle of it all.

'Order!' Judge Hanks screamed. 'Let's have order!' She banged her gavel on the table. 'Everyone please sit down!'

The commotion slowly subsided, and people began to return to their seats. But Gardner, Jennifer and Granville still stood in silence in the centre of the room.

Suddenly there was another commotion at the front door. A man rushed in and ran over to the prosecutors.

'Brownie!' Gardner exclaimed. 'What happened?'

The police officer's clothes were muddy, and he was sweating profusely. 'Fell in a grave,' he puffed. 'Call me as a witness!'

'What's going on, Mr Lawson?' Hanks asked.

Gardner looked across at the bench. He was so confused now that he could hardly talk.

'Call me as a witness!' Brownie whispered.

'One moment, please, Judge,' Gardner said. Then he turned to Brownie. 'Granville's still testifying.'

'Take him off, and put me on,' Brownie persisted.

'But ...'

'Just do it!' Brownie said. 'Call me. Set me up. And I'll take it from there!'

'Mr Lawson, please!' Hanks was getting impatient.

'We'd like to call a new witness, Judge,' Gardner said. 'Admittedly out of order, but it's an emergency.'

Jacobs had risen to his feet. 'Objection!' His normal calm was gone. 'You cannot allow this!'

Hanks looked over at King. He, too was standing, but for the last few minutes he'd been busily conferring with his client.

'What's your position, Mr King?' Hanks asked.

King shrugged, and smiled. 'No objection.'

'What are you doing?' Jacobs whispered.

King didn't answer.

'OK!' Hanks responded. 'The State will be permitted to take a witness out of turn. Go ahead, Mr Lawson.'

Brownie walked towards the elevated chair.

'Call Sergeant Joseph Brown,' Gardner announced. He

had no idea what was going on, but what the hell? Maybe they'd soon find out. 'Take Gran outside,' he told Jennifer.

'But I want to hear,' she argued.

'Me, too,' Granville said.

'Move it, State,' Hanks said impatiently.

'OK,' Gardner whispered 'Sit over there and stay quiet.' He motioned to the prosecution table.

'State your name and occupation for the record, please,' Gardner said.

'Objection!' Jacobs was still standing. This was not supposed to be happening. 'Judge, I beg you to put a halt to this abomination, now!'

'Mr Jacobs,' Hanks said sternly. 'I shall not. Proceed, Mr Lawson.'

'Name and occupation?' Gardner asked.

Jacobs slumped into his chair.

'Sergeant Joe Brown. Detective. County police.'

'And did you have occasion to investigate these cases: State *v.* Miller and State *v.* Starke?'

'Yes, sir, I did.'

'And can you tell the court and the jury your findings?' That was as far as Gardner could go. The set-up. From here on, Brownie was on his own.

'Yes, I can,' Brownie said. 'It all began many years ago, in the battlefields of Europe, during World War Two . . .'

'Objection,' Jacobs said weakly. 'This is blatant hearsay.'

'Overruled,' Hanks replied, and her expression made it clear that she was going to allow Brownie to say what he wanted.

'Anyhow,' Brownie continued, 'two men formed a friendship back then. Two fine, decent men. They fought side by side throughout the toughest combat of the war. And, one day, one of the men saved the other's life. Crawled through murderous gunfire. Got wounded himself, but pulled the other man through.'

The courtroom was mesmerized again. The only one stirring was IV Starke, shifting nervously as each word came out.

'And then the war was over,' Brownie went on, 'and the men returned to the United States. One was rich, the other,

340

poor, but there was a strange turn of fate. The rich man and his wife had a problem. They wanted a family. An heir to the fortune. A child to carry on the name. But it was not to be; the wife was infertile.'

Gardner looked at Jennifer. The picture was beginning to materialize.

'But the poor man was blessed with a son: a fine boy-child with a not-so-promising future in the Maryland hills, barely scratching out an existence. And then, fate stepped in.' Brownie's voice dropped dramatically low. 'The obligations of the past came due. One life was saved, and that created a debt. A debt that could be satisfied only by a trade . . .'

'Oh, God,' Gardner said under his breath. He suddenly saw the whole tragic story. The secret exchange that ultimately led to murder.

'So the poor man gave the rich man his own son, to raise and keep and pass on the fortune and the name. And the rich man gave the poor man three million dollars cash . . .'

'Which he never spent,' Gardner whispered sadly.

'And no one knew about the switch,' Brownie continued. 'They faked the death of the poor man's child, and falsified the records of the rich man's. And no one ever knew.'

Gardner looked at Jennifer. She had tears in her eyes. He reached over and squeezed her hand.

'But, as the years went on, fate struck again. The poor man's wife couldn't have any more children. The first was all she was ever going to conceive, and, as far as the world knew, that child was dead. But the poor man grieved, in his own way. And he was rewarded. His own son, with the rich man's name, was enrolled in a boarding-school nearby. Purposefully, so the poor man could see him, but only from a distance . . .'

'The football games,' Gardner whispered as Jennifer squeezed his fingers.

'So the poor man watched his own son play ball, and grow up, and become a fine person. And in his honour, the poor man gave money to the school. Every year, in August, a hundred thousand dollars. A secret donation. But the son never knew his real father. And the poor man never told.'

Gardner looked at Granville. The boy's eyes were wide.

341

'But the poor man got old, and he continued to grieve for his child. And, once again, fate stepped in. A grandson came to the school. A young man who looked a lot like his father. But the resemblance was only skin deep . . .'

IV Starke began to stand up, but Gardner motioned the sheriff to hold him down. He fell back without a struggle.

'The boy had a history of bad behaviour. He was a bully and he liked to hurt people, but because of his money and his power, the family was able to cover it up. But the poor old man didn't know anything about that side of his grandson's personality, and that's when he made his fatal mistake. He contacted the boy. Violated the pact that had been made so many years before. In his grief and his pain, the poor man let it slip. Told the grandson who he was . . .'

'Bullshit!' IV Starke yelled from the back of the room.

'Quiet!' Judge Hanks ordered. 'Keep your mouth shut or I'll have you gagged!'

'But the boy wasn't impressed,' Brownie continued. 'In fact, he was devastated. In his twisted mind, this couldn't be. He was from a line of blue-bloods, not shopkeepers. He tried to disprove it. There had to be a mistake.'

The room was hypnotized, hanging on every word.

'So he hired a private detective from New York. Behind the poor man's back, even behind his own father's back, because his own father didn't know where he had really come from. The parents never told him. But the grandson had to check it out. And when he did, he learned the truth. He *was* the old man's grandson!'

'Damn!' Gardner said. Poor, dear, Henry.

'This revelation made him angry – very angry. He couldn't let it stand. He devised a plan. He took up with a local thug who worked at the school, became his pal, offered him money to drive down to the poor folks' store one day. It was a great set-up. There was even a resemblance between the two. But why not? It was his own flesh and blood, his own cousin. Blue-eyed, and dark-haired, and all . . .'

'No!' Starke screamed.

'Gag him!' Hanks told the deputy.

There was a brief struggle, and IV Starke suddenly had his mouth stuffed with a handkerchief.

342

'So they went to the store, and the grandson obliterated his past with two bullets from a special gun, a unique weapon that the rich man had used during the war. The grandson stole it from the family gun collection and used it to kill his real grandparents. And then, later, he killed Purvis Bowers to shut him up. He was afraid Purvis knew the truth about the relationship and was going to tell the police. The whole scheme would have worked. No one would have ever known, but there was an unexpected interruption. A child ran in . . .'

'And *he* tried to kill him,' Roscoe Miller yelled suddenly, standing and pointing to Starke. 'I tried to stop it, knocked the gun up, and the bullet hit the wall . . .'

'Object!' Jacobs cried.

'You can speak, Mr Miller,' Judge Hanks said.

'Bastard threatened to kill me!' Miller snorted. 'And I believed him! But I don't give a damn any more!' His eyes blazed with righteous anger.

King stood and faced Gardner. 'Ready to talk plea?'

Gardner's head was reeling. A few minutes ago he was ready to strangle Miller with his bare hands, now they were talking plea bargaining. 'Accessory,' Gardner said.

King nodded and put out his hand to Gardner. 'Deal.'

Gardner returned the handshake, and looked at the judge. 'I request that we conclude these proceedings, Judge. There will be a plea regarding Roscoe Miller's case, and we'll be resubmitting Starke's case to the Grand Jury on multiple murder charges. I also request that he be held without bond in the meantime.'

Jacobs stood up shakily. 'You can't do that!'

Judge Hanks smiled. 'Oh yes, I can. Mr Starke is remanded to the custody of the sheriff without bond. I hereby declare a mistrial on all charges against both defendants. Pending new indictments or plea agreements, trial dates will be re-set. Court is adjourned!'

Bedlam returned to the courtroom. The sheriffs hauled out Starke. King and Miller were gloating. And Joel Jacobs looked as if he'd just been shot.

'Can you come up here, Mr Lawson,' Judge Hanks called from the bench, 'and bring your son?'

343

Gardner and Granville walked up to the platform.

'I just wanted to compliment the young man,' Hanks said. 'It took a lot of bravery to do what he did.'

Gardner nudged Granville's arm. 'Say Thanks, son.'

'Thank you,' the boy replied.

'You're welcome,' Judge Hanks said.

Brownie came down from the stand, and patted Granville on the back. 'You did a super job, boy!'

Granville's face was still pale, but he managed another smile.

Gardner turned away from the bench, seized Brownie's hand and simultaneously grabbed Jennifer round the waist. 'You two are the best,' he said. 'The absolute best! Thanks for getting me through.'

'You can be a pain sometimes,' Brownie said, 'but you're OK.'

'Congratulations, Gard,' Jennifer added.

Then Gardner bent down to Granville's eye-level. 'You are really something,' he said. 'A very strong young man. I'm so proud of you!'

Granville put his arms round Gardner's neck. 'Did we get the bad guy, Dad?'

'We got him, Gran. Thanks to you. He's never going to hurt anyone again.' Gardner stood up and took Granville's hand. And the two of them led the entourage out of Bowers Corner, into the light of the summer day.

EPILOGUE

'Hit it, Dad!' Granville called.

It was late October, and the leaves were turning red. The air was warm, but the chill of night still clung to the turf. Gardner and Granville were in the park, playing baseball for a last time before the ground froze. The boy was living with his mother again, and this was a visitation day.

The Bowers cases were finally over. Roscoe Miller had entered a guilty plea to accessory to murder, and received a five-year sentence in the county detention centre. His testimony had cemented first-degree murder convictions against Starke and guaranteed three consecutive life sentences. Starke's cases were still pending appeal, but Gardner wasn't worried. Brownie's evidence had rendered them watertight. There was no way Starke could buy his way out.

Ironically, Kent King had lost the Bowers money. Miller had finally filed a claim to the estate, and because he'd only been convicted of a misdemeanour, he was permitted to collect it. When he got out of prison, he was going to be rich. King wouldn't get a cent.

The saddest part had been meeting Wellington Starke the third, Starke's father. His tearful plea for lenience had been heartrending, but Gardner didn't flinch. Fathers and sons could be an unbeatable combination, for good or for evil. Gardner had to tell the father 'No'.

'Hit it, Dad!' Granville called again.

Gardner looked at his son. The boy was in his 'ready' stance. Primed, and raring to go. He had on his Orioles warm-up jacket and cap.

Gardner raised the bat and cracked the ball hard. It was a sinking line drive, streaking down the field. The boy took off

345

at first contact, and raced to intercept it. Gardner held his breath. He'd never make it. The ball was falling too fast. Granville was at top speed now, still ten feet away from the ball. Gardner scolded himself silently for hitting it so hard. Granville was too small, too inexperienced, for one that tough. Suddenly the boy dived, and stretched, and fell. 'Gran!' Gardner called with alarm.

Granville rolled over twice, and leaped to his feet, holding his glove high in the air. The ball was neatly tucked in the web.

'Way to go!' Gardner cheered, jumping up and down. 'Way to go, Gran! That was major league! Best catch you ever made! Best catch you ever made!'

Granville smiled, and heaved back the ball. 'Hit me another!' he said.